Endgame

Books by **CJ Daugherty**

Night School
Night School Legacy
Night School Fracture
Night School Resistance
Night School Endgame
Night School the Short Stories
The Secret Fire
The Secret City
Number 10

As **Christi Daugherty**

The Echo Killing
A Beautiful Corpse
Revolver Road

NIGHT SCHOOL

Endgame

C J DAUGHERTY

MOONFLOWER

Published by Moonflower Publishing Ltd.
www.MoonflowerBooks.co.uk

2nd Edition

ISBN: 978-1-8382374-6-2

1st Published in the United States 2013

Printed in the United States of America

Moonflower Publishing Registered Office: 303 The Pillbox, 115 Coventry Road, London E2 6GG

If you sit by the river long enough,
you will see the body of your enemy float by.
Japanese Proverb

RUINS
TERRACED GARDEN
FOLLY
WALLED GARDEN
CIMMERIA ACADEMY
CHAPEL
SUMMER HOUSE

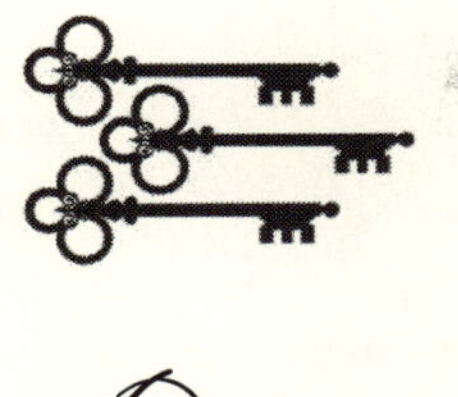

One

‘The black Land Rovers roared down dark London streets. Stopping for nothing and nobody, they hurtled across the crowded metropolis, thundering through red lights, tearing over intersections.

Alone in the back seat of one of them, Allie Sheridan stared out the window without seeing anything. Her eyes were red and sore from crying.

She couldn’t stop remembering Carter alone in the dark street, fists raised. Nathaniel’s guards swarming.

He got away, she assured herself for the thousandth time. *Somehow. He got away.*

But in her heart she knew it wasn’t true.

It all made sense now. Jerry Cole told her to take someone she trusted to the parley. And now she knew why.

Take someone you trust so Nathaniel can take him away from you.

Take someone you trust so Nathaniel can kill him. Like he killed Jo.

Tugging hopelessly at the unyielding door handle, she stifled a sob. She couldn’t get out. Couldn’t go back to him. The doors were locked through a central system.

This car was a prison.

She'd tried fighting, begging, weeping… the men in the front seats were unmoved. They were under orders to bring her back to Cimmeria. And that's what they were going to do.

Frustration raged inside her. She struck the door hard with her fist.

The vehicle careened around a corner with a screech of tyres, throwing her to one side.

As she scrabbled for the safety handle, the guard in the front passenger seat turned to look at her.

'Put your seatbelt on, miss. This is dangerous.'

She glared at him balefully.

I watched my own grandmother die five hours ago, she thought of saying. *And you're telling me this is dangerous?*

At the thought of Lucinda, everything that had happened that night seemed to hit her at once. The sour taste of bile filled her mouth. She lunged instinctively for the window, but that was locked, too.

'I'm going to be sick,' she muttered.

The guard said something to the driver. The window rolled down with a smooth, mechanical whirr.

Cool air flowed in.

Allie stuck her head out of the car, inhaling deeply. Her hair flew around her face in a tangled cloud.

Now that it was OK to vomit, though, she couldn't seem to. Still, she stayed where she was, resting her clammy forehead on the cool metal of the window frame and taking deep, steadying breaths.

The air had that city smell of exhaust and concrete. Vaguely, she considered climbing out and jumping to freedom, but they were moving too fast for her to be certain she'd survive.

She was so tired. Her whole body ached. Her scalp burned where one of Nathaniel's goons had pulled out a clump of hair. Blood had coagulated on her face and neck, tightening her skin unpleasantly.

In her mind she went through the evening's catastrophic events step by step.

The plan had been simple. Meet Nathaniel for a peaceful parley on the neutral ground of Hampstead Heath. Hand over his spy, Jerry Cole. In exchange, Nathaniel would back off long enough for the Cimmeria leaders to regroup.

But then Jerry had a gun. And the night had spun out into an awful chaotic maelstrom of violence. In the midst of it, Lucinda collapsed, blood pouring from a gunshot wound.

And Nathaniel.

Allie shook her head, still puzzled by what she'd seen.

Nathaniel had been in tears. Trying desperately to save her grandmother.

Until that moment she'd thought he hated Lucinda. But she'd never seen anyone more heartbroken.

She could still hear his tormented voice in her head, pleading with her grandmother. *'Don't leave me, Lucinda...'*

Almost like he loved her.

But she had left him. She'd left all of them.

Now, all Allie knew was that she didn't understand Nathaniel at all.

If he didn't hate Lucinda, why was he fighting her in the first place?

What does he really want?

Letting go of the door, Allie leaned back against the tan leather seat. The guard in the front passenger seat turned to look at her.

'Better now?'

She levelled a silent glare at him.

After a second, he shrugged and turned back around.

Next to her, the window closed.

They gained speed as they pulled on to a motorway, desolate at this hour. They were nearing the city limits. Behind them London was a canopy of light. Ahead, the English countryside lay shrouded in darkness.

Allie's chest tightened around her heart. She was so far from Carter now. God knew what was happening to him.

A tear traced a line down her cheek; she reached up to brush it away. Her hand never reached her face.

A bone-jarring jolt threw her off balance. Before she could react, the vehicle swerved wildly, hurling her across the back seat. She slammed into the window with such force she saw stars.

She never had put that seatbelt on.

'What's going on?' Her voice sounded far away; her head rang from the blow.

No one replied.

Pulling herself up, Allie saw the driver wrestling with the steering wheel. The guard was talking into a microphone, his voice low but tense.

She looked around to try and see what had happened but all she could see was darkness and headlights.

The driver swore and spun the wheel. 'Goddammit. Where are they coming from?'

Allie was clinging to the door handle, but the sheer force of the turn threw her against the door so hard her breath hissed through her teeth from the pain.

'What is going *on*?' she demanded again, louder this time.

Without waiting for an answer, she reached over her

shoulder for the seatbelt and strapped herself in, latching it with a metallic click.

Then she turned to look out the back window. What she saw made her breath catch in her throat. There weren't four vehicles anymore.

There were ten.

'Are those ours?' she asked, her voice faint.

No one replied to that question, either. But they didn't have to. She knew the answer already.

A large, tank-like vehicle swung up next to them, revving its engine. Suddenly the Land Rover seemed small.

Allie stared at the monstrous thing, her heart contracting. Its windows were tinted – she couldn't see who was inside.

Without warning it gunned the engine and swerved sharply towards them.

'Look out!' she cried, ducking low.

The driver yanked the wheel. The Land Rover swung right, so sharply Allie's stomach dropped.

They dodged the collision but the car wobbled wildly and the driver struggled to keep control. He clung to the wheel, muscles bulging from the effort as the tyres squealed and they swung across two lanes.

'Six to seven vehicles, affirmative,' the guard in the passenger seat said into his microphone. He was clutching the safety handle above his door to try and hold himself steady as another massive machine swung towards them with an angry roar.

'Convoy disrupted and separated. Other vehicles using diversionary tactics… Look to your *left*!'

He shouted the last words at the driver, who saw the car heading straight towards them at the last minute and wrenched the wheel hard. Too hard.

The Land Rover spun sickeningly. Allie couldn't feel the road beneath their tyres anymore. They seemed to be flying.

The scene took on a dream-like feel. The world outside blurred. They swirled in a deadly dance towards the flimsy guardrail.

Allie closed her eyes.

Nathaniel had found them.

Two

Inside the Land Rover, the noise was deafening. The driver and guard shouted orders at each other. The engine roared. Tyres shrieked.

It sounded like war.

Clinging to the door handle, Allie bit her lip to stifle a scream. Ahead of her, the driver fought the steering wheel, sweat beading his forehead from the effort, tendons in his neck cording as he struggled to regain control of the wildly spinning vehicle.

'Pull out!' The guard kept saying. 'Pull out!'

'It's not…' the driver replied through gritted teeth '… responding.'

The acrid scent of burning rubber filled the air as they neared the edge.

'We're going to hit!' the guard shouted.

The Land Rover struck the guardrail with an awful, crunching thud.

Allie gave a frightened cry as she was thrown forward against the seatbelt.

The guardrail bent but didn't give way. The force of the impact broke their spin. The vehicle swerved left, then right, and then the driver had control at last.

'We're good,' he announced, relief evident in his voice.

With her heart still thudding in her ears, Allie sagged back in her seat. But Nathaniel's cars were still all around them.

The guard pointed to the left. 'There! Take that exit.'

Looking where he indicated, Allie saw an exit ramp looming.

'Roger that,' the driver muttered.

He waited until the last second, then turned the wheel and accelerated hard. They hurtled off the motorway at incredible speed.

Craning her neck, Allie looked through the rear window. Nathaniel's cars had overshot the exit. It would cost them valuable seconds to backtrack and follow.

The driver must have thought the same thing, because he sped through a red light and tore around a roundabout before turning on to a dark country road. Allie kept her eyes on the road behind them – no headlights followed. With an audible exhale, she turned to the front.

The lane was so narrow and winding, it was impossible to get up much speed but the driver did the best he could.

From the passenger seat, the guard relayed the directions coming through his earpiece. 'Left. Right at the next exit. Here. NO! Here. Down that lane…'

Clearly, someone was tracking their progress by satellite and providing a safe route. Allie found this oddly comforting. They weren't entirely alone out here in the dark.

Soon they'd lost themselves in a tangle of winding country lines, roaring over hills and taking hairpin turns so fast she started to feel queasy again.

'Right at the crossroads,' the guard said as they approached a junction.

The hedgerows on either side of the road were very high. The driver approached at speed, gearing up to turn. At the last minute, though, he slammed on his brakes so hard they were all thrown forward.

At first, all Allie could see was blinding headlights to their left. She had to squint to see the vehicle. When she did, her heart plummeted.

It was the tank-like car from the motorway. And it was headed right at them.

Swearing under his breath, the driver shoved the gearshift. They reversed with such force the engine gave a shrill warning whine, like a siren.

'There.' The guard, who had momentarily fallen silent, pointed at a dirt track behind a metal gate, barely visible in the darkness.

Apprehension rose inside Allie as she stared at the road the guard indicated. It was little more than a tractor path across a corn field. The gate in front of it was locked and chained.

How are we going to get through that?

The guard handed the driver a pair of glasses with a kind of gold tint, which he put on without question. Then the driver switched off the headlights.

Allie stopped breathing. The darkness was claustrophobic. Complete.

'Wait…' she started to say, but before she could get the word out the driver gunned the engine and they shot towards the closed, locked gate.

She couldn't seem to move. Or to scream. She just stared straight ahead into the black.

They hit the gate with a screech of metal on metal. The impact rocked the Land Rover with such force, Allie's chin banged into her shoulder. Something scraped across the roof before falling behind them with a clatter.

Then they were tearing across the field. The ground was so rough that even with her seatbelt on she had to grind her teeth together to avoid biting her tongue.

Long leaves and cornstalks slapped the windows like hands trying to reach in.

The driver and the guard had stopped talking; the only sounds were the scream of the engine and the crunch and creak of the tyres.

Suddenly, headlights swung in behind them, illuminating the field with a ghostly white glow.

'You guys…' Her voice trailed off as the driver accelerated, turning sharply and leaving the rough track behind.

Everything went dark again.

They weren't on any road now. They were just jostling across the uneven field, tyres spinning in the soft dirt. Things Allie couldn't see thudded under their wheels.

She heard herself whimper.

For what felt like a lifetime she was thrown around the smooth, leather seat and then…

'*There.*'

The guard pointed at something in the night. Without a word, the driver turned the wheel.

The Land Rover hit something big and metal.

Another farm gate, Allie guessed.

A piece of metal sailed onto the Land Rover's hood and crunched into the windscreen. Allie ducked.

'Great,' the guard muttered as a cobweb of cracks spread across the glass.

Like a gate nearly killing him was a minor annoyance.

Then they were thumping out of the fields and fishtailing on to a tiny, paved country road.

The driver kept the headlights off as they roared into the dark night.

From the back seat, Allie could still see nothing ahead. She turned to look over her shoulder.

No headlights.

The guard began murmuring instructions again. They took a complicated route up steep hills, and down deep, isolated ravines.

Finally, the driver took off his night vision glasses and switched the headlights on.

The guard turned back to look at Allie, who still clung in mute terror to the door. He looked grimly pleased.

'Lost them.'

Two hours later, the Land Rover turned onto a rugged, forested dirt track. The sky was aglow with vivid pink and gold. Dawn had broken.

Allie leaned her forehead against the cool window as Cimmeria's long black fence loomed ahead of them. It was meant to be forbidding – each metal bar culminated in a sharp point ten feet above the ground.

Beyond it was the only safe place she knew.

She was home. But what about everyone else? They'd sent at least twenty guards and Night School students to fight Nathaniel in London. She'd seen none of the others in hours.

The gate opened with a shudder, and they followed the long drive through the forest. It was strangely peaceful – the only sound the rumble of the engine and the crunch of tyres on the gravel drive. But Allie was tense in the back seat, her gaze missing nothing.

After a mile, the trees lining the lane gave way to smooth grass, and the drive coiled into a question mark in front of the massive, Gothic school building, its jagged roof and chimneys thrusting up into the pale sky.

The driver cut the engine. The silence that followed was deafening.

Allie looked at the empty front steps, her chest tight around her heart.

Where is everyone?

The driver and guard climbed out first. Allie followed stiffly. Every muscle ached.

She was limping towards the steps when the front door flew open and a small crowd rushed out to surround her.

'Allie, thank God.'

Allie caught only a glimpse of Rachel's familiar heart-shaped face before she was pulled into her arms.

She clung to her, wanting to cry but unable to summon any more tears. The night had used them all.

'You're OK,' Allie kept saying. 'You're OK.'

Nicole was right behind Rachel, a small wound neatly sutured on her chin.

'Allie! *Dieu merci.*' Her huge brown eyes flooded with relief. 'We were so worried.'

As the two clustered around her, Allie stepped into the light. Rachel's breath caught.

'You're hurt!' Turning, she called up the steps, 'Allie's

bleeding.'

'It's nothing,' she said but no one was listening.

'Stand back.' Pushing the girls aside, Isabelle le Fanult made her way to Allie's side. Without ceremony the headmistress took Allie's chin in her hand, tilting her face towards the light from the open door.

Allie had a sudden memory of seeing her, a whirling dervish of power and speed, fighting Nathaniel's guards in Hampstead Heath.

She'd been almost happy to see her then. Now she stared at her, unblinking, as a tidal wave of blame and anger swelled inside her.

Isabelle's light, wavy hair was pulled back tightly. A purpling bruise covered one cheekbone. She still wore her black Night School gear.

'You should see the nurse.' Isabelle pressed her fingertip lightly against Allie's head wound.

It stung but Allie didn't flinch. She had a question for the headmistress and she intended to ask it.

'Where is Carter?'

The others fell silent.

At first, Isabelle didn't react. But then, releasing her hold on Allie, she let out a long exhalation. She looked exhausted; Allie thought she saw new lines etched in the delicate planes of her face.

'I don't know.'

The softly spoken words hit Allie like a punch in the stomach.

And she didn't hesitate to punch back.

'They made me leave him there,' she said, her voice low and accusing. 'On the street. *Surrounded.*'

The headmistress looked away, her lips trembling.

Allie wasn't sorry. She wanted Isabelle to suffer. This was *her* fault. Leaving Carter had been her call.

A rush of rage and pain swept into her veins like fire. She walked up to the headmistress and shoved her, hard.

Caught off-guard, Isabelle stumbled back, almost falling. Allie heard someone gasp.

'You did that, Isabelle.' Her voice rose. 'The guards were following *your* orders. You left him there.'

Isabelle held up her hands in a weak, calming gesture but Allie shoved her again. And again.

'Why, Isabelle? Why did you make me leave him? How could you do that to him?'

Each time Allie pushed her, the headmistress took another step back. Allie followed her.

'Where is Carter, Isabelle? Is he dead? Did Nathaniel kill him, too?'

'I don't know.' Isabelle repeated, her voice a whisper now. Her golden brown eyes were bright with unshed tears but Allie hardly noticed as she pushed her one last time.

She thought of Carter, lifting her into the black SUV, slamming the door and pounding his fist against the metal, shouting, '*Go!*' at the driver. The fervent gleam in his eyes – like he thought he was going to die, and he was willing, even eager, to do it – was burned into her memory like a brand.

'He's just a kid. If he dies it's *your fault*, Isabelle. Your fault.'

Her voice broke. She crumpled to her knees.

For a split second, no one moved. Then Rachel was next to her, an arm draped across her shoulders.

She lifted her to her feet.

Nicole put her arms around both of them, holding them

together.

Allie had never felt more helpless. She didn't want to hurt anyone anymore. She just wanted Carter to be alive.

Three

The infirmary was in the classroom wing on a mezzanine level where tall windows lined one wall, letting in sun so bright, Allie squinted in the glare. In tired silence, the three girls made their way past ghostly rooms where desks sat in empty rows, waiting for students who might never come back.

Allie ignored it all as she ignored the blood on her face and her own weariness. She wasn't even thinking about how defeated Isabelle had looked outside. She was compiling a list of the missing in her head.

'Where's Zoe?'

'She's fine.' Rachel answered quickly. 'She volunteered to help the nurses.' A ghost of a smile flickered across her tired face. 'She's decided she likes the sight of blood.'

'Everyone else? Raj? Dom? Eloise?'

Nicole answered this time. 'All safe.'

'Dom, too?' Allie couldn't hide her surprise. The last time she'd seen the American girl, she was fighting her way through a crowd of Nathaniel's guards to get to Carter.

'Carter…' Nicole began and then stopped for a second. 'He got her into the car. Got her out of there. He had her back.'

Allie's heart twisted.

'That arsehole,' she whispered, striking a tear away with the back of her hand. 'He is so freaking stupid.'

But everyone knew she didn't mean it.

'Don't give up hope, Allie,' Rachel said, squeezing her arm. 'Nobody saw him get hurt. We have to believe he's all right and Nathaniel's just holding him. To get to you.'

Before Allie could reply, they reached the main medical ward. A large room had been turned into a triage area. Medics clustered around a guard in a black uniform, stitching a wound on his arm.

The smell of rubbing alcohol combined with antibacterial cleaning liquid and the rusty tang of blood made Allie's stomach churn.

'Snip please.' The cool, uninflected voice came from a small, plump woman with a stethoscope draped around her neck and narrow glasses perched on the end of her nose.

A nurse leaned where she indicated. A pair of silver scissors flashed in the light.

She bent over to examine her work, then straightened and threw bloodstained bandages into a bin. 'You're done, my dear.'

Glancing down at his arm, the man tested the stitches, flexing his hand into a tight fist before loosening it again. His muscles bulged.

Seeing this, the doctor sighed. 'Do that a few more times and I'll be stitching you up again. Shall we both attempt to avoid that little reunion? I so hate repeating myself.'

'Sorry.' The man's voice was contrite.

As he stood to leave, Allie saw Zoe. She'd been standing behind the nurses, watching avidly.

Some of the tension left her body.

Spotting her, the younger girl gave an excited bounce.

'You're back!'

She shoved past the injured man without apology and raced to where Allie stood with Rachel and Nicole and hurled herself at her. It was more a tackle than a hug, but Allie didn't mind at all.

'You OK?' Allie searched her smooth face for signs of injury and found none. 'All in one piece?'

Zoe nodded, her ponytail bouncing with her enthusiasm. 'Totally. I hurt a lot of people last night. It was *ace.*'

'Zoe…' Rachel spoke quietly.

The younger girl paused. Allie could see her thinking, figuring out the reasons why what she'd just said was inappropriate, and struggling to correct the oversight.

'I'm sorry about your grandmother.' Her tone took on a curious flatness, as if she was reciting something she'd memorised. But then she grew animated. 'And Carter. I am *so* pissed off about Carter.'

Someone cleared their throat and Allie looked up to see the doctor watching them.

'Look what the cat dragged in,' she said, not without empathy. She patted the seat the guard had vacated. 'What've you done to yourself this time?'

Ordinarily Allie would have smiled at that. The doctors and nurses at the infirmary had treated her on more than one occasion. Today she couldn't seem to fake it.

'It's not as bad as it looks,' she said as she climbed into the chair, still a bit warm from the prior occupant.

The doctor snorted and snapped on her gloves. 'I'll be the judge of that.'

'It's good and bloody.' Zoe sounded approving.

She hadn't noticed how destroyed Allie was, or how

frightened. And Allie was glad of that. Inside, she felt numb and confused and lost. But she had to get it together. No one would listen to her if they thought she was hysterical about Carter. No one would want to follow her if she tried to lead.

If they were going to work together to get Carter back, they had to believe she was fine.

She *was* fine.

Allie glanced at Zoe, forcing a brighter tone. 'Rachel says you're into blood now?'

'I think I want to be phlebotomist.'

'What's that?' Allie said. 'It sounds like a kind of caterpillar.'

'Blood doctor!' Zoe enthused. 'All you do, all day long, is play with blood.'

'Oh good.' Allie sighed. 'So, basically a vampire.'

Zoe beamed. 'Awesome.'

'There is money,' the doctor murmured, snipping Allie's hair away from the wound with a small pair of scissors, 'in phlebotomy.'

The girls exchanged looks of blank incomprehension.

For a while after that Zoe chattered about fighting and diseases while the medical team cleaned the blood from Allie's forehead and stitched her scalp back together. Across the room, Rachel rested her head on Nicole's shoulder.

Everything was horrible. Everything was wrong.

But Cimmeria was home. And this was the closest thing to normal Allie could imagine right now.

A few hours later, Allie hurried down the school's sweeping main staircase. After a shower and a change of clothes, she felt a little more like herself. Ready to figure out what to do now.

Her head throbbed, and her hand strayed unconsciously towards the stitches in her scalp, now mostly hidden by her thick, golden-brown hair.

She hadn't taken the pain pills the doctor gave her. She wanted to keep her head clear.

It was time to plan.

When she reached the ground floor, she turned into the wide formal hallway. The polished, oak-panelled walls gleamed. Sunlight danced off the gilded frames of the oil paintings, making them sparkle. The crystal chandelier hanging above the wide staircase glittered like diamonds. The marble statues on the landing could have been carved from snow.

Allie could never remember loving any place as much as she loved this school. But already she felt she was losing her grip on it.

Without Lucinda, how could they stay here? She'd held this place together.

And now she was gone.

As she passed the headmistress' office, tucked away under the grand central staircase, Allie's footsteps hesitated. She knew she needed to talk to Isabelle – to explain her actions. But she couldn't bring herself to do it. She wasn't ready to be that grown up yet.

Still, she needed information now. She needed to talk to someone she could trust.

At that moment, a guard walked by, dressed all in black. Allie caught his eye.

'Where can I find Raj Patel?'

Allie and Raj sat across from each other in the mostly empty common room. Allie perched on the edge of a deep leather sofa. Raj was in a chair, watching her with unreadable dark eyes, almond-shaped, exactly like Rachel's. He'd come as soon as she'd asked for him, even though he must have been busy. And she saw no judgement in his expression.

'I just have to understand what happened,' Allie said.

Raj didn't look surprised by this.

'The plan went smoothly,' he said, 'until it didn't.'

She listened quietly as he went over everything that had gone right. She and Carter had made their way across Hampstead Heath just before midnight, as planned. They'd found Allie's grandmother right where she was supposed to be, on Parliament Hill. And Nathaniel had joined them only a few minutes later than expected.

The mood had been calm – even jovial at times.

Until Jerry and Gabe appeared, each holding a gun.

'Lucinda left Jerry shackled in a van near the park,' Raj explained. 'He was guarded by two members of her personal security team. We don't know how Nathaniel discovered the location she'd chosen. But he did. Her guards were overwhelmed. Jerry was freed.'

Allie sagged back in her seat. It was so sickeningly obvious. The best plan foiled by the simplest means.

The most complicated design in the world can be

destroyed in seconds by a basic hammer.

'Where did they get the guns?' she asked.

'Gabe, I'd imagine.' Raj's voice dripped distaste. 'He's the only one insane enough to bring guns to a parley.'

Allie glanced at him. 'You don't think it was Nathaniel's idea?'

He shook his head. 'I got a good look at Nathaniel when he saw those weapons – he didn't seem happy.'

This was a surprise. Nathaniel was a control freak. Surely he didn't encourage off-roading among his minions.

'As soon as we saw the guns we had to move,' Raj continued. 'I threw everything we had at them. And it worked. Eventually. But…'

His voice trailed off and he rubbed his eyes.

'But Lucinda was shot.' Allie finished the thought for him. She leaned forward intently. 'Raj, did anyone see who shot her? Was it Jerry?'

Jerry Cole was the science teacher who had betrayed them all – who'd cost them Jo's life when he sided with Nathaniel. It would make sense if he'd done this, too.

But Raj shook his head, lips tight. 'It wasn't Jerry. Isabelle was close enough to see it all. It was Gabe. And there's something else you should know.' He met Allie's gaze. 'Isabelle swears Gabe was aiming at Nathaniel.'

Allie took a sharp breath. '*What?*'

'I didn't see it myself,' he said, 'but Isabelle's convinced Gabe was aiming at Nathaniel and, at the last minute, Lucinda stepped into the path of the bullet. Isabelle thinks…' He hesitated as if deciding how much to reveal. 'Well, it seemed to her Lucinda saw what Gabe was about to do. And she took the bullet. To save Nathaniel.'

Allie's lips moved but no sound came out. She felt as if she was sinking. She couldn't breathe.

Lucinda let herself die? She left me on purpose?

She shook her head so hard her stitches stung. 'No, Raj. Isabelle's wrong. Lucinda wouldn't do that. She wouldn't. Not for Nathaniel.'

He didn't argue with her. 'I find it hard to believe myself. I'm only offering it as a qualified explanation.' He paused. 'Allie, I'm not going to tell you what to do. But Isabelle is heartbroken about this – about everything. I wish you'd talk to her. Get her side of things.'

Allie's expression hardened, but Raj didn't back down. He lowered his head to catch her gaze. 'Leaving Carter wasn't Isabelle's call. Carter knew what the drill was going in. He knew everything that could happen – every possible way it could go wrong. He was ready for this.'

She didn't want to argue with him but cold anger was creeping back into her veins like ice water. She squeezed her hands into fists, waiting to speak until she had her emotions under control.

'Where is he, Raj?' she said, letting the earlier conversation drop. 'Is he alive?'

He didn't answer right away. When he spoke, his voice was low.

'I wish I knew.'

Four

The rest of the day passed in a haze of exhaustion.

Allie went to the dining hall at lunch time to prove to the others how fine she was.

Completely fine.

As soon as she walked in the room, though, Katie Gilmore ran to her and wrapped her in an entirely unfamiliar hug.

'Thank God you're OK.'

After hating her for years, it felt weird being her friend. Not bad weird. Just… *weird* weird. And yet, Allie found herself hugging her back, clinging to Katie's lean shoulders, her face buried in her long, red hair. She smelled of the world's most expensive perfume.

'It was awful,' Allie heard herself whispering. And she wished she would stop.

How was anyone going to believe she was fine if she kept saying she wasn't?

But Katie seemed to understand. Her beautiful face looked sombre – all of her arrogance stripped away.

'I'm so sorry about Lucinda. I admired her so much.' Katie's voice was low; her words were meant for Allie alone. 'She was a *giant*.'

Mention of her grandmother made Allie's heart lurch.

Unlike Allie, Katie had grown up with Lucinda Meldrum – always head of Orion, always a tangible part of her life.

It would have been wonderful to grow up with Lucinda always there.

'She was amazing,' Allie agreed softly, 'wasn't she?'

The two exchanged a look of understanding. Then Katie cocked her head to one side and narrowed her gaze. 'You should eat. You look like crap.'

And just like that the moment was over.

Lessons were cancelled, of course. And Night School. Having nothing to do felt like failure. If Allie hadn't been so exhausted she would have run back to Raj and shouted at him. Demanded they all get back to work. Find Carter. *Fix this*.

But she didn't. What good would it do? The truth was, they *had* lost. They were defeated. They'd failed.

Besides, the teachers were locked away somewhere having secret strategy meetings. She hadn't seen any of them since she'd returned to the school. There was no one to shout at.

After lunch, the others succumbed one by one to the lack of sleep, disappearing to their rooms. But Allie refused to follow them.

The last time she'd slept she'd been lying in Carter's arms in the safe house in London. The memory of that moment haunted her now.

She didn't want to be in her room. Didn't want to be alone.

She didn't want to be safe when Carter wasn't.

By late afternoon, though, she was punch-drunk with exhaustion. She hadn't slept properly in two days.

She reeled through the tangle of hallways alone, trying to stay awake.

'Someone to talk to,' she muttered to herself as she turned into the common room. But it was empty, save for the cleaners, who were silently stacking used cups and plates on trays. The delicate clattering of the china echoed in the stillness.

She walked along the formal hallway as far as the classroom wing, where a cluster of marble statues kept watch. Then she turned and paced back again, fingers tracing the grooves of the carved panelling.

Eventually, she found herself standing outside the library, unable to remember exactly how she'd got there.

The door swung open with a soft sound, like an intake of breath.

This room was as familiar to Allie as her own bedroom. The long rows of tall bookcases with their tilted, rolling ladders. The dim, low light. It felt like refuge.

She walked in slowly – the high-ceilinged space felt hollow and empty. There was no sign of Eloise, the librarian. Or of any students or guards. The big metal light fixtures hanging from chains had been left on, as they always were. Green-shaded lamps glowed on every empty table.

Allie found herself walking slowly across the room. She was so tired her feet felt light. Like she was floating through the fiction section. Thick Persian carpets muffled her footsteps, adding to the sense of unreality.

Maybe she was asleep right now, and dreaming this whole thing.

When she reached the modern history section she turned. Her fingertips lightly brushed the gilded spines of the old books as she looked for one title. When she found what she sought, she slid it off the shelf and clutched it to her chest.

It was a heavy book with a leather cover. The title

was *Conquering the World.*

Allie closed her eyes.

A month ago, she'd stood right here with Carter, bickering about their history assignment.

'Here's a good one,' he'd said, handing her this book.

In science class she'd learned all objects constantly exchange electrons. If you sit in a chair long enough eventually the chair has all your electrons, and you have the chair's.

Jerry Cole had taught her that.

She put her hands where Carter's had been, trying to *feel* him in the book. Yet she could feel nothing beneath her fingertips but the hard, unyielding cover.

Allie gave a muffled sob.

Who knew where he was? She'd failed to keep him safe.

Failed to protect him.

I should have done something. But I lost him.

Still holding the book in her arms, she slid slowly down to the floor and lowered her head to her knees.

Carter, please be alive.

'Allie Sheridan?' The gruff voice was unfamiliar, dispassionate.

Allie blinked awake. The world had tilted sideways. Her cheek was pressed against the rough weave of an antique Persian rug.

Slowly she sat up and looked around blearily.

The library.

She could only vaguely remember coming in here. She must have fallen asleep. She still cradled a book in her arms.

One of Raj's guards stood at the end of the row, his expression inscrutable. 'Isabelle le Fanult would like you to come to her office.'

'She would, would she?' Fully awake now, Allie rubbed the back of her hand across her gritty eyes. 'Well, maybe I'm not interested in talking to her right now.'

The guard opened his mouth, then closed it again. Clearly he hadn't expected that.

'She said it was important?' A touch of uncertainty had entered his voice.

It's always important, Allie wanted to snap at him.

But she didn't. It wouldn't be fair to take it out on him; this wasn't his fault. She didn't even know his name.

Heaving a sigh she waved him away. 'Fine. I'll go see her.'

Unable to disguise his relief, he gave a curt nod and left hurriedly, before she could change her mind.

Allie climbed to her feet – her muscles ached from last night's fight and from sleeping on the hard floor.

Moving stiffly, she made her way out into the hallway. The windows were dark. Night had fallen while she slept. She'd been out for hours.

At the foot of the grand staircase she turned to where Isabelle's office was tucked away, the door virtually hidden in the elaborately carved oak panelling. She paused and took a deep breath. When she felt steady enough, she tapped once.

'Come in.'

The door swung open at Allie's touch. The headmistress sat at her desk, a laptop open in front of her.

She glanced up briefly. 'Please have a seat.'

Her expression gave nothing away.

Isabelle's antique, mahogany desk dominated the small office. Two, deep leather chairs faced it; Allie sat on the edge of the closest one.

Isabelle typed with quick, sure movements, her gaze fixed on the screen. She'd changed out of her Night School gear into tailored dark trousers and a white silk blouse. A cardigan was draped across her shoulders. She didn't look as pale as she had earlier. At first glance, in fact, she appeared almost… normal.

When the seconds ticked by and she kept typing, Allie knew a message was being sent. Isabelle was reminding her who was in charge.

As she waited, she glanced around the room. Everything was in its usual place – low cabinets lined one wall beneath a large, romantic tapestry of a knight and a maid with a white horse.

At last, Isabelle finished whatever she was doing. She closed the laptop with a decisive click and leaned back in her chair, fixing Allie with her fierce, leonine gaze.

'Raj and Dom are working flat-out to find where Nathaniel has taken Carter,' she said without preamble. 'I wanted you to be the first to know that we believe he is alive.'

Something about the cool simplicity of that last sentence undid Allie. She pressed her palms against her eyes.

He's alive. He's alive…

Isabelle waited for a moment before continuing. 'Please believe this: we will get him back. And Nathaniel will pay for what happened last night. We will get through this. And we will start over.'

Her tone had turned ice cold and, to her own surprise, Allie found she *did* believe her.

They may have been beaten in London but one thing was

clear: Isabelle wasn't giving up. Not in the slightest.

The fight was still on.

Dropping her hands to her lap, Allie raised her gaze. 'Where is he?'

'We don't know that yet, but we are monitoring Nathaniel's conversations and that has given us reason to believe Carter and the two guards are being held somewhere outside London. I suspect Nathaniel wants to use them as a bargaining chip.'

She sounded furious. But Allie's whole body felt lighter. As long as Carter was alive she could deal with anything.

This burst of optimism came hand-in-hand with instant guilt for the way she'd behaved towards Isabelle that morning. The cruel things she'd said came back to her in a flood.

Nathaniel was the enemy. Not her.

'Look…' she said hesitantly. 'About what happened this morning —'

Isabelle's hand snapped up, stopping her.

'Please don't,' she said. 'It wasn't your fault. I handled it very badly.'

But Allie wasn't about to accept that.

'I was wrong,' Allie said. 'It was an awful night and horrible things happened but I know…' She paused for a second before finishing. 'I know you love him, too.'

Spots of colour had appeared in Isabelle's cheeks – the only sign of the tidal wave of emotion Allie suspected she was suppressing.

'Yes, I do love him,' the headmistress said. 'Very much. And, with your help, we'll have him back. Will you fight with me, Allie? For Carter?'

Allie didn't hesitate. 'Yes.'

Isabelle stood and walked around the desk to sit in the chair next to hers. This close, Allie could see the strain in her face. Her eyes were red-rimmed, underscored by shadows. But her expression was determined.

'Allie, there have been times when, perhaps, I didn't appreciate that this was as much your fight as it is mine. When I assumed you were too young to be involved in running this… struggle with Nathaniel,' she said. 'I won't make that mistake again. You are at the heart of this. You have a right to decide what happens in your own life. And you have a right to know what my plans are.'

She took a deep breath. 'I'm leaving the Organisation. Leaving Cimmeria. And I'd like you to come with me.'

The news hit Allie like a punch in the stomach. She felt winded. Betrayed.

Abandoned.

Hot tears prickled the backs of her eyes. For a second, she couldn't seem to make her mouth work. 'You're… you're leaving?'

'We have to, Allie,' Isabelle said gently. 'You and me. Raj… Everyone. Whatever happens next, we have to leave Cimmeria Academy. We can wait until Nathaniel throws us out, or we can simply go. We can walk out of here on our own. I intend to do the latter.'

The bottom had fallen out of Allie's world.

Do I have to lose everything?

She wanted to run out of this room and never come back. To sit in a dark corner somewhere and lick her wounds.

But she made herself stay.

'I don't understand.' Her voice was thick with unshed tears. 'Where will you go?'

Isabelle didn't answer the question immediately. She ran her hand affectionately across the top of her polished, mahogany desk. Her face looked pensive.

'Did I ever tell you I inherited this desk from my father?'

Puzzled by the turn the conversation had taken, Allie shook her head. She knew Isabelle and Nathaniel had the same father, different mothers. That they'd grown up together, and their father had left everything to Isabelle, even though Nathaniel was his eldest child.

But she knew little else about her family life.

'He specified it in his will.' Isabelle's voice was soft. 'It had been in his office as long as I could remember. It belonged to his father before him. He left it to me.'

She pressed her hands flat on the desktop, her eyes flashing with repressed anger.

'I don't want my half-brother to touch this desk. I cannot bear to think of him in my school.' She lifted her hands. 'But the simple truth is, he has won. And we have to start thinking about how we intend to lose.'

Too horrified and angry to be diplomatic, Allie raised her voice. '*No*, Isabelle. Don't even say that. It's not over. Not yet. We can't give up. I won't let you. Not after what he did. Not after Jo. Not after Carter.'

Putting those two names – those two fates – in the same sentence was hard. But they were being honest with each other now. And Isabelle had to know how she felt.

'Oh my dear, how can you have so little faith in me?' The headmistress leaned back in her chair, studying her with a melancholy half-smile. 'If there's one thing Lucinda and I have both tried and failed to teach you, it's how to win by losing. I think you have no choice now, except to learn this painful lesson.'

'I don't even know what that means,' Allie snapped. She wasn't interested in word-play right now. She needed Isabelle to stop giving up.

'Then let me explain it to you.' The headmistress held her gaze steadily. 'First, we will lose when we leave this school. I accept that. But what you don't understand is, I'm not giving up. I'm starting over.'

Allie's brow creased. 'Starting over how?'

'We will close Cimmeria Academy,' the headmistress explained. 'And open again with the same teachers, the same students, someplace else. Far away.'

Allie was stunned. 'What? You want to move the school?'

'Effectively… yes.'

'But… how? Where would we go?'

'We have a lot of support abroad, and there are many possible locations. There's a lovely old school in the Swiss Alps. A beautiful place, high in the mountains. It was a Victorian finishing school.' Isabelle glanced at her father's desk. 'I can see us there.'

Allie wanted to argue, but when she put it like that, it made worryingly good sense. An easy out. An end to the fighting. A fresh start. But there were flaws in the plan.

'Wouldn't Nathaniel just follow us?'

The headmistress shrugged. 'Possibly. But perhaps not. You see, if we left Orion and Cimmeria voluntarily, he'd have no reason to pursue us.'

'Then he's won,' Allie said flatly.

'That's what we'd want him to think.' Isabelle gave her a meaningful look. 'Once we're out of his reach we will find a way to undermine him. To destroy everything he builds. To defeat him.'

Allie let out a breath she hadn't known she'd been holding. She felt suddenly numb.

'So the same fight would continue.'

Isabelle shook her head emphatically.

'No, Allie,' she said. 'A new fight would begin. For the soul of everything. With us in the drivers' seat.' She leaned forward. 'This is what I mean when I talk about losing cleverly. To come back and win another day.'

Allie hated how plausible it sounded. The idea that this war with Nathaniel could go on, even after they'd lost Cimmeria, was more than she could bear right now. With Lucinda still to be buried, and Carter…

She straightened. 'What about Carter? You're not giving up on him are you? Because I won't go anywhere without him.'

Isabelle held up her hands. 'No,' she said. 'No one is going anywhere without Carter. We need to get him back first and then we leave. That's what I'm focusing on now. Please believe me. I would never do anything that would hurt Carter.'

It was a good plan. Or rather, it was the least-worst plan.

Even so, Allie hated it. You can have all kinds of fancy words for losing, but whatever you call it, you've still lost.

On the other hand, getting away – starting over. That *was* enticing. Leaving Nathaniel behind, at least for a while. Escaping. Being safe.

The thought was almost inconceivable. And she wanted it as much as Isabelle did.

However, she couldn't imagine how this could be explained to the other students. They seemed so defeated. So exhausted. If she told them Isabelle's big plan was to lose really, really well…

They'd give up. The way she kind of wanted to give up

now.

They had to find a way to make everyone believe losing really was victory.

She could hear no sound at all coming from the corridor. The school was quiet as a church. So her voice seemed startlingly loud when she spoke again.

'We have to get Night School going again.'

Isabelle's head jerked up. 'I'm sorry?'

Now that she'd said it, Allie knew this was the answer. 'You've cancelled training, and classes,' she said, urgency strengthening her voice. 'Bring them back. Get everyone back to work. Right now.'

The headmistress looked taken aback. 'Allie, after what happened to Lucinda, I really believe we need a few days to mourn.'

But the more she thought about it, the more Allie was certain she was right. Having nothing to do was making everyone feel hopeless.

'Don't you see? We don't need time to *cry*. Crying is losing. We need to get to work. When we work – when we train in Night School – we feel powerful. We *are* powerful.' She took a breath. 'Besides. If we're going to get Carter back we don't have days to wait. We have to get started right now.'

Isabelle still appeared doubtful. 'But the teachers are exhausted. The students are demoralised…'

Allie didn't waver. 'Then let the teachers sleep tonight. Tomorrow, they should *teach*. The students are depressed because they think we've lost. Worse,' she said, 'they think we're giving up. We need to make them understand we're still fighting. We still have a chance… Because we do.'

Five

The next morning, when Allie walked down for breakfast, a hand-written notice was posted on the door of the dining hall.

Normal lesson schedules resume today at

9 a.m. All students are expected to

attend classes as per the Rules. Night

School resumes at 8 p.m. Henceforth,

ALL students at Cimmeria Academy

are to train with Night School.

THERE WILL BE NO EXCEPTIONS.

'What's this?'

Katie leaned over Allie's shoulder to read the letter.

'All students at Cimmeria Academy are to…' She read the words aloud, dismay growing with every word.

'Not *me*, of course.' She looked at Allie, her face a perfect mask of disbelief. 'She can't mean *me*?'

Allie knew they were friends now, and she should be sympathetic, but she grinned at her and turned into the dining hall.

Suddenly she was ravenous.

Katie followed on her heels, panic making her voice rise. 'You *volunteer* for Night School. That's the way it's always been. They can't forcibly enlist you. This isn't the army. I am not a *conscript*.'

Rachel and Nicole were already at their usual table as the two of them walked up, Katie in mid-complaint.

Seeing Allie's pleased expression and Katie's outrage, Rachel's eyebrows winged up.

'Ah. You've seen the notice.'

Katie turned her attention to her. 'Rachel, I can't be forced to join Night School, can I?' she implored. 'There must be a law. Freedom of… individuality. Some sort of protection. Human rights. I'm human, aren't I?'

Allie snorted. Rachel's lips twitched. 'Well…'

'Oh God.' Katie sank into the seat next to Nicole, whose long, dark hair gleamed in the light like spilled ink.

Nicole patted her shoulder. 'I think you'll be very good at Night School.'

'Of course I will.' The redhead glared. 'But I don't want to. I'll speak to Zelazny. He'll put a stop to this.' Jumping up from her seat, she sped across the room, copper-red ponytail streaming behind her.

'Poor Zelazny,' Rachel murmured, watching as she disappeared through the doorway.

'He can handle her,' Allie said.

Rachel's cinnamon-coloured gaze scanned her face. 'You look a lot better. Did you sleep?'

In fact, after her talk with Isabelle Allie had slept properly, in an actual bed, for the first time in days.

'I had a talk with Isabelle,' Allie said. 'Cleared the air a little.'

'Did you learn anything new? Any news on Carter?'

Allie filled Rachel in on what she knew. The other girl absorbed this with less joy than Allie'd expected.

'But nothing concrete?' Her brow creased. 'They don't know where he is?'

Her doubt was instantly deflating. Rachel was one of Allie's smartest friends. If she didn't believe Carter was fine…

Allie didn't want to think about that.

'Anyway,' she continued firmly, 'I told Isabelle we should get back to work…'

Nicole leaned over. 'Are you responsible for lessons beginning again?'

'Was it Allie?' Zoe walked up to the table with Lucas. 'Way to go, Allie!'

She emphasised her happiness with an air-kick that barely missed a nearby table of younger students. Allie hadn't even noticed they were there until they ducked.

'Don't kill the little ones,' Rachel chided Zoe mildly.

Zoe blinked at them, as if she, too, had failed to note their existence.

'Hi Zoe,' a boy at the table said shyly. He had glasses, olive skin and wavy dark hair and looked at Zoe with undisguised admiration.

She fixed him with a blank stare until his cheeks flushed and he turned back to his breakfast.

'Whoever did it is a hero.' Lucas pretended to punch Zoe who promptly punched him back for real.

Lucas clutched his arm. 'Ow! Dammit, Shortie,' he

complained. 'You have to work on your anger control.'

'Don't call me Shortie,' Zoe replied, unrepentant.

'So Night School starts tonight.' Rachel raised her voice, in an attempt to restore order. 'And this time every student left in the school's going to be there. And every teacher. What's that going to be like?'

A determined smile spread slowly across Allie's face.

'A start.'

Allie was hurrying to class when someone called her name. Turning, she saw a young woman with glasses and long dark hair twisted up on her head hurrying towards her.

'Eloise!' Allie ran to the librarian and hugged her. 'You're OK.'

Eloise was the youngest of the Night School instructors – the one closest to their age. She'd always been the one they would go to with their problems – the one most likely to still remember what it was like to be seventeen years old.

But the stress of the last year had changed her – she looked older. No one would mistake her for a student now.

'I'm just fine.' Her warm gaze swept Allie's face, catching on the stitches barely visible at her hairline. 'Mostly fine, anyway.' Her smile faded. 'I'm sorry about your grandmother.'

Allie took a step back. 'Thanks.' She mumbled the word. She still didn't really know how to react to expressions of sympathy. What to say.

Seeing this, Eloise didn't linger on the subject.

'Dom's looking for you,' she said. 'She wants you to come to her office right away.'

Allie's heart leaped. 'Is it Carter? Did she find him? Is he OK?' Eagerness sent her words tumbling over each other.

Eloise held up a hand. 'I don't know. I was just told to find you.'

'OK,' Allie said, nearly hopping with excitement. 'I better go.'

She spun on her heel and took off down the hall, class completely forgotten.

Maybe they'd found Carter. Maybe they were going to get him right now.

The thought spurred her on, and she ran even faster. The only problem was, she didn't actually know where the tech's office was.

She searched the main school building without success before trying the classroom wing. Students were still in classes, and most of the doors were shut. She could hear the teachers talking, a faint drone in the background as she hurried upstairs to check the next level. It was much the same – there was no obvious place for Dom here.

The top floor of the classroom wing was dedicated mostly to seminars for senior students, so the classrooms were smaller and more numerous. All were empty at this hour – the corridor was gloomy and too quiet. Allie found herself tiptoeing – as if not to disturb the silence. That was when she first heard the faint tapping sound.

She paused to listen. The noise was arrhythmic but constant.

She traced it – going from door to door until she reached one where the sound was louder. This close she could hear something else as well.

Music.

She knocked.

'Enter.' Dom's American accent flattened her vowels and elongated the 'r'.

Allie burst in, already talking. 'What's happening? Is it Carter? Have you found him?'

Her words poured out in a breathless race.

'Sort of.' Dom stood up from a desk at one end of the room. Allie's hope began to dissipate instantly – she looked too serious for this to be good news.

Allie's chest tightened. 'What do you mean, sort of?'

'I've heard his voice.' Dom's tone was calm. 'He's definitely alive. I just… can't exactly find him.'

Like Eloise, Dom was young, twenty-one according to gossip, but she was a technical genius. She had started a software company while still at Harvard, and sold it for millions of dollars.

A former Cimmeria student, she'd returned to the school to help them deal with Nathaniel, but her distinctive, androgynous style always set her apart from the school's conservative teachers. Today she wore a button-down shirt of a heavy creamy material, with baggy trousers cinched tight around her narrow waist. Her burgundy brogues had been polished until they gleamed. With her dark skin and short-cropped hair, she was so sophisticated, Allie was usually a little in awe her.

But today all she cared about was Carter.

'You've heard his *voice*?' Allie wanted to shake the news out of her. 'How? When?'

Dom stepped back. 'You better come in, and close the door.'

Allie did as she was told. The room had once been a

classroom, but it had been transformed into a spacious office. The desks had all been removed, leaving only an oak teacher's desk, which Dom had accessorised with a sleek, black office chair. Three laptops sat side by side on the desktop. A widescreen monitor was mounted on the wall. Four leather chairs Allie thought she recognised from the common room surrounded a round wooden table that might have been harvested from the dining hall. A red Persian rug with a design of gold stars covered the floor.

Allie could hear the faint sound of jazz – the discordant kind, rather than the jolly World War II kind – swirling from hidden speakers.

'Have a seat.' Dom pointed at the chairs by the table, but Allie shook her head. She didn't want to sit down. She wasn't here for a *chat*.

'Please, Dom. If you know something, just tell me.' She couldn't keep a pleading note out of her voice. 'Where is he?'

Behind her glasses, Dom's eyes were sympathetic. 'That's the one thing I don't know.'

Allie wanted to scream in frustration. It took all her determination to keep her voice steady. 'What do you know? Is he hurt? Where did you hear him?'

'I hacked into Nathaniel's comms system. I've been listening to them all night.' Dom hurried back to her desk and began typing rapidly on one of the laptops. This was the sound Allie had heard from the hallway. 'His system is well-protected. His people are very good, but…' She paused to glance at the monitor. 'I'm better.'

The jazz disappeared, replaced by a cold voice. 'Item secured. Team Eight en route. Over.'

The sound crackled but Allie recognised it instantly: Gabe.

Her hands clenched and unclenched at her sides. The last time she saw Gabe he killed Lucinda. It turned her stomach to hear his voice.

It was hard to be here. Hard to know he lived on, while her grandmother's life was over. But she made herself focus on small things. In the background, she could hear an engine rumbling – a vehicle of some sort – and other voices talking.

Then a second voice replied to Gabe. 'Copy Team Eight. Gold Command requests verification of condition of item. Over.'

Gabe responded a moment later. 'Item is conscious and aware. Condition good.'

Time passed. Then the second voice spoke again. 'Gold Command requests verbal verification from item.'

Allie couldn't put her finger on it, but something in that voice – a cool, undertone of distaste – told her the person didn't like Gabe.

There was another long silence, broken suddenly by harsh breathing, and the clunking sound of a microphone being fumbled with.

Gabe spoke from a slight distance. 'Verify your condition.'

A new voice replied, sardonic; unafraid. 'How the hell do I do that?'

Allie's heart leaped. It was Carter. She'd know that voice anywhere.

Six

'Speak into the microphone. Tell Gold Command you're being well treated.' Gabe was emotionless. The cold, efficient voice of a soldier.

'Sorry. What exactly do you want me to say?' Carter said.

He was being stubborn on purpose, and Allie found herself smiling, even as a tear rolled down her cheek.

It was just so *Carter.*

Gabe muttered something low and threatening the microphone didn't catch.

Carter cleared his throat. 'Uh… Hey, Gold Command. This is the *item*. I am being very well treated. If by "well" you mean handcuffed and carted off by some murderous arsehole and stuffed in a…'

Muffled sounds of a struggle followed. The microphone clicked off abruptly.

Seconds later, it clicked again.

'Verification complete.' Gabe sounded slightly breathless.

I hope Carter punched you in the face, Allie thought.

'Copy that, Eight Leader,' the voice from headquarters responded. 'You are advised to use Protocol Seventeen. Repeat, Protocol Seventeen. Verify that you receive and understand.'

'Protocol Seventeen. Received and noted.'

The voices disappeared.

Allie wiped the tears from her cheeks with the back of her hand and took a tremulous breath.

'When did you record that?'

'Last night,' Dom said. 'Shortly after 3 a.m. I've been trying to trace it ever since without much success. Like I said… they're good.'

'What was happening exactly?' Allie was trying to piece together what she'd just heard. 'Where were they taking him?'

'We believe he was being moved from wherever they've been keeping him to a new location. Someone – Nathaniel probably – was monitoring his location and condition.'

'Is there more?' Allie asked hopefully. 'More of Carter?'

Dom shook her head. 'That's all we got. They gave Nathaniel proof he was alive and well.' She met Allie's gaze. 'That itself is pretty interesting, though. It indicates a lack of trust between Nathaniel and his lieutenants. Which ties in to what Isabelle saw in the fight on the heath – Gabe turning his gun on his boss.' She leaned back in her chair. 'There's definitely something going on there.'

Allie lowered herself into a nearby chair. She needed to process everything but her brain kept having its own celebration – *Carter's alive! He's alive!*

Still, the last bit she'd heard puzzled her enough to keep her focused.

'What's Protocol Seventeen?'

It was the right question. Dom shot her an approving look.

'We've been talking about that all day. We're assuming it's a humane treatment protocol similar to the one we used for Jerry Cole. If I could just get into Nathaniel's system, we'd know more.' Dom ran a tired hand across her short hair. 'His security is damn good. I'm going to need time and help.'

'But where is he?' Allie couldn't keep the frustration out of his voice. 'Are they even in the country?'

'We think so. At least, he was last night.'

Dom's words left Allie hollow. Between that recording and now, Carter could have been bundled onto a private plane and spirited across the Channel. Nathaniel had the means. Nothing was beyond him.

Her desolation must have shown on her face because Dom left her desk and came to stand near her.

'Look,' she said with uncharacteristic gentleness. 'The thing you need to take from it is this: Carter is fine. And we are going to get him back. I need you to be positive, OK?'

She knew Dom was right. But hearing Carter's voice had been a kind of sweet torture. He'd seemed so close. So *reachable*.

And now he was gone again.

She bit her lip so hard it hurt. Then she nodded. 'I'll try to be patient.'

To her surprise, Dom shook her head. 'Don't be patient.' Her dark eyes flashed. 'That's bullshit. Be angry. Use your anger to help you think clearly. That's what Carter needs from you now.'

That night, all the senior students were early for Night School. No one could wait. They wanted to get started.

Everything was different now.

When Allie told the others she'd heard Carter, Rachel and Zoe tackle-hugged her.

Lucas had walked away from the group for a moment to gather himself. Allie thought she'd seen tears of relief in his eyes.

The mood at the school had changed. There was a kind of barely controlled energy – it fairly crackled in the air.

Everyone wanted to win. Just this once.

Allie decided not to tell the others what she and Isabelle had discussed. They needed to believe in their own power first. They needed to believe they could win. If she told them now it would deflate them at precisely the worst time.

As they headed downstairs, for the first time ever Katie was with them, albeit lagging just a little behind.

In the end, Zelazny hadn't helped her out of Night School training after all.

The girls' changing room was a simple white cube lined with brass hooks above a polished wood bench. Each hook held a single set of black, Night School training gear, draped like shroud. Above each hook was a name.

Katie surveyed the room with open distaste.

'And you come here every night… on purpose?'

'It's great,' Zoe chirped. Not waiting for the others, she started to change. As she pulled the white blouse of her uniform off, Allie saw a row of deep purple bruises on her narrow back.

She drew in a sharp breath. 'Zoe! Is that from London?'

Zoe twisted to see her back in the wall mirror.

'Yeah. Some tosser ran right over me. Lucas dropped him with a spin kick.'

She sounded pleased.

But Allie stood for a long moment, looking at those marks on Zoe's narrow back. Her delicate shoulder-blades, the tiny knobs of her spine – they looked so fragile.

Pressing her lips together, she turned to her own hook and began to change.

We all have bruises, she reminded herself.

In the mirror, she met Nicole's expressive dark eyes. She could tell the French girl understood how she felt.

This was all getting harder to take.

'So, what am I to do?' Katie still stood in the middle of the room. 'Change or drift elegantly through the room offering useful and badly needed fashion advice?'

Zoe opened her mouth to reply but Allie didn't give her the chance.

'Change,' she said tersely. 'You're one of us now.' She took a set of black leggings and matching tunic hanging from a hook with the name 'Jules Matheson' above it and held them out to her. 'Shoes are under the bench. Take any that fit.'

Chagrined, Katie accepted the clothes with a silent nod.

Allie returned to changing her own clothes, but out of the corner of her eye she watched as the redhead began to get ready. She could see the nervous set of her jaw, and the way she fumbled with the top as she pulled it on over her expensive lace bra.

She knew this wasn't easy for her – she was faking the arrogant act. But, for her own good, she had to do this the hard way.

As they emerged from the training room a few minutes later, Allie dropped back to whisper to Rachel. 'Keep an eye on Katie.'

Rachel, who'd only joined Night School recently herself, inclined her head.

'I'll stick with her.'

Training Room One was squat and ugly – grey stone walls,

dim fluorescent lighting and floors covered in blue exercise mats. A perpetual smell of warm sweat hung in the air.

Lucas was already there. The small group clustered together stretching, talking in low voices.

Allie turned a slow circle, taking in the emptiness of the room. The first time she'd ever come in here, it was packed with Night School students. Cimmeria's best and brightest. There must have been fifty students in here then. Maybe more. Now there were six.

And one of them was Katie Gilmore.

Others were coming – but most of them were new to Night School. They'd be starting with the very basics. No one would mistake them for the real thing.

Most of the Night School students had gone when Nathaniel laid down his first ultimatum, forcing parents to choose between his way and Lucinda's. They'd almost all chosen his.

Out of fear, probably, but it didn't matter what their reasoning was. The effect was the same. An empty school. A hollow training room.

'Who are our partners going to be?' Zoe asked. Her voice echoed in the quiet.

Allie's heart sank. Of course, with Carter and Sylvain both gone they'd have to rearrange. Find a different system. Suddenly it seemed overwhelming. Everything was such a mess. Everything they'd thought so permanent was crumbling around them.

The others were looking at her as if she should have the answers. She just stared back at them, panic rising in her chest.

I don't know how to do this, she thought. *How can we even go on with just us? It's not Night School anymore. It's not anything.*

It was Nicole who came up with the solution.

'I think Rachel should pair with Katie,' she said, pointing at the two girls who were newest to the training. 'Zoe, you pair with Lucas. I'll pair with Allie.'

Lucas punched Zoe lightly on the shoulder. 'Come on midget, let's see what you got.'

'Don't call me *midget.*' Leaping effortlessly to her feet, Zoe swung a kick at him. This time he dodged the blow.

Their sparring lightened the mood, and soon the group had arrayed themselves in pairs. While Rachel walked Katie through some basics, the others worked on the last self-defence moves they'd been practising before the parley.

Within minutes the room had warmed up. They'd forgotten how empty it was, how few of them were left. They were really fighting – sweating from the exertion. They didn't notice when the door swung open.

'Uh… guys…'

Something in Rachel's voice made the others stop and look up.

At one end of the room, a group of younger students clustered by the door, watching them with wide eyes.

Slowly, they all noticed what was happening and stopped fighting. As a group they turned to face the new recruits.

'What's wrong with them?' Zoe squinted at the younger students critically. 'Why are they just standing there?'

'I think you're scaring them,' Katie said. She waved cheerily. 'Come in, little ones, come in. Welcome to Hell. Don't be afraid.'

'Oh great, Katie,' Rachel said. 'Scare them more.'

'What's going on here?' Zelazny pushed his way through the crowd of new trainees. 'Move along. Move along. Stop crowding the doorway. They don't bite. Spread *out.*'

With obvious reluctance, the youths moved a step or two further into the room where they clustered together, surveying this new world with suspicion. Most were twelve to fourteen years old, but a few were younger.

Allie found herself staring at them. They looked so *small*.

Eloise arrived a few seconds later, with Raj and a troupe of his guards. More teachers poured in, too.

Allie and the senior students stood at the back of the room, arms crossed, surveying the increasingly crowded space as Zelazny and the other instructors took their place at the centre of the room.

The history teacher was in his element.

'Good to see the advanced students here early,' he said, with a nod to Allie's group. 'And welcome to the new trainees. You'll find we work very hard here. We will ask much of you, but we will also teach you how to keep yourselves safe. And to *fight back*.'

He walked the length of the room, studying the new students, who watched him warily.

'I think we should start by showing you what the senior students can do.'

Crossing the room to where Allie stood next to Nicole, he spoke quietly. 'The move you were working on last week – the spin and escape. Do that again but slowly, so they can see how it works.'

They went through the steps with ease; Nicole performed the kick while Allie blocked the blows, catching her foot as it neared her face and twisting it, a move Nicole parried with a forearm to Allie's throat.

The new students looked impressed and terrified in equal measure.

The other senior students applauded sardonically.

'Now' Zelazny had turned back to the new students. 'We're not starting with something as complicated as that. I think first we must work on your conditioning. We will start, as they say, at the beginning.'

For the next hour, Eloise and Zelazny worked the new students through stretches and sit-ups, while Raj and his guards took the senior students through a complex krav maga and martial arts moves.

Allie was glad to be moving. She was stiff from the fight in the park but her muscles wanted to move.

After a while, she and Nicole stopped to rest, leaning against a wall side by side. A short distance away, Rachel and Katie were trying out a basic spinning kick. While Rachel struggled a bit, the redhead performed the move with easy grace – leaping through the air and landing on her feet with the lightness of a cat.

Nicole and Allie exchanged a surprised look.

'What the hell?' Allie murmured.

As they watched, Katie executed the move again, just as perfectly the second time.

A smile of understanding flickered across Nicole's even features.

'Of *course*. I forgot she studied dance,' she said, her French accent gilding each word. 'She'll be a natural at this.'

A short distance away, Zoe and Lucas were speed-fighting – doing the same moves the others had been doing, but much faster. Allie knew they were trying to see how quickly they could do it without missing a step or hospitalising each other.

Raj walked up behind her with soundless steps. 'I was going to stop them,' he said. 'But they're having too much fun.'

Allie's gaze searched his face. 'Anything new from Dom? About Carter?'

'Not yet. But she's working on it.'

At that moment, Zelazny clapped his hands to get their attention. His voice boomed across the room: 'Three mile run. Lucas and Zoe.' He turned to where the two had stopped mid-fight, fists still raised. 'Guide the junior students. Don't,' he added sharply, 'lose any of them.'

Zoe dashed for the door. Lucas gave Allie a grin as he sped by.

'Don't worry,' he said. 'I won't let her hurt them.'

'I hope Zelazny knows what he's doing.' Allie turned back to Raj, but he'd already gone.

Nicole was gone too. She was over talking to Rachel, whose expression brightened instantly as Nicole whispered something to her.

Seeing the two of them together sent a sharp stab of loneliness through Allie. They were so close now – always together. She and Rachel were close too, of course, but… not like that.

'Allie.' Katie waved for her attention.

It was annoying how she managed to look effortlessly beautiful even now. Exercise had brought a glow to her cheeks and sent her shoulder-length ponytail bouncing into copper curls.

'This running thing…' Katie cast her a coy look. 'Do I have to?'

Allie rolled her eyes. 'You're going to fight this every step of the way, aren't you?'

'Of course.'

Taking her by the arm, Allie dragged her into the shadowy corridor.

'Everything we do here? You have to do it, too.'

'God. Running is so dull,' Katie complained.

In that instant, her crisp, upper-class accent reminded Allie so strongly of Jo it made her chest ache.

'Running is boring unless someone's chasing you,' she said. 'Which around here is almost guaranteed. Let's go.'

Seven

By the time Allie and Katie emerged through one of the old Victorian building's many hidden doorways into a moonlit night, the other students had already disappeared.

Allie didn't like this – the group shouldn't be separating right now. Especially when the younger students were out for their first night run. She could only hope Zoe and Lucas would keep them together.

Katie peered around them. 'Where do we go now?'

'Let's just take the usual route.'

Katie held up her perfectly manicured hands. 'Which is…?'

'Which is *follow me.'* Allie took off at speed, and Katie followed, complaining under her breath as they hurtled across he smooth grass.

When they reached the woods, all light disappeared. Allie knew the forest footpaths like the back of her hand, but Katie didn't. Almost immediately in her struggle to keep up, she tripped over a tree root and nearly fell.

After that, Allie reluctantly slowed her pace. It was a quiet night – the only sound the rasp of their breathing and the drumming of their feet against the hard ground.

Allie cast a sideways glance at Katie. She had an easy natural stride and moved lightly, but she was already breathing heavily.

Sensing her gaze, Katie glanced up – her eyes a flash of green in the gloaming.

'Are we there yet?'

Allie snorted. 'You wish. We're just getting started.'

They still hadn't seen any of the others. Allie squinted into the darkness ahead, straining for any sign that they were gaining on them. But they were alone.

'Could we… slow… down…' Katie was panting heavily. '… just a little?'

Reluctantly, Allie gave up on finding everyone else and dropped her speed to a gentle jog.

'Thanks,' Katie gasped, clutching her side. 'Dying.'

Her face was bright red.

'You're actually doing really well,' Allie said. 'You should have seen me on my first run. I nearly passed out. Carter practically…'

The sentence died on her lips. Saying his name aloud reminded her where he was right now.

It hurt like a punch.

The look Katie gave her then was surprisingly sympathetic. 'He'll be OK, you know.'

'I know,' Allie said, her voice low.

'Nathaniel will have taken him for a reason,' Katie said. 'He doesn't do things just to be a wanker. He's too smart for that. He only does what he thinks will increase his chances of victory. He knows how you feel about Carter so he'll want him alive. To him, Carter is a weapon.'

If this was supposed to make Allie feel better it failed

dismally.

Nathaniel was ruthless. Carter was his knife.

Allie desperately needed Katie to stop trying to cheer her up.

'I think I see Rachel and Nicole ahead,' she said. 'Let's catch up to them.'

She increased her speed.

Behind her she heard Katie say, 'Oh bugger.'

From then on, Allie ran as fast as she needed to in order to be certain Katie didn't have the breath to talk.

They really did find Rachel and Nicole near the old stone wall that surrounded the chapel. Rachel had stopped to catch her breath; Nicole, who didn't even look winded, was waiting patiently in a pool of moonlight when Allie and Katie jogged up.

Katie slid down the stone wall to the ground next to Rachel, her face dripping sweat.

'Can't… breathe…' she gasped.

'Right there with you.' Rachel looked exhausted.

Allie turned to Nicole. 'Any sign of Zoe or Lucas?'

The French girl shook her head. 'I think they took a different route.'

'And I've been slowing us down.' Climbing stiffly to her feet, Rachel pressed her foot against the wall to stretch. 'As usual.'

Nicole's smile was indulgent. 'It's not a race.'

It kind of was a race, but it seemed mean to say that.

'We should get going,' Allie said instead.

She glanced down at Katie who had folded her torso over her outstretched legs and was pressing her face to her knees with apparent effortlessness. 'You ready, Katie?'

'Yep.' The girl's tone was curt. She lifted her head and

fixed Allie with a sharp look. 'If we can go at a less suicidal pace.'

'Stick with me.' Rachel answered before Allie could. 'I'm all about slow and steady.'

They all heard the noise at the same time. The crack of a twig breaking. The rustle of branches. Footsteps.

Rachel's voice trailed off.

Allie and Nicole exchanged a frozen glance. In silent unison, they grabbed Rachel and Katie and pushed them behind them.

For once in her life, Katie didn't argue.

Allie crouched down, prepared to spring. She looked around for a weapon – a heavy stick, anything. But there wasn't time.

The thick shrubs that lined one side of the path shook violently as someone crashed through them.

Allie held her breath.

Two of Raj's black-clad guards burst out of the shadows. With them was one of the new trainees – a lanky boy, about fourteen years old, dark hair in a tangle, glasses askew. He looked pale and scared. Allie thought she'd seen him somewhere before but she couldn't place him.

Dropping her fists, Allie drew a deep breath.

As soon as they spotted the girls, the guards' expressions changed from tension to relief. They murmured something to each other then turned towards them.

'This one got lost,' one of the guards explained, pushing the boy towards them. 'Could you take him back?'

The next morning Allie awoke early. At first, she wasn't sure what had disturbed her but when she climbed out of bed, yawning, she discovered a square, ivory envelope on the floor of her room near the door.

She eyed it with suspicion.

The envelope paper was thick, creamy. Soft as fabric. No name was written on the back.

It opened easily to reveal luxurious note paper. At the top, the paper was engraved with a simple 'I' in deep blue.

Isabelle.

The message was terse. 'There's a meeting at 7.30 a.m. in the grand ballroom. Please be there.'

Instantly wide awake, Allie looked at the clock. She had fifteen minutes.

Senior staff meetings were held early in the morning. She knew this because Sylvain and Jules always went when they were prefects. Allie had never been invited before. Isabelle had told her she'd be stepping into Lucinda's shoes.

Now it was happening.

After showering quickly and throwing on her uniform, she ran downstairs, damp tendrils of hair clinging to the shoulders of her blazer.

The air smelled enticingly of bacon, but there wasn't time for breakfast.

When she reached the grand ballroom, she skidded to a stop. Took a calming breath. And knocked politely.

The door was opened by a guard, who waited impassively for her to walk in then locked it behind her.

A table had been set up in front of the towering fireplace.

Isabelle sat at the head. Around the sides were Eloise, Zelazny, Dom, Raj, Rachel, and Lucas. Two guards stood by the door, like sentinels.

'Welcome, Allie,' Isabelle said.

Allie gave Rachel a 'You, too?' look. Rachel mouthed 'prefect' at her.

It made sense. And Lucas must be standing in for Sylvain.

She slid into an empty seat.

'We were just beginning to discuss Dom's plans,' Isabelle explained. She turned to the tech. 'Please continue.'

Neatly turned out as usual in an oversized blazer and perfectly pressed blue button-down shirt, Dom stood to speak, a notebook in one hand.

'I'm assembling a small group that can work twenty-four hours. They'll be listening in on Nathaniel's comms and attempting to hack into his computer system. It's well protected but I'm convinced we can find a way to crack it.' She flipped a page in her notebook. 'I've chosen students and guards who've demonstrated technical abilities beyond the norm. Rachel is the most obvious one.'

Rachel flushed and looked down at her hands.

'Also two younger students – Alec Bradby and Zoe Glass. They've both shown a natural ability. In addition, Raj, I'd appreciate it if you'd allow me to borrow your guard, Shakir Nasseem. I've checked his background files.' She gave Raj a pointed look. 'I can't believe you never told me one of your team was an ace hacker.'

'I was hoping you wouldn't steal him.' Raj's tone was resigned. 'But you can borrow him for this purpose. Anyone else?'

'Katie Gilmore has offered her assistance,' Dom continued, glancing at her notes. 'She has no technical skills to speak of, but her personal knowledge of the locations Nathaniel might be likely to use as a base could prove invaluable.'

'This is all fine with me,' Isabelle said. 'When will you start?'

'I've already begun.'

Raj briefed the group on security patrols, how many guards, which areas each covered.

'No attempted incursions have been noted since the parley,' he said. 'But we believe that could be simply because Nathaniel is regrouping.'

'Agreed,' Isabelle said. 'We should maintain the same level of security until we have better awareness of what Nathaniel is planning.'

And so it went until all the adults had given their reports, and the information had been fully discussed. Allie's stomach was starting to rumble and she was thinking longingly of breakfast when Isabelle spoke again.

'I have one final announcement.' Her gaze lingered on Allie. 'A funeral will be held for Lucinda tomorrow afternoon at the chapel. Her… body will arrive tonight.'

Allie went cold. She didn't know what to do – what expression to have on her face. She felt as if everyone was looking at her.

'The story in the papers,' the headmistress continued, her face devoid of expression, 'is that she fell while walking on the heath late at night, and suffered a heart attack.'

Everything involving Orion and Night School was covered up. Orion owned newspapers, TV stations. Its members had huge influence over the police and the courts. As a result, they had control over how things were reported. When Jo was murdered, the papers said it was a car accident. When Ruth died, it was reported as suicide. Allie knew the drill. But she hated the lies.

Hated them.

Resting her hands on the table she stared down at them. Her nails were ragged and uneven. Suddenly this bothered her. Lucinda valued neatness.

The headmistress was still talking. 'I'll be handling the arrangements. You'll all be made aware of the time for the funeral. No one is required to go but all students and staff will, of course, be welcome to attend.' She paused. 'Now. On to other business…'

For the rest of the day, Allie tried to pour herself into her work and forget about the fact that her grandmother would be buried the next day.

It wasn't easy.

Part of the problem was, while everyone else was busy working to find Carter, she really wasn't. She had no technical skills – nothing to offer that would help right now.

At lunch time the others bubbled with excitement. Dom had set up an action centre in her office.

'We all have laptops,' Rachel enthused. 'And this guard, Shak, he's an *ace* hacker. He's teaching us all how to do it.'

'It's amazing,' Zoe joined in. 'He taught us how to hack into unprotected systems first. This afternoon we're going to start on Nathaniel's system.'

For her part, Katie had spent the morning briefing a detail of guards on the homes of the country's rich and famous.

'Basically we sit with a map and a list of my dad's friends

and track down all the houses they hide from the tax man,' she said, her green eyes glinting in the light like gems. 'There are loads of them. I had no idea my parents' friends were such hideous liars.' She paused to reconsider this statement, pressing one perfectly manicured fingertip against her lips. 'Well, maybe I did, actually. They're all perfectly ghastly.'

Their enthusiasm and newfound hope left Allie feeling oddly left out. Yes, she got to go to the strategy meetings now – Isabelle and Raj asked her opinions. But the others were actually *doing* something.

When classes ended for the day, she couldn't find any of the others. She searched the library, the common room and the gardens without success. They all had to be up in Dom's office. Looking for Carter.

Allie made her way back to the common room. The big, windowless room was busy with students doing their homework and chatting, and guards off-duty, still in their black uniforms but sprawled on the deep leather sofas, mugs of coffee clutched in their hands.

Finding a seat in a corner, she pulled out her history book. But her mind wouldn't focus on medieval Europe in a time of plague. No matter how she tried not to, she kept thinking about Lucinda. And Carter.

And Sylvain.

She hadn't phoned him once since he'd left for France. She told herself it was because his family needed him right now. But she knew the real reason was because she was afraid he'd hear in her voice that she had chosen Carter. Not him.

The very thought of telling him the truth made her feel like a cheat and a liar. She couldn't even imagine how much it would hurt him.

Guilt unfolded in her heart like a knife.

Enough.

Allie slammed her book shut with such force, nearby guards snapped around to look at her.

Shoving her books into her bag, she jumped to her feet and ran from the room into the school's wide hallway. She ran past chatting students and patrolling guards, under the gaze of the elegant nineteenth-century men and women who gazed down at her dubiously from the oil paintings hung high on the walls. When she reached the section where the school's wings met and the hallway widened to hold marble statues on heavy plinths, she turned into the classroom wing. She pelted up two flights, and down the shadowy corridor, skidding to a stop in front of Dom's office.

The once peaceful room was now a crowded hive of activity.

Rachel sat with Zoe and a young guard, all of them typing furiously on laptops. A gigantic map had been spread across one wall and Katie stood in front of it with two guards talking animatedly. None of them even noticed Allie.

A low hum of voices crackled through the speakers.

Dom was at her desk, talking on a cell phone. Spotting Allie hovering in the doorway, she motioned for her to enter. 'Anything you can do to get us some of that satellite time?' she said into the phone.

The light streaming through the windows that lined one wall of the office gave her dark skin a bronze sheen as she ended the call and turned to look at Allie.

'I'm not supposed to bother you,' she said, 'until after your grandmother's funeral.'

So that was why Isabelle hadn't given her anything to do.

'If I don't do something I think I'll go crazy.' Allie looked around the crowded room. 'Isn't there something I could do? I'll sweep floors, bring coffee. Anything.'

For a long moment Dom said nothing. Her expression was hard to read. Allie tensed, readying herself to be sent away.

But that didn't happen.

'I'm glad you're here,' the tech said. 'I was just about to ask Isabelle for another volunteer.' She pushed back her chair and stood up. 'Come with me.'

Allie was grateful for the lie.

Dom headed over to the round table where the others were working, Allie at her side. Rachel waved; Zoe was too involved in her work to notice her.

She tapped the shoulder of the young guard in headphones. He was obviously involved in whatever he was listening to, because her touch made him jump. When he saw it was Dom, he slid the headphones off hastily.

'What's up?'

He was small and muscular with short dark hair and skin a shade or two lighter than Dom's.

'Shakir Nasseem, This is Allie Sheridan. She's going to help monitor the communication from Nathaniel's unit.'

Shakir didn't ask any questions.

'Aces.' He pointed to an empty chair and handed her the silver headphones he'd just taken off.

'Thanks, Shakir,' Allie said, as she sat down.

'Call me Shak,' he said. 'Welcome to the Situation Room.'

Eight

Nathaniel's guards talked constantly.

'I think they're bored,' Shak explained. His disapproving expression told her what he thought of that. 'They say a lot of stuff they shouldn't ever say. Raj would kill us if we pulled that kind of shizzle.'

He had a contagious smile that Allie liked instantly. He seemed laidback, despite his intimidating black uniform.

He showed her how to toggle between conversations on the computer, so she could listen to multiple guards at once. 'Give us a heads up if you hear anything useful.'

She frowned. 'What's useful, though?'

'Clues about their location. Anything at all. A street name. A restaurant. A shop. Anything we can track down.' He turned back to his own laptop, where the screen held only a mystifying series of numbers. 'Just keep your ears open. Don't miss anything.'

Hesitantly, Allie slid the headphones on. Instantly the sound of typing and chatting disappeared. Voices filled her head. They were all male, speaking in the crisp truncated language she associated with soldiers in films.

There were so many of them, at first it was a bit

bewildering. A tangle of words. Gradually, though, she began to identify unique voices barking orders, giving locations, making jokes. Saying 'copy that' a lot.

'Going to the shops. Want anything?'

'Copy that. Get me some crisps. And something sweet.'

'Copy that. How about that sweet blonde behind the counter? No wait. I forgot. She's mine.'

'That's not what she told me last night…'

'(Muffled laughter) Copy that.'

There was no way she could imagine Raj's guards having conversations like this on Cimmeria's comms system. He'd have their heads.

They never used names, only numbers. After a while she got to know their voices. Nine had a gravelly voice and an Essex accent. Six had a distinctive high-pitched voice and a London accent.

As the hours passed, and she listened to them talk about lunch, their cars, their girlfriends, she imagined faces for them. She decided Nine had a square jaw and dark hair. Six was slim with an overbite.

There was only one guard whose real name she knew. He called himself One.

'One to Six. You bringing me those papers? Over.'

When she heard that voice, Allie started so violently her earphones unplugged. The guards' voices flooded into the room.

Shak glanced up at her questioningly.

Her hands had gone cold and clumsy, and she fumbled with the cable.

'It's Gabe.' She whispered the words, as if Gabe might somehow hear her. 'Gabe Porthus.'

Shak didn't seem surprised. 'Number One,' he said. 'What

a wanker.' He gestured at her laptop. 'Make a note of what he talks about. We're keeping an eye on that guy.'

Allie finally got the earphones plugged in. Gabe's voice filled her head.

She hated that voice. She'd heard it the day before, but only for a second. Now it made her skin crawl.

His face she didn't have to imagine. She knew it all too well. He was beautiful – with blond hair and perfectly even white teeth. He had a chiselled jaw and warm brown eyes. The kind of boy any girl would fall for.

He was Jo's murderer.

His voice was a little deeper than she remembered; the corners had been shaved off his plummy accent, but it was definitely him.

'Do it now, Six,' his voice crackled through her headset. 'I don't have time for this.'

'Copy that. En route.' Six sounded sullen but he didn't argue.

'Too late,' Gabe muttered. 'Again.'

For a while after that, the other guards seemed subdued, using the radio more carefully. Soon, though, they slid back into their old ways, talking too much and wasting time.

There was nothing useful in what they said – quite a bit of disgusting talk about women. A bit of gabbing about football. Then, late in the afternoon, Six reappeared. Whatever had happened with Gabe, he hadn't been fired. He seemed relatively jolly.

The others teased him about getting in trouble and he brushed it off.

Then Nine said something that made Allie sit up straight.

'So… the boss. He still holed up in there with his

pictures?'

She made a note: *Nathaniel = boss? Pictures?*

Six replied. 'Yep. One says he hasn't eaten anything in twenty-four hours.'

There was a pause. Then Nine responded. 'In all seriousness, mate, is the guy losing it? Ever since that old lady got shot no one sees him.'

'One says he'll be fine.' But even to Allie's ears, Six didn't sound convinced.

'Yeah, One gets paid to think that. What's it feel like to you?'

There was a pause.

'Too early to tell.' Six's tone was terse.

'Mate, this whole thing's getting strange. We've done nothing since London. We should be moving in on them. Finishing this. I didn't sign up to be a wet nurse in a loony bin.' Frustration was clear in Nine's gravelly voice.

All the other guards had fallen silent. Allie got the feeling they were listening to this conversation – hanging on every word. She willed Six to say something useful.

But when Six replied it wasn't at all what she was hoping for.

'I got a break in twenty. Meet at the usual place? We need to take this off the air. One's on the rag again.'

As the others returned to normal chatter, Allie wrote feverishly: *Ever since Lucinda died Nathaniel has been locked away. No one sees him. Guards are restless.*

She paused to consider how to explain what she'd heard. Then she wrote it straight.

They think he's going mad.

All through dinner that night the students chatted excitedly about working with Dom, finding Carter. There was a tangible sense of hope in the air.

But Allie was distracted. Unable to join in. The conversation she'd heard that afternoon was still bothering her. The idea that Nathaniel was locking himself away and mourning his dead stepmother – who he'd helped to kill – had really thrown her.

It brought too many images of that night. Images she'd tried to forget.

Lucinda's hand, slick with blood, clutching her wrist.

Red blood soaking through a crisp, Burberry raincoat.

She didn't want to think about that. She'd tried really hard not to think of it.

Rachel must have seen how distracted she was, because as soon as dinner ended, she pulled her to one side.

'Hey, are you OK? You look so sad.' Her warm brown eyes searched Allie's face.

They stood in the wide hallway, out of the way of the bustling crowd pouring out of the dining hall. Everyone was talking and laughing. Allie felt utterly cut off from that world.

'It's nothing,' she said, dodging Rachel's gaze. 'I don't know, Rachel. I guess I'm just not looking forward to this whole funeral thing.'

'Oh honey,' Rachel put her arm around her shoulders. 'Do you want to talk about it? My grandmother died a few years ago…' She paused, before adding hastily, 'Of course, it's not the same as what happened with Lucinda. This must be much worse for you than it was for me. But I was really sad. It was hard to imagine life without her.'

Allie thought for a second about not telling her the truth, but then she couldn't seem to lie.

'Here's the weird thing, Rach,' she said. 'I know I should be sad, but I can't seem to feel very much right now. It's like I'm numb.' She swallowed hard. 'I feel like such a monster. I mean… Lucinda's *dead*. Dead forever. But whenever I think about it, it's like I'm kind of… I don't know. Empty.'

She squinted at Rachel, expecting her to be repulsed. But it wasn't repulsion she saw in her eyes. It was understanding.

'Do you know what? I think that's perfectly normal,' Rachel said. 'You saw her get killed. One of your best friends was kidnapped. And it all happened so fast. Your brain – your heart – they need time to catch up with you. With what happened.'

Allie wasn't convinced. 'But it's weird, isn't it?' She kept her voice low so the guards passing by couldn't overhear. 'She was my *grandmother*. It should hurt more.'

'Don't do that,' Rachel scolded her gently. 'You're torturing yourself for no reason. You are not doing anything wrong. There aren't rules for being sad. We all handle it our own way. And you *are* sad. I can see it in your face. Even if you can't quite let yourself feel it yet.'

Trust Rachel to know the right thing to say. She'd been reading psychology textbooks for fun since she was fourteen.

'Thanks for saving my sanity, Rach.'

Rachel smiled and pulled her into a warm hug. 'The doctor is in, whenever you need her.'

Her hair smelled like jasmine flowers. Odd. Jasmine was a scent Allie always associated with Nicole.

Maybe they use the same shampoo now…

'You can get through this,' Rachel said, her cheek pressed against Allie's shoulder. 'We'll all get through this together.'

The two of them joined the others who were already gathered in the common room. The conversation was lively. Zoe and Lucas played a bizarrely aggressive type of chess.

Allie sat back, watching the others. Rachel's words made sense, but she hated being numb. She wanted to feel grief. She wanted it to hurt.

It wouldn't be real until it hurt.

She thought of Nathaniel, weeping over pictures of her grandmother. How was it possible Lucinda's enemy felt worse about her death than her own granddaughter?

Why couldn't she feel anything?

She didn't want to chat or play. When the others weren't looking, she slipped away.

Two guards sat on chairs on either side of the heavy front door, with its elaborate system of hand-forged black iron locks hundreds of years old.

'I'm going for a walk,' she said. 'I won't be long.'

The two glanced at each other. She could tell that they knew who she was.

Everyone knew Allie Sheridan now.

One stood and opened the door for her.

'Be careful,' he said.

Allie inclined her head. 'Always.'

The door closed behind her with a solid thud. The evening was cool and grey – there'd be no vivid sunset tonight. A hint of rain hung in the air like a threat.

Allie took a deep breath, and then struck out across the grass towards the woods.

It was time to talk to Lucinda.

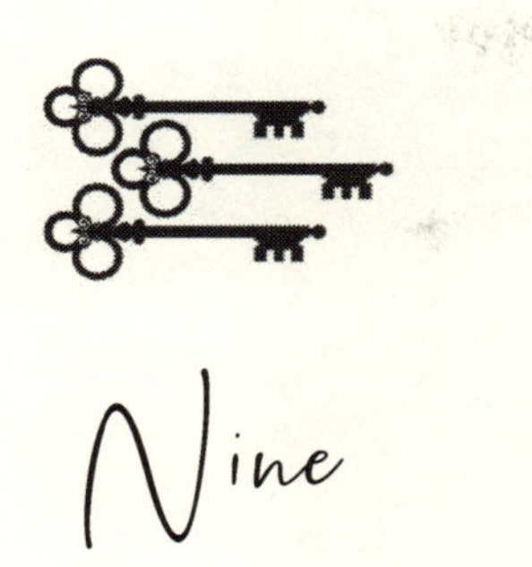

Nine

The chapel was hidden deep in the woods not quite a mile from the main school building. When Allie reached the old church wall, she slowed to a walk. Her heart began to quicken.

She didn't want to do this. But she had to. She would see her grandmother again. She would say goodbye.

And she would feel something.

She followed the long path that ran beside the wall until she reached the arched, wooden gate. She flipped the well-oiled metal latch. The gate swung open.

Inside the churchyard, she saw that someone had cut the grass recently – maybe even today. It still smelled green and fresh. All the bushes had been neatly trimmed, making the grey, lichen-covered gravestones seem taller.

In the middle, an ancient yew tree spread its long, smooth branches over the graves. Its gnarled roots rose out of the ground. The tree was said to be as old as the chapel, and the chapel was more than nine hundred years old.

Just beyond the tree the ground had been disturbed. Fresh dirt lay in a neat pile at the end of a rectangular hole.

It took Allie a second to realise what she was looking at.

When she did, her lungs contracted until her breath

disappeared.

Tearing her gaze away, she stumbled the last few steps to the church door. It took both hands to turn the iron ring that served as a handle, and she had to shove her shoulder against the door to force it open.

There was no electricity in the chapel, and she expected to find darkness inside. Instead, she was greeted by a warm, flickering glow.

Candles had been lit in all the wall sconces, ceiling fixtures, candelabras. They glimmered from the pulpit, the tables and on the windowsills.

The flames caught the breeze coming through the open door and shivered. Allie hurried to shut the door.

The room was small, with ten rows of high-backed, mahogany pews neatly aligned on either side of a central aisle. A plain pine coffin had been placed on a stand at the foot of the pulpit.

The lid was shut.

Allie's back was pressed against the solid oak door. Every muscle in her body was stiff. She didn't want to be here.

But she had to do this. After all, she'd made it this far.

Slowly, she made her way down the aisle, her feet scuffing softly on the flagstone floor, eyes glued to the pine box ahead of her.

She glanced around nervously – the walls were elaborately painted in medieval style, with devils, dragons, trees and doves. In the candlelight, the paintings seemed to move.

The dove's feathers fluttered. The dragon's scales shimmered.

By the time she reached the front row, Allie's heart was pounding. She couldn't breathe. Every instinct told her to run away. But she lowered herself stiffly onto the hard wooden pew.

I can do this. I have to.

The room was so quiet, she could hear the melting wax sizzle.

Knotting her hands in her lap, she made herself think about Lucinda. The first time she'd seen her, standing on the landing in the school building, looking out at the snow. Regal as a queen; an emerald the size of an almond on her finger.

And later, her calm cool voice coming through the phone, giving orders, but also listening. Understanding.

Then, on a hilltop, looking down at the lights of London. One last time.

The coffin was so simple, no ornamentation at all. That was wrong. It should be covered in diamonds.

'I wish…'

She hadn't meant to say the words aloud, and her own voice startled her to silence.

The candles flickered, sending light dancing on the vivid walls. The dragon's painted eyes seemed to watch her.

'I wish I'd known you,' she told the box. Her voice was low and shaky. 'Really known you. Sometimes I…' She paused, then made herself continue. 'Sometimes I pretend I grew up with you in my life. You took me to plays. To Parliament. We went to Washington, DC, together. I called you "grandmother" and it didn't feel weird. It just felt… normal. I pretend that's the way things were. Because… I would have liked that.'

She was shaken by a sudden overwhelming sense of loss. As if a hole had opened in front of her unexpectedly and she was falling down into it.

Hot tears stung her eyes.

Here was the emotion she'd been hiding from herself. The

pain she'd dodged since that night on the heath.

She dropped her feet to the floor, leaning forward to look at the box earnestly, letting her tears fall unimpeded.

'I know you thought I didnt always listen to you. But I *did.* I really listened. And I want to be like you, someday. To be brave. To try and make things better. Only now…' She paused, seeking the right words. 'Sometimes I don't believe things *can* be better. Like, maybe better is impossible. And when you try to make one thing better you make something else worse. Something you never thought about before. Like you tried to help Nathaniel and it ended up killing you.'

She could hardly see the coffin now, through the blur of tears.

'I don't know what to think about that. Because I don't want to stop trying to fix things.' She looked up at where her grandmother lay. 'You always tried.' She swiped a hand across her wet cheeks.

'I guess that's what I wanted to tell you. Thank you for trying.'

Something crashed behind her, and she jumped to her feet, whirling as the door swung open, striking the wall.

Isabelle stood in the doorway, the hood of her black raincoat all but obscuring her face. She held a large bouquet of lilies in her arms. Water streamed from her hood.

Allie hadn't noticed it start to rain. But now she could hear the drops pattering against the roof and stained glass windows. The wind shook the trees.

The headmistress closed the door, and turned back around, pushing the hood off to reveal her face, pale and stern.

'What are you doing here?'

Feeling instantly like a trespasser, Allie wiped her tears

away. 'I'm sorry. I just…'

Isabelle's expression softened. 'Please. Don't apologise. I was just surprised – I thought I was alone. You have every right to be here.'

She crossed to the front of the chapel and arranged the flowers carefully in a large vase in front of the coffin.

'Did you light the candles?' Allie asked, her voice tentative.

Isabelle glanced at the candelabra near her as if she'd only just noticed it. 'We're keeping them lit. Myself and the other teachers.'

She had her back to Allie again, straightening the purple and gold satin that covered the altar table. Moving it one way, then shifting it back again.

Allie didn't know what to say, but she had to say something.

'I'm here,' Allie found herself explaining, 'to say goodbye.'

Isabelle stopped fidgeting. When she glanced up, Allie saw her eyes were bright with unshed tears. She looked so heart-broken. And of course she would be – she'd known Lucinda all her life. Lucinda had treated Isabelle like her own daughter.

The same way Isabelle treated Allie.

The realisation took her by surprise. She'd been so focused on herself, she hadn't thought about how devastated Isabelle must be right now. Between Carter and Lucinda – her whole life had just fallen apart.

Maybe she had things to say to that pine box, too.

'Would you like to… to sit with me, for a while?' Allie held out a hand. 'We could say goodbye together.'

The next day was Lucinda's funeral.

That morning, Allie brushed her hair until it hung in smooth waves over her shoulders and carefully applied her makeup. Her grey eyes looked back at her from the mirror, serious but clear. Her nose was still pink from last night's tears, but that was the only giveaway.

She and Isabelle had sat in the chapel talking about Lucinda until the candles began to burn down.

The conversation that started with tears, had gradually morphed into the headmistress telling stories of her childhood, with Lucinda as her de facto stepmother. Soon they were both laughing about a Pekinese puppy given to Lucinda by a foreign ambassador.

'She didn't want to keep it, but I loved it,' Isabelle recalled. 'I named him Socks. He slept in my bed when I visited during school hols. He was so cute, but he was utterly, hopelessly stupid. Lucinda was Chancellor at the time, so she lived at Number 11 Downing Street. It was her house and her office. One day the prime minister came over for a meeting and Socks peed on his handmade lamb-skin wing-tips. He said…' Isabelle lowered her voice into a passable impression of the former prime minister's gruff, Scottish demeanour. '"Luce, it's Socks or me, and I've got to tell you I don't think the dog will back your eight-point plan for economic recovery."'

Allie laughed.

'She never did get rid of that dog,' Isabelle said. 'He lived to be fifteen. She always said she hated him but I think she loved him as much as I did.'

'What about Nathaniel?' Allie asked. 'Was he close to Lucinda then? As close as you were?'

Isabelle's expression grew thoughtful.

'He was always an odd one, Nathaniel. A skinny kid with a chip on his shoulder. Our dad pushed him too hard, I think. Always demanding a kind of perfection from him that he didn't ask of me. And his life was so sad – losing his mother like that when he was still a child. Everyone wanted to help him but…' She held up her hands. 'He just wanted to be alone.'

Allie told Isabelle what she'd overheard earlier from Nathaniel's guards. 'They say he's locked up with old pictures. He doesn't eat.'

Isabelle's face tightened; she stared into the shadows at the end of the chapel.

'Nathaniel's relationship with Lucinda was… complicated,' she said after many seconds had ticked away. 'I think he did love her in his own way. But he pushed her away because…' She heaved a sigh. 'I guess because he wanted her to prove she'd come back. That she'd always be there. No matter what he did.'

Allie's thoughts drifted to her own parents. She hadn't seen them since Christmas. They talked occasionally on the phone but their conversations were stilted and brief.

She blamed them for not wanting her. They blamed her for being difficult.

It was like they wanted a different daughter. And she wanted different parents.

Maybe Nathaniel felt the same way about his father.

You can't choose your parents. But if you could… Life would be a hell of a lot easier.

From outside she could hear the rumble of engines and the crunching of tyres on the school's gravel drive. The funeral guests were arriving.

Allie stood up and headed for the door.

Lucinda would never forgive her for being late to her funeral.

Rachel, Nicole and Lucas were clustered by the front door. Allie saw Rachel glance at her watch. When Allie walked up, she didn't hide her relief.

'There you are,' was all she said. Then, gently, 'We should probably get going.'

Everyone wore clothes in sober shades of black and grey. Lucas wore an elegantly tailored suit, and had actually combed his hair.

Allie's black silk sheath dress and matching flats had been sent to her room that morning by Isabelle. They fit perfectly. She had no idea where the headmistress had found them with such short notice.

Together, they all headed out across the lawn. The air was chilly, and smelled clean and fresh. As if last night's rain had washed away the last of the summer.

They walked in near silence. Rachel held one of Allie's hands. Nicole held the other.

They were just entering the woods when Zoe ran up to join them.

'I'm here,' she announced, adding with unnecessary

honesty, 'Isabelle made me.'

Her straight brown hair had been pulled into a glossy braid, her smooth face scrubbed. Her short, grey dress made her look younger than fourteen. The solemnity of the moment seemed to affect even her. She walked with them, instead of dashing ahead as she usually would.

Nobody tried to make small talk. It wasn't the day for it.

When they reached the chapel, they found it crowded – every seat full. People stood at the back. Guards, out of their usual black gear and clad instead in dark suits, leaned against the walls.

On the pews, alongside the teachers and students, Allie recognised famous politicians from several countries, including the prime minister who Socks had peed on so long ago.

From the front row, Isabelle motioned for Allie to join her. Allie saw her parents next to the headmistress, twisting around to try and see her.

To her surprise, at the sight of her mother, her heart jumped. She fought the urge to run to her.

'I better go,' she said.

Rachel followed her gaze – her eyes widened. 'Crikey O'Reilly. Is that your parents?'

Allie shrugged. 'I guess Hell froze over.'

But she was already crying as she made her way down the aisle, squeezing past the guards.

As soon as she saw her, her mother's eyes filled with tears, too. She pulled her into her arms.

'Oh Alyson.'

And Allie let her call her that. Let her hold her.

Her father stood beside them, patting her awkwardly on the shoulder.

'It must have been terrible,' he said gruffly.

Allie couldn't remember the last time she'd been so glad to see them. She breathed in her mother's familiar sent – Coco by Chanel. She always wore it for important events.

'I'm OK,' she said. 'Really.'

And she was.

The pine box was still at the front of the room as it had been last night, but it was no longer bare. Now it was covered in flowers.

Hundreds of white roses were spread across the top like a thick, creamy blanket. Other bouquets pressed against it on all sides. Flowers covered the altar table, the floor, even the windowsills held bouquets.

The candelabra was still lit, but the other candles had been put out. They were no longer needed; light flooded through the stained glass windows, filling the room with brilliant streams of gold and red.

A vicar she'd never seen before conducted the service. Some hymns were sung. Famous people said wonderful things about Lucinda.

Allie was fine until the coffin was carried out. She couldn't bear to see it put in that hole in the ground. So she slipped away from the crowd.

She stood alone near the gate, arms wrapped tightly across her torso. Looking up at the grey sky.

It's a perfect day, she found herself thinking, *for a funeral.*

'Hello Allie.'

The voice came from behind her. French accent. Familiar.

She spun around to look into a pair of eyes the same clear blue as the sea on a sunny day.

'Oh, *ma belle*,' Sylvain said. 'I'm so sorry.'

Ten

'Where did you come from?'

'How's your dad?'

'Why didn't anyone tell us?'

The others surrounded Sylvain, exclaiming, demanding information and hugging him. Even Lucas, who had never been fond of him, pounded his shoulder in a kind of violent guy-hug.

'Glad you're back, man,' he said gruffly.

They clustered near the towering hearth in the great hall talking and laughing, relieved to have something to be happy about.

Allie stood to one side. She'd already had a chance to talk to him. They'd slipped away from the funeral and walked back to the school together before the others had seen him.

'I flew in as soon as I could get away,' he'd explained. 'I had to be here. For you… for Carter.'

'What about your dad?' she'd asked. 'Is he… better?'

His muscles tightened almost imperceptibly at mention of his father, badly injured in an assassination attempt a week ago.

'He's out of intensive care. The doctors say he's going to come through.'

'Thank God,' Allie said with genuine relief. 'I'm so sorry

we're taking you away from him. He needs you.'

Unexpectedly, he'd stopped then, turning to face her. He held both her hands in his.

'*You* need me.' Before she could react, he'd leaned forward, brushing his lips gently against the top of her head.

Allie had shivered at his touch. She'd missed him so much. They'd both been through hell. It was a crappy day. When he wrapped her in his arms, she leaned into his touch.

'It's been horrible, Sylvain. Horrible.'

'I know,' he'd whispered. His breath stirred strands of her hair.

Now, as she watched the others chatter excitedly to him, he glanced over to check on her. His gaze a lightning flash of vivid blue.

The protectiveness and worry in his expression made Allie's heart ache.

Oh God, she thought. *What am I going to do?*

Sylvain had still been her boyfriend when he went away. Now she had to tell him the truth about Carter.

And then she would lose him forever.

Looking at him now, his wavy hair perfectly tousled, his cheekbones high and fine, standing tall and slim as he listened patiently to the others, she felt hollow inside.

She had to let him go. It had already taken her too long to listen to her heart. Too long to realise who she wanted. He'd be right to be angry with her about that.

She shook herself. She couldn't think about this today.

Turning, she looked around for her parents. People were streaming in from the chapel, but she didn't see them in the crowd.

The room was set up with tables draped in pristine white linen. Pale yellow flowers topped every table.

Along one wall, buffet tables were piled high with food – charcuterie and sliced cheeses, cold roast chicken and at least a dozen salads. One entire table held just decadent desserts – cheesecake and chocolate puddings, something covered in blood red raspberries and glossy blackberries.

With the sunlight streaming in through the towering windows, it looked more like a wedding than a wake. Allie knew that was intentional. Lucinda would have hated people standing around weeping over her.

Waiters in black suits circulated with trays of red and white wine, and juice. Allie was accepting a glass of iced orange juice when her parents appeared at her side, looking a little red-faced and hot from the walk back from the church.

'There you are.' Her mother lifted a glass of white wine from a passing tray with relief in her eyes. 'You disappeared.'

'I'm sorry,' Allie said. 'Turns out I'm not so great at funerals.'

'I'm the same,' her father said, taking a glass of iced water. 'Maybe you inherited it from me.'

'I'm not sure bad manners are genetic.' Her mother's reply was tart but Allie smiled.

She hated their dysfunctional family relationship, but she'd been away from them both so long it was almost nice to encounter it again. The warm glow of familiar antagonism.

'I'm glad you guys are here.'

If she'd said 'I'm thinking of piercing my nipples' they couldn't have looked more astonished.

'What?' she said innocently. 'I'm not allowed to like you?'

'Well, it is a bit unorthodox,' her father murmured, sipping his water, but he looked pleased.

Her mother recovered quickly.

'Of course you're allowed to like us. It's virtually required.' She took a gulp of wine and glanced at her husband, who inclined his head in some silent communication. 'Actually, seeing as we are together… there are some things we need to discuss.'

Something in her voice made Allie's stomach clench. Her moment of near-contentment evaporated.

'What's going on?'

The noise in the room was increasing – everyone was back from the church now.

'Let's step outside for a second,' her mother said.

They walked together up the grand staircase to the landing, where Allie first met Lucinda, the night of the winter ball.

They stood at the banister, looking down over the hallway. A low rumble of voices rose from the grand ballroom below. But they were alone and could talk quietly.

'So, what's going on?' Allie's gaze skipped from her mother's face to her father's.

'First,' her mother said, 'we owe you an apology for the way we handled things. I never told you who Lucinda was. Or about my connections with Cimmeria.' She rested a hand cautiously on the highly polished oak banister, as if she didn't quite trust it. 'That was wrong. We should have told you the truth. But in all honesty, we never suspected things would turn out like this.'

'It's fine,' Allie assured her, without hesitation. 'I've kind of worked that bit through.'

'There was a time when I thought I'd never see this place again,' her mother said. 'Hoped, even.'

'And now?' Allie shot her a sideways look.

Her mother's lips curved into a tight smile. 'I still don't

like it.'

Downstairs, someone laughed. She saw Zoe dash down the hallway barefoot in her little grey dress, shoes clutched in her hands.

'And we are very sorry that you had to see… what you saw that night in London.' Her mother dropped her gaze. 'What happened to Lucinda was awful. And she wouldn't have wanted you to see that.'

Allie thought of the look in Lucinda's eyes as she'd clutched her wrist with bloody hands. A look of trust. Of acceptance.

'Yes she would.' Allie didn't like the turn this conversation was taking. 'I actually think she had a very good idea something like that might happen. She wanted me there to see it.'

Her father looked taken aback. 'Why on earth would she have wanted that?'

'So that I would understand what the stakes are.' Allie hadn't thought about this much before now – there hadn't been time. But as soon as she said it, she knew it was true. 'She wanted me to understand what I was facing. What I *am* facing.'

'You're not facing the same danger as Lucinda,' her mother argued. 'That's absurd.'

Maybe she didn't mean to sound as sharp as she did, but Allie's temper flared with the speed of a match strike.

'Do you have any idea what the last year of my life has been like?' Her voice was low and cold. 'Lucinda is not the only person who's died. Jo died. And Ruth. Other people were hurt. Including me.' She held up her hair so they could see the jagged wound at the edge of her scalp. 'I am*covered* in scars.'

Her mother made a small sound, and covered her mouth with her fingertips.

Allie took grim satisfaction from that.

'I'm lucky to be alive. And I might not be for long if we don't win this thing. So don't tell me what Lucinda wanted or didn't want.' She took a breath. 'I think I know better than you.'

Her mother opened her mouth to argue but her father cut her off.

'Hang on.' He held out his hands. 'Let's just stop there. Fighting won't get us anywhere. Besides, this is a funeral, remember?' He turned to Allie. 'Alyson.' His voice was steady. 'We know this is a terrible day, and we don't want to make it worse. Your mother just wanted you to know that we are aware of what's happening here, on some level. We're worried about you. And that… well. We're here if you ever need us.'

He was talking to her almost like a grownup and, for once, Allie was grateful for his unerring calm.

'Thanks, Dad,' she said. 'I appreciate that. I love you guys, too.'

He gave her a sad smile.

We would hug now, Allie thought, *if we were a normal family.*

'There's something else you should know,' he said. 'Lucinda's lawyers have been in touch about the will.'

Allie flinched. She didn't care about money or Lucinda's belongings. None of that mattered. She'd give every penny to have her grandmother back.

But she knew that wasn't what her father wanted to hear.

'Fine.' She shrugged. 'Let me know what they say.'

'That's the thing,' he said. 'They didn't want to talk to us. They want to talk to you.'

She blinked. 'Me? Why would they want to talk to me?'

'We think she must have left something to you. Or at least

mentioned you in her papers.' Her mother's voice was calmer now. Her anger seemed to have dissipated. 'We gave them the phone number here and told them to contact Isabelle. But we only received the call this morning and with everything that's happening today, she probably hasn't had a chance to speak with them.'

'We'll mention it to Isabelle as well,' her father said. 'They seemed rather urgently interested in contacting you. I suppose Lucinda owned several companies and was on the boards of numerous corporations. Her affairs will be complicated.'

By now, Allie was eager for this conversation to end. She wondered what the others were doing downstairs. Where Sylvain was.

'Fine,' she said shortly. 'I'm sure Isabelle can handle it. Should we go back down, now?'

'Alyson.' Her mother took a step towards her. 'We want you to be safe. That's all that matters to us. I don't like seeing you so caught up in Lucinda's world. It was this I tried to protect you from.' She gestured at the building around them – the crystal chandelier, the marble statues, the towering windows. 'Now I feel as though it's sucked you in.'

Allie bit back the angry words she wanted to say.

She hated that her instinctive reaction to anything her mother said was to fight.

But she also hated how little her parents knew her.

'I know,' she said gently. 'And thank you for that. But this is where I belong. I'd rather be here than be safe.'

She turned towards the stairs. Then she thought of the one thing she really wanted to say to them.

She stopped and looked back.

'One more thing. Please don't call me Alyson anymore.

My name is Allie.'

'I can't eat another bite.' Nicole pushed her plate away. 'I don't know why I ate so much. I wasn't hungry to start with.'

Next to her, Zoe had made a 'cakewich' of chocolate and Victoria sponge slices stacked together.

'If I have any more sugar,' she said hopefully, 'maybe my pancreas will explode.'

Rachel smiled. 'It's good to have goals.'

The party was winding down. Students had begun drifting to the common room. Some of the more famous guests had already departed, their Jaguars and Audis purring down the drive.

Sylvain stood in a corner of the room near the fireplace, talking to Lucas and Katie. Allie's eyes lingered on him. Despite everything, she was so glad he was here. She felt safer when he was around.

As if he'd felt her gaze, he looked up. Their eyes met across the room.

Allie's stomach flipped.

She didn't understand herself. Would there *always* be this thing between them? It was a kind of electricity. As if their wires were connected in some inexplicable way.

What had happened with Carter – the decision she'd made – it didn't erase her history with Sylvain. She knew what it was like to be held in those arms. To be kissed by that mouth.

When you've been that close to someone, how do you just… forget that? Is there a way to shift gears from tearing each other's clothes off on the roof to being friends?

If there is, she thought, watching his smooth, dangerous long stride, *I haven't figured it out yet*.

At that moment, someone called Allie's name. She spun around to see Dom in the doorway.

Even today, the tech wasn't wearing a dress – she wore perfectly creased black trousers, with a white shirt and long, black blazer.

Her face was alight with excitement.

Allie hurried towards her, only vaguely aware that Sylvain had caught up and was walking alongside her.

'What is it?' Allie asked.

Dom motioned for her to follow. If she was surprised to see Sylvain it didn't show on her face.

'Come with me. We've found something.'

Eleven

Dom moved fast down the hallway, her long jacket flowing behind her. Sylvain and Allie stayed right on her heels. She stopped only long enough to grab Isabelle and Raj along the way.

'What have you found?' Sylvain asked her as they hurried through the classroom wing to the stairwell.

Allie glanced at him. His face was set, his blue eyes clear and focused. He'd stepped back into Cimmeria's crisis situation seamlessly. As if he'd never gone away at all.

'We've been tracing their communications, trying to triangulate their location. Looking for any indication of where they're keeping Carter,' Dom explained.

'Nathaniel has no idea we can hear every word his guards say,' Isabelle added. 'It's a useful tool.'

'Or it should be,' Raj said. 'If they'd say something useful.'

'They just did,' Dom said, shooting him a look. 'At last.'

When they reached her office, Shak was at the table typing furiously, headphones perched on his head.

'Has there been more?' Dom asked as she hustled across the room.

He nodded without looking up. 'They're still talking.'

Sylvain turned around, taking in the room that had become a command hub. Allie tried to see it with his eyes – maps stretched across one wall, tagged with dozens of photos of expensive mansions owned by supporters of Nathaniel, a cluster of laptops dominating the round table, metres of wires snaking across the floor.

Dom hurried to her desk calling over shoulder, 'Give me a second and I'll show you what I'm talking about.'

Isabelle and Raj followed her, talking quietly. Allie and Sylvain stayed by the door, waiting.

The room fell quiet, the only sound the machine gun rattle of computer keys as Shak and Dom typed.

Then Dom glanced up. 'Here we go.'

Crackling male voices filled the air from hidden speakers.

'He says he wants you to pick up a package.' Allie recognised the nasal voice as belonging to the guard they knew only as Six. 'From that place in the village.'

There was a pause than another voice swore. It was Nine. 'What are we now? His sodding delivery boys? This is ridiculous. Waste of our time. Tell him to pick up his own package.'

The guards engaged in creative criticism of their boss, whose name they never mentioned. But it was clear they were talking about Nathaniel.

'I've had just about enough of this,' Nine's voice sounded cold with anger. 'Someone has to tell One this is over.'

'Go right ahead.' Six's voice was a snarl. 'But someone's still got to go down to the Half Moon and pick up the bloody package and it isn't going to be me.'

Raj took a sharp breath.

Dom pushed a button, cutting off their voices.

'That was their first mistake,' she said. 'There are forty-seven establishments in England called the Half Moon. Fifteen are in the south of England. Only four are within the Home Counties where we believe Nathaniel to be hiding.'

She typed something into her keyboard, and a map flashed up on the widescreen monitor mounted on one wall. A bright red circle had been drawn on it.

Allie's heart skipped a beat. Suddenly she knew what Dom was going to say.

'Nathaniel is somewhere in that circle.' Dom thrust a finger at the screen. 'I'd bet this building and everyone in it that's where Carter is, too.'

'Well, it's a start.' Isabelle glanced at Raj, whose expression was set and brooding. 'But no more than that.'

Raj nodded his agreement.

Allie wanted more. 'If we know where he is, we should go get him,' she said. 'What are we waiting for?'

Raj typed something into Dom's computer, and brought up a satellite image of green countryside, dotted with houses. He thrust his finger at the monitor.

'There will be no fewer than five hundred houses in that area, Allie,' he said. 'That's five hundred places to hide.' He pointed at a long building, a rectangular white blob on the screen. 'Then there are industrial structures. Farm buildings. Barns. We can't break into all of them.'

Allie's heart fell. When he put it that way, it didn't seem like they knew much at all. Carter was still lost.

Her unhappiness must have shown on her face.

'A start isn't nothing,' Dom chided her gently. 'It's a beginning. You have to have a beginning before you can get to the end.'

'I know,' Allie mumbled.

But it felt like nothing. Worse than nothing. It felt like someone had held out the answers to all of Allie's prayers. And then taken them away again.

The room was growing crowded. Word must be spreading. Zoe, Nicole and Rachel burst in and raced to Allie's side.

'Everyone's saying they found him,' Rachel said breathlessly. 'Are they right?'

It was Raj who told the others what had happened.

'Rats,' Zoe muttered, disappointment written on her face. 'I knew it was too good to be true.'

Without sticking around to hear more, she went over to join Shak at the round table. Soon the two of them were deep in code.

Rachel turned to Dom. 'What can I do?'

Dom walked across the room with her and Nicole, explaining something in a quiet voice. Raj and Isabelle left the room, heads close together as they talked.

Allie looked around. The room was full now. Buzzing with energy.

In the midst of all of the excitement, she'd forgotten about Sylvain. She scanned the room, but he wasn't there.

He must have slipped away while she wasn't looking.

Some of the tension left Allie's shoulders.

She was glad he was gone. She needed some time to think. His arrival had been so unexpected. She'd thought she'd have more time – weeks even – to decide what to do.

She knew she had to break up with him. She just couldn't bear the idea of telling him what had happened.

Sometimes truth is a weapon.

This time it felt like a loaded gun.

By the time Allie left Dom's office, the wake was over. The grand hall was empty again, the tables had been stacked away. She looked around for her parents, but they weren't in the common room, and the dining hall was empty, too.

They must have gone while she was upstairs. Her mother would be cross.

As she walked the shadowy corridor, she let out a sigh. No matter how she tried to fix things with them, something always happened to ensure everyone ended up wounded.

Then she heard a low rumble of voices. It seemed to come from upstairs.

Whirling, she hurried back that way, pausing at the foot of the grand staircase. Only then did she realise the noise was actually coming from under the stairs – Isabelle's office.

The door was closed, but she could hear the sound of many people talking.

Maybe they're in there.

She knocked tentatively, but it was noisy inside – everyone seemed to be talking at once. No one came to the door.

After a second, she turned the handle.

The small office was full of people. Some she recognised from the funeral, others she didn't. There were too many for the room, which had only two chairs aside from Isabelle's own. Everyone stood, although some leaned against walls or perched on cabinets.

With so many people, it was too warm. The air felt uncomfortably short of oxygen.

Allie didn't see her parents anywhere.

She was just thinking of sneaking back out again, when Isabelle spotted her through the crowd.

'Allie.' Isabelle motioned for her to join her by her desk. 'Over here, please.'

The room fell silent. Everyone turned to look at her. The crowd parted, forming a path.

Allie shot Isabelle a questioning look as she made her way to her, but the headmistress wore her best professional blank expression.

Isabelle stretched out her arm to take in the room. 'These people are from the Orion Group.'

Allie stifled a gasp. Orion was Nathaniel's group now. He'd wrested control from Lucinda, taking over completely after her death. As far as she was concerned, Orion was part of her grandmother's murder.

'What's going on here?' Her voice was low and ominous and Isabelle didn't miss the underlying message. She gave her a reassuring look.

'Allie, these are the people who stood with Lucinda against Nathaniel. They've been through the wars, just as we have.' She smiled at the group with obvious affection. 'And they've come here today to talk to you.'

'Oh.' She looked out at the sea of faces, still suspicious but with increasing curiosity.

A man about her father's age stepped forward. He was very tall and lanky, with dark hair and eyes, his expensive-looking silk tie perfectly knotted.

'My name is Julian Bell-Howard.' His voice was plummy, rich. The kind of voice you'd expect to hear on the news. 'I think I speak for everyone when I say we were all enormously fond of your grandmother. Lucinda Meldrum was the greatest leader Orion has ever seen – its first female president. We shall miss her terribly. And we are so sorry for your loss.'

A low murmur of agreement swept the room.

Allie was touched. 'Thank you,' she said. 'I miss her very much.'

'I know Lucinda thought very highly of you,' Julian continued, taking another step forward. 'She spoke about you often, especially after you enrolled at Cimmeria. She believed you would one day step into her shoes.' He glanced around at the people beside him. 'That's why we're here. You see… we'd like to invite you to join us.'

That, Allie hadn't expected.

'Join you?' She stared at him. 'I don't understand. How can you even invite me? I thought Nathaniel ran it now.'

Julian's smile tightened. 'We are the core group – the real Orion, if you will. It's our goal to wrest control of the organisation back from Nathaniel. Seize back the leadership that is rightfully ours. Return Orion back to the high standing it has held for centuries. Expel the Neanderthals and close the gates.'

'Hear hear,' someone murmured. The group rustled with approval.

Julian smiled. 'We would very much like it if you were at our side, as Lucinda was for so many years.'

Her frozen expression seemed to deflate some of his enthusiasm. His voice faltered very slightly at the end.

Allie felt as if the handsomely dressed group in front of her had walked in with machine guns and deposited a time bomb in her lap.

She wanted to shout at them about how their stupid battle had cost her grandmother her life. How other people she loved had been caught up in it and paid a horrible price.

But she didn't. She squared her shoulders and looked out at the group.

'I'm sorry you wasted your time coming here today.' Her voice was low but perfectly clear. 'I'm afraid I cannot accept your invitation.'

If the people in the room had known her better they would have heard the suppressed anger in her tone. But they didn't know her at all.

'Perhaps I wasn't clear —' Julian seemed befuddled.

Allie didn't let him finish. 'You were perfectly clear. Now let *me* be clear. Lucinda Meldrum died trying to end this thing once and for all. That is all she wanted. This fight ruined her life, Nathaniel's life, my life, and the lives of all the kids in this building.' She took a breath, ignoring the stunned expressions on the faces looking back at her. 'So, I will not join you to fight for control of Orion. I don't want anything to do with Orion at all.'

No one met Allie's gaze as she threaded her way through the crowd in Isabelle's office – all she wanted was out.

But just as she stepped into the corridor, taking a grateful gulp of the cool air, Julian caught up with her.

'Allie, could I speak to you for a moment?' He closed the door behind him, so no one could overhear their conversation.

He was very tall – he towered over her. She looked up at him cautiously, expecting him to chide her. But he didn't do anything like that. Instead, he apologised.

'My timing was terrible. Please forgive me. I put you in the most appalling position in there.'

His contrition appeared real; Allie was disarmed.

'I'm sorry, too,' she said, her cheeks colouring. 'I lost my temper a little.'

'Everyone loses their temper.' His lips twitched mischievously. 'I've seen your grandmother throw a stapler so hard it left a dent in a wall.'

'No *way*,' she said. It was unimaginable. Calm, controlled Lucinda, losing it?

'Absolute way,' he said. 'You don't get anywhere in life by being placid. Greatness comes from passion. And passion is almost always twinned with anger. You can fight that in yourself or you can accept it, and use it as a force for good. Which is what she chose to do.'

Allie studied him curiously.

He was an interesting-looking man – all angles and elbows, like an overgrown teenager. His hair flopped over his narrow forehead, and he kept shoving it back absently. She liked that his quick smile always reached his eyes.

'Perhaps I was overly exuberant in my timing, because Lucinda was an inspiration to me,' he continued. 'She helped me many times when I was young, and we remained friends and colleagues throughout my life. I named my daughter after her.' He paused. 'Lucy's eight now. I'd always hoped to send her to Cimmeria when she was old enough so she could walk in her godmother's footsteps. Now I wonder if she'll ever get that chance.'

It was heartbreaking to think of Cimmeria in Nathaniel's hands – out of all of their reach. But if that was what it took for there to be peace, Allie would let it happen.

'I wish there was another way,' she said. 'I just don't think there is one.'

His reply came without a second's hesitation.

'Actually, I'm certain there is,' he said. 'We just have to find it.'

Twelve

Classes resumed the next morning.

Allie, who had longed for any kind of normality, none the less endured the lessons with ill grace. It was hard to stay focused on what the teachers were saying. She wanted to be in Dom's office, helping to find Carter.

She was also avoiding any situation when she might be alone with Sylvain. She wasn't ready to deal with their confused relationship.

As soon as classes ended for the day she raced up to Dom's office, working there until Night School began in the evening.

She hadn't told anyone about her meeting with the Orion Group. If she told them that, she'd have to tell them she was leaving Cimmeria. And that was a conversation she wasn't going to have with anyone until Carter was back.

And he would be back.

But she kept thinking about it. Julian had seemed so reasonable. He seemed to have absolute faith that they'd find a way to beat Nathaniel.

She wanted him to be right so badly it hurt.

Night School training resumed that evening. Isabelle suggested Allie should skip it ('You've had a terrible week…'), but she refused.

She had to stay busy or she'd go insane. She wanted to run. To kick things. To knock everyone down.

Now the students were arrayed in Training Room One under the flickering fluorescent light. On one side of the room, Zelazny and two of Raj's guards were working with the younger students, walking them through basic stretching and strength building.

On the other side of the dim room, senior students were working with Eloise, practising techniques for disarming attackers.

Sylvain was there, too. He looked relaxed, focused. He didn't seem to have noticed she was avoiding him.

To Allie's relief, Eloise paired him with Nicole, assigning Allie to practise with Katie.

So, thirty minutes after training began, Allie held a fake handgun in her hand, pointed at Katie's face.

'Bang,' she said.

Katie rolled her eyes. 'Very funny.'

'It was the best I could come up with,' Allie said. 'I didn't have much time to prepare…'

Without warning the redhead leapt into the air, directing a perfect flying kick at the weapon.

Before Allie could react, the gun flew out of her fingers, thudding against the wall.

Katie landed weightlessly in front of her. Allie stared at her, open-mouthed.

'Bang that, girlfriend.' Katie dusted her hands against her hips. She looked very pleased with herself.

'Remind me never to get into a fight with a ballerina,' Allie muttered, as she looked around for the lost weapon. But Katie found it first.

Picking it up, she pointed the barrel at Allie's heart. 'Your turn, rock chick.'

Allie's eyebrows shot up, making her stitches sting. '*Rock chick*?'

'It's street talk.' Katie gave a disinterested shrug. 'Don't blame me if you're not down with the kids.'

'I'm not down with the kids. I *am* a kid.'

'Are you going to kick this gun?' Katie asked evenly. 'Or not?'

Allie noticed that her nails were beautifully manicured in pale pink. How did she have time to paint her nails when Carter was a hostage and Lucinda was dead and the world had gone to hell?

For some reason this small detail galled her. Anger, always close to the surface, flared.

'I'm going to kick that gun.' She gritted her teeth.

Whirling on the toes of one foot, she performed the same move with less balletic grace, and more violence. The gun flew ten feet, just missing Nicole and Sylvain.

'Careful,' Eloise cautioned from where she was training with Zoe. 'Nobody's supposed to get hurt tonight.'

Allie waved an unrepentant apology.

Katie examined her wrist. 'That was unnecessarily brutish.'

'Thanks,' Allie said. 'I tried.'

Katie craned her neck to look to where Rachel was training with Lucas. She was struggling to reach the gun with her foot, even though Lucas kept lowering his hand to make it easier for her.

'I want to train with Rachel again. She has excellent

manners.'

'You mean she's not very good at the fighting.'

'That too.' Katie picked up a towel to dab her face. 'Let's take a break while I plot my revenge.'

Grabbing a bottle of water from the floor, Allie took a swig. She wouldn't have admitted it to anyone but she liked training with Katie. She was a quick student. Interesting to spar with. And funny.

She took her mind off things. At least five minutes had passed since she'd last worried about Carter.

Katie stretched an arm above her head, bending so far to one side she looked broken. 'You must be glad to have Sylvain back.'

Allie followed her gaze. At the opposite end of the room, Sylvain and Nicole were practising with smooth, well-matched precision. Sylvain's movement were as graceful as Katie's – he had a dancer's perfect balance. He defied gravity.

His muscles flexed as he whipped the gun from Nicole's fingers.

So much for taking my mind off things.

'I am glad,' she said, not entirely dishonestly. 'We need him.'

'*We* need him?' Katie's gaze sharpened. 'That's an odd way of putting it.' She turned to look at her more closely. 'Now that I think of it, you two have hardly spoken all day. You used to be so lovey-dovey. What's going on?'

'Nothing,' Allie lied. 'It's just been a rubbish few days.' She looked down at her feet, as if something interesting had just appeared there.

'Hmm.' Katie didn't sound convinced. 'Try harder. I was watching the two of you even before that thing happened with his dad and he had to leave. I saw signs of strain. Something's definitely up. You might as well tell me.'

She didn't sound happy or unhappy about this fact. Just intrigued.

'You were watching me? That's so creepy.' Allie tried to appear bored. But the conversation was making her increasingly uncomfortable. 'Whatever it is, it's none of your business.'

'I'm right, then.' Katie pounced. 'I knew it. There *is* trouble in paradise. What's going on? Did you argue? Did you lie? Did he cheat on you? Did you cheat on him?'

Allie's cheeks flamed. Hurriedly, she turned away, pretending she was just collecting the gun from where it had fallen.

By the time she returned, she'd smoothed all the guilt from her expression.

She pointed the gun at Katie.

'Fight me,' she said darkly. 'Or something that rhymes with that.'

Katie rolled her eyes. 'Nice try. I'm not giving up. Tell me what happened.'

'Whatever. *Bang*.' Allie twitched the gun. 'You just keep getting killed, Katie.'

But the redhead was relentless. 'Tell me the truth. Did you and Sylvain fight? Did something happen in France? What did he do?'

'Nothing happened.' Allie had begun to sweat. 'We did *not* fight.'

She glanced over her shoulder to ensure the subject of this conversation couldn't overhear them. But Sylvain and Nicole were laughing about something. Well out of earshot.

'Fine. Then something must have happened in London

with you and Carter,' Katie persisted. 'You professed your undying affection. Something like that.'

Allie dropped the gun.

She didn't know how it happened. Her fingers just went nerveless.

The gun hit the blue rubber mat on the floor without a sound.

Katie's green eyes widened. Wordlessly, she picked up the gun and pointed it at her.

Allie held up her hands; to a casual observer it would have looked like a hold-up.

'Please,' she whispered. 'Stop this.'

'Never.' Katie's cat-like eyes had gone cool. 'That's it, then. Something happened in London, that night. With Carter. And you. You fought. You kissed. He was cruel. You're in love.'

There was too much truth in her litany of guesses.

Allie dropped her hands. Her shoulders slumped.

She thought of Carter, kneeling above her on the bed in the Kilburn safe house. Pulling her into his arms, pressing her body against his hard chest. Their whispered promises whirled through her memory, tainted by the guilt and loss she'd felt ever since.

She hadn't told anyone about it. Not even Rachel. And it was killing her.

She couldn't keep it a secret. Couldn't lie anymore.

It was time to be honest with someone. Time to come clean.

Besides, if there was one thing Katie knew about aside from money, it was boys.

'We didn't fight, OK?' Allie's voice was barely above a whisper.

'What did you do, Allie?' Katie challenged her.

Allie took a long breath.

'We had sex.'

'You *didn't.*' Katie stared.

Her condemning gaze made Allie's insides curdle.

Suddenly telling her the truth seemed like a really stupid idea. But it was too late to change her mind now.

'We didn't mean to,' she said, defensively. 'It just… happened.'

Katie had gone so blank Allie could project anything onto her. Contempt. Disbelief. Ridicule.

When she finally did speak, her voice was low and angry.

'Did you think *once* about Sylvain? About how he'd feel? With everything that just happened to his dad…' She looked away, her jaw tight. 'Bloody hell, Allie. You're much more ruthless than you let on.'

The familiar bite of guilt cut deep into Allie's heart.

She dropped her gaze, unable to take the disapproval she saw in the other girl's gaze.

'I just don't understand you.' Katie lowered her voice. 'What were you *thinking*?'

Allie thought of Carter's dark eyes. His voice saying, '*Oh God, Allie. I love you, too.*'

How could she explain that to Katie? How could she describe the relief of listening to her heart at last? Or how it felt to have – if only for a few minutes – the one thing she wanted in the world?

She didn't have words for that.

'We weren't thinking,' she whispered. 'It just happened.'

'It *just happened*?' Katie's stare was incredulous. 'Jesus Christ, Allie. That's even worse. At least tell me you were safe.'

Allie flushed. Somehow, Katie asking her if she'd used

protection was worse than anything else.

'Of course we were.' She mumbled the sentence, staring down at the feet.

'Thank God for that.'

'Look,' Allie said. 'I love Carter. I'm sorry about… everything. But I *love* him. It's the most real thing in my life.' She took a shaky breath. 'Maybe the only real thing.'

If she'd hoped to move Katie, she was to be disappointed. The redhead squinted at her sceptically.

'Come on, Allie. You have form on this. You love him today and hate him tomorrow. So ask yourself this. Is it *love* love? Like, actual love? Not the pretend…' she waved her hand in an impatient gesture, 'things are dangerous and you have muscles so let's just do it' love. But the messed up, ugly, painful, no-makeup love. Because if it's not that kind and you break Sylvain's heart…' She took a step closer, fixing her fierce gaze on Allie's. 'I swear to God I'll never forgive you.'

'It's that kind.' Allie's voice was ragged. 'The ugly kind.'

Maybe Allie was imagining it, but it seemed like Katie's face softened, just a little. Still, her response was cutting.

'If it's real love, I feel sorry for you. Because it's going to hurt a lot of people. This kind of love leaves scars.'

A tear escaped and slipped down Allie's cheek, but she didn't reply.

There was nothing to say.

From the centre of the room, Zelazny's harsh voice interrupted them. 'All senior students: a five-mile run begins now. Junior students remain in the room, please.'

Relieved, Allie took a step towards the door, but Katie grabbed her arm, holding her back.

'Allie…' Her voice was low and urgent. '… be very

careful how you handle this.'

The other students streamed past them towards the door. Rachel shot the two of them a curious glance as she passed. Across the room, Allie saw Sylvain turn back, his eyes scanning the crowd. Looking for her. As he always did.

'Sylvain loves you,' Katie whispered. 'Ugly love.' Her fingers were tight on Allie's wrist.

'This will *demolish* him.'

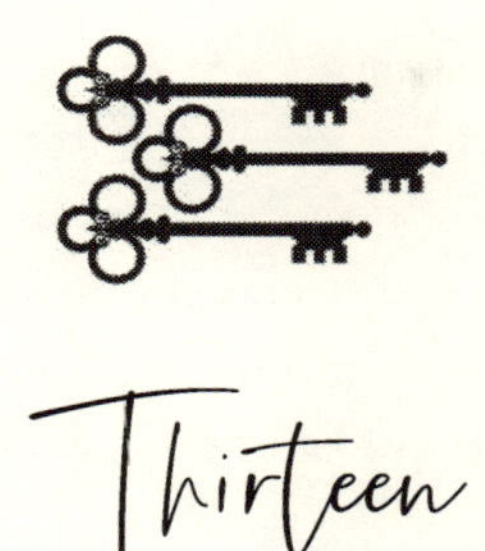

Thirteen

The conversation with Katie made everything worse. The next day, Allie could hardly look Sylvain in the face. Katie's condemnation had left her feeling like a criminal.

Every time she passed her in the corridors, the redhead shot her a warning look. *Sort this out*, the look seemed to say.

But how the hell was she supposed to do that? With Carter missing and Sylvain utterly unaware of everything that had happened while he'd been away, Allie couldn't see a way to handle this that didn't end badly.

The only thing she could do was avoid the situation altogether.

As soon as her last lesson ended that afternoon, she tore up the stairs so fast her skirt fluttered around her legs from the breeze she created.

When she walked into Dom's light-filled office, the faint sound of jazz swirled softly from hidden speakers. The room smelled of fresh coffee and Earl Grey tea.

Shak and another guard were working at the table. Isabelle and Raj were talking quietly in a corner.

'Hi Allie,' Dom said, looking up from her laptop. 'What's up?'

'Any news?' Allie asked, as she always did.

Dom shook her head, as she did every time. 'Not yet. Hang tight, kiddo.'

Her pragmatic American sayings usually made Allie feel better. Today it made her want to cry. It must have shown on her face, because Dom got up from her desk and followed her across the room.

'Look, Allie,' she said, 'this isn't going to be fast, no matter what. It's a big world out there, and we've got to find one seventeen-year-old boy in it. The people hiding him are very good at what they do. We *will* find him. But this could be a long slog. Nothing will happen overnight.'

'I know,' Allie said, biting her lip. 'I just wish… it was faster.' She glanced over to where Shak's gaze was glued to his screen. 'Look… I know my shift doesn't start until eight. But I don't have anything else to do right now. Do you want me to help out for a while?'

'Sure. We can always use more ears.' Dom waved at the table. 'Grab some headphones.'

Rachel and Zoe walked in a few minutes later, as Allie was setting up.

'Hey Allie.' Rachel stopped beside her. 'I thought you weren't working in here until later.'

Ignoring them both, Zoe leaned over to see what Shak was working on.

'Ooh,' she said, staring at the incomprehensible code on his screen. 'Awesome.'

'I'm impatient,' Allie said. 'Overeager.'

There was truth in this explanation, and Rachel accepted it without question, but Allie felt a little bad about not telling her.

She knew it might seem like an odd decision to tell Katie

the truth about Carter instead of her best friend. But Rachel would always find reasons to understand, to sympathise. Katie, on the other hand, would tell her the cold, hard truth.

And that was what she needed right now. Still, it sucked. And she had to tell Rachel soon.

She slipped the earphones over her head and plugged them into the laptop. The room disappeared, replaced by the harsh male tones of Nathaniel's world.

The voices of his guards were increasingly familiar. Some had such distinctive personalities, she felt like she was getting to know them.

The guard known as Nine was the most interesting – he seemed grumpy and bitter, but also funny and irreverent. He really didn't like Nathaniel or Gabe at all.

Six, on the other hand, was whiny and unpleasant. He seemed the type to toady to anyone in power. Sucking up to anyone who could help him get more power himself.

He made her skin crawl.

When, after half an hour of idle chit-chat among minor guards, Nine's gravelly voice appeared in her headphones, Allie was secretly pleased.

'What's the news?' His question was apparently directed at anyone who happened to be listening.

The others ribbed him. 'What kind of time do you call this?' one of them asked him.

Allie recognised the voice as belonging to Five. He sounded younger than the others, and he and Nine often teased each other in a way that indicated they might be friends.

'I call it early enough,' Nine growled good-humouredly.

Then Six's nasal voice interrupted them.

'Our man is up.' He sounded smug. 'Back on his feet. One

says he's his old self.'

Allie straightened, instantly alert.

She typed, *Nathaniel is better*, into her laptop.

'Hallelujah,' Nine replied dryly. 'Does this mean we're getting on with things? Are we all through crying?'

'There's a meeting at 1700,' Six said, ignoring his sarcasm. 'At headquarters. You should be there. Things are happening.'

'Well, miracles never cease,' Nine said. 'Maybe we'll get to do something useful at last.'

A voice she didn't recognise spoke up. 'Hey Six – any idea what's going on?'

There was a pause.

'All I can tell you is something's happening,' Six said, clearly pleased to be the one in the know. 'Tonight. We're making a move.'

Allie took the news straight to Dom. By the time five o'clock arrived that evening, the office was packed.

Isabelle and Raj were there, along with several of Raj's guards, Zelazny and Eloise. Dom put Nathaniel's comms through the wall speakers so everyone in the room could hear. Then they waited.

The minutes ticked by slowly. Allie began to doubt herself. Maybe they hadn't said 1700. Maybe she'd overblown the importance of what she'd heard.

When it reached six o'clock, and still not one guard had

spoken, the mood in the room changed from eager curiosity to disappointment.

Raj turned to Allie. 'You're certain they said five o'clock?'

Despite her unspoken doubts, Allie nodded. 'Positive.'

The instructors exchanged dubious looks.

'Could they still be in the meeting?' Eloise asked.

No one replied.

An hour was a long time just for Nathaniel to give his guards an assignment. If Allie had been right about the meeting time, something was definitely up.

Sylvain walked up to Raj and murmured something too quietly for her to hear. Raj nodded, looking at his watch.

'We'll give it five more minutes,' he said.

Allie looked away quickly, but she could feel Sylvain looking at her. There was no way he hadn't noticed she'd been avoiding him by this point.

At that moment, a voice rumbled from the speakers. 'Well, that was illuminating.'

Allie's breath caught.

It was Nine. Sarcastic as ever.

'Wasn't it just?' Five sounded amused.

'Well,' Nine sighed, 'I guess that's me cancelling all my plans for tonight. I had big plans, too, with that hot blonde from the other night…'

'Copy that.' The other man snorted a laugh. 'She'll have to wait while we go pay the boss' family a little visit.'

Allie stiffened. *The family? Does he mean Nathaniel's family?*

Across the room she saw Raj pull his phone from his pocket.

The only family Nathaniel had left was Isabelle.

The headmistress stood very still, one hand gripping the back of the chair in front of her, listening intently.

'When are we rolling out?' Nine's voice was loud in the frozen silence of the room. 'Did he say eleven?'

'That's affirmative,' Five replied.

'Just let me powder my nose,' Nine said. 'And I'm good to go.'

The two fell silent.

Isabelle turned to Raj. She looked pale, but when she spoke her voice was steady. 'Eleven, then.'

He headed for the door at speed, his phone pressed to his ear. His reply was crisp.

'We'll be ready.'

Allie was still hunched over the computer an hour later, earphones pressed to her head, when Eloise tapped her on the shoulder.

'I want you to take a break,' the Night School trainer said. 'It's dinner time. And you've been here too long already.'

'I'm fine,' Allie insisted. 'I'm not hungry.'

Eloise scanned her face. 'When was the last time you took a break?'

When Allie, who had actually not stopped since eight o'clock that morning, hesitated, Eloise pulled her from her chair.

'Nothing's happening for hours,' she said. 'There's plenty of help here. And you look hungry to me.'

Soon the headphones had been handed to one of Raj's

guards and the librarian was shooing her out the door.

'Don't come back for at least an hour,' she said. 'There are child labour laws, you know.'

Allie, who had no idea what she was talking about, made her way downstairs, grumbling to herself.

She knew in her heart she was unlikely to miss anything – there'd been nothing new for hours. Nine had disappeared, along with Six and several other guards. Raj believed they were preparing for whatever they had planned for later tonight.

But she still wanted to keep listening. Just in case.

When she reached the ground floor, the rumble of conversation from the dining hall let her know most people had already gathered for dinner.

Rich cooking smells floated from the kitchen. Candles glittered on the tables, which were set, as always, with heavy silver cutlery and crystal glasses. Allie couldn't decide whether she was glad that the staff so determinedly ignored the school's crises, or found it absurd.

The others had already gathered at their usual table. There was an empty seat next to Sylvain. Allie knew she had to take it. Anything else would be impossible to explain.

Taking a deep breath, she slid into the seat. 'Hey everyone.'

Sylvain turned to her. His expression was neutral, but Allie thought she sensed a new distance. He didn't smile.

'Hey.' Rachel waved from across the round table where she sat between Zoe and Nicole. 'Any news?'

Allie shook her head, then glanced at Sylvain again, conscious that he hadn't spoken.

'Hey,' she said. 'You OK?'

His response was immediate. 'I'm fine.'

But his tone was cool.

Before Allie could think of what to say, Zoe distracted her with a question. It was a while before she looked back at him. By then, Sylvain was eating silently, stony faced.

Allie felt terrible. She'd effectively ignored him since the moment he arrived. He had no idea what was going on in her head. In her life.

'I'm sorry I haven't had a chance to talk to you,' Allie said.

Sylvain stopped eating. When he turned to look at her, she thought she saw a flicker of hurt in his eyes.

'Things have been crazy,' she explained, not very convincingly. 'Maybe we can talk later.'

'Maybe.' He studied her for a moment without speaking. 'Or maybe it's something else.'

Then he turned away and resumed eating, as if she wasn't there.

Allie froze. Had he guessed? Had Katie told him?

She didn't dare ask what he meant – she wasn't sure she wanted to know.

From across the table, Rachel watched their exchange, puzzlement knitting her brow.

Allie turned back to her plate. She had to tell everyone the truth.

Soon.

'Anything happen while I was gone?' Allie asked, slipping into the chair next to Shak. She was so glad the stressful dinner was over, she could have hugged her headphones.

'Radio silence.' Shak leaned back in the chair and stretched. 'Nathaniel's boys suddenly got discipline.'

Allie slid the headphones on anyway. 'Maybe they'll start talking.'

But he was right about the silence – not one of Nathaniel's guards spoke on the comms system for nearly two hours.

During that time the room filled steadily, until it seemed all the senior students and instructors were there. Everyone wanted to know what Nathaniel was up to – whatever it was, it couldn't be good.

Dom was in constant motion – on the phone, on the comms, coordinating Raj. Rachel sat in a chair at her desk, acting as an assistant. Nicole sat next to Rachel while Zoe and Lucas worked with Shak.

Sylvain stayed away from the other students, with Raj and Isabelle in one corner, talking quietly. He never looked at Allie.

After the long silence, at eleven o'clock precisely, Nine's voice rumbled from the speakers at last.

'Roll out, boys.'

'Copy that,' someone said.

Allie stared at her laptop, willing them to say more. But the wall of silence descended again.

A sense of unease crept up her spine. This didn't feel right.

Nathaniel's guards had been talking non-stop for days. All of a sudden they were far too quiet. It was as if Nathaniel knew they were listening. As if he was taunting them.

Everyone fell silent as they waited for any sound from Nathaniel's guards. Any clue as to what they were planning.

In the quiet, they all heard the footsteps pounding down the hall, growing steadily closer. The door flew open with such violence, Sylvain had to jump out of the way.

It was Eloise. She looked winded and pale.

'It's Nathaniel.' She looked at Isabelle. 'He's here.'

Fourteen

The room erupted.

Voices tumbled over voices in a chorus of panic.

'What?'

'Where?'

'How did he get in the *building*?'

Allie found herself standing, although she had no memory of leaving her seat. She felt numb with fear; her hands had turned to ice.

Isabelle and Zelazny huddled with Eloise by the door. Seconds later, Zelazny sprinted from the room, Eloise right on his heels.

'I need everyone to be calm.' The headmistress held up her hands for quiet.

Slowly the room fell silent.

'Nathaniel is *outside* the gate. He is not on the grounds.' Isabelle surveyed the room. 'We have been here before. I need everyone to follow protocol for this. Security team, please report to Raj. Night School students – Zelazny and Eloise will coordinate. For the moment, I need you all to stay inside the building. Nathaniel has asked to speak with me.' Her eyes searched the group until they found Allie face. 'And Allie.'

There was a collective intake of breath.

'Allie… no,' Rachel whispered.

But Allie didn't hesitate. She jumped to her feet and crossed the room to join the headmistress.

The headmistress studied her, concern clouding her eyes. 'I don't have to tell you how dangerous this situation is.' She lowered her voice to a whisper. 'We have no idea what he's planning. You don't have to come with me. Nathaniel has no right to ask that of you and neither do I.'

Allie thought of Carter, shoving her into the car. Slamming the door behind her. Knowing he'd be left behind.

He's not the only one who can be stupidly brave.

'I'm going with you.' Her voice emerged strong and steady. 'I'm not afraid.'

The look Isabelle gave her then was bittersweet. 'And to think, I just promised your mother I'd keep you safe.'

They turned towards the door, but then Sylvain stepped between them, his eyes blazing. 'You can't do this, Isabelle. You can't take Allie out there. It's incredibly dangerous.'

Allie opened her mouth to argue, but Isabelle didn't give her the chance.

'Sylvain, Allie is neither your possession nor your responsibility.' Her words sliced through the air. 'Nor is she mine. She's quite capable of making her own decisions. Now, let us get on with what we have to do.'

Allie was astonished. She'd never heard the headmistress speak to Sylvain like that. She'd always treated him like an equal.

Colour rising to his face, Sylvain pivoted towards Allie. 'Don't do this,' he pleaded. 'Don't you understand? You can't trust Nathaniel. He could kill you.'

Allie's fury flared. There was a time when his

protectiveness made her feel safe. Now it seemed insulting. Didn't he know that she could look out for herself? Didn't he understand how much she'd learned?

'I'm not an idiot, Sylvain,' she snapped. 'I know how dangerous this is. I don't need your advice.'

She saw the hurt in his eyes and felt the quick sting of remorse. Then Isabelle pulled her away.

'We must hurry, Allie.'

Together they ran from the room. Soon Sylvain was forgotten behind them.

Allie kept her focus on Carter. He could be outside right now.

She clung to that hope as Isabelle talked low and fast. 'There are five vehicles, each holding at least four guards. Eloise believes Nathaniel is among them.'

'What about Carter?'

'No one has seen him. But it's dark.' Isabelle glanced at her. 'He could be there.'

They ran down the stairs, their voices echoing. Below, Allie could hear the rapid-fire footsteps of the guards racing into position. Her heart thudded hard in her chest.

She loved this feeling. The adrenaline. The danger.

She felt wide awake for the first time in days.

'Is there anything else I should know?'

Isabelle's lips tightened. 'Nathaniel says he has a message for you. He insists on giving it to you directly. That's the only reason I'm willing to put you in such danger right now.' She looked away. 'He hasn't left me any choice.'

They reached the foot of the staircase and headed down the hallway at a run. In the shadows around them Allie could hear the sound of activity – people rushing in all directions, urgent voices, doors slamming.

The front door stood open. Dozens of guards were on the lawn, scanning the grounds through night-vision binoculars.

Zelazny intercepted them as they turned into the drive. 'Everyone's in place.' His eyes darted from Isabelle to Allie and back again. Perspiration dotted his high forehead. He lowered his voice, directing his words at Isabelle. 'I don't like this. The situation's too fluid. We don't know what he's up to.'

'I'm aware of all of this, August,' Isabelle said evenly. 'Keep the students safe. I'll look out for Allie.'

Without waiting for his response, she headed down the long, gravel drive. Allie hurried after her.

She kept trying to think of more questions – there had to be more to know. A better way to prepare. They hadn't even changed into Night School clothes. Isabelle wore black trousers and a white silk blouse. Her office shoes were all wrong for running. Allie was still in her school uniform.

There was no moon tonight. The darkness was so complete, they could barely make out the road ahead.

It was nearly a mile to the front gate. Their steps took on a kind of rhythmic synchronicity. Despite her shoes, Isabelle ran with fluid ease. Her hair had begun to spring loose from the clips that held it back; stray golden-brown strands tumbled into her eyes.

'Do you think,' Allie asked after a long time had passed, 'this is a trap?'

Isabelle didn't reply immediately. 'Probably,' she said after a moment. 'With Nathaniel, everything's a trap.' Unexpectedly, she smiled. 'In a strange way, he's predictable.'

It was an odd response. Even after what had happened to Lucinda, Nathaniel didn't seem to intimidate her. He seemed, more than anything, to disappoint her.

But then Allie thought of Christopher. Her own brother had sided with Nathaniel, but then saved her from his thugs in London. He'd helped her escape. Maybe Isabelle's relationship with her stepbrother was just as conflicted as Allie's own.

Suddenly, she saw something in the distance. A faint, sulphurous glow flickered through the trees. Allie squinted at the light, trying to understand what she was looking at. Then it struck her.

Headlights.

Soon they were close enough to see the source. Several large vehicles, arrayed in a row, faced the school's intimidating front gate. She recognised the biggest one – the huge tank-like vehicle that had pursued them on the way back from London.

Her stomach flip-flopped. The thing was so big – surely Nathaniel could just bash through the fence with it if he wanted.

The closer she got to the fence line, the less she could see. After the darkness, the light was blinding.

Shading her eyes with one hand, she peered into the glare. She thought she could make out figures facing them but she couldn't tell if they were men or women, armed or unarmed.

'Nice trick, Nathaniel.' Isabelle's voice rang out in the silence. 'Turn off the lights.'

For a moment nothing happened. Then all the lights went off at once.

Now Allie was even more blind. She blinked hard but it was as if a curtain had fallen, hiding everything.

She stopped walking. She didn't dare take a step.

She felt helpless. Exposed.

'Stay close.' Isabelle's whisper came from the darkness right next to her; Allie couldn't see her at all.

How am I going to stay close if I don't know where you are? she thought.

'What do you want Nathaniel?' Isabelle asked from a few feet away. Allie took a cautious step towards the sound. 'There's no need for all this drama.'

'Aren't you glad to see me, Isabelle? How disappointing.' Nathaniel's familiar voice sent ice into Allie's veins. 'I've brought you a present.'

'It's not my birthday,' Isabelle said with veiled sarcasm. 'You didn't have to bring anything.'

'Oh, but I did.'

Allie's vision began to clear. She could make out a hazy image of the scene on the other side of the fence. There were about ten large men. They appeared to be pulling something from a car.

On the other side of the fence from this group, she and Isabelle were alone. Surreptitiously, Allie peered around, looking for any sign of Raj's guards nearby – but she saw no one.

They had to be there, though. Somewhere.

Nathaniel's guards shoved two men towards the gate. They were handcuffed and blindfolded. Each wore the distinctive black gear of Raj's security team.

'I've brought your men back,' Nathaniel said, a touch of glee in his voice. 'A peace offering.'

He was as handsome as ever. His dark hair was neatly combed, his expensive tie perfectly straight. He might have been going to a business meeting, instead of a nocturnal prisoner exchange. But Allie knew better than to underestimate him. There was nothing ordinary about Nathaniel.

The guards surrounding him all, like him, wore dark suits and ties. As far as Allie could tell, all were male, with short hair. She scanned their prisoners quickly, searching for Carter.

He wasn't there.

Isabelle must have been thinking the same thing. 'What about the boy? Where is Carter West?'

Nathaniel spread his hands. 'Regrettably, he couldn't accompany us today. He was… otherwise engaged.'

All the breath seemed to leave Allie's lungs. She stared at Nathaniel in stunned disbelief. She'd been so certain he'd be here. That she'd see him now.

His amused gaze swept across her face. 'Oh dear,' he said. 'You did expect him, didn't you? How upsetting for you.'

He was mocking her. Enjoying her pain.

Allie's hands curled into fists at her sides, nails digging into her palms. She wanted to punch Nathaniel's smug face. To claw her nails across his smooth skin.

Isabelle, too, seemed to have lost her patience.

'What is the point of this, Nathaniel?' The headmistress stepped closer to the fence. All the humour was gone from her voice. 'Lucinda is dead because of your endless vendetta. Isn't that enough for you? Haven't you done enough damage? Can't we stop now?'

'Lucinda is dead,' Nathaniel said coldly, 'because she couldn't accept the truth. That her time in charge of Orion was over. The future has arrived.' He held out his arms. 'I am the future.'

Isabelle fairly crackled with fury.

'Maybe you are. But Lucinda loathed the future you represented.' She moved closer to the fence until they were staring at each other. 'It's not a future. It's the past. You would take the power much greater men gave to all people, and keep it for yourself.' She was within his reach now, but Nathaniel didn't move. He was watching her, expressionless. 'She was right to fight you. And now that she's gone… I'm going to fight you in her place.'

Allie thought of their plan to leave the school – to give up and start over somewhere else – and lowered her gaze. Isabelle didn't want Nathaniel to know anything until Carter was returned to them – just in case.

Nathaniel's eyes glittered like broken glass. 'It's nice to know where we stand, *sister*.'

His gaze shifted to Allie. 'What about you, little one? Will you fight me, too?'

She raised her eyes to meet his, forcing herself not to flinch. 'To the death.'

She meant it, too. Maybe they would leave. But she would come back some day. And make him pay.

He arched one eyebrow. 'Well, let's hope it doesn't come to that.' He glanced around, looking into the darkness behind them. 'By the way, where is that brother of yours, Allie?'

She frowned. 'What do you mean?'

'Don't play games, little girl.' Nathaniel tapped his heel against the ground impatiently. 'Christopher has been missing since the parley in London. I presumed he came running to you. Is he here?'

So Chris hadn't been caught. He'd run away.

This was stunning news. Allie fought to keep her expression neutral.

Maybe he was telling the truth – he really did defy Nathaniel.

'Christopher is none of your business,' she said.

He ran a hand across the smooth line of his jaw. His gaze was piercing. 'You have a smart mouth.'

'So do you.'

For a second he stared at her. Then he threw back his head and laughed. 'Oh Allie. If you'd chosen the right side, I think I might actually like you.'

'I did choose the right side,' she fired back.

His smile faded. 'You're wrong about that.'

He rocked back on his heels. In the dark, on a dirt road, surrounded by his guards, he still managed to appear relaxed, in his element. He seemed to enjoy sparring with them.

'You made a promise to me, in London, Allie. Do you remember?'

At first, she had no idea what he was talking about. Nothing seemed important about that night except Carter and Lucinda.

Then it came to her in a flash of images. Nathaniel and Lucinda, standing together – the lights of London spreading out behind them like a glittering carpet.

'I will need you to promise, Allie, that you will never seek to take control of the Orion Group while I am still alive.'

Lucinda had tried to stop her from agreeing. But Allie had insisted. She never wanted anything like that anyway.

'I remember.'

'Good.' He made a quick gesture.

She watched with narrow suspicion as one of the guards produced a stack of papers, which he pushed through the bars of the fence.

Allie took a step forward, but Isabelle gestured for her to remain where she was. She took the papers.

As she scanned the first page, her lip curled in disgust.

Nathaniel was still talking. 'These papers bind you to that promise. I'll need you to sign them.'

'Allie will never sign this,' Isabelle said, contempt in her voice. 'How dare you even ask her?'

'Come on Izzy, she's a big girl,' Nathaniel replied. 'Surely she can decide for herself.'

'She's a minor,' Isabelle snapped. 'No, she can't.'

Nathaniel waved his hand. 'There are ways around that and you know it.'

As they argued, Allie tried to decide what to do. In the end, it didn't matter what they said. The decision was hers.

When she'd agreed to Nathaniel's demands that night, it had been in direct opposition to what Lucinda wanted her to do. She hoped it would make him leave them alone.

It had been a miscalculation.

She'd never known Lucinda to look at her with such disappointment as she had at that moment. As if she'd failed her.

She wouldn't fail her now.

Allie stepped forward until she stood close to the gate. Eye-to-eye with Nathaniel. She wanted him to see how unafraid she was.

'I will sign your papers.' Her sudden announcement seemed to surprise them both. Isabelle shot her a frustrated look.

'Excellent.' Nathaniel reached for his breast pocket, as if to take out a pen.

Then Allie finished her thought: 'As soon as Carter West is safely back at Cimmeria Academy – and after you agree to leave us in peace – you will have your signature. Until then, I won't sign anything.'

Nathaniel's expression darkened. He'd gone very still. Colour rose in his cheeks.

Suddenly, one of the guards arrayed behind him – a muscular man with a baby face and a brush of stubble on his cheeks – caught Allie's gaze and made a subtle gesture with his hand.

Get back, it said.

Allie took a hasty, stumbling step away, just as Nathaniel reached through the bars and swung for her. He missed her by inches.

Then he lost it.

'What the hell is *wrong with you*?' He kicked the metal gate over and over again. The fence shuddered from the force of the attack.

Behind him, the guards stood stoic, as if what he was doing was perfectly normal.

Her heart pounding, Allie scanned their faces until she found the one with the baby face. Like the others, he gazed steadily over her head, as if she wasn't there.

Why had he warned her?

What if that's Nine?

It had to be him.

She made up her mind. She would find a way to meet him. To explain.

Allie cast a sideways glance at the headmistress. She was watching Nathaniel's tantrum with a strange mixture of sympathy and revulsion.

Panting, Nathaniel stepped back from the fence. The night seemed quieter after that burst of violence.

She and Isabelle watched him warily.

'Listen to me, little girl.' His voice was a snarl. 'If you ever want to see your boyfriend alive again, I suggest you sign that document now…'

'Enough.' Isabelle held up her hand. 'You wouldn't dare. If you hurt Carter West, you lose all your leverage. You need him like you need her signature. You have your answer, Nathaniel.

Give us Carter. And you can have everything you want.'

Nathaniel could have no idea how true that was.

Holding the document he'd given her up, Isabelle tore it in half. The pieces fluttered to the ground, scattering around her like flower petals.

Nathaniel's face was red with rage.

'You should be careful, Nathaniel.' Isabelle's tone was taunting. 'I hear everyone in Westminster is talking about how Lucinda died. Nobody believes the cover story. A heart attack. Really?' She shook her head. 'Rumours spread fast in Parliament. How long do you think you're going to last?'

Allie expected Nathaniel to lose it again. But his response was chilling.

'You are sailing,' he said, 'too close to the wind, little sister.'

Isabelle just smiled. 'That is right where I like to be. *Big* brother.'

For a long moment the two stood, locked in a silent battle. Then Nathaniel held up one hand.

'Let's go.'

As one, his guards turned back to their vehicles. Allie searched the crowd but she couldn't see the baby-faced guard anymore – he'd disappeared into the shadows.

The headlights switched on in a blinding display. Isabelle stood at the gate, unafraid, staring right into the bright light.

Backlit like that, her hair golden and waving around her face, she looked like a goddess. Or like a warrior queen.

The SUVs lumbered around and, one after another, roared away.

When they were gone, the night fell silent. Allie heard birds – disturbed by the engines – grumbling in the trees. Wind rushed softly through the branches of the pines.

The only people left on the other side of the fence were the two returned hostages. They stood helpless, blindfolded, their hands still tied behind their backs.

They lifted their faces, in a curiously animalistic way, trying to see through the fabric that covered their eyes.

Allie knew they were bait.

This was classic Nathaniel. He could have stopped the cars a short distance down the road. He could have left men hidden in the woods, waiting to signal him as soon as the gate opened.

There'd been no reason for him to bring these men back at all.

The whole situation screamed *trap*.

She couldn't imagine what would happen now. It was too dangerous to open the gates. But they couldn't just leave the hostages standing there.

Like her, the headmistress was staring at the two men. She might have kept her cool throughout the evening, but now she was pale with fury.

'Are they really gone?' Allie asked hesitantly. 'Is it safe?'

'I don't care.' Isabelle pulled a phone from her pocket and pushed a button. Every muscle in her body was tense as she spoke into the phone.

'Open the bloody gate.'

Fifteen

With a jarring screech of metal, the gate began to roll open.

Allie stared at the headmistress in utter disbelief. Opening the gates now was insane.

This kind of recklessness was utterly out of character for cautious, protocol-obsessed Isabelle.

The headmistress stood in the middle of the drive, inches from the moving metal.

It was almost, Allie thought, almost like she *wanted* Nathaniel to come back.

This was scarier than anything that had happened all night. The teachers at Cimmeria had been pushed to the brink by Nathaniel over the last few months.

Maybe this had been a step too far. Pushing the headmistress over the edge.

'Isabelle…' she began hesitantly.

Before she could finish the sentence, Isabelle lifted her phone again.

'Now, Raj.'

As if by magic, security guards in black fighting gear poured from the woods behind them. There must have been fifty of them. They moved without a sound.

In the inky darkness, they were like night in motion.

Allie had known they must be nearby – the guards were never going to leave the two of them out here alone – but she hadn't seen any sign of them until now.

With silent swiftness, they streamed around the two women and rushed towards the gates.

Raj was in the lead, his face set and focused. He didn't glance at them as he sped by.

They hurtled through the gate to the two blindfolded men. There they divided in a movement of silent precision. Most headed off to search the surrounding area. The others searched the bound men before hustling them on to the school grounds.

As quickly as it had begun, it was over. The guards raced back towards the fence, stealth forgotten now. Zelazny shouted orders as he ran. The gates shuddered and began to close.

Once safely inside, the guards arrayed themselves in a long, black line in front of the slowly closing gate. They stood poised, ready to spring.

Raj was the last one back, slipping through the bars like a shadow, just before the gate closed with a clang.

Zelazny headed straight to Isabelle, disapproval in his pale, blue eyes.

'That was risky,' he said, sotto voce.

Isabelle kept her gaze on the two bound men. Someone produced a knife and sliced the plastic cuffs from their wrists.

'It is time,' she said after a moment, 'for risk taking.'

She strode away to talk to Raj. Zelazny glowered, but didn't pursue her.

Allie watched the guards dealing with the returned hostages, a hollow, helpless misery growing inside her.

No Carter. It was all a trick.

She didn't know what to do.

Everything felt so pointless. No matter what they did, they lost. Nathaniel read them like a book. They couldn't force him to do anything he didn't want to. He was just toying with them now.

They were the mouse. He was the cat.

She couldn't see that ever changing. Especially now that Lucinda was gone. He'd play with them until he was bored. Whenever he was ready, he would take everything. Game over.

'Don't worry.'

Allie glanced up in surprise to find Zelazny watching her, a rare hint of sympathy in his expression.

'Nathaniel will pay for this,' he said.

If she hadn't been so dazed by the speed with which events had transpired, she might have been surprised that he'd noticed her pain. Or that he cared.

But that would only occur to her later. Now she just nodded her thanks.

'Everyone back inside.' Raj's voice sliced through the night.

Zelazny whirled, the momentary kindness disappearing.

'Let's go,' he bellowed. 'Everybody move! Now!'

With one last longing look through the gate to the empty darkness beyond, Allie did as she told.

As soon as they reached the main school building, Isabelle took the two released prisoners to be debriefed.

'August, Eloise – with me.' Her tone was so clipped and

cold, Allie knew better than to ask if she could come, too.

The small group disappeared into the office underneath the stairs. The door slammed behind them.

Quiet fell.

For a while, Allie waited outside Isabelle's door, hoping for news. Maybe the guards knew something about Carter. Maybe they could give them some clues as to where he was being kept.

But the ornate carved door stayed stubbornly shut.

She leaned against a wall, trying to remain cool and composed, but her right foot tapped nervously against the polished wood floor. She couldn't seem to make it be still.

'Allie.'

Sylvain had walked up behind her soundlessly; she'd never heard him coming.

No chance of escape.

'We need to talk,' he said.

He was still in his black Night School gear; his expression was thunderous.

Allie's heart sank.

She tried to affect nonchalance, but tension crept into her voice. 'Sure. What's up?'

'Not here.' He pointed at the sweeping staircase behind them. 'Up there.'

He climbed the stairs with a cat's smooth stride. Allie followed as slowly as possible, gripping the banister.

She had a bad feeling about this.

On the landing, he stopped in front of the towering windows. Resting one hand on the plinth for a marble statue he drummed his fingers briefly – the only sign that he was nervous, too.

She wanted him to say something. But he just stood there.

'I'm sorry I shouted at you earlier,' she said. Because someone had to say something. 'That wasn't on.'

'This isn't about that,' he said.

He was avoiding her gaze.

'Oh.' Her stomach flip-flopped. 'What *is* this about?'

His eyes met hers for just a second then skittered away. 'Don't you know?'

'No,' she said, but it came out as an unconvincing whisper.

His expression told her she wasn't fooling anyone.

'Something happened while I was gone. I can tell. I know there's a lot going on but… Everything's different now. With us.'

Panic left a fine sheen of perspiration on Allie's skin. Her heart beat out an erratic rhythm.

He knows, she thought with wild certainty. *How does he know?* And then: *Katie.*

The redhead had betrayed her after all. She should have guessed that would happen. Bloody Katie. Always looking for an angle. Always trying to get ahead.

Well, it was too late to fix it now. She had to think. Fast.

'I don't know what you mean,' she lied.

He smiled at her sadly. 'Yes, you do.'

At that moment, Allie hated Katie with a white hot rage. She hated her more than Nathaniel.

She couldn't pretend any longer.

'What did Katie tell you?' she asked heatedly. 'You shouldn't believe anything she says.'

'Katie?' Sylvain's brow creased. 'I haven't spoken to her today.' He stared at her then, a sudden realisation in his eyes. 'What should she have told me?'

Allie froze. Now she really had blown it.

She couldn't think of any more lies to tell.

When she didn't reply, he waved his hand. 'Never mind. I can guess. So I was right. About everything.'

This was so awful. So spectacularly amazingly awful.

She'd caused all this with her indecision. And then, at the end, made it even worse by making up her mind.

She took a step towards him but didn't dare go any further. He seemed suddenly so out of reach.

'Sylvain, please,' she said.

He nodded as if she'd just confirmed all his suspicions.

'I knew before I left things weren't right between us. I guess I was hoping that – after everything…' His voice trailed off. His hands clenched and released. 'But I was wrong.' He lifted his piercing blue eyes to meet hers. 'Wasn't I? You want to break up with me. Don't you?'

How do you even answer that?

It's a trick question. The answer is already inside it.

Allie felt as if the floor was shifting beneath her feet.

This couldn't be happening now. She'd planned to deal with it all later. After everything was resolved. When Carter was back and…

When she was ready.

But when was that going to be? She'd never be ready to break Sylvain's heart.

The school had gone horribly quiet. Nothing stirred. It felt as if the whole building was watching them fall apart.

His question still hung in the air. Unanswered.

Don't you?

'Yes,' she whispered.

He let out a quick breath, as if she'd punched him.

'At last,' he said. 'The truth.' He held her gaze. His eyes were unnervingly steady. 'Is it Carter? Did something happen with you two?'

'Yes,' she repeated, sorrow in her voice.

He flinched then, although he tried to hide it.

'I always knew,' he said. 'But it still…'

He never finished the sentence. He didn't have to. She knew what he was going to say.

It still hurts.

Tears burned the backs of her eyes.

'You know,' she said, 'you told me a long time ago that I had to figure out who I was and then I'd know what I wanted. Well, I figured it out. The thing is, I *wanted* to be in love with you.' Her voice grew unsteady. 'But I wasn't. I just… wasn't.'

He kept his eyes on his hands, letting her talk. When he finally looked up, the pain on his face cut her heart like broken glass.

'You're in love with Carter.' He said it flatly.

Allie couldn't bear this. She couldn't hurt him anymore.

'I'm sorry,' she whispered.

'Don't.' He held up his hand as if to physically stop her words. 'I don't want…'

A tear slipped down his cheek. He swiped it away with a look of utter disbelief.

Without another word, he turned and walked away – his steps fast but even – across the landing and into the shadows beyond.

Away from her.

Allie almost made it to her room.

She was on the stairs to the dormitory wing, tears streaming down her face, when she heard angry voices from downstairs. She turned back, hurrying down to the landing.

She leaned over the banister, trying to make out words.

Suddenly Zoe shot out of Isabelle's office and hurtled up towards her, her ponytail bouncing with each rapid step. She spotted Allie when she was halfway up.

'Isabelle says for you to come quick.' She squinted at her. 'What's wrong with your *face*?'

'Nothing,' Allie wiped her cheeks with her sleeve. 'Just… nothing.' She cleared her throat. 'What's going on?'

'I don't know.' Zoe motioned for her to hurry. Before Allie knew what was happening, she was following her down the stairs. 'She just came out of her office in a bad mood and called for you. And you weren't there and then she shouted.' She paused. 'Isabelle never shouts.'

Side by side, they sped down the curved staircase, hitting the ground floor at a run, skidding to a stop in front of the common room door. Zoe went in first.

'Where's Isabelle?' she said, looking around. 'I found Allie.'

Rachel and Nicole were waiting by the door.

'In her office. She said for us to all come.' Rachel's eyes scanned Allie's face, missing nothing. Her eyebrows arched up. Allie hurriedly turned away.

Zelazny stood just inside Isabelle's office.

'In,' he growled. 'Now.'

The two guards Nathaniel had returned earlier that night sat nervously in the chairs in front of Isabelle's desk.

Isabelle and Eloise stood behind the desk, looking at

something on a laptop screen – it was turned away from the girls, so Allie could see nothing.

Isabelle's cheeks were pale, her lips set in a thin line.

Zelazny closed the door behind them.

'Thank you for coming.' Isabelle's raised her eyes from the screen. 'I'm afraid there's something you need to see.'

Allie's chest felt tight. She couldn't breathe in this room. Everyone was scaring her.

He can't be dead. God, please don't let him be dead.

She couldn't speak. Her lips felt nerveless.

'What is it?' Rachel asked, frowning.

The headmistress nodded at the two guards. 'Tell them what you told us.'

Allie turned to them. Outside they'd just been shadows. This was the first time she'd got a good look at them. The one on the right had blond hair, cut short, and freckles. The one on the left had dark skin and short dark hair; he had a similar athletic build but looked a little older – more like Raj's age.

'He said to give you a web address,' the older guard said hesitantly. 'He said you should see what you'd done. He said… if you don't give him the school the boy dies. He said "The clock is ticking."'

A strange fuzzy sound filled Allie's ears. She could see the others talking, but it was all muffled, distant.

The headmistress held up her hand, and the room fell silent.

Then she turned her laptop so they could see the screen.

Allie saw a body in a chair, chained, dark head slumped forward. At first, because of how the body was placed, she couldn't make out his features. But she still knew. She recognised those shoulders. The line of his back.

Then he shifted on the hard wooden seat and looked up. It was Carter.

Sixteen

Allie ran from Isabelle's office to the girls' bathroom down the hallway. Crashing through the doors of the first cubicle, she threw herself down on the cool tile floor, her stomach heaving.

When she'd finished vomiting, she didn't get up. She just stayed where she was, her forehead resting on her crossed arms on the toilet seat. She kept seeing Carter in chains. It had been dark, and the picture was grainy but there was no question. It was him.

She wanted to weep but she had no tears left. This day had finished her.

First Nathaniel, then Sylvain. Now Carter.

She'd never felt more defeated.

She just wanted it to stop.

She didn't know how long she'd been there when the bathroom door opened with a faint creak. 'Allie? Are you in here?'

It was Isabelle.

Vaguely, Allie considered saying nothing. Maybe she'd just go away.

But she knew that wouldn't work. The headmistress would search every cubicle.

Still, it took all of her strength to respond. 'I'm here.'

There was a pause. 'Are you OK?'

Allie didn't want to talk to her. She didn't want to talk to anyone. But she couldn't hide forever.

With slow reluctance, she dragged herself to her feet and opened the cubicle door.

'I'm fine.'

Isabelle ignored the lie. Her golden brown eyes scanned Allie's face.

'We've been monitoring Carter for nearly an hour now,' she said gently. 'He has water. He doesn't look starved or drugged. We had the doctor take a look at the footage and she sees no signs of dehydration or catastrophic injury…'

'He's in chains, Isabelle.' Allie cut her off. 'He's been there for *days*.' Saying those words made it all real again. Her hands trembled. She crossed her arms tightly to hide the shaking. 'He's tied up like an… an animal…'

'I know.' Isabelle pulled her into a tight hug. Only when she felt the warmth of her body did Allie realise how cold she was.

'We're going to figure this out,' the headmistress vowed, still holding her close. 'We'll get him back. I promise.'

Allie didn't want promises now. She wanted facts. And the truth.

She extricated herself from Isabelle's arms.

'How though? We don't even know where he is. And Dom's tried and tried.'

Isabelle studied her thoughtfully for a moment. Then she turned the water on and soaked a hand towel in the stream.

'Here's the thing.' Turning back to Allie, she dabbed the warm, damp cloth against her cheeks and forehead. 'Nathaniel just made one huge error. Until now all we had was his comms system. He just gave Dom a poorly protected computer system and an open web cam. She can use it to track his location.' She leaned forward, holding Allie's gaze; excitement glittered in her golden eyes.

'We're going to get him back.'

The next morning, Dom's office was packed. Rachel, Dom, Zoe and Shak were at the table with Allie, all working furiously. Across the room, Nicole, Eloise, and several security guards milled around maps and photos of enormous rural houses. Isabelle and Zelazny hovered around Dom's desk in a tight cluster.

Outside, rain tapped a staccato beat against the windows. Inside, the room buzzed with energy. Everyone believed they had a chance now. They had the information they needed to beat Nathaniel, and he didn't even know he'd handed it to them.

He'd be undone by his own arrogance.

The mood was contagious, and Allie could buy into it now and then, for a few minutes. Until her eyes fell on the wall-mounted screen.

And there was Carter, chains fixed to his wrists and ankles.

He wore a grey, ill-fitting t-shirt and oversized trousers. His hair was a mess. He didn't look like he'd been beaten. Mostly he just looked bored. And furious.

Nathaniel had left the feed live for hours now – a boon to Dom, but excruciating at the same time.

'He thinks he's torturing us,' Isabelle had told her earlier.

'But he's giving us the weapon we need to kill him.'

To Allie, though, it just felt like torture.

There was a clock on the bottom of the screen. She'd missed it last night in her panic, but she was very familiar with it now. The red, digital numbers glowed like dragons' eyes: 72:45:50

The last number was going down.

49, 48, 47, 46…

Those numbers were all the time they had left. Seventy-two hours, forty-five minutes.

Three days.

If they weren't out of the school by then, Nathaniel swore Carter would die. The returned prisoners had explained it all, in tones of regret and muted outrage.

It was Nathaniel's 'little flourish', Isabelle said bitterly. 'He's trying to scare us.'

The only problem was, it worked.

Allie couldn't keep her eyes off the numbers. Her gaze strayed to them, over and over again. Their inexorable decline fuelled a constant sense of borderline panic. Her heart never stopped racing.

Faster, she kept thinking. *We have to be faster.*

She was exhausted. Isabelle had thrown her out of Dom's office at four in the morning – ordering her not to come back until she'd rested. But her attempts to sleep had been plagued by nightmares of bombs with clocks on them, ticking down, down, down…

She'd been back in the office at seven.

She wasn't alone. Dom, Shak and Zoe were working to hack into Nathaniel's computer systems. Raj and his guards were out systematically identifying and searching mansions owned by

Nathaniel's supporters – looking for signs that Carter was being held there.

With one last, long look at Carter, she slid the headphones back on her head. All she could do was listen to Nathaniel's guards.

And hope they made a mistake.

'Another day in the salt mines, eh Five?'

Nine sounds tired today, Allie thought. She sat at the table, her feet propped on a nearby chair, munching on a granola bar. The headphones blocked all sounds except the guards' voices; she kept forgetting anyone else was in the room.

'It's the glamorous life,' Five replied, his voice thick with irony.

'Isn't it just?' Nine replied. 'How's the boss today? He's been in a good mood ever since the last excursion.' He paused. 'Gives me the creeps.'

'Christ, Nine.' Allie could almost hear Five rolling his eyes. 'Does anything ever make you happy?'

'Shagging your wife cheers me right up,' Nine replied without missing a beat.

Five responded with a creative string of expletives.

'You're a company man, Five,' Nine said when Five's enraged sputtering ended. 'You don't see the truth because you don't want to. Our boss is a nutter. And we're all looking at ten years if he loses this thing. Hard time.'

Allie nodded in agreement.

'Don't be so wet, Nine.' Five scoffed. 'He'll win. And if he doesn't… So what? You get three squares a day at Her Majesty's pleasure. I'd be happy with that.'

'You would, too.' Nine didn't sound like he thought it was funny. 'I bloody well wouldn't.'

They exchanged insults for a while. Allie was reaching for a cup of tea when Nine said, 'You see that girl, last night? At the school? The one in the uniform?'

She froze, the mug halfway to her mouth.

'Yeah,' Five said, dismissal in his tone. 'So what?'

'It ain't right,' Nine said. 'That's all I'm saying.'

'What ain't right?' Five's tone was not encouraging. Like he only half-wanted to know. Or like he wanted Nine to shut up.

Even though he must have got that, Nine kept going.

'What he's doing… She's just a kid. My own kid'll be that age in a few years. It's one thing when he's fighting with his sister. But that kid, or the one upstairs… It ain't right.'

There was a pause. Then: 'You should mind your own business, Nine,' Five warned him. 'Keep your nose out of this.'

For a second Nine didn't reply. When he spoke again, all he said was, 'I don't like what I don't like.'

Elation flared in Allie's chest.

For the ten thousandth time, she thought of that one little gesture. The hand pressing back at the air. The warning in his eyes.

She was certain now it had been him. That was Nine. He'd saved her.

Now she just had to figure out how to reach him.

Seventeen

For the rest of the day Allie stayed glued to the headphones, hoping Nine would say something more. But he was quiet after that. When he did speak, he seemed subdued. She was still at the table, male voices filling her head, when Eloise tapped her on the arm. Allie pulled off her headphones and glanced up at her.

'Isabelle wants you downstairs.' The librarian held out her hand for the earpieces. 'I'll take over. You need a break anyway.'

It didn't feel like Allie had been sitting all that long but when she stood, her muscles protested. She glanced at her watch, surprised to discover it was already four o'clock in the afternoon. She'd been here for hours.

As she left the room, Allie glanced up at Carter. He sat in a wooden chair, looking down at his hands. It was hard to tell if he was awake or asleep.

The clock in the corner of the screen glowed red: 64:12:31.

The numbers were falling so fast.

The school was quiet – all the activity was in Dom's office or outside in the school grounds. Allie was mostly alone in the wide hallway. When she reached Isabelle's office, the door was closed.

She could hear the low rumble of quiet voices inside.

She knocked lightly.

'Come in,' Isabelle said.

Isabelle was at her desk. Two men in expensive looking grey suits sat in the leather chairs facing her; both had turned so they could see Allie standing uncertainly in the doorway.

'Oh good, Allie,' Isabelle said brightly. 'We've been waiting for you. Please shut the door.'

A chair had been set next to Isabelle, and the headmistress gestured at it. 'Have a seat.'

The men didn't hide their curiosity. They were both middle aged, one was a little younger than the other, with sandy brown hair and designer glasses. The other had greying hair and kind blue eyes. He smiled when their eyes met.

It was a fatherly smile but Allie looked away quickly.

'Allie, these gentlemen worked for your grandmother,' Isabelle explained. 'They've come here to talk to you about her will.'

Allie stared. 'Her… will?'

Until that moment she'd entirely forgotten the conversation with her parents at Lucinda's wake. Her father's words came back to her now: *Lucinda's lawyers have been in touch.*

'Yes.' Isabelle was using her most pleasant voice, and it made Allie anxious. 'Lucinda included you in her will. And these men are here to explain this to you.'

Now Allie noticed the briefcases at their feet – the stack of documents the older one held.

'My name is Thomas Granville-Smith,' he said. 'This is Will Ainsworth. We work for a firm of attorneys employed by Lucinda Meldrum.' He glanced at Isabelle. 'Is it fine if I just explain the situation?'

Isabelle inclined her head.

He turned his attention back to Allie. 'Your grandmother left strict instructions for what should happen in the unfortunate event of her death.' He paused. 'And, if it would not be untoward of me, I'd like to take this opportunity to tell you how sorry we are for your loss.' His eyes darkened with what looked to Allie like genuine emotion. 'I worked closely with Lucinda for many years. I cannot conceive of this world without her in it.'

Allie, who'd found it hard to accept sympathy from even her closest friends was, for some reason, touched by this.

'Thank you,' she said, meaning it.

Clearing his throat, the man glanced down at his papers for a moment before continuing.

'Now, as she was quite specific, I think the best thing to do would be to read what your grandmother wrote.' He pulled a pair of glasses from his breast pocket and put them on, then held up the documents.

'I, Lucinda St John Meldrum, being of sound mind, do hereby bequeath and bestow upon my granddaughter, Lady Alyson Elizabeth Sheridan, all my worldly goods and possessions. All companies in their entirety, all bank accounts as listed herein, my houses in London, Scotland and St Barts, detailed below. Other entitlements and holdings, without restriction.'

He held up the thick stack of paper. 'There's a complete list here for you of the properties, both corporate and domestic.'

Allie just stared at him, her lips parted in surprise. The words were simple but she couldn't seem to process them. Her grandmother had been one of the most successful businesswomen in the country.

If she'd left her everything…

She couldn't even conceive of what that would mean.

I don't even know where St Barts is. And I've got a house there?

She turned to Isabelle as if she might be able to make sense of it, but her attention was focused on the attorneys.

'Tom. Please read her the section we discussed. I think it's important she should hear this, as it impacts her directly.'

'Of course.' He flipped a page and searched until he found the passage in question. 'Here we go.'

'To my stepson, Nathaniel Ptolemy St John, I leave neither money nor possessions. Instead I leave a word of warning that is more valuable than either. Nathaniel, your place within this world is not to sit atop it. That location belongs only to God. Your role is to walk among men as an equal. Do that, and you will find all you seek.'

He took off his glasses and put them away. For a moment no one spoke.

'I don't understand.' Allie turned to the headmistress. 'Isabelle, how is this possible? I'm only seventeen years old. I can't own companies.'

'That's a good question.' The headmistress turned to the two men. 'I suppose this is the time to discuss trusts and holding corporations.'

'That's where I come in.' The younger man cast a deferential glance to Tom, who nodded. 'I specialise in financial planning at the firm, Miss Sheridan. And I'm here to explain your options.'

He pulled a very thick binder from his briefcase.

Allie's heart sank.

'Oh good,' she said weakly.

'So, wait.' Rachel stared at Allie. 'She left you *everything*?'

'Everything. I have a house in St Barts.' Allie paused. 'Where's St Barts?'

'Someplace very pretty.' Rachel's tone was light, but Allie could see the stunned surprise in her expression.

Dinner had just ended and the two were in the empty library. Allie had kept the secret of Lucinda's will as long as she could. She could hardly bear to be away from Dom's office – from Carter – but she had to tell someone.

The second the meal ended, she'd dragged Rachel away from Nicole.

For more than an hour in Isabelle's office, Will Ainsworth had explained trusts and inheritance tax, handing Allie sheets of papers with enormously long numbers on them, and others with endless lists of corporations.

Allie wasn't completely certain what any of it meant.

'Lucinda owns Nabisco?'

'Uh… No.' Will's smile had become fixed. 'She owned *stock*. That is your list of stock derivatives.'

'Oh,' Allie had replied without comprehension. 'Derivatives.'

Now she and Rachel were sitting on the floor in the Ancient Greek section, talking quietly. The library was mostly empty – just a few students were at tables in the front – too far away to overhear them.

For a while, they tried to amuse each other by calculating

how long it would take Allie to spend all of Lucinda's money if she started spending a million pounds a day. They gave up when they reached a hundred years.

'This is bonkers, Allie,' Rachel said. 'Lucinda had more money than the Queen. What are you going to do?'

'I don't know. It doesn't seem real. She owned everything. I thought for a second I owned Weetabix. But it turns out she was just on the board. Whatever that means.' She leaned back against a row of leather-bound books with a sigh. 'Help, Rach. How can I be on a board when I don't know what a board is?'

Rachel shook her head. 'I guess you'll have to learn what a board is.'

'The bosses?' Allie guessed.

'Kind of… I think they're like extra bosses.'

'*Extra* bosses?' Allie was baffled. 'I'm an extra boss?'

'I think you get paid for nothing, if that helps?'

Allie held up her hands. 'Oh, I don't know, Rach. Lucinda must have thought it would help me but it just seems like crazy responsibility. It's all going into some trust until I'm twenty-one, and Isabelle's going to help but… she says I have to understand it all.' She pulled a string from the binding of one of the books. 'I'm not ready for any of this.'

'At least you're rich,' Rachel said. 'Which is nice.'

'Beyond my wildest dreams.' But Allie's tone said what she thought of that.

Rachel stretched out her legs until the soles of her shoes pressed against the book shelves across from her.

'My dad always says there's nothing like being rich and powerful to make you hate wealth and power.'

Allie blinked. 'He says that?'

She couldn't imagine the always circumspect Raj Patel

saying something even mildly rebellious.

'He says lots of things.' Rachel changed the subject. 'Will it be weird for you? Being so rich, I mean?'

Allie considered that. 'Will it be weird for *you*?'

'No.' Rachel's reply came without hesitation, and Allie cocked her head.

'Really? You don't have any doubts?'

Rachel's face grew serious. 'Allie, after everything we've been through, I'll always be your friend. If you had no money and lived in a cardboard hut or you had all the money and bought Buckingham Palace… it doesn't matter to me. I'm your friend for life.' She grinned crookedly. 'I hope you like me. Because you're stuck with me.'

There was no way she could have known how much that meant to Allie. It was just what she needed to hear.

Allie launched herself at her, pulling her into a rough hug.

'You old softie,' she said. 'I thought you hated me.'

'I do secretly.'

As they laughed at that, at the end of the row of towering bookcases where they were hidden, two students approached chatting.

For a horrible second, Allie thought one of them was Sylvain.

She hadn't spoken to him since the break-up. He hadn't been at the debrief, after the meeting with Nathaniel. He'd avoided all meals in the dining hall. He'd just disappeared.

She wasn't ready to see him yet.

Releasing Rachel abruptly, she crawled to the end of the row and peered out to see if it really was him.

It wasn't. It was one of the junior exchange students – not Sylvain at all.

It took a second or two for her heart rate to return to normal. Her cheeks felt hot.

When she looked up, Rachel was watching her quizzically. 'What's the matter?'

'Nothing…' Allie lied. 'I just… thought it might be Sylvain.'

Rachel's eyebrows winged up. 'And that totally freaked you out because…?'

Allie hesitated. She hadn't had a chance to tell Rachel what had happened. Everything had been too crazy since last night.

'Because… we broke up. And I don't want to see him.'

'*What?*' Rachel stared at her. 'When did this happen?'

'Last night.'

'So, *that's* why you looked like you'd been crying.' Rachel reached for her hand. 'Oh, bollocks, Allie. I'm sorry. I should have asked what was going on but with Carter and Nathaniel…'

Allie waved her apology away. 'I didn't want to talk about it anyway.'

'What happened?' Rachel studied her face. 'Was it rough?'

Allie thought of the look on Sylvain's face when he saw the teardrop on his own fingertip.

The memory made her heart ache.

'It was hard,' she admitted. 'Really hard.'

Haltingly, she told Rachel what had happened in London. The night with Carter. Her sudden realisation that he was the one she wanted.

Rachel knew better than to interrupt. She just let her talk until she'd told her everything.

When Allie was finished Rachel leaned back. 'Wow,' she

said. 'Everything makes sense now. I knew something was up but I just didn't know what it was. And you've been carrying all that around by yourself for days?'

Allie nodded. 'I kept waiting for a time to tell you about it…'

'But it's hard to share personal stuff around here lately.' Rachel finished the thought for her. 'Don't worry. I don't mind that you didn't tell me. I'm just worried about you. How are you dealing with all of this?'

'Badly,' Allie confessed. 'The thing is, this is all my fault. I made everything so much worse by not making up my mind earlier. That made Sylvain believe I'd chosen him. So when I told him the truth… it really hurt him.' She blew out a breath. 'I wouldn't blame him if he hated me now.'

'Hey, don't do that.' Rachel's voice was passionate. 'It's not like you *meant* to fall in love with Carter. You tried with Sylvain. I watched you try. You can't help who you love. No one can.'

'Yeah, but… I could have made it easier.'

Rachel shook her head. 'Come on. You can't blame yourself for this and I won't let you. You did the best you could.' She must have seen Allie wasn't convinced, though, because she leaned forward, reaching for her hand. 'We're young. This is the age when we're *supposed* to make mistakes. You have to let yourself learn. We're still figuring out what we want. Who we are. All of us are.'

The intensity with which she said those last words caught Allie's attention. She frowned, suddenly aware that Rachel might be hiding secrets of her own.

'Hey. Is something going on with you, too, Rach?'

Rachel dropped her hand. She didn't answer for a long time. Colour rose to her cheeks.

'Actually,' she said when the silence had stretched on too long, 'there's something —'

'Allie! Rachel! Are you in here?' Zoe's high-pitched voice floated across the library, cutting Rachel off.

'Back here.' Allie shot Rachel an apologetic look but, to her surprise, Rachel appeared almost relieved.

'You're late for Night School.' Zoe appeared at the end of the row, already in her black training gear, hopping from one foot to another.

Allie glanced at her watch – it was five past eight. They'd been here much longer than she'd thought. Only now did she notice how quiet the library had become.

'Shit,' she muttered. 'We're screwed.'

Zoe nodded so hard her ponytail flew. 'Zelazny says to get your arses in motion or he'll put you in detention until you don't know any other way of living.'

She emulated the history teacher's gruff bark so perfectly Allie had to laugh, despite everything.

'Zoe, sometimes you're actually scary,' she said, climbing to her feet.

'Really?' The younger girl beamed.

Allie and Rachel followed her across the mostly empty library.

'We'll talk later, OK?' Allie said, keeping her voice low. 'I want to know what you were about to say.'

'Sure,' Rachel said. 'No worries. It's not important anyway.'

Eighteen

When Allie and Rachel ran into the training room a few minutes later, shoe laces dangling and still straightening their Night School gear, the room was packed.

'You're late,' Zelazny barked.

'Sorry Mr Zelazny,' they chorused.

Allie braced herself for a lecture, but he let it go at that, turning back to the junior students he was training without another insult or complaint.

She and Rachel exchanged surprised looks. The teachers were definitely not themselves right now.

The older students had gathered at the back of the room, where they'd carved out a space from which younger students were banned. They threaded their way across the room to join them.

With the guards, teachers, and all the students, the small, square room was pretty crowded. So it was only when she reached the back section that Allie saw Sylvain.

His head was down and he was listening to something Lucas was saying.

Allie's chest tightened.

When he raised his head, even though he was still mostly

turned away, she could see the high planes of his cheekbones, his finely carved jaw. She searched for signs of pain or imminent collapse, but he looked exactly the same. No scars.

Spotting her, Lucas said something to Sylvain, who glanced up.

For the tiniest fraction of a second their eyes met.

Then he turned away again, shifting his position so she couldn't see his face.

Blood rose to Allie's cheeks. For a second, she just stood there, momentarily uncertain of what to do. When she saw Rachel, Nicole and Katie were talking in a corner, she hurried to join them.

'Hey, so, what's going on? Anything happening?' The words came out unbelievably cheery, but none of the others seemed to notice.

'Apparently we're patrolling tonight.' Rachel sounded disapproving.

'And we get to play teacher.' Nicole, too, seemed less than happy.

Allie looked back and forth between them. 'Play teacher?'

'We're taking the juniors out,' Rachel explained. 'It's their first patrol.'

No wonder she didn't seem happy. The junior students were far too young to be put into such danger.

'Why is all this happening all of a sudden?' Allie asked. 'I thought the guards were handling the patrolling now.'

'Apparently, so many guards are off searching for Nathaniel, they're spread thin here.' Rachel's voice was low. 'They need us to fill the gaps.'

'*Bollocks*,' Allie whispered, unable to disguise her shock. What a stupid night to be late. If she'd been on time, she could have at least tried to talk Raj and Zelazny out of this.

This was the worst time for the school to be unprotected. Nathaniel had to be watching them like a hawk right now.

'Listen up, people.' Zelazny's voice cut through the buzz of conversation like a chainsaw. 'Raj Patel will hand out your assignments. He's overseeing tonight's activities. I want *quiet.*'

Raj, who Allie hadn't even noticed before now, stepped into the pool of light at the centre of the shadowy training room.

He was tall with a commanding presence – powerfully built but not overly muscular, with dark skin and piercing eyes. His ability to command attention without a word and then – five minutes later – disappear into the shadows like a wraith, never ceased to astound her.

'The rules tonight are simple,' he began. 'You'll be patrolling in teams of three. Senior students are each assigned two juniors to oversee – your teams are here.' He waved a sheet of paper that crackled in the stillness. 'Each team is assigned a zone to cover. That is where you will stay. Now, you should be aware my guards are patrolling, too. You're not alone out there. Each team leader will have radio equipment, connecting them to base.' His gaze moved from face to face, as if searching for signs of weakness. 'But this is the real deal, make no mistake. This is what Night School is all about.'

Allie studied the junior students who stood rapt, watching him with wide, fascinated eyes.

She wished she still believed anyone held all the answers. She longed for the old days, when Night School was all weird philosophy questions and nocturnal jogging. Back when she still thought the teachers could keep them safe.

It would all be gone soon, anyway. Once Carter was back.

As Raj talked to the junior students, she found herself

wondering what it would be like when they moved. Would the new school have the same kind of massive grounds as Cimmeria? Would they need to patrol it?

No matter how she tried, it was impossible to imagine being at school anywhere except Cimmeria. Whenever she tried to envision a place they might escape to, it looked exactly like this.

Across the room, Raj was wrapping up. 'Remember your training. Stay with your senior students. Do as they tell you. And be safe.'

Allie heard Katie murmur, 'God I hope I'm not a senior student…' to herself as Raj stuck the piece of paper to the wall.

She and the others crowded around the list. Allie found her name midway down the page. 'Allie Sheridan, Charlotte Reese-Jones, Alec Thomason. Zone 6.'

'Awesome,' Zoe said. 'Minions.'

'*Trainees*, Zoe,' Rachel corrected her.

'Whatever.' Zoe dashed across the room shouting, 'Stephen and Nadja! You are *mine.*'

Rachel watched her despairingly. Catching her eye, Nicole smiled.

'Poor minions.'

From the doorway, Zelazny barked, 'Time is money, people. Get moving. Senior students, your comms devices are here.'

Rachel, Nicole and Allie exchanged a look.

'Here goes nothing,' Allie said.

Nineteen

Charlotte turned out to be about Allie's height, with shoulder-length golden-brown hair pulled into a pontytail. Her serious hazel eyes seemed to miss nothing. Alec was loose-limbed and laconic, with dark hair and glasses. Both looked to be about thirteen years old.

They stood just outside the school building, waiting as Allie hooked the comms device to her ear. Even though it was tiny, it was hard to get it into place. While she struggled with it, most of the other groups had moved off, heading to their areas, although a few still lingered, asking questions, going over the rules.

'Balls,' Allie muttered, as the earpiece tumbled out again.

'I think you've got it backwards,' Alec suggested after a while.

Muttering to herself, she tried flipping it around as he demonstrated.

It fit perfectly.

'Thanks,' she said, looking at him properly for the first time. Something about him was familiar.

'I've seen you before.'

Spots of colour appeared on his thin cheeks. 'That night,'

he mumbled. 'I got lost. You guys brought me back.'

Instantly Allie recalled the boy shoved forward by the guards on the dark night a few days earlier. Glasses crooked. Face pale and terrified.

'That was *you*?'

He shrugged, eyes on his feet. 'Zoe's too fast.'

'Can't argue with that.' Allie's tone was dry. 'Haven't you been working with Dom, too?'

'A little.' He glanced up at her from beneath thick straight brows. 'When I'm home I like hacking. You know, for fun. Games and stuff.'

Allie tried to imagine herself at his age, hacking for fun. It was inconceivable.

The last group of remaining students struck off into the woods reminding Allie that they needed to get moving.

'Right,' she said. 'We're Zone Six, which is down by the chapel. We'll take it slow and steady. Don't leave my side. Don't get lost.' She shot Alec a look. 'If we're lucky, we'll all come back in one piece. We just have to get through the next two hours.'

As inspirational messages went, even she knew it wasn't brilliant. But, under the circumstances, it would have to do.

They headed out across the broad expanse of lawn at a steady jog.

It was a clear night, and cool. The nearly full moon hung low on the horizon. A silvery dusting of stars shimmered above the trees as they headed across the lawn towards the forest.

'It's dark,' Charlotte said.

'Your eyes will adjust,' Allie replied. But she slowed down a little to give them time to get used to the night.

As they ran, she kept an eye on her charges.

Charlotte wasn't slim – her chubby cheeks made her look

even younger than she was – but she handled the pace well. She had a smooth, natural gait as if, like Allie, she was born to run.

It was Alec who got winded easily. He was gasping for air within minutes.

'Try to breathe from your diaphragm,' Allie advised him, running alongside him.

'What does that even mean?' he groused.

'It means,' she said, 'breathe deep. Use your entire lungs. They have a lot of space. Unless you have asthma. Do you have asthma?'

'I don't have asthma.' He wouldn't meet her gaze. He seemed embarrassed. Actually, everything seemed to embarrass him. He was hopelessly awkward.

Allie forced herself to be patient. She tried to think about how she ran.

'Get a rhythm going. Breathe in and then out, every second step. So in, left foot right foot. Then out, left foot right foot.' She ran alongside him, watching him critically as he tried the method with obvious reluctance.

Even though her own running was going well, Charlotte joined in, breathing rhythmically as Allie had demonstrated. Keeping an eye on Alec.

Allie was starting to like her.

'Does it help?' she asked.

The boy shrugged. 'I don't know. Maybe.'

But he looked better. Some of the purple tinge seemed to be fading from his skin.

'Good.' Allie pretended he'd thanked her. It made it easier not to hit him. 'Now work on your foot placement. It's not thump, thump. It's heel toe, heel toe.'

'Jesus,' he muttered.

Allie, who had now used up all her patience, moved until she was running alongside Charlotte.

'How are you doing, Charlotte?'

'Everyone calls me Charlie,' the girl said, apologetically. 'Only my mum calls me Charlotte.'

Allie, who had said virtually the same thing a million times in her life, smiled.

'Charlie it is.'

The cool glow of the moon disappeared the second they entered the woods. It was much darker here. The only sound was the thudding of their footsteps, and the harsh burn of Alec's still imperfect breathing.

Allie ran a little ahead looking out for any sign of danger. They were running much slower than her usual pace and she longed to move faster. But she didn't want Alec to collapse or Charlie to break an ankle. Because of all that, it took them a good fifteen minutes to reach the chapel wall.

They were well behind schedule now, but Allie tried to keep her tone positive.

'This is our zone,' she announced quietly.

The junior students exchanged puzzled looks.

'Uh… What happens now?' Alec asked.

'We move quietly through the zone, looking for anything out of the ordinary.'

'Like what?'

'Murder and carnage, Alec. Use your imagination.'

'God,' he muttered. 'Attitude.'

I will never be a teacher, Allie promised herself.

When they reached the chapel gate it was closed and secure, but she decided they should search it anyway. Just in case.

The latch opened with a metallic jangle, and the gate

creaked open.

Inside, the churchyard was still. It no longer smelled of fresh cut grass. Allie didn't let herself look at Lucinda's grave.

With cool discipline, she scanned the yard for anything amiss, but all was in place.

With the other two right behind her she headed up the path to the front door of the church, and tried the handle. It turned with effort.

Inside, the darkness was complete. There was no electricity out here – no light switch to flip.

Allie pulled a torch from her pocket.

'Oh my God. You had a torch all this time?' Alec's voice was too loud.

Allie motioned urgently for him to shut up.

Stepping into the chapel, Allie squinted into the glow of the flashlight. She could see the wall paintings – the dragon, the Tree of Life. The pews lined up in neat rows, waiting for the next service.

The next death.

A faint scent of lilies hung in the air. Reminding her of the hundreds of flowers that had filled this room not long ago.

Still. It was empty now.

'All clear. Let's go.' She switched off the light.

They all heard the faint scuttling sound at the same moment.

A chill ran down Allie's back. She'd seen nothing in there.

She heard Charlie gasp.

Hurriedly switching the torch back on, Allie swung the light at the back of the room. The church was completely empty.

The sound came again. It sounded like hands beating the walls, very softly. Or like nails against stone.

It didn't sound… human.

Suddenly something shot out of the darkness directly at Allie's light. She jumped, dropping the light.

Charlotte stifled a scream. Alec grabbed her, pulling her out of the way.

The thing fluttered past Allie's face, brushing her hair with its webbed wing.

Her heart hammered in her chest – for a split second she couldn't catch her breath.

Seeing that the other two were terrified, she forced herself to breathe.

'It's just a bat, you guys,' she said.

'*Just* a bat?' Charlie hissed with such disbelief, Allie might as well have said it was *just* a triceratops.

For some reason this struck Allie as hilarious, and she found herself shaking with silent laughter.

The two junior students stared at her.

'I'm sorry,' she whispered, regaining control. 'We're safe. I promise.'

Retrieving the torch from the ground, she pulled the door shut behind them. In a straight line, with Allie in the lead, they headed down the path towards the gate, which they'd left open.

There's something about the aftermath of a frightening moment that makes you let your guard down. That exhilarating sense of survival takes away all fear, just for an instant.

Maybe that was why she didn't see him until they reached the gate.

He stood just on the other side, in the shadows. The moonlight caught his hair and turned it blond.

'Allie,' he said. 'I can't believe it's you.'

Charlie squeaked and scrambled backwards, running hard

into Alec who caught her before she could fall.

But Allie didn't run. She just stared at the man in the gateway.

'Christopher?'

Twenty

Allie felt dazed. Like she'd stepped into a dream. He looked good – his hair was a little shaggy, but he looked strong. He was casually dressed in jeans and a black t-shirt, Converse trainers on his feet.

The suit he'd worn when he was working with Nathaniel was gone.

'What… What are you doing here?' She stumbled over her words.

She'd forgotten about Charlie and Alec. Forgotten what her role was here. All she saw was her brother. Standing where he should not be.

His nervous smile disappeared as quickly as it arrived. 'Looking for you, Allie-cat,' he said.

'How did you get in?' Allie looked around, as if the dark woods around them might hold the answers. 'How did you get over the fence?'

'Um… yeah.' He stuffed his hands in his pockets, and rocked back on his heels. 'We should probably talk about that. For now, let's just say I got in.'

Something about his stance reminded her so strikingly of Nathaniel, it acted like a slap in the face. Allie suddenly realised where she was. What she had to do.

'You shouldn't have.' She pressed the button on the radio mic connected to the neckline of her top. 'This is Allie. I'm at the chapel.'

'Allie, don't.' Christopher looked at her pleadingly.

But she couldn't protect him. Not this time.

'There's an intruder.'

Christopher took a nervous step back, glancing around furtively as if he thought SWAT teams might spring from the forest.

'I don't understand,' he said. 'I've left Nathaniel. I saved you in London. I sold everything I had to get here without going on the grid.' He held out his hands – his wrists bare. 'The watch dad gave me. It's gone.'

He seemed genuinely upset, but Allie could no longer say for certain if she knew her brother well enough to know when he was faking an emotion. He'd run away a long time ago. She'd been a child the last time they'd had a real conversation.

She wasn't a child anymore.

'If you're really not working for Nathaniel, we'll figure that out, and you won't have any trouble.'

Her voice was cool and dispassionate. Like she was talking to a stranger.

Christopher shot her a look of pure disbelief. 'I can't believe you're doing this to me. I'm your brother. They'll tear me apart, Allie. They think I'm on Nathaniel's side.'

In the distance, footsteps pounded towards them out of the darkness. Dozens of them. Allie could see torch beams bobbing and dancing firefly-like through the trees.

Everyone was coming.

She turned back to her brother, who was backing towards

the fence as if he might, foolishly, decide to run.

She couldn't blame him. It sounded like an army was coming for him.

Too late, Allie questioned her decision.

'I'm sorry, Chris,' she said, panic fluttering inside her chest. 'I had to.'

At that moment, the first guards sprang into the courtyard.

'Get *back.*' A muscular, dark-skinned man clad all in black leaped in between Allie and Christopher, pushing her away from her brother.

Around her, voices shouted rapid-fire commands.

'Down on your knees. *Now.*'

'Hands behind your head.'

'*Move.*'

As the guards surrounded her brother, Allie backed slowly away.

Holding her gaze with desperate eyes, he did as he was told, lowering himself to the ground and bracing his hands behind his head.

The guard slipped plastic handcuffs on his wrists; another guard searched his pockets, finding only a phone, which he confiscated.

Straightening, one spoke into his radio. 'Intruder in custody.'

The guards pulled Christopher roughly to his feet. He wasn't looking at Allie now. He kept his gaze on some indefinable point in the distance.

The whole scene made her uneasy. Christopher's placid acceptance of everything they were doing. The guards' aggression.

She hated that it had come to this.

It was over in seconds. They hustled him out of the churchyard gate, and down the footpath towards the school building.

Then the night fell silent again.

Allie inhaled with gasping suddenness. Shaking herself as if waking from a nightmare, she looked around for the others.

Charlie and Alec were huddled together in the shadows by the chapel door, watching her with trepidation. As if *she* was the intruder.

Straightening her shoulders, she motioned for them to join her.

'Come on. We need to get going.'

Emerging slowly from the safety of the sheltered doorway, they followed her down the footpath with clear reluctance.

It was a while before anyone spoke.

Charlie broke the silence when they were halfway to the school.

'Who was that guy?'

'My brother.' Allie's voice was flat.

'Wait.' Alec panted behind them, struggling with the pace. 'Your *brother* just broke into our school?'

'Yep. He used to work for Nathaniel.' Allie kept her eyes on the dark woods ahead. 'Any more questions?'

After that, Charlie dropped back to run with Alec.

When they reached the school building, Allie stopped and pointed towards a side door.

'Go back down to the training room and let Zelazny know what happened.'

She was breathless, but not from running. With every step she'd grown more anxious. If Christopher had come here, he was either working for Nathaniel or he needed her help.

Which one is it?

Alec did as she said, but Charlie hung back. Her eyes watched Allie worriedly.

'What about you?' she asked. 'What will you do now?'

Allie was starting to like her. She had potential.

But she didn't say that. Instead, she turned towards the front door.

'I'm going to find out what the hell my brother is doing here.'

Her footsteps were all Allie could hear as she sped to Isabelle's office.

'Isabelle?' she called, knocking harder than was entirely necessary. 'It's Allie.'

The office door was locked – no light seeped from the crack around the door.

Trying to think, Allie walked slowly back into the corridor, pressing her fingertips against her lips.

Where would they take him? Eloise had been held in an outbuilding, near the pond at the fringes of the school grounds. Jerry had been locked up in a disused wine cellar deep in the school's foundations.

Would they consider Christopher such a threat that they'd lock him up like that? She just didn't know.

'Allie. What's happened?' Sylvain appeared on the staircase, heading down towards her. 'Isabelle said you found an intruder.'

Out of habit, Allie's heart jumped, then sank again as he stepped into the light. His expression was cool; enigmatic. He stayed a safe distance away.

'It was my brother.' Her throat went suddenly tight. 'It's Christopher.'

'What? On the *grounds*?'

He was shocked and she couldn't blame him. She couldn't decide which was worse, that she'd just turned in her own brother, or that somehow he'd managed to get into the school grounds undetected.

She nodded.

'I don't know what he's doing here or how he got in. I didn't have a chance to talk to him. The security guards took him away so fast.' She looked at him imploringly. 'Sylvain, I have to talk to him. I have to know why he's here.'

'Allie…'

She could hear the conflict in his voice. The last thing he probably wanted to do right now was help her. She'd told him flatly she didn't want that from him. And yet, here they were again.

'He's worked with Nathaniel for years,' he said. 'He was fully immersed in that world. There's no reason to believe he's changed his mind.'

'But in London he saved my life. He risked everything.' It felt good to defend Chris, and she warmed to the cause. 'Maybe Christopher really wants to be on our side now. What if he wants to help us? To help me? I can't let them put him in the dungeon or whatever they're going to do to him.' Seeing the doubt in his eyes, she took a tentative step towards him. 'Sylvain, he's my *brother*.'

He raked his fingers through his wavy hair. 'I know it's difficult, but you have to think about this rationally,' he said. 'Pretend he's not your brother. Perhaps, instead, he's *my* brother. And he's been on Nathaniel's side throughout all of this. He was indoctrinated years ago. Then he does one thing to help me. One thing.' He held up one finger. 'Do I believe he's changed all of his beliefs? Or do I suspect that's what he wants me to think.'

Allie's shoulders slumped. He had a point. But she wasn't ready to give up. Not without talking to Christopher first.

'I know it's possible this could be a trick. But I still don't want them to question him without me.' He opened his mouth to argue and she spoke over him. 'I know how they work, Sylvain. So do you.'

He held up his hands in tacit acknowledgement.

'I just want to make sure he's safe. That's it.' She held his gaze. 'Will you help me?'

He didn't answer immediately.

Allie wasn't going to beg him. She was almost certain he'd know where Christopher was being held. He was very close to Raj and Zelazny, always involved in high-level decision making. It was just the sort of information he'd have.

But if he didn't want to tell her, she'd find out on her own.

She thought she saw a flicker of emotion in the ocean blue of his eyes – a hint of the loss she felt, too. And of the connection that always existed between them. Different from the one she had with Carter. Not a love like that. But no less real.

'I must be insane.' Sylvain let out a long breath. 'Come with me. I think I know where they'll take him.'

Turning on his heel, he headed down the hallway with long, confident strides.

Allie hurried after him. 'Are you sure?'

'No. But if it was me, I'd put him in one of the old storage rooms in the cellar. Secure, private…' He glanced at her. 'Soundproof.'

The lights were off in the classroom wing when they reached it, but they both knew it well enough to find their way through it in the dark. Sylvain moved with lithe grace. Allie matched him step for step.

She knew Isabelle wouldn't be happy to see her, but it didn't matter.

What she'd told Sylvain was only partially true. Yes, she wanted to protect Christopher, but she also wanted to decide for herself whether or not he was telling the truth. Whether or not she could trust him.

They were nearly to the end of the hallway when Sylvain stopped with such abruptness Allie slammed into him, full force. He grabbed her shoulders to keep her from falling.

Even in the dark, the look he gave her scorched. 'Careful.'

She took a hurried step back.

'Sorry,' she mumbled.

But he'd already turned away. He opened an unmarked door to reveal a staircase going down into complete darkness.

'This way.' His voice was devoid of emotion.

The old stone spiral staircase had a musty smell. Unable to see even an inch ahead, Allie clung to the metal banister. She couldn't see Sylvain anymore – she could hear his feet scuffing on the steps as they descended.

'What do you think he wants?' His voice echoed, disembodied.

'I don't know,' she said. 'Maybe he really has given up on Nathaniel. Maybe he's really on our side.'

'If not?'

'Then it's a trick.' Her own voice rang back at her mockingly. 'And Nathaniel sent him to sabotage us. Or to spy.'

The stairs ended abruptly, and Allie suddenly found herself standing in a small, dark room, with corridors branching off in several directions.

The cellars were a tangle of old tunnels and rooms that had

been added to over the years. Some were centuries older than the building that stood there now.

They headed into a long, narrow corridor. The ceilings were low, and the only light came from ancient wall sconces. The sconces emitted a flickering, ghostly glow, making shadows that jumped and ducked in an almost human way, setting Allie's nerves on edge.

After a long, straight stretch, the corridor turned sharply to the right.

Just as they reached the bend, two guards appeared out of the darkness, blocking their path.

'You're not supposed to be here,' one said.

Next to her, Sylvain stiffened but, before he could speak, Allie stepped forward to confront the two guards.

'My name is Allie Sheridan,' she announced. 'I need to speak with Isabelle. Now please. Get out of the way.'

The two guards exchanged a look. Then they stepped back and let them pass.

Allie couldn't believe it worked. The rules of Cimmeria's game really had changed now that Lucinda was gone. She wasn't just a normal student anymore.

If she ever had been.

'Interesting,' Sylvain murmured. 'Would you care to explain what just happened?'

'Long story.' Allie pointed to the end of the hallway. 'I think we found them.'

Raj and Isabelle stood with a group of guards outside a battered door.

It was the same room where they'd kept Jerry Cole.

Allie knew what was inside. Bare, stone walls. And chains.

'Isabelle.' The word came out sharper than she'd intended,

and the headmistress spun around to face her.

'Allie? What are you doing here?' Isabelle frowned. 'Sylvain? What's going on?'

'You have Christopher in *there*?' Allie pointed at the door. 'The same room where you kept Jerry? Why would you do that? What are you doing to him?'

The headmistress held up her hands. 'Now, just one second, Allie…'

'He's not chained.' Raj stepped up to join them. His expression was serious. 'We just needed a safe place to keep him while we evaluate the situation.'

When he put it like that it didn't sound unreasonable, but Allie still didn't like the symbolism of it.

'I was planning to come and get you as soon as we knew what we were dealing with,' Isabelle said.

'Well it's good to know that I'm involved in major decisions as long as I can *find you.*'

'Your brother is not in any danger,' the headmistress said evenly. 'We didn't even know who he was when the guards first brought him in. He was treated like any other intruder until he told us his name. Now things are different. Obviously.'

Everyone was being so rational, Allie had no choice but to calm down.

'Fine,' she said grudgingly. 'What has he told you so far?'

She was vaguely aware that Sylvain stood at her shoulder, listening to everything but not joining in.

'Not much,' Raj said. 'We were planning to start the real questioning now.' Seeing the stubborn look on her face he added, 'Since you're here you can help. In fact, you can start by telling us what you know about what he's doing here.'

'The last time I saw Chris was the night of the parley. He

hit Gabe in the face with a club to get him to let me go. He told me…' Allie tried to remember the conversation that happened amid deadly chaos. 'He said he was on our side.'

'Allie.' Isabelle's voice was gentle. 'You mustn't put too much faith in that. Nathaniel is very good at brainwashing people. And his people are very good at lying.'

Allie thought of Nine, and his disgruntled tone. 'I know,' she said. 'But I think it doesn't work on everyone.'

She could see they weren't convinced.

'Look, I know this might be a trap, OK?' she said. 'All I'm saying is, let's hear him out. In case it isn't.'

'This gives me an idea.' Sylvain looked at Raj. 'You should use this in your interview. Let Allie take Christopher's side. You and Isabelle act just like this – like you don't believe her.'

Raj's expression grew thoughtful.

'That could work,' he said slowly. 'If Christopher thinks there's someone on his side…'

'He could make a mistake.' Sylvain finished the thought for him.

'Or,' Allie said, 'if he's not trying to trick us he won't.'

She looked around the circle of faces, knowing no one except her believed for one second that Christopher might not be trying to trick them.

Even she wasn't at all certain.

'Let's get started,' Raj said, turning for the door. Isabelle went with him.

Allie started to follow. She was almost to the door when she realised Sylvain hadn't moved.

She turned back. 'Aren't you coming?'

He shook his head. She saw a hint of the old Sylvain in his

expression.

'This isn't my fight,' he said. 'It's yours. Go save your brother.'

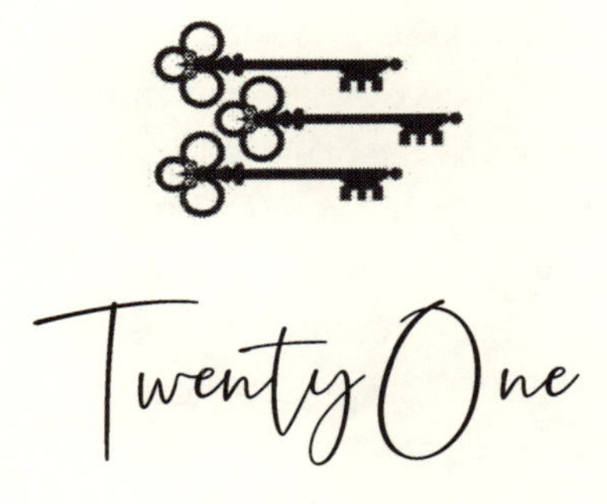

Twenty One

The wine cellar was a long, narrow vaulted room, with grey stone walls and floor. It was cooler in here than it had been in the corridor.

When Jerry Cole had been held here, all furniture had been removed save for a chair, and he'd been shackled and chained. By contrast, Christopher sat at a small table, unbound. Someone had given him a mug of tea, which steamed in front of him, untouched.

He looked tense but not afraid. When Allie walked in, he looked up at her eagerly, relief in his eyes.

Allie joined Isabelle and Raj across the table from him.

'Christopher, I am Isabelle le Fanult, the headmistress at Cimmeria Academy.' Isabelle's tone was distant but not unfriendly. 'This is Raj Patel, my chief of security. We need to ask you a few questions.'

'Of course,' Christopher said politely. 'I understand.'

'Tell us first how you got into the grounds.'

'It's something Nathaniel showed me a long time ago. There's an old entrance on the north side. A gatehouse.' He cleared his throat. 'It's, uh… Well. It's how Nathaniel gets in.'

Raj looked stunned. 'It's my understanding that gatehouse has been sealed for decades.'

'That gatehouse *used* to be sealed,' Christopher corrected him. 'If you look closely, you'll see the locks have been removed. I used it the last time I came. Tonight I gambled that you hadn't noticed it yet.' He held up his hands apologetically. 'You hadn't.'

Isabelle turned to Raj, her expression disbelieving. He leaped to his feet and stalked out of the room.

When he returned a few seconds later Allie could tell he was seething, even as he kept his expression blank. His jaw was tight and set.

'I'm having that information checked. Let's continue.' He turned his gaze to Chris. 'Is that the only access to the grounds you're aware of?'

Christopher gave a non-committal shrug. 'It's the only one Nathaniel ever mentioned to me. He considers it hugely valuable. You'll see how well he's disguised it. It's not your fault you didn't notice before. He's very, very good at what he does.'

Raj didn't seem mollified by his sympathy. If anything it seemed to make him angry.

'Is that why you joined him?' he asked. 'Because he's so "good"?' He said the last word with contempt.

Christopher didn't immediately respond; he templed his fingers on the table.

'I know you're being sarcastic but in a way, it's true,' he said at last. 'He was very good at befriending me when I was young. Very good at convincing me my family couldn't be trusted. Very good at undermining everything I believed, leaving me confused and vulnerable. I trusted him.' He let out a long breath. 'And he's the last person I should have trusted.'

Allie watched him closely, looking for signs of duplicity. But he seemed entirely candid. He looked like Christopher, the way he used to be.

'You're saying he lured you to his side, and you later regretted it?' Isabelle didn't sound convinced. 'Forgive me but, you've been with him since you were seventeen. You're nearly twenty years old now. It took you a long time to decide you made a mistake, didn't it?'

Colour rose to Christopher's cheeks. But he met her gaze without flinching. 'If you're asking was I stupid? I guess the answer is yes. I wanted Nathaniel to be right. I wanted to believe I was this great, rich guy, who should have the world at his feet. I wanted to believe you were my enemy and Nathaniel was my friend. Instead I learned he was just some messed-up guy who wanted to use me to get back at his family. Just like I was using him to get back at mine.' He gave a hollow laugh. 'Ain't life grand?'

'Christopher,' Isabelle leaned towards him. 'You're asking us to take a huge leap of faith for no reason other than your word, and Allie's belief in you.'

His gaze flickered to Allie. 'I wouldn't lie to her. Or to you.' He turned back to Isabelle. 'I'm truly here because I know how dangerous Nathaniel is now. I've seen what he's willing to do. And the only people in the world I know of who are fighting him are in this room.'

There was a pause. Then Allie cleared her throat.

'Chris, Nathaniel is holding one of my friends. The one you met in the fight in London, the one who helped me.'

'I remember him,' Chris said. 'Dark hair, lots of muscles?' He gave a wry smile. 'I thought for a second he was going to kill me.' He paused. 'I'd hoped you guys got away.'

'We did,' she said. 'Nathaniel followed us.'

'Shit,' he said, not without sympathy. 'And now he has him?'

She nodded, unable to hide how miserable this fact made her. 'He says he's going to kill him. We've got to do something, but we don't know where he is. And we're running out of time.'

Christopher held her gaze for a long moment. Then he turned back to Isabelle and Raj. 'You've checked the London townhouse?'

They nodded.

'It's been monitored ever since the parley,' Raj said. 'He hasn't been back there.'

Christopher rubbed his hand across his jaw thoughtfully.

'That leaves two distinct possibilities. The Gilmore's country place in Surrey or the old St John estate in Hampshire.'

Allie blinked. *The Gilmore place – Katie's parents.*

'We've checked the Gilmore place. He's not there.' A file folder had lain untouched in front of Raj throughout this meeting. Now he opened it and flipped through the papers. After a second he looked up.

'We don't know of the St John place. It's not on our lists.'

'That's strange.' Christopher's brow creased. 'It was the only thing his father left him in his will. Or at least, that's the way Nathaniel tells it. He says his father left almost everything else to you.'

He addressed the last line to Isabelle.

She frowned. 'I thought that old place was sold off after my father died. Are you saying it wasn't?'

Christopher shook his head. 'I've been there many times. Nathaniel goes there a lot.'

Raj and Isabelle exchanged a look – Allie could sense their growing excitement although they were both trying not to give anything away.

'Where is the St John place, precisely?' Raj's expression

was studiedly neutral.

'Farm country. Near some tiny nothing village called Diffenhall,' Christopher said. 'It's just a crossroads, really. If you bring me a map I can show you.'

Raj crossed the room to the door with long quick strides, and yanked open the door. He had a quick, whispered conversation with a guard.

While he was gone, Allie studied her brother surreptitiously. He looked the same as she remembered, and yet... different somehow. More grown up. She couldn't put her finger on what it was – but the last few years had changed him. He wasn't a boy anymore. His cheeks bore a fine, golden dusting of whiskers.

When Raj returned, he studied Christopher with new interest.

'You were right about the old gatehouse. The guards say all the locks had been removed and replaced with imitations, seamlessly.'

'I really won't lie to you about anything,' Christopher said with apparent earnestness. 'I am here exactly for the reasons I gave.' He paused. 'You shouldn't leave the gate like that. If Nathaniel finds out I'm here, he'll use it.'

'The door's been barricaded.' Raj's reply was gruff. 'It'll be bricked over tomorrow.' He didn't take his seat, standing with his fingertips light on the battered table top. 'We'll get you that map. I want you to show me where that house is.'

He motioned for Isabelle and Allie to rise. 'Could you come with me, please? I'd like a word.'

They headed out together. At the door, Allie looked back. Christopher was watching them go.

She'd never seen him look more lonely.

'What do you think?' Isabelle asked Raj.

His ran a hand across his jaw. 'I don't know. If it's an act, he's very good.'

'Well,' Isabelle reminded him, 'he's had a good teacher.'

They'd gathered in the shadowy cellar corridor. A short distance behind them, four of Raj's men guarded the cell holding Christopher.

Isabelle turned to Allie, who was standing quietly beside them. 'What do you think? You know him better than us.'

Allie hesitated. 'I wish I could be certain,' she said. 'That seemed like the real Christopher but…'

'But he could be a good liar.' Raj finished the sentence for her. 'So we are in agreement.'

Allie didn't argue with him but inside, she was torn. She was betraying Christopher by not believing him. But he'd done so little recently to merit her trust.

Even if he really had changed his mind, her loyalties had to lie with Cimmeria. With the people upstairs. Not with the brother who, not all that long ago, tried to burn this building down.

'We'll know more when we have a chance to check on that house.' Isabelle called over her shoulder impatiently, 'Where is that *map*?'

A guard spoke into his radio, then looked up at her. 'On the way now.'

Isabelle turned to Raj, her gaze sharpening. 'We will have to talk about that gatehouse, by the way. How was that allowed to happen?'

His lips tightened. 'I wish I knew. Apparently the work was extremely professional, but I will take personal responsibility for that security lapse. It was unacceptable.'

It was very unusual for the headmistress to allow a student to observe her criticising her staff. Allie felt uncomfortably like an eavesdropper. She tried to find other things to look at.

'Hmph.' Isabelle seemed about to launch into a more heated complaint when Dom appeared out of the gloom, a laptop tucked under one arm, papers clutched in her hand.

She'd clearly run all the way down from her top floor office, and she was breathless by the time she reached them.

'It's real,' she said before Isabelle could ask the question. 'The house is real.'

Setting the laptop down roughly on a dusty ledge, she flipped it open. The screen lit up and a map appeared.

A location had been marked with a red dot. Dom tapped it with a fingertip.

'There's a farm here called St John's Fields. It's been in the St John family for generations.'

The computer screen was the brightest light in the dim hallway. Its glow gave everyone's faces a ghostly hue.

'And it's the right St John?' Isabelle's voice sounded tight. 'My father?'

Dom nodded. 'It was in your father's property portfolio until shortly before he died. At some point it was signed over to Nathaniel St John.' She handed Isabelle a piece of paper. 'The reason it didn't come up in our property searches is because Nathaniel transferred ownership to a property portfolio trust, Ptolemy Properties Limited, more than a decade ago.' Her glasses glinted in the light. 'Basically, he sold it to himself.'

'Which took it out of his name.' Raj sounded impressed.

'Exactly. The only property he didn't transfer was the London townhouse.' Dom glanced from Isabelle to Raj. 'We've checked all the properties in the portfolio for other possibles but there are none in the region where we believe Nathaniel is hiding. We're still going through them all thoroughly, though. Just in case we've missed something.'

'Thank you, Dom.' Isabelle looked grimly pleased. 'This could be the place.'

Raj was already pulling his phone from his pocket. 'We'll need to readjust the satellite to give us a look at the house as soon as the sun comes up. I'll get some of my guys out there. And anything you can find on the security he's got in place out there…'

Dom nodded. 'We're working on that now.'

Raj glanced at his watch. 'I think there's not much we can do tonight until we can get a look at that house. It would be a good idea to let everyone get some rest. It might be a long time before we get another chance.'

Allie thought of the clock on the screen upstairs. Counting down, down, down.

'Come on, Raj,' she objected, 'we don't have *time.*'

She didn't normally talk to him this way – like an equal. But, to her surprise, he didn't object.

'I know how you feel,' he said. 'And we're going to move fast on this. I just need a few hours to gather some intel, then we'll hit the ground running at dawn. Dom's team will work on this through the night.' He held her gaze. 'If he's in there, we've got to do this right.'

Twenty minutes later Allie stood in Dom's office in front of the wall-mounted monitor. The screen was almost too dark to make out Carter's face. He sat in a chair, his head bowed, apparently asleep – or something like sleep. There was a tension in the way his body hunched forward, as if he was resisting rest. Trying to force himself to stay awake.

Just like she was.

Across the room, at the round table, a group of guards she didn't know were at the laptops. One, a woman with a long, blonde braid, had the headphones on, listening to Nathaniel's guards.

They cast occasional curious glances at her, but no one bothered her.

Raj, Isabelle and Dom had gone down to Isabelle's office to make plans – they'd ordered her to bed. She'd come here instead.

The clock on the screen read 52:21:38.

The numbers were going down so fast. It was breathtaking.

She longed to see Carter's face. To hear his voice. She wanted to pass him in the hallway and say 'Hey.' Really casually. Because they saw each other every day, and seeing each other was no big deal. They'd see each other again in a few minutes.

'Hey back,' she imagined him saying. And it made her feel worse somehow.

Because it was all in her head. And he was in so much danger.

Tentatively, she raised her hand, touching the screen. It

was cold beneath her fingertips.

'Stay alive, Carter,' she whispered. 'We're coming to get you.'

Sometime later, Allie awoke with a start and looked around, disoriented. It was so dark that it took her a moment to realise she was in her room.

She had only the vaguest memories of climbing into her bed. She'd been so exhausted after leaving Dom's office, it was all a blur. She was still in her skirt and blouse, the duvet thrown over her legs haphazardly.

She felt groggy, as if she was dreaming. But she was certain she wasn't.

Something had disturbed her. A sound.

She fumbled for the switch on the desk light, knocking over the alarm clock. It fell with a musical crash.

The light, when she finally located the switch, seemed insanely bright; it blinded her.

That was when she heard it again.

Tap. Tap. Tap.

Three taps in quick succession. From the door.

Suddenly, she was wide awake.

Throwing back the duvet in one smooth movement, she leaped out of bed. Her bare feet made no sound on the whitewashed wood floor as she crossed the room.

She pressed her ear to the cool wood of the door and held her breath. Her heart had begun to pound.

'Who is it?' she asked, her voice still rough from sleep.

At first there was nothing. Then, 'Allie? It's Dom.'

She exhaled, all the tension leaving with the breath, and yanked the door open. Dom stood in the darkened corridor.

She wore the same clothes she'd had on earlier. Her narrow glasses made her eyes hard to read, but there was something in her expression – something that made Allie's stomach clench.

'What's happened?'

'It's Carter,' Dom said. 'Nathaniel cut the feed.'

Twenty Two

When Allie slammed into Dom's office a few minutes later, Isabelle stood by the map talking to three of Raj's security guards. She'd changed at some point into neat grey trousers and a white blouse. A black cashmere cardigan hung loose from her shoulders. You wouldn't know she hadn't slept, were it not for the circles under her eyes.

Standing next to Dom at the back of the room, Raj was clean shaven, a mug of coffee in one hand. Dom was explaining something, and he was listening attentively.

Shak and Zoe sat at the table, each in front of a laptop, but they weren't typing. They were looking up at the wall-mounted computer screen.

She followed their gaze. Carter was gone. All that was left was darkness, and a warning carved out in stark white letters: DO AS I DEMAND AND YOU WILL SEE HIM AGAIN.

In the bottom corner of the screen the red clock still glowed: 47:53:15.

'What happened?'

Her words came out as a stunned whisper. But Isabelle heard and walked over briskly.

'Allie, good. I'm glad you're here. Now, listen. Nathaniel

cut the feed. Dom and Shak are trying to get it back – there may be a way to hack into the webcam. She's trying that now. In the meantime…'

Allie didn't let her finish.

'I don't understand. Why did he do this? What is going *on*?'

The bottom seemed to have dropped out of her world.

They'd been *so close* to getting him out. And now they didn't even know if he was still there.

'Allie,' Isabelle said, 'this is how Nathaniel works. He loves a performance.' She turned to Dom. 'Show her.'

Dom typed something. Suddenly, Carter reappeared on the monitor, chained to the wall. Something was taped across his mouth. He looked pale. Seconds later, Nathaniel walked into view.

As always, he wore a perfectly tailored suit, his tie was neatly knotted. Cufflinks glinted at each wrist. It was perverse that someone so horrible should be attractive.

Moving without any apparent urgency, he approached the camera, his face looming as he leaned towards it. He did something they couldn't see. Suddenly, the sound came on. Allie could hear Nathaniel's footsteps. Hear Carter's chains jangle when he shifted uneasily.

Whistling to himself, Nathaniel walked away. The tune echoed eerily as he crossed to stand behind Carter's chair. When he was ready, he lowered his hands onto Carter's broad shoulders and smiled at the camera.

Carter flinched at his touch. A muscle worked in his cheek. Allie could see hatred flickering in his eyes.

'Isabelle. Allie.' Nathaniel's lips curved into a perfect, smooth hateful smile. 'I've given you the chance to see where we stand. You've received my message. As you can see, time is running out. Let's end this now.' His voice was rich, almost pleasant. As if he was talking to old friends. 'We all know the game is over. It ended that night in London. Admit your defeat. Leave the school and never come back. Tell Lucinda's few remaining supporters that you're done. And you can have Carter West back.'

Carter shook his head and tried to talk, but the tape across his mouth made his words unintelligible.

Nathaniel continued. 'If you don't then you can watch Carter die. Live on camera.' He patted his shoulder in a sickening mock of sympathy. Watching it made Allie's skin crawl. 'You can see the clock. You know how much time you have. My phone lines, as they say, are always open. But I'm turning this off for now. I think you've seen enough.'

He gestured at someone off screen. Instantly the image disappeared, replaced by a series of white numbers.

'Nathaniel's phone number,' Isabelle explained, contempt dripping from her voice.

Then the message that Allie had seen when she walked in the room flashed up on the screen.

Isabelle turned to face her. 'And that's how it's been since.'

A tidal wave of panic seemed to hit Allie all at once. 'I can't stand any more of this. We have to do something.' Her voice rose. 'There must be *something*.'

The room fell silent. Everyone was watching them now.

'We are doing something, Allie.' Isabelle's reply was measured. 'This is a tactic. Surely you can see that? You have to think with your head, not your heart. Look at this rationally. Nathaniel gave us the chance to see Carter, because he knew it would make us panic. Now he's taking that away for the same reason. He wants us to panic. That's why he's doing it. Don't give him what he wants.'

Allie didn't know how she was going to do that. It felt like her heart was being torn in two.

Raj joined them, his expression grave. 'Allie, I genuinely believe Carter is fine. Nathaniel is a businessman – he wants something we have. There's no logical reason for him to harm Carter.'

'Maybe he is fine right now.' Flinging out a hand, Allie pointed at the red clock on the screen, ticking inexorably down. 'But what happens in two days, Raj?' He opened his mouth to answer but she didn't let him speak. 'I want him back.' Tears burned the backs of her eyes. 'This can't happen. Nathaniel has to pay for this. We have to get it right this one time…'

Her voice quivered with emotion, and she bit her lip hard.

Raj answered her.

'It's nearly dawn. I'm heading out to St John's Fields with a group of my best guards. Dom has secured satellite time. As soon as the sun comes up we'll be all over this place. I believe Carter is in there. And if he is, we'll get him.' He leaned forward, his gaze unwavering. 'I swear to you. We're going to get him back.'

As promised, Raj's team headed out just before dawn, staking out positions all around the sprawling acreage of St John's Fields.

When daylight finally broke, Dom's satellite company contact came through. Just after 6 a.m., Nathaniel's message disappeared, replaced with a hazy green image of rural England.

For a second, everyone stopped what they were doing to look. The view was of a ribbon of winding narrow road. Peeping through a thick canopy of trees, Allie could see a large brick house with a chimney. Set further back from the road were several hulking barns.

Cars were parked haphazardly on the grass in front – whatever this place was, it was crowded.

Allie stared at the house fixedly, as if it might give some hint as to what it held. But nothing moved.

It all looked empty.

Dom patched the feed through to Raj.

After that… nothing happened. They waited for ages. Occasionally cars arrived and a flurry of excitement arose. But by that afternoon, neither Nathaniel nor any member of his immediate circle had been seen.

Slowly, the faint flame of hope Raj had lit began to dim.

Allie found herself doubting everything. Her thoughts became a tangle of fears.

What if this isn't the place? We have a day and a half left. So little time! Why are we wasting it on this house?

And finally, inevitably, a suspicion.

What if Christopher lied to us?

That last thought kept nagging her.

And so, late that afternoon, she slipped away and went in search of her brother. She found him sitting alone in the common room, a book open in his lap. The two guards assigned to watch him sat a short distance away.

Somebody had loaned him trousers and a dark blue

Cimmeria pullover. He looked comfortable – like he'd always belonged here. And something about that enraged her.

Why should he be sitting warm and safe while Carter was a prisoner?

She was determined to get the truth out of him.

'You look better,' Allie said, dropping into the leather chair across from him. 'Did you sleep?'

'Yes.' His eyes searched her face. 'You look worse. I'm guessing you didn't?'

'No time,' she said. 'There's too much going on.'

'You haven't found him yet.' He stated it as fact. And Allie's suspicions grew.

'No,' she admitted. 'Nathaniel set up a feed for a while, so we could see him in his… prison.' It was the only word for it. 'But he cut it last night.'

Christopher's breath hissed between his teeth.

'God, Allie. I'm sorry. That's a classic Nathaniel move. The guy's such a douche.' He glanced at her. 'He's messing with you, you know that, right? Whatever he's asking for right now, it's just a game to him.'

Allie didn't know what to think. He was completely believable. He looked genuinely frustrated with Nathaniel. Sympathetic, even.

But what if it's all an act?

'That's what Raj says,' she replied, a little grudgingly. 'But it's hard to believe it when Nathaniel's put a clock up on the screen counting down a day and a half, and says he's killing Carter at the end of it if we're still here.'

She searched her brother's face for clues to what he was thinking. 'Chris, we're staking everything on your word that he's at St John's Fields. When there's no sign of him there. At all.'

She leaned forward to meet her brother's surprised gaze. 'Please tell me you're not playing us,' she said. 'I'm your *sister*. If you ever loved me, don't do that to me now. Because if you are I swear to God, you are not part of my family.'

Despite all her efforts to keep it steady, her voice quivered. For a second she looked away to gather her emotions.

When she turned back, he caught her gaze and held it. 'I swear on our mother's life, Allie, I'm not playing you. This is real. I'm done with Nathaniel. I'm here because I don't want anything to do with him ever again. Please, I'm begging you. Believe me.'

Allie didn't blink, searching for any sign of duplicity. But there was nothing in his voice but pleading. Nothing in his familiar face but candour.

She sagged back in her chair. 'I want to believe you, I really do. But I'm just so scared. You've been gone so long. You've been with him all that time. I can't trust you now. I want to, but I can't.'

He looked stung.

'Come on, Allie,' he said. 'That's not fair. I risked my life to get to you. I risked everything. At least give me a chance to prove I am who I say I am.'

'I don't know how to do that.' Allie's voice rose, and she forced herself to lower it again. 'Everything's so dangerous. Giving you a chance is freaking dangerous. Not giving you a chance?' She held up her hands. 'Well that's dangerous too. So I can't bloody win.' He looked like he wanted to speak but she didn't let him. 'The thing is, Christopher, if you're not real anymore – if Nathaniel has messed with your brain so much you aren't *you* any longer – Carter could die. And I can't let that happen.'

Christopher rubbed his eyes hard before replying.

'Nathaniel messed with my head when I was a kid. I was vulnerable and he took advantage of it. I've never denied the mistakes I made. But I'm telling you – I'm *swearing* to you – that I'm done with him. I see who he really is now. He kills people. Or at least, he hires people to kill for him. And that scares the crap out of me.' He hesitated, his eyes locked on hers. 'I thought he'd kill you, Allie. I really did. And I still think he would, if he thought it was useful for you to die. So… if you want to know why I'm here now, that's why.'

For a moment, Allie couldn't think of anything to say. She'd thought many times that Nathaniel might kill her. Or get Gabe to do it. But hearing Christopher tell her she was right was somehow even scarier.

Perhaps more importantly, though, she believed him. The passion in his voice, the veiled loathing for Nathaniel – no one could fake that. No one. He might have been lying about some things, but she believed this part. He was here because he was afraid for her.

'OK,' she said. 'Then, here's the thing. I need your help.'

He searched her face hopefully. 'You believe me?'

'More than I did before,' she conceded. 'But if you want everyone here to accept that you've changed, help us get Carter back.'

His brow creased. 'Al, I was right about St John's Fields. I still believe that's where Nathaniel would hold him. He doesn't trust anyone in the world enough to let them hold an asset as valuable to him as your friend. He's too cautious for that. He's going to keep this guy on his own property.' He thumped his finger against the table for emphasis. 'He's there, Allie.'

Her heart jumped, but she kept her expression steady.

'We've got people watching the grounds,' she said. 'If

you're right, we'll know soon. But, even if Carter is there, we still need to get in. And that doesn't look easy. I've been listening to Nathaniel's guards – there seem to be loads of them.'

Christopher didn't disagree. 'He's got his own army. And he likes that farmhouse for a reason – it's set back from the road. Like this place.' He glanced at the guards watching them from across the room. 'He has a good electronic security system inside the house…' He paused. 'Basically, the guy's obsessed with security.'

This was just what Allie had expected.

She schooled her voice to sound casual when she broached her idea. 'We think the key is the guards. We need one of them on our side.'

She hadn't exactly told Raj this. But she was sure she was right. Nine would help. And now that they were so close, she needed to know as much about him as she could.

Christopher considered this, nodding thoughtfully. 'That could work. You get a guard on your side, he distracts the others, helps you get in and out safely. Yeah.' He looked impressed. 'That's probably the best way, actually. Has Raj been working on one of them in particular?'

'I think so,' Allie lied. 'But we need to know more about them. That way we could know how to reach them.'

He seemed to accept this. 'What do you want to know?'

'Why are they loyal to Nathaniel?'

He didn't hesitate. 'Money.'

'Money?' Allie didn't hide her surprise. 'What, he just pays them? That's it?'

'Almost. Nathaniel chooses his recruits well and pays them a fortune.' He leaned forward, warming to the subject. 'Most of these guys have real financial problems when he hires them.

Child support, bankruptcy, gambling debts… Their lives are a mess. That's what he looks for. Ex-military or ex-police with problems. He swoops in and offers them a solution to all their troubles.'

Allie must have looked sceptical because his tone grew a little defensive. 'We're talking life-changing money here, Al. You work for Nathaniel for a few years, if you're a regular guy, you're made. You just won the lottery. All your worries go away.'

Allie thought of the things she'd heard Nine and the other guards say on the radio. That no money was worth what they were being asked to do.

'After a while, though,' she said, 'why don't they quit? This can't be an easy job.'

'Because money is addictive,' he said. 'They start out thinking it's the perfect job. By the time they realise how dodgy it is they're trapped. If they leave, they slide right back into the problems that brought them to Nathaniel in the first place. And they want a new car, a new house, a new girlfriend… There's always something more they can buy to make it all worthwhile.' He sighed. 'That kind of money's like a prison without walls.'

Allie thought of all the zeros on the papers she'd signed the other day with Lucinda's lawyers, and blood rushed to her face. Was she in that wall-less prison now?

She forced herself to stay focused on the subject at hand. 'Do you know any of them by name? On the radio they only talk in code.'

Christopher's eyes widened. 'You hacked into Nathaniel's system?' When Allie nodded in reply, he smiled. 'You guys really are smart as hell.' He ran a hand across his head as he thought it through. 'I know a few, but there are dozens of them. If you showed me some pictures of them, I could tell you all I know about them. But it's hard without images.'

Allie made a mental note to ask Raj for images of the guards.

'How can we get to them?' she asked next. 'I mean, you say they're in it for the money… could they be bribed? Like, if we offered to pay them more than he was paying, do you think they'd help us?'

He considered this. 'It could work. I don't think most of them are with him because they agree with him or they like him. But you'd need a lot of money.'

'Money isn't a problem.'

Christopher shot her an amused look. 'Where are you going to get that kind of money, Al? Mum and Dad have never even seen the kind of money we're talking about. These guys will need *real* money.'

She opened her mouth then closed it again.

He didn't know what had happened. Didn't know about their grandmother's will. She didn't have to tell him. She could tell him it was Isabelle's money she was talking about. But she wanted to tell him. Because she wanted to know how he'd react if he knew.

The students who'd been sitting by the door talking, walked out of the room. Now it was just the two of them and the guards.

'The thing is… Lucinda,' she said cautiously. 'When she died she left me… a bit of money.'

'Did she now?' His gaze sharpened. 'How much is *a bit* of money?'

'A lot.'

'Right.' He leaned back into the soft leather chair and studied her, realisation dawning in his eyes. 'She leave you everything, Allie?'

She thought about Nathaniel and Isabelle – how an inheritance had destroyed their relationship, their family, their lives. A parent's decision – something neither of them could control – had all the impact of a wrecking ball.

But Christopher had done the same thing to their family when he walked out. Maybe there was nothing left to destroy.

She lifted her gaze to meet his. 'More or less.'

He blew out his breath. When he spoke his voice was low. 'Allie, our granny was a billionaire. Does that mean…?'

'That I'm a billionaire now?' she asked. The word sounded *insane*. But she'd seen all those zeros. And there was no point in denying the truth, to herself or her brother. 'I think so. Kind of. Yes.'

He stared at her for a long second and then, a smile slowly spread across his face. His shoulders shook with suppressed mirth. Until he threw back his head and laughed.

'Bloody hell, Allie. That is *amazing*. I am so freaking glad she left it to you and not Nathaniel.' He slapped his hand on his knee and the guards both glanced at him reflexively. 'He's going to be so deeply pissed off when he finds out. First his dad, now Lucinda – twice he's been left out of massive wills that could have given him everything he wanted. That is…' He wiped his eyes '…perfect.'

Even as Allie smiled, she watched him closely. But he gave no hint of rancour or rage. Not even the slightest flicker of indication that he wished Lucinda had left the money to him instead of her.

She allowed herself to relax a little. 'Well, I don't feel rich,' she grumbled. 'For one thing, I'm still in sodding school…'

For some reason, that left Chris doubling over with

laughter.

'Oh, our family,' he said, as his laughter subsided. 'What a strange, messed up bunch of crazy rich bastards we are.'

Twenty Three

After she left Christopher, Allie pelted it up the stairs, adrenaline bubbling through her veins, sending her heart racing. She had all the information she needed now to present her plan to Isabelle and Raj. If they agreed, the whole thing could be over tonight.

It was time to talk to Nine.

She'd appeal to his hatred of Nathaniel. Offer him a lot of money.

It would work.

But when she burst through the door of Dom's room, prepared to launch into her spiel she found everyone gathered at one end of the room, listening to voices emerging from speakers.

The tension in the room was palpable; no one spoke or moved. Everyone seemed glued to the voices.

Before she could ask what was going on, Dom caught her eye and held up a hand for quiet.

Allie closed the door behind her carefully.

Dom spoke into the radio. 'What are you seeing right now?'

Raj's voice crackled through the speakers. 'We've personally identified two of Nathaniel's vehicles here. We're seeing guards in black uniforms in the grounds, apparently patrolling.'

Dom and Isabelle exchanged a look.

Isabelle took leaned towards the radio. 'What's your assessment, Raj? Is this the place?'

There was a pause before Raj replied.

'I think so.' But he struck a cautious note. 'I need clearer identification. It could still be a decoy.'

Isabelle bit her lip. Allie could see she was trying to contain her frustration. There was so little time. They were so close.

'What do you need, Raj?' Her voice was measured. 'Is there anything we could do with the satellite footage?'

'I won't be happy until we have a visual on Nathaniel,' he said. 'We need to be certain. There are cars warming up now – this looks like a convoy. If we're lucky, these could be his personal vehicles. Can you see anything on the screen there?'

As one, everyone turned to look at the wall-mounted screen. Allie squinted at the increasingly familiar satellite image of a farmhouse rooftop and scattered buildings in the sprawling yard. It looked like three cars had pulled up to the front door, but overhanging trees were blocking her view – it was hard to see much beneath the leaves.

Dom seemed to come to the same conclusion. 'We need to zoom in,' she muttered, typing something into the computer.

A few seconds later, the camera inched closer. Now Allie could see the dark roofs of the car glistening in the late afternoon sun. She could just barely see the front door.

'We can see the cars, Raj,' Isabelle said. 'But no people.'

'Give it a minute,' he said. 'They've just gone inside. I haven't got the best angle here to see their faces. I'll be able to see them when they get to the gate, but I was hoping you could see more.'

On the monitor, the front door of the farmhouse swung open, and a group of men walked out.

'We have motion,' Isabelle said, tensely. 'I count four… no, five men. All in suits, no black gear.' She looked down at the radio. 'This could be it, Raj.'

'Copy that,' he replied. 'Can you see their faces?'

Isabelle had moved closer to the screen to get a better view, so it was Dom who replied. 'That's negative, Raj. There's a tree blocking our view at this time.'

Unconsciously, Allie moved closer to Isabelle, staring up at the image.

All she could see was glossy dark heads, shoulders in tailored navy blue and dark grey, clustering under the branches of a sprawling chestnut tree.

Then: motion. The doors of the cars opened and the men disappeared inside. The doors slammed shut. The satellite brought them no sound, but she could see the way the cars moved slightly from the impact, the way the dust jumped and floated from the disturbance of the air.

Silently, the cars began to roll forward.

'Raj – they're on the move,' Dom said urgently. 'We've got no face visuals here.'

'Copy that. I can see them. Stand by.'

Allie heard Raj say something quietly to one of his guards before the signal went completely quiet.

As the cars rolled with slow deliberation down the short drive, the room took on a kind of breathless anticipation. No one dared even move.

Isabelle stood in front of the monitor, one hand covering her mouth, watching the procession.

Next to her, Allie stared at the screen.

Come on, she thought. *Come on.*

The satellite showed the sturdy gate opening slowly in the dappled shade. The first car rolled out onto the road. The second followed closely.

The third was just turning out of the drive when Raj's voice crackled from the speakers.

'Visual identification made. Nathaniel is in car number two. Repeat: visual identification confirmed.' Allie could hear the grim satisfaction in his voice. 'We've got him, guys.'

Everyone whooped at once. Isabelle sagged forward for just a second before standing tall and striding back towards the radio. Shak high-fived Allie.

Even Dom allowed herself a moment's celebration. 'Hell's yeah,' Allie heard the tech say to herself. 'Now we've got ourselves a party.' Her usual decorum returned quickly, though, and she switched the microphone back on, raising her voice to be heard above the jubilation in the room. 'Copy that, Raj. Visual identity confirmed.' She added after a pause, 'You'll be able to hear how that news was received, I imagine.'

'That's affirmative,' Raj said. Allie could hear the smile in his voice. 'Further information, one of my guards is following Nathaniel's entourage now. The rest of us are keeping watch on the house.'

They continued to talk through technical details, making arrangements. Then Isabelle headed towards the door, motioning for Zelazny to follow her.

'There are some things we need to work out,' Allie heard her say. 'I'm concerned about the logistics of the next step. And the speed.'

Allie waited for them to make their way into the corridor,

then she slipped through the door after them.

'Isabelle.'

The two glanced up at her in surprise.

Allie took a deep breath. 'I have an idea.'

'Absolutely not.' Isabelle shook her head firmly. 'There is no way I will allow this.' The look she gave her was scathing. 'I can't believe you would even suggest such a thing.'

'Now, hang on.' Zelazny held up his hands. 'I'm not sure it's the best idea either, but I can't really think of a better one. Can you?'

Allie sat next to him on one of the chairs facing Isabelle's desk. She'd given them the gist of her plan, and now she was letting them argue it out. She'd expected Isabelle to say no at first.

What she hadn't expected was that Zelazny would say yes.

'If we let her speak to one of Nathaniel's guards, we are putting a great deal on the line,' Isabelle leaned forward. 'Not least Allie's safety.'

Zelazny didn't back down. 'We can make sure it all happens in a public place, we'll stay with her at all times. Nothing can happen to her if we do this right.'

When Isabelle paused to think of a response, Allie jumped in.

'Look, I know it's a gamble, but I've been listening to Nine for days now. He's not just a little unhappy. He really hates Nathaniel. He helped me the other night, and he didn't have to do that. He talked about me – about how what Nathaniel was doing was wrong. I can use that.' She pointed at her face. 'I'm just a kid, right? Nine has a daughter, I've heard him talk about her. He sees me and it makes him think of her. So he's not going to want to hurt me.'

Isabelle shook her head, her lips pressed in a thin line. 'Even if I was willing to risk your life, I'm not convinced he'd listen to someone your age.'

'Actually, you're wrong. He wouldn't listen to someone like you or Raj – any adult. He doesn't seem to trust grownups.' Allie took a breath. 'I think he'd listen to me.'

The headmistress met her gaze speculatively, then shook her head. 'I'm sorry. I know you want to do this but it's just too dangerous.'

Allie wanted to tell Isabelle this wasn't her decision. That Lucinda would have backed her on this. She wanted to shout that she was going to do this either way so they might as well help her.

But she knew if she said any of those things she'd lose her advantage.

'Hear us out first,' Zelazny said, stepping smoothly into the tense silence. 'Allie's done her legwork here. She's researched the guard. Monitored his conversations. Made contact. We know he's unhappy. He's not loyal to Nathaniel.' He banged a closed fist lightly against his crossed knee. 'I think she's right. I think we can turn him.'

'I'm sorry but you're not using Allie.' Isabelle's voice was still firm. 'Not for this.'

'I don't like how closed minded you are on this. Your emotions are getting in the way.' The history teacher gave her a stern look. 'Allie's intelligent, capable and trained. She's one of our best students. You can't be afraid to use your best.'

'August, I can't believe you would even consider sending

a student into such an unpredictable environment,' Isabelle said reprovingly. 'After what happened in London, I thought we'd agreed to change our approach.'

Forcing herself to sound calm, Allie spoke up. 'Isabelle, I know why this makes you nervous. And I get that it's dangerous. You know I do.' She held her gaze until Isabelle lowered her own in acknowledgement. 'I know how he thinks. How his mind works. I know he doesn't trust his peers – he thinks they're all after something. I think he got caught up in this situation because he was desperate. Christopher says all these guys are in debt. Nine must have been in a lot of trouble. Now I think he wants out. And I think he might listen to me because I'm young. And he feels sorry for me – we have to use that.'

'Even if that was the case, Allie, it's not reason enough to let you walk up to one of Nathaniel's guards and identify yourself as the one person Nathaniel would love to grab.' Isabelle looked from her to Zelazny. 'Surely you can both see that.'

Zelazny was ready for that argument. 'That's why we do it in a public place,' he said. 'That's why we send half a dozen guards with her. If he tries anything? We're ready.'

'I'm sorry August, but the answer is no.' Isabelle's expression was closed. Her tone indicated the argument was over.

Her earlier bravado fading, Allie began to despair. If Isabelle thought this was a terrible plan then… maybe it was. What did she know, anyway?

But even as her hope began to slip away, she thought again of that moment at the gate. The intensity in Nine's eyes. The subtle warning signal.

And his voice on the radio. '*It ain't right…*'

Her determination returned. Isabelle had to understand. If they didn't let her meet with Nine, then all they could do was continue to sit outside St John's Fields as the clock ticked down. Or try a dangerous home invasion that could end very badly for everyone.

They had just over twenty-four hours left.

One day.

Allie leaned forward. 'Isabelle, I know why you're afraid but *please* trust me. This man, Nine. He could get us inside. If we take this chance, he really could help us get Carter home.' Seeing Isabelle about to argue she spoke quickly. 'If he says no, the worst thing that happens is we reveal our hand. It doesn't really help Nathaniel. All he would know is that we know where he is.'

'Actually, I think the worst thing that happens is we end up with both you and Carter on our computer screens in chains.' The look Isabelle shot her was challenging. 'Are you ready for that?'

Allie suppressed a shudder. But when she spoke her voice was firm.

'You know Raj better than that,' she said. 'It won't happen.'

'Isabelle.' Zelazny said her name with uncharacteristic gentleness. 'I think you know she's right. She's trained and experienced. She's willing to take this chance. We can protect her.'

The headmistress held his gaze for a long moment, then lowered her head to her hands.

'I can't do it, August.' Her voice grew unsteady. 'I can't dig another hole in that churchyard.'

Zelazny paused. When he spoke, his tone was firm. 'You won't have to. I promise you that.'

The headmistress let out a long breath and straightened her shoulders. With obvious reluctance she said, 'If I were to agree to this, when would you want to do it?'

Allie's heart jumped. She tried to disguise her triumph behind a solemn expression.

'As soon as possible. But first we'll need to find out everything we can about him. We don't even know his name, do we?' Zelazny glanced at Allie.

'Yes we do,' she said, fighting the urge to grin. 'Christopher said his name is Owen Moran.'

Christopher hadn't known much about the guards, but Moran had been assigned as his driver for two months.

'Doesn't talk much, that guy,' he'd said. 'Never told me anything about himself. Seemed angry about something all the time, but I never knew what.' He'd paused to think. 'Hell of a good driver.'

Isabelle picked up her pen and wrote it down. She spoke without looking up.

'I want to be included in every element of this plan.' Zelazny nodded, as if this went without saying but she was still talking. 'And I want Dom and her team to find out absolutely everything there is to know about this man. I want to know what he thinks, what he eats, where he sleeps. Nobody goes anywhere to meet anyone until I know him as well as I know you.'

She fixed them both with a steely glare. 'I don't like this. Not after everything we've been through. But I fear we don't have any choice. We need to get Carter back, and then get out of this school as fast as we can. It's time.'

Twenty Four

When they walked out of her office Allie turned right, to head back to Dom's office, but before she'd taken a step, Isabelle grabbed her arm with a firm grip.

'Oh no you don't,' she said. 'You're exhausted. You've hardly eaten or slept all day. I've already told Dom and the teachers, now I'm telling you: all students are to get some rest. I'm banning you from work for the next hour, and I'd rather you took three. The staff have left food out in the dining hall for those who missed dinner. I want you to eat and rest. Come back later.'

'No *way*.' Allie stared at her in disbelief. She glanced to Zelazny for help, but he'd already headed down the corridor.

This battle he was leaving her to fight alone.

'You can't do this. Not right now.' In her mind she could still see that red clock, ticking down.

Isabelle was unmoved. 'I'm giving in on a lot of things Allie. But I'm not having students passing out from exhaustion. Now, go.' She pointed down the hallway towards the stairs. 'Eat. Rest.'

Seeing the stubborn look in Allie's eyes, she sighed and dropped her hand. 'If Dom needs you I promise we'll send for you, OK? Now will you go?'

Allie accepted her fate with ill grace. 'Fine. But I'm only taking thirty minutes.'

The thing was, now that she had a moment to think about it, she was starving. She'd been up since before dawn and she really hadn't eaten much all day.

In the dining hall, buffet tables had been set up along one wall and stacked with food. Sandwiches and salads, vast bowls of fruit and platters of biscuits were arrayed in a tantalising display.

Copper urns of coffee and tea steamed. Nearby, bottles of energy drinks poked out of frosted silver ice buckets.

It was nearly ten o'clock and the atmosphere had a nervy late-night buzz. Students clustered at tables talking and clutching energy drinks. Guards relaxed nearby, their feet propped up on chairs, steaming mugs of tea at their elbows.

Cimmeria was always at its best when everything was going wrong.

After piling a plate high, Allie turned to look for a place to sit.

The tables had been rearranged for the late-night crowd; no elegant white table cloths or glittering candles at this hour.

A flash of copper and a sudden burst of bell-like laughter drew her gaze to where Katie was sitting with Lucas. They were snuggled close together, whispering and laughing. Allie hadn't talked to Katie once since she and Sylvain had broken up.

She decided it was time.

'Hey,' she said, setting her tray down on their table.

'Oh.' Katie looked at her with the distant hauteur of a Persian cat. 'It's you.'

Lucas grinned in his usual amiable way. 'Hey. How's it going? Ace news about St John's Fields.' He cracked his knuckles. 'Looks like we're going out.'

'Don't do that.' Katie cast a pointed glance at his hands.

'Sorry, babe.' He dropped his hands.

Rolling her eyes, Allie took a bite of her toasted cheese sandwich and tuned them both out. It was the first hot food she'd eaten all day. It melted in her mouth.

With a glance at his watch, Lucas stood and stretched. 'I want to track down Zelazny. Find out how this is all going down.'

To Allie's surprise, Katie responded seriously. 'Go,' she said. 'Do what you need to do.'

He brushed his lips against her cheek and then hurried away.

Allie watched as he walked across the room. His long, loping stride reminded her achingly of Carter.

She dropped her gaze to her plate.

'I heard about the break-up.'

Katie's words caught Allie off guard. Her mouth went suddenly dry and the sandwich turned to paste in her mouth.

She swallowed painfully.

'Where did you hear it from? I haven't told anyone.'

Katie gave her a pitying look. 'From Sylvain, of course.'

'Oh, yeah,' Allie mumbled. 'Of course.'

'I want you to know I never told Sylvain anything.' The redhead took a prim sip of water. 'He guessed.'

'How?' Her appetite now gone, Allie pushed her plate to one side. 'How did he guess?'

On some level, she thought she already knew. She could imagine every excruciating second of his thought process. But she was tired and feeling guilty.

She wanted Katie to salt her wounds.

'The way you were acting he knew something was wrong. You were short-tempered. Distant. Changed.' She toyed with the label on her water bottle. 'I didn't tell him, Allie.'

Allie thought of the look on Sylvain's face, the knowing, hurt look.

She exhaled. 'I'm glad he figured it out.'

'What?' Katie stared.

'I wanted to break up with him but I kept bottling it,' Allie admitted. 'I don't know how it would have gone if he hadn't finally broken up with me. I really care about him, Katie. Despite everything. So I'm glad he knows and he can just, like… move on.' She held her gaze. 'Look out for him, OK? I know he won't want to talk to me but… make sure he takes care of himself. That he doesn't do anything crazy.'

'Sylvain would never do anything stupid.' Katie's tone was prim, although her expression was surprisingly sympathetic. 'But don't worry. I'll make sure he eats something now and then.'

'Is he…' Allie cleared her throat. 'Is he… OK?'

Katie leaned back in her chair with a sigh. 'Of course not. He's devastated. He loved you. But he'll be fine, Allie. You did the right thing.'

Those were five words Allie never expected to hear Katie Gilmore say. The two of them exchanged a look of quiet understanding.

'Allie! There you are.' Rachel ran into the room with Nicole at her side. 'Isabelle banned us from working. I thought you might be banned, too.'

Rachel's wavy hair had been clipped back loosely, but curls escaped to frame her heart-shaped face. She looked happy.

The two slid into seats next to Allie.

'I never thought I'd say this… But I'm tired of those computers.' Rachel glanced at Nicole who took a bite from a perfectly round apple. 'I need a break.'

'Personally, I cannot wait for Raj to come back and tell us we can go get Carter.' Nicole's French accent was like a silky blanket over every word. 'I'm ready to go in today.' She leaned back, her long hair draped over the back of her chair. 'I hate waiting.'

With her dark hair, rosy cheeks and creamy pale skin, Nicole had never looked more like Snow White. Her beauty appeared so unconscious – she never seemed to really think about it. But she looked amazing – perfect figure, perfect oval face.

Why did she and Sylvain never get together? Allie found herself wondering, as she had many times before. *Why me instead of her?*

Nicole swallowed a bite of apple and met Allie's gaze. 'I hear you met with Isabelle earlier – does she think we'll really be able to do it? Will we get Carter back?'

Allie didn't hesitate. 'We're getting him back.'

Katie's green eyes glittered. 'The thing I don't understand is what happens then?'

Allie fell silent. She'd never told the others about the plan she and Isabelle had concocted. In fact, she and Isabelle rarely spoke of it. They'd both tacitly agreed that all their energy was on getting Carter back. They'd worry about tomorrow when it arrived.

She wanted to tell them. She wanted them to know there was a plan. To start over somewhere safe.

But was this really the time?

She was still trying to decide when Nicole gave an elegant shrug.

'Well,' the French girl sighed, 'we will not solve it tonight. We need a distraction. Rachel and I are going for a walk. We have to get out of this building.' She glanced at Allie and then looked away. 'Sylvain and Zoe are coming with us. You could come too…'

Katie met Allie's gaze and arched one eyebrow.

'No thanks,' Allie said. 'I've got to go back upstairs for something… in a minute.'

Everyone at that table knew she was lying.

'If you change your mind, seriously… come if you want,' Rachel urged her. 'It would be fine.'

No it wouldn't, Allie thought.

She wondered if there would ever be a time when she and Sylvain could be in the same room together without it all being a confusing, tense mess.

'I might come out in a bit,' Katie said, waving a hand at the room around them. 'I'm sick of this place.'

Nicole and Rachel left a few minutes later, walking in perfect sync, their heads close together.

As she watched them go, Katie sighed. 'They're so cute.'

Bemused, Allie shrugged. 'I guess.'

'What?' Katie blinked. 'You don't think they're basically the cutest couple at Cimmeria right now? Honestly, Allie. What's *the matter* with you?' With an indulgent smile, she glanced back to where the two were just disappearing through the door. 'I think they're adorable.'

At first, Allie couldn't understand what she was talking about.

'What do you…?'

Her voice trailed off.

Then, with the sudden impact of a hammer strike, Katie's words made sense. Complete and absolutely stunning sense.

Katie's gaze floated from the door to her, and stopped. Her eyes widened.

'Oh Allie. Come *on.*' She didn't even try to hide her disbelief. 'You can't not know this. Rachel is your *best friend.*'

Mute, Allie just shook her head. Blood rose to her cheeks.

Because she hadn't known.

'I don't understand.' Katie watched her with dismay. 'Everyone knows. How can you not know? They're "Cimmeria's Adorable Lesbian Couple TM".'

She made air quotes around the words.

'I mean, everyone always knew about Nicole, of course. Although I have to say Rachel was a bit of a surprise.' She tapped a nail against her chin as she considered Rachel's sexuality as if it was a menu option in an expensive restaurant. 'But they've been together for… I don't know. Months.'

Allie couldn't believe this was happening. Had Rachel intentionally deceived her? Had she hidden it?

Or was I just a self-absorbed idiot?

Across the table, Katie was still working through the puzzle of Allie's ignorance. 'I guess we all just assumed you knew about Nicole. Especially after that kiss.'

Allie's head jerked up. When she didn't speak, Katie shot her an exasperated look.

'Remember? During Truth or Dare? God, Allie. Do you just sleepwalk through your whole *life*?'

A sudden memory flooded into Allie's mind: a bonfire, Nicole's unexpected embrace, all soft lips, expensive perfume and long hair.

It had never once occurred to her that Nicole hadn't kissed her solely to shock people. That she might have just… wanted to kiss her.

Katie was still looking at her as if she should be explaining herself, but she didn't know what to say.

Yes, we kissed but I thought it was a game?

It was all coming together now. Rachel and Nicole, always together. Rachel and Nicole holding hands. Nicole's protectiveness of Rachel in Night School. The laughter she'd heard from Rachel's bedroom.

It was so obvious.

Her face felt hot. Her eyes had begun to burn with unshed tears.

How could I be so stupid?

Katie was watching her piece it together. 'You two have never talked about this?'

Allie shook her head.

'And you never noticed…?'

She never said a word.

A tear rolled down Allie's cheek, warm at first but leaving coldness in its wake. She felt so stupid. So betrayed.

Everyone knew.

'I have to go,' she whispered and stood so suddenly her chair screeched against the polished wood floor.

'No, Allie, wait…' Katie began. But Allie was running away even as the words left her mouth.

In the quiet of the formal hallway, she stopped, uncertain where to go. She couldn't go outside. She might run into *them*. Then she'd have to explain how unbelievably stupid and naive she was. In front of Sylvain. Who hated her.

She didn't understand how Rachel could keep this from her. This was huge. Best friends don't keep secrets like that.

Best friends trust you.

Don't they?

'There's something going on in my life…' Rachel had said once. 'I'm going through something…'

But you didn't bloody tell me, did you?

Allie gave an involuntary choking sob.

A trio of guards were approaching, and she spun around to face the wall. She didn't want them to see her tears.

They ambled by without glancing at her.

When they were out of sight, Allie wiped her cheeks with the back of her hand. She couldn't stay here, standing like a complete loser in the hallway with tears running down her face.

She ran up the grand staircase, taking the stairs two at a time. Then up another flight to the girls' dorm, quiet at this hour.

When she reached her room she didn't bother to turn on the light. She felt her way across the room and scrambled up on to her desk, shoving books and papers out of her way. The desk lamp fell to the floor with a crash.

Flipping the latch up, she pushed the shutter-like window open so hard it banged against the wall, and let the fresh air wash over her damp face.

Outside, the moon was nearly full, casting everything in a wash of blue. It was a cool night.

For a second, she just sat there, letting herself weep.

She felt dangerous – a volatile cocktail of pain and anger and exhaustion frothed inside her. She wanted to break things.

She needed to breathe.

Most of all, she wanted *Carter*. She wanted to run across the roof to his room. Tell him everything. Have him help her piece it all together, calm her down. If he was here she'd know what to do.

But he wasn't. She was all alone.

Still. That didn't mean she had to sit here.

She slid to the edge of the desk and, without hesitation, swung her legs out the window, into the void. Then she climbed out onto the ledge.

She stood there for just a moment, clinging to the window frame, waiting for her eyes to adjust to the dark.

Far below, she could hear voices and laughter, floating up to her on the breeze.

The sound made her flinch. What if Katie had run out and told the others how stupid she was? That could be them, laughing at her now.

Some rational part of her knew that wasn't logical – that Rachel would never laugh at her, but she was too upset now to think reasonably.

It hurt so much.

She began to make her way across the roof, sliding her feet along the narrow ledge too quickly to be safe. Her vision blurred with tears but she didn't slow.

She walked recklessly, letting her feet find their way.

The first window she passed was Rachel's. The lights were off – the room behind the windowpane, dark.

You didn't tell me. She imagined shouting those words at her. *Why didn't you tell me? Did you really think something like that would change our friendship? Don't you know me at all?*

'You should have trusted me,' she whispered, touching the cool glass of Rachel's window.

Hurriedly, she moved on, one foot and then the other, half wishing something bad would happen. Wishing she'd be hurt.

But her steps were sure; she'd done this many times.

When she reached the point where the roof dipped down, she remembered the night Sylvain pulled her up.

But she didn't need a boy to help her. She was strong.

She didn't need anyone.

Grabbing the sturdy lead drainpipe she pulled herself with

easy grace onto the slate tiles.

She didn't slip. Didn't lose her balance.

She was just fine.

She climbed up the sharp peak to where one of the towering chimneys thrust up into the sky. There, finally, she stopped.

The breeze ruffled the pleats of her skirt against her bare thighs and blew strands of her hair into her eyes. She pushed her hair back, tucking it behind her ears, letting the wind cool her face.

The moon seemed bigger up here – a spotlight in the sky, shining down on her.

Sometimes to see clearly, you need a great height. From here, she could see everything. The grounds where so many tremendous things had happened. In the distance through the trees she could just see the low steeple of the chapel. The white stone peak of the summer house was easier to find – it seemed to glow.

The steep slate roof itself held many memories. This was the place where Jo had nearly fallen to her death. Where Sylvain had told her he loved her. Where Carter first told her about Cimmeria.

Jo. Carter. Sylvain. All lost to her.

Was Rachel gone now, too? Could her lack of faith really destroy a friendship Allie considered the one sure thing in her life?

She lowered herself down to the roof, her back against the sturdy bricks of the chimney, and pulled her knees up close to her chest. She forced herself to breathe. To try and think things through.

Gradually she calmed down. Her tears dried. She tried to see things from Rachel's perspective.

But why...

'Hello, Allie.'

The voice that interrupted her thoughts was horribly familiar.

Allie froze.

Standing casually at the edge of the roof, Gabe grinned at her. The moon turned his dark blond hair gold.

'I've been looking for you.'

Twenty Five

Leaping to her feet, Allie stood with her back against the chimney.

'Gabe…? What the hell?'

Her heart was pounding, her lungs had compressed until her breath trickled through in short, quick bursts. Not enough to give her the oxygen she needed. Not enough to think.

'Nice to see you, too,' he said.

He was athletic and tall, all blond hair and muscles. Smiling coldly as he tossed a pebble up in to the air and caught it with ease. Even so, knowing what she knew about him, Allie couldn't believe she'd ever thought he was handsome.

She was looking at a viper in human form.

She cast a desperate glance across the empty roof, as if help might suddenly appear. But she was all alone. Just the way she'd wanted it.

'How did you find me?'

His grin widened. 'You should turn on the lights in your room, Allie. I was this close to you.' He held out his hands so only a tiny gap of air separated them.

A chill ran down her spine, raising the fine hairs on the back of her neck.

She thought of all the shadowy corners of her room – he'd

been in one of them, and she never knew.

He tossed the pebble in the air again, watching her with a knowing look.

'I thought about killing you then, while you were cry-babying it all over your desk. But then you went out the window.' He caught the pebble. 'And that gave me a better idea.'

Allie couldn't seem to get her mind to work properly. Fear had frozen her synapses.

This can't be happening. He can't be here.

He was in a farmhouse with Nathaniel. None of this was remotely possible.

How did he get in? she asked herself, as she fought to stay calm. *We sealed the gate.*

Gabe tossed the pebble aside. Allie heard the faint clatter as it hit the tiles and rolled down and over the edge. She never heard it hit the ground.

'This is getting boring,' he said, an irritated look on his face.

She had to talk to him. Distract him. Somehow she had to make enough noise so somebody could hear them up here.

She thought through the things she'd learned from the guards. Nine's derision for the boy who called himself Number One.

Use that.

'What do you want, Gabe?' She adopted a cool attitude, hands on her hips. 'Does Nathaniel even know you're here? I thought he was keeping you on a short leash after you screwed up in London.'

His eyes narrowed. 'Screwed up? What the hell are you talking about, Sheridan? I was perfect. Ask your grandmother how perfect I was.' A malicious smile spread across his face. 'Oh wait. She's not around anymore.'

She was too scared to get angry.

'I got the impression Nathaniel kind of thought that was the opposite of perfect,' she said. 'It seemed like he thought you messed up.'

He snorted a laugh but she could see the tension in his shoulders.

'Nathaniel doesn't know how to thank me for solving his problems,' he snapped. 'That guy has issues.'

'Really?' Allie struck a sympathetic note, although it made her stomach churn. 'I guess he was a little unfair.'

'He's a tosser,' Gabe said. 'But he won't be here for long.'

What did that mean?

The more Allie thought about it, the more this didn't make sense. Dom's team had been listening to Nathaniel's guards nonstop. They weren't planning any operations.

Nathaniel had Carter. He was working a trade. It didn't seem logical that he would send Gabe now to attack her. He needed her to sign those papers. Surely, this kind of confrontation was the last thing he'd want.

She stared at Gabe who was reaching behind his back.

'Gabe,' her voice came out barely above a whisper. 'Does Nathaniel know you're here?'

Later she would never remember seeing him move. Sylvain had always said 'Gabe is the best of us.' And it was true. He was fast. So fast.

One minute he was standing by the chimney glaring at her. The next he was behind her, pressing the cold blade of a knife against the skin of her throat.

'I don't answer to anyone.'

He whispered the words, his lips pressed against the

sensitive flesh of her ear, his breath warm against her skin.

She couldn't move. She hated that he was touching her. But the sharp edge of the blade dug into the vulnerable skin of her throat, rendering her powerless.

'This is crazy,' she said, swallowing hard. 'If you hurt me Nathaniel will kill you. Raj will kill you.'

He stroked the knife lovingly against her throat. The blade seemed to scald her skin.

'I'm not going to hurt you. I'm going to kill you, Allie. And then I'm going to kill my boss.'

There was no hesitation in his voice. No sense that what he was doing would have ramifications he couldn't imagine. No doubts. He seemed to find all of this utterly reasonable.

The part of Gabe that should stop him from doing deadly things was missing. Killing her would be simple for him.

'Wait.' Her voice was breathless. 'Wait, wait…'

But what could she say? What could she do? He had her right where he wanted her. It was over.

Tears stung her eyes, turning the moon into a hazy, thousand-pointed star.

I'm going to die.

Everything that had been so important to her five minutes before suddenly seemed utterly meaningless.

So what if Rachel hadn't told her she liked girls?

Everyone had secrets.

So what if Sylvain was upset right now?

He'd get over it.

It all seemed so clear.

She could live without Sylvain in her life. Live without Cimmeria.

If only she could *live* at all.

She became acutely conscious of everything around her.

The way the wind had quieted. The way the hairs on her arms stood on end. The rise and fall of Gabe's chest against her back. The sinews of the muscles in his arm. The point of the knife, cold and deadly against her skin.

She could hear every beat of her heart as loudly as if it played from speakers. Each beat a hammer strike against her ribs.

Her senses had never been so sharp.

This is how it ends.

There was something she'd read somewhere. *Everyone dies suddenly.* It was in English class, when they were working on a paper. Her teacher had encircled her description of Juliet's death, 'Her death was not sudden.'

In the margins the teacher had written: 'Everyone dies suddenly.'

Now she knew she was right. A flick of Gabe's wrist. And she would die.

Suddenly.

'I kind of hate to do this.' Gabe pulled her closer, pressing his body closer against hers. 'You look so good. What is it about you Cimmeria girls? That uniform… It does something to me.'

He ran his free hand down her shoulder to her breasts.

Allie couldn't breathe. His touch made her feel ill. She struggled in his grip, but he pressed the knife tighter against her neck, reminding her of the control he had over her. She froze.

'That's better,' he said. And she wanted to kill him.

'Stop it,' she said without hope.

But his hand kept moving. He was enjoying humiliating her. Enjoying the horror she felt.

'Killing you seems like such a waste. Maybe we could have a little fun together first…' When his hand reached her thighs and began to find its way under her skirt she made up her mind.

Even if he killed her in the end, she had to fight him.

I'm alive right now.

Turning her head as far to the right as she could, she lowered her mouth to his shoulder as if to kiss him. Then she sank her teeth into him.

He recoiled but she held on. He tried to yank free, but she dug her teeth in further, her jaws ached but she wouldn't let go.

Swearing loudly, he punched her in the head with his free arm. Her left ear rang and her jaw hurt so much she thought she'd dislocated it.

Only then did she let go. At the same time, though, she dropped her weight, forcing him to grapple for her with both hands.

In the struggle he lost control of the knife. As the blade slipped, it sliced into her neck with a burning pain she felt through the entire right side of her body.

She screamed. A hot flow of blood ran down her neck soaking the collar of her shirt.

'Shut up.' He tried to cover her mouth but she was fighting like a wildcat now. Using her elbows. Her hands. Her feet. She stomped hard on his instep and he cried out in pain.

There was so much blood. His hands were slippery with it when he grabbed her and she screamed again driving her right elbow into his ribs.

She felt his body buck from the impact.

'You bitch,' he gasped and raised the knife. It glittered silver in the moonlight. Allie raised a fist to block the blow, striking his wrist with all her strength.

The hilt was slick with her blood, and the knife flew out of his hand and sailed across the roof.

Swearing, Gabe let her go and scrambled after it. Picking it up, he spun back towards her.

'You're dying now, bitch,' he growled, his eyes blazing. 'No matter what.'

'No she isn't.'

Zoe stood on the edge of the roof, eyes fixed on Gabe.

Dread filled Allie's chest with ice.

Not Zoe. Please, not Zoe.

Looking at Allie, Gabe held up his hands in frustration. 'Who the hell is this child?'

But she was focused on Zoe. She wanted to run to her side, but Gabe stood between them.

'What are you doing here? Go back down. You have to go back down *now.*' Allie kept her voice low but forceful.

'I came to your room.' The younger girl never took her eyes off Gabe. She seemed to find him fascinating. 'Katie said you were upset. I heard you talking.' For just a second her gaze flickered around them appreciatively. 'I've never been up on the roof before. It's awesome.'

Gabe held the knife in one blood-slick hand. His arms were spread wide and he was crouched low, bouncing on the balls of his feet, a look of cold calculation in his eyes.

The three of them stood in a tense triangular formation – Zoe still too near the edge of the roof, Allie across from her, afraid to move any closer but desperate to protect her. Gabe, by the chimney facing them both.

He focused on Zoe. 'Listen little girl. You should take her advice. Otherwise, I'm going to kill your friend Allie and then I'm going to kill you.' His tone was so casual, he might have been telling her what he had for dinner.

She cocked her head with bird-like curiosity. In her pleated skirt and white blouse, she looked younger than fourteen.

'You're Gabe,' Zoe announced. 'I saw you in London.'

His lips curved into a cruel smile, but then she finished the thought. 'You were unconscious.' She studied his head. 'Did that leave a scar? It looked like it hurt.'

'Enough.'

With a sound like a snarl, he rushed at her, knife raised. Her centre of gravity was low and she danced out of his reach, ducking with such speed and smoothness he nearly lost his balance. At the edge of the roof, he swung his arms hard until he regained his footing.

Zoe stood next to Allie.

'You're bleeding,' she said, eyes on her neck. 'It looks superficial to me. It's not arterial. But you should apply pressure.'

Allie blinked. Then she remembered Zoe's new-found fascination with all things blood. She must have been hanging out with the nurses. Asking them questions. Collecting information whenever she wasn't working in Dom's office.

Allie didn't know what to do. She couldn't keep herself safe, much less take care of Zoe, too.

'Come on, little girl,' Gabe waved his knife. 'Don't be afraid.'

'What a wanker,' Zoe murmured, eyes following the blade.

Allie watched the knife, too.

'He's good, Zoe,' she said. 'Fast.'

'I'm fast, too,' the other girl kept her voice low. 'Break left when he comes. I'll break right.'

Allie had no chance to argue.

Gabe ran at them, scrambling up the steep roof.

At the last possible second, Allie sped left, her eyes on Zoe the whole time. The younger girl was a bullet, flying low and fast away from Gabe. They met together near the edge of the roof.

It was steep, and Allie had to work to keep her balance. They were momentarily safe, but now Gabe had the advantage of height. He glared down at them with open irritation.

'I'm sick of your games.' He waved the knife. 'Allie. Come here or I swear I'll kill the other one.'

'Don't,' Zoe warned her.

None of them was lowering their voices. Allie couldn't understand why nobody had heard them and come up to see what was going on. A guard. A teacher. *Someone* to help them.

She didn't know what to do. They could hold Gabe off, but they couldn't beat him. Eventually he'd get what he wanted.

She couldn't feel the wound in her neck anymore. All she could feel was panic for Zoe. She couldn't bear for Gabe to hurt her. Couldn't stand the idea that he would do to her what he'd done to Jo. She'd rather die than see that happen.

'Fine.' She held up her hands. Zoe shot her a furious look but Allie ignored her. 'I'll come to you. But first you have to let her go.'

Gabe's stance relaxed. He glanced from Allie to Zoe, and tossed the knife into the air. It spun twice, deadly beautiful in the moonlight.

Catching it with practiced ease, he pointed the tip at Zoe and motioned towards the sloping section of the roof that lead down to the ledge and escape.

'Fine. Get lost kid. You're saved.' He turned to Allie and smiled horribly. 'She's the one I want, anyway.'

Zoe didn't move. Her lips were set in a tight line.

'Zoe, you have to go.' Allie had begun to shake again but

she was resolute. 'I won't lose you.'

Zoe looked up at her, eyes too bright. 'You lose me if you die.'

But it would hurt less, Allie thought, holding her gaze.

Grabbing Zoe's narrow shoulders, she gave a forceful shrug, propelling her down the roof.

'Just go,' she said again, raising her voice.

Zoe shot Allie a betrayed look, and took two reluctant steps away.

Gabe rolled his eyes and tossed the knife in the air again.

'I can't handle the emotion,' he said.

Something about that seemed to make up Zoe's mind. Allie saw the sudden determination in her face. But Gabe didn't know her well enough to notice it.

Without warning she pivoted and shot up towards him – a slim arrow of muscle and bone, flying across a century-old roof, her hair streaming behind.

Too late Gabe realised what she was doing. 'What —?'

She loosed a high, brutal kick, straight to his midsection. Taken by surprise, he grunted from the blow and lost his balance, rolling twice on the roof before stopping himself with sheer, brute strength.

Zoe whirled back towards him. Fast and light.

'Zoe!' Allie cried, and ran after her. Knowing what would happen next. Knowing how quickly Gabe recovered. Knowing Zoe had never seen him fight.

Time slowed.

The tiles were solid under Allie's feet, and gravity was her friend, pulling her down to where the two figures were haloed in moonlight. Zoe looked so small. So fragile.

Allie couldn't seem to hear anything at all – not her

footsteps, not her heart. She ran in a vacuum of terror. Unable to breathe or think.

With sickening smooth purpose Gabe rose and reached for Zoe – fast as a snake strike. He didn't need to turn to see where she was – he just knew. He always knew.

He is the best of all of us.

Allie had no doubt he would throw her from the roof just like that pebble earlier. With as little thought or conscience.

Just before his hands could touch Zoe's slim arm, though, Allie reached him. Bending low as she'd been trained, she let her weight and her speed drive her shoulder into his abdomen. Knocking him off his feet.

Even as she hit him, though, she was pulling back, reaching for Zoe who, wide-eyed with surprise, grabbed her hand in a move that was pure instinct.

Gabe reached for her, too, grappling for anything to hold on to as he tumbled backwards.

But she was just out of his reach. His fingers caught only air.

There was nothing to hold him back. No one to pull him from the edge.

In the bright, cold moonlight, his confused gaze locked on to Allie's for what seemed like forever but must have been a fraction of a second.

Then, with a look of utter surprise, he fell from the edge of the high, slate roof, disappearing into the night with no more sound than a rush of wind.

Twenty Six

Allie wouldn't let go of Zoe's hand.

They sat in Isabelle's office, surrounded by a hubbub of frantic activity – guards and teachers all shouting and arguing.

A nurse had come down from the infirmary to clean and bandage her neck wound. Allie was still as a stone as she worked. Dazed and unaware. When the nurse gave her an injection, Allie barely noticed the sting.

All she knew was Zoe's slim, small hand, warm and alive in her own.

For a while, Zoe endured this contact, her emotionless face puzzled but polite. After a while, though, she leaned towards Allie.

'You're hurting my hand.'

It took everything in Allie to let go. But she did.

Zoe flexed her fingers and tightened them into a fist. Deciding Allie hadn't done lasting damage, she beamed at her.

'I have to go tell Lucas what happened. He won't believe it.'

She was gone in an instant – a bullet of energy shooting through the crowded room.

'There you go.' The nurse bustled around her, gathering

her supplies into a black plastic case. 'All done.'

Isabelle left a cluster of teachers to join them. She rested a hand on Allie's shoulders.

'How is she?'

'Stitched back together again.' The nurse sounded disapproving, as if it was Isabelle's fault this had happened. 'The cut wasn't deep and the knife hit no major arteries, thank goodness.' She closed her bag with a snap. Her lips were stretched tight, as if holding back many unflattering words. 'I've given her an injection as you instructed.'

'Thank you, Emma.' Isabelle's voice was measured. 'My apologies for dragging you out of bed.'

'I'm used to it,' the nurse said sourly before marching away, her green scrubs swishing.

Isabelle sighed and glanced down at Allie.

'Are you in much pain?' She brushed a fingertip against the bloodstained collar of her blouse. The gesture was subtle but tender.

Allie, who couldn't seem to feel much of anything, ignored the question.

'Isabelle, promise me Gabe's really dead. You're sure?' She'd already asked this question many times. She couldn't seem to stop herself asking it again.

She hadn't seen the body – no one would let her. She'd heard, faintly, the concussion when it hit. And the commotion that arose four storeys below.

But she couldn't see anything. She'd nearly tumbled after him, pulled by her own forward motion. But Zoe had held onto her arm with a relentless grip, using her entire weight to pull her back to safety, digging her heels against the hard tiles.

By the time they'd climbed down, the school was in

uproar. Guards surrounded the body. Students had been ordered into the common room. Teachers and guards ran everywhere searching for other intruders.

Cimmeria was in lockdown now – no one allowed in or out. On some level, everyone knew it was futile. The place was too big to fully secure. They could find every hole, close every gate. But a ten-foot fence couldn't keep out someone absolutely set on getting in.

Gabe and Nathaniel kept proving that.

Still, they had to try.

'He's really dead,' Isabelle said. 'I swear it.'

She lowered herself into the leather chair next to Allie's.

'What happens now?' Allie looked down at her bloodstained hands. 'Should we call the police…?'

'Of course not.' The headmistress cut her off, her expression indicating the suggestion was absurd. 'His body will be… taken care of.' She leaned forward to catch Allie's gaze. 'No one will ever know what happened. It's all been arranged. Please don't worry about that.'

It didn't make Allie feel any better to know she'd never face justice. Because that also meant no judge would ever hear her side and exonerate her for what she'd done. It would always sit on her conscience – a horrible secret she could never share with anyone.

She didn't feel guilty, exactly. On some level she could completely vindicate her actions – self-defence, protecting Zoe – but that didn't make Gabe any less dead.

I've killed a human being. Even though it had just happened, the fact was impossible to fathom. How would she feel in a year? A decade?

By then she probably wouldn't believe it herself.

Her neck was stiff from the cut and the bandages. She couldn't turn her head without burning pain. Whatever the nurse had given her was making it hurt less, but it was also making her feel fuzzy. The edges had begun to blur.

Isabelle kept talking, explaining what the teachers were doing. The guards. But Allie found it hard to focus. Her gaze wandered, taking in the teachers, their faces creased with worry, and the guards. She wanted to ask something, but she couldn't seem to form the question.

She felt warm all of a sudden, and very tired. Her eyelids had begun to droop.

What did that nurse give me?

'I can't…' She tried to tell Isabelle what was happening, but the words were slurred.

'You need to rest.' Through a tired haze, Allie saw Isabelle motion to two guards. One was a woman, her hair in a long, blonde braid that hung down her back like rope. Allie thought she knew her from somewhere.

'Take her upstairs,' the headmistress instructed. 'The nurse gave her a tranquiliser and I don't think she should walk. I'll come with you to clean her up.'

A tranquiliser?

'Up you get.' The male guard put his arm under her shoulders and gently lifted her to her feet. But her knees felt oddly unstable; soft as custard.

She sank slowly towards the floor.

'Oopsy daisy.' He swept her up in one smooth move – one arm beneath her knees, and another behind her back.

She blinked at him blearily. Like the woman, he looked familiar. Pale hair and kind eyes. But her brain wouldn't work. Every thought seemed like such hard work.

It was easier to close her eyes.

'It's time to go sleepybye…' he said heading towards the door. And the words floated over her head like birds.

Allie woke in her own bed. The shutter had been closed over the arched window, but bright daylight bled through the cracks around it.

She needed to know what time it was, how much time Carter had left, but when she turned her head to look at the clock the wound on her neck stung like fire and she groaned, rolling back.

It all came rushing back. Zoe. Gabe.

It was like waking into a nightmare.

With effort she managed to sit up, and turn her body, holding her neck stiff.

Befuddled, she looked down at her clothes. She was in her pyjamas – the blood was gone from her hands. Someone – Isabelle she guessed – had cleaned her up and changed her clothing, which was unpleasant to think about. But she had no memory of it at all.

Whatever the nurse had given her had knocked her out cold.

Every movement hurt, but she put her feet on the floor and stood slowly, her breath hissing between her teeth.

She moved slowly, gathering her shower things, and then headed down the hallway. In the empty bathroom, she showered carefully, struggling to keep the bandage dry and failing, generally.

Afterwards, she brushed her teeth, studying herself in the mirror. Her grey eyes were sober. Aside from the bandage on her neck, the night had left no visible marks.

A stranger would never know she'd killed a man.

After hurriedly dressing, she made her way downstairs. The school looked exactly the same – elegant high ceilings and polished wood, marble statues and crystal chandeliers. Everything just where it should be.

But with each step Allie was conscious that *she* had changed. She felt different. As if she'd aged ten years overnight.

No one ever deserved to die more than Gabe. But she was not a judge and jury. The seriousness of what had happened could not be ignored. Everything might be covered up – all the evidence hidden away forever – but she would always know what she'd done.

The ground floor was busy – students, guards and instructors filled the common room. Allie turned right by and headed for Isabelle's office.

Her office door was closed, but Allie could hear voices within.

She knocked sharply on the oak door, carved with an elaborate pattern of acorns, leaves and fruit, as familiar to Allie now as her own hands.

'Come in.'

The door swung open.

Isabelle was leaning back in her chair, her mobile to her ear. When she saw Allie, she straightened abruptly.

'I'm sorry, Dom,' she said, 'Allie's here. I have to go.'

Setting the phone down on her desk, she hurried to where Allie stood.

'How are you feeling?' Her critical gazed swept across

Allie as if looking for new damage.

'You drugged me.' Allie shot her an accusing look. 'I feel drugged.'

'I'm sorry.' The headmistress spoke without a hint of apology in her tone. 'You were exhausted and in shock.' She motioned for her to enter. 'Come in. Sit.'

'How long was I out?' Allie asked. 'How much time is left?'

Isabelle didn't ask what she meant. 'Seventeen hours,' she said.

Allie's breath caught. No time at all. Not even a day.

'Why did you drug me?' she said, fighting to control her temper. 'I was out *six hours*. I could have helped.'

'Come on, Allie.' Isabelle's tone was even. 'You were no good to anyone last night. You still look wobbly. Now, please.' She gestured at a chair. 'Sit.'

Allie didn't want to admit she needed to sit down but she did feel light-headed. Reluctantly, she did as she was told.

The headmistress bustled to the corner of the room where she kept the kettle. Allie tried to focus on the job at hand. But the residual drugs in her blood made her brain sluggish.

'Has anything happened since last night?' she asked.

Isabelle shook her head. 'There's nothing new. The feed to Carter is still down. Raj has been out at the farm most of the night.'

She poured hot water into cups, steam rising in a cloud. Allie watched her for a moment, gearing up for the next question.

'Does Nathaniel know? About Gabe, I mean?'

The headmistress handed her tea in a white mug with the Cimmeria crest on the side in midnight blue.

'His absence has been noticed.' Isabelle walked around the

desk to her chair and sat down. 'It doesn't appear they have any idea what happened to him.'

Neither of them used the 'D' word.

Allie took a sip of tea. It was sweet and strong.

She made herself think about how Gabe had acted on the roof last night – the things he'd said about Nathaniel.

'I don't think Nathaniel knew what Gabe was up to.'

Isabelle's eyebrows winged up. 'Explain.'

Allie told her what he'd said – his criticisms of Nathaniel. 'To me, it sounded almost like he was standing up to Nathaniel.' She frowned as she thought it over. 'Defying him.'

'Interesting.' Isabelle tapped a finger against her chin. 'If Gabe acted outside of orders, Nathaniel won't be looking for him. In fact, I suspect he'll be glad he's gone. If we continue as normal, he won't know he's lost his rogue henchman. He'll still be afraid of what he might do. That could distract him.'

It was easier to think of everything from last night like this – looking at the technical side of it, the strategy. Like a giant game.

The headmistress glanced up. 'There's something else I need to tell you.'

Allie didn't like the look on her face. It was like she was gearing up for a fight.

'Raj is going to meet Owen Moran this afternoon.'

'What?' Allie set her tea cup down on the table next to her with a thud. Hot tea sloshed on her fingers. '*Raj* is going to meet him? Since when?'

'Allie, you're injured…' The headmistress sighed.

'I know I'm injured.' Allie pointed at the bandage on her throat. 'It's kind of hard for me to miss. But that doesn't mean I can't sit and *talk to a man*.'

'Don't be unreasonable, Allie,' Isabelle said evenly. 'If it went wrong you'd need to run. To fight. And you must know you're in no fit state —'

'Isabelle, enough.' Allie slammed her fist against the arm of the chair with such force the headmistress stopped talking and looked at her in surprise.

'I am fully aware I'm injured. I am also aware that makes this meeting more dangerous for me.' The headmistress opened her mouth to speak but Allie held up her hand to stop her. 'But this doesn't change the fact that I have a better chance of convincing this guy to join our side than Raj does. He knows what Nathaniel's doing is wrong. But if a security expert he doesn't trust tells him it's wrong, I think he'll swing at him. If a wounded girl tells him it's wrong… I think he'll listen.'

'Allie, it's too dangerous,' Isabelle said.

Allie held up her hands. 'And I am willing to accept the danger. Just as willing as I was last night.'

'What if *I'm* not willing?' The headmistress met her gaze defiantly.

'It's just not your decision, Isabelle,' she said. 'Not this.'

The headmistress looked stunned – as if Allie had unexpectedly betrayed her. Spots of colour rose high on the planes of her cheeks.

'I think you'll find I still run this school.' Her voice was haughty. 'You'd do well to remember that.'

'I'm sorry.' Realising she'd gone too far, Allie softened her tone. 'But you *can't* protect me, Isabelle. Not anymore. No matter how hard you try.'

'That's not true,' Isabelle said, although her expression suddenly lacked conviction.

'It *is* true. We all know it's true.' Allie brushed her

fingertips against the soft fabric of the bandage on her neck. 'Isabelle, this has to end. This whole thing. Raj can't end it. You can't end it.' She dropped her hand. 'But I can.'

'Allie.' The headmistress let out a breath. 'I want you to go too, but it's simply too dangerous. You'd have to be in a public place with this man. A place we couldn't begin to control. We have no idea if he's unstable, or even if we're right about which side he's on. We are pinning a lot on a few overheard words and a single hand gesture.'

Allie didn't back down.

'We've done more based on less,' she said.

She'd never felt more sure of herself. She had to make her understand.

'I know I'm right about Nine, Isabelle. And not because I really want to be right, or because I want Carter back so much I'm looking for a way to be right. I did the *work*. I listened to every word he said. You can research this now – find out who he is, help me understand who I'm dealing with. But I've played every second of this by the rules. Your rules. And now you have to let me finish this.'

The headmistress rested her chin on one hand, studying her with those leonine eyes. Allie knew that look well – she was making up her mind. Weighing the arguments.

'I don't like it,' Isabelle said, almost to herself.

Allie held her breath.

'But you're not a little girl, anymore. You have a right to make up your own mind – you've proved that. So I'm going to let you do this. We will do all we can to protect you, but you know perfectly well how impossible it is to control this situation. This very well could go wrong.' She paused. 'Allie, this scares me. We don't know this man at all.'

Allie could have lied. Could have pretended she had it all

under control, but she didn't. Instead, she met Isabelle's gaze, and told her the truth.

'It scares me, too.'

Twenty Seven

When Allie left Isabelle's office a short while later, she walked with new confidence. Dom and Raj were already researching Nine – or Owen, as Allie now knew he was called. They were going to meet to hear her report in an hour.

So she had just enough time to take care of something very important.

If Isabelle's fears were right and she never came back from this meeting with Nine, she wanted to be certain Rachel knew how she felt.

After a bit of searching, she found her with Nicole in the otherwise empty library, at a table stacked with enormous old books of what appeared to be maps.

The library door opened with so little sound the two didn't hear her come in. The Persian rugs that covered the floor absorbed her footsteps.

'Here's one,' she heard Nicole say as she leaned over a book nearly as big as the table beneath it. 'This looks like the right area.'

'It's very old, though.' Rachel sounded doubtful.

'Does the earth change?' Nicole purred, in her soft, French accent.

Their heads were close as they leaned over the book. Rachel's glossy curls next to Nicole's long, straight hair. Nicole's fair skin contrasted with Rachel's tawny colouring.

They looked beautiful together.

How did I miss this? I must have been blind.

Allie cleared her throat. The girls looked up in surprise.

Allie kept her gaze fixed on Rachel, whose cheeks gradually reddened, until she dropped her eyes.

It was Nicole who ran over to greet her. 'We heard what happened. Thank God you're OK.' She tilted her head to see her bandage. 'Does it hurt?'

'A little,' Allie admitted. 'But it's not too bad.'

'Good,' Nicole said. 'Zoe's been telling us about it in the most excruciating detail.'

Allie rolled her eyes. 'I'll bet she has.'

Through all this, Rachel hadn't said a word.

Allie glanced over to where she stood, her head bowed over a map.

'I'm sorry to ask, Nicole. But… would it be OK if I talked to Rachel alone for a second?'

Nicole nodded. Her expressive brown eyes were inquisitive but she didn't ask what was going on.

'Of course. I was going to get some coffee anyway. Rachel?' She glanced back at her girlfriend. 'Would you like some tea?'

Her head still lowered, Rachel just shrugged.

'Well.' Nicole flashed a sympathetic smile to both of them and left the room. The door closed behind her soundlessly.

Allie walked over to where Rachel stood staring blindly at the old book of yellowed maps. A teardrop fell onto the page in front of her.

'Rach,' Allie said, 'I'm so sorry.'

Rachel's head jerked up. Her cheeks were wet with tears.

'*You're* sorry?' she said. 'Why on earth are you sorry? I'm the one who kept things secret.' She stifled a sob. 'I'm the one…'

'I'm sorry,' Allie said gently, 'because I have been such a self-absorbed arsehole, I didn't notice this huge thing happening in your life. I was too busy worrying about my own stupid love life to see you were dealing with things, too. Really important things. I'm sorry because I'm such a crap friend. You deserve so much better. I seriously do not understand why you hang out with me.'

Rachel shook her head hard, her jaw set.

'No, Allie. Stop it. I'm the crap one. I kept trying to tell you about me and Nicole… but I just… bottled it. I don't know why.' She brushed the tears from her cheeks with the side of one hand. 'I was just scared, I guess.'

'Scared of what?'

Rachel held up her hands. 'Scared it would change our friendship. Scared you wouldn't feel the same way about me. I kept thinking maybe everything would be different if you knew. Like… What if I hugged you and you… I don't know. Pulled away.' She took a sobbing breath. 'I didn't want anything to change with us.'

Allie's throat tightened with unshed tears. She didn't know how to reply to this. How to tell Rachel that she should never be afraid of losing her. She didn't care who else Rachel loved as long as she still loved her. As long as they were still friends.

Lost for words, she let her actions speak for her. She walked around the table and, grabbing Rachel by the arms, pulled her into a fierce hug.

'I want you to hug me forever,' she said, crying now, too.

'And I want you to trust that I will always hug you back. Because I swear I will. I swear it.'

Her face buried in Allie's hair, Rachel clung to her.

'I'm sorry,' she kept saying. 'I'm sorry.'

This time Allie did know what to say. 'You have nothing to be sorry for.'

Dom pulled a stack of printed photos from her file folder and handed one to Isabelle, who sat at her desk, and another to Allie.

'Meet Owen Moran, thirty-one years old,' Dom said. 'Number Nine.'

Allie stared at the photo. It showed the baby-faced man from the fence – the one who held up a hand to warn her. The picture was grainy – it looked as if it had been taken from far away and then zoomed in. But it was definitely him.

'I took that photo this morning.' Raj's voice emerged from the phone on Isabelle's desk. 'I've been following him since last night. Dom, tell them what we know.'

Dom typed something into the laptop propped on her knee. 'He was born at Liverpool General Hospital. Lived in Liverpool until he was six years old, at which point his parents divorced and his mother moved to London, where she worked as a waitress and part-time carer. His father does not appear to be part of his life after that. Mum remarried when Owen was ten, to a James Smith, long-distance lorry driver.' She glanced up at Isabelle; her glasses glittered. 'It was a bad move. They had a tough relationship.

James has a criminal record longer than we have time to read – GBH, public drunkenness… you get the picture. Police were called to their flat many times for domestic disturbances.' She scanned the screen on her laptop. 'They divorced when Owen was sixteen.'

Allie suppressed a shudder – what a horrible childhood.

Dom continued at a brisk pace. 'Owen scored well on his GCSEs, but left school at seventeen to join the Army Infantry Division. When he was nineteen he served his first mission in Iraq. He was there off and on for two years before he transferred to Afghanistan. Served with honour for two more years in Helmand Province. Numerous commendations for bravery.'

Pausing, she handed Allie and Isabelle another photo. It had been taken against the backdrop of a lush green field. Moran was opening the door of a car. He wore the plain black gear of Nathaniel's guards. He appeared to be looking directly at the photographer.

'Raj took this yesterday afternoon at St John's Fields.'

As she stared at the photo, Allie covered her lips with her fingertips.

The man's light brown hair was kept short and neat, the well-groomed stubble on his cheeks was probably there to make him look more mature – or tougher.

Her gaze was arrested by his expression. His hazel eyes held a look of bitter disillusionment so striking it took her breath away. It wasn't just in his eyes, but in the set of his shoulders, in his posture. He exuded cynicism and anger.

'While he was in the military, one incident in particular stands out.' Dom tilted her screen to see it better. 'His unit was pinned down by enemy gunfire. Moran's commanding officer was hit and killed, and his second in command badly injured.

Moran took over leadership of the unit, rescuing two wounded men, risking his own life many times, until an air unit arrived to get them out of there.' She glanced up. 'He was the last one in the helicopter. Received a medal for bravery. Then left the service.'

Isabelle nodded briskly. 'Since then?'

'Nothing striking,' Dom said. 'No criminal record. Married at twenty-six, divorced at thirty. One child, a girl…' She glanced at her screen. 'Annabelle; five years old. The mother has custody. Career history not so great – he had a few jobs but never held them for long. Mostly security work. Applied to be a police officer but his application was rejected for suspected mental issues – PTSD, apparently.' She leaned back in her seat. 'He started working for Nathaniel eight months ago.'

Allie thought about what Christopher had told her.

'Does he have debts?'

Dom shot her a surprised look. 'Loads. Couple of years ago he got behind on his child support and rent. Racked up big credit card debts. A loan was turned over to a collection agency. Within the last year, though, he's started paying everything off. All of a sudden, he's a model citizen.'

Allie suppressed a relieved sigh. So far her brother hadn't been wrong once.

'Thank you, Dom,' Isabelle said. She leaned closer to her phone. 'Raj, what's the plan?'

His voice emerged tinny but clear from the phone's small speakers. 'Moran eats every meal at a pub called the Chequers. It's not far from St John's Fields at the edge of Diffenhall. Your basic village joint, nothing fancy. None of the other guards join him, he likes to eat alone. I suggest this is where we catch him.'

Dom typed something into her computer then turned it so Allie and Isabelle could see it. 'This is the place.'

Allie leaned forward to see the image. It was a traditional looking old inn at the edge of a country road. Vines grew up the walls and over the roof.

'Last night he had dinner there before six o'clock. I suspect he goes early because he likes it empty. Here's the plan: I'll place six of my guards in there, sitting two to a table. Allie will remain with a separate team outside until Moran enters the establishment. Once he's inside, I will contact her team by radio. Allie…' She sat up straight. '… you are to walk in and go directly to his table. How you handle this moment is up to you. I suggest you quickly introduce yourself, using your real name and identity, and do not ask permission to sit. Take control of the situation from the start. Isabelle can go through this with you.'

His tone was the same cool, efficient one he used when briefing his guards.

'You will have no more than two and possibly less than one minute to make your case,' he continued. 'You need to have your facts lined up and your offer ready. You must not hesitate. State your case and make your points and, only when you have done so, give him the opportunity to ask questions. I believe he will have quite a lot of questions under the circumstances.' He took a breath. 'So you must be ready with answers.'

The sound of a car engine roaring by, momentarily drowned him out. He'd explained at the start of the call that he'd parked on a layby not far from the farmhouse. She waited until the noise faded.

'I'll be ready,' she assured him.

She tried to sound confident, although nervousness had settled on her chest like a weight.

Nine was a grownup. A veteran. He'd had a life so tough it made her own look like a cake walk by comparison. Why would he listen to some pampered teenager from a private boarding school?

Why should he pay any attention to her at all?

Somehow, she had to reach him. She had to make him listen. For Carter. For herself.

For everyone.

'I'm glad to hear it,' Raj said after a long beat. 'Because this is the only chance we get at this. Isabelle and I have both made it clear we're worried about this plan. You're in no condition to fight. If he takes against you, I will do all I can to help. But this is dangerous, Allie. There's no way around that fact. Moran is a highly trained ex-soldier. He could kill you in an instant. I suggest, if you start to believe he's going for you, you run.'

Allie swallowed hard – the wound on her neck gave a twinge, as if to remind her it was there.

'I understand,' she said, her voice steady.

Isabelle shook her head but didn't argue with her.

'Good,' Raj said. 'Now, let's go over it again. From the beginning.'

Twenty Eight

The Chequers Inn sat at the edge of a village so tiny, it was really little more than a crossroads.

The inn had to be very old, Allie thought, as she waited in the back seat of the SUV parked a short distance down the road. Its stone walls were pitted and worn with age. Its windows were tiny, as windows all used to be in the days before glass became plentiful and cheap. A flowering vine grew up one wall and over the top of the roof.

Aside from the inn and a village green surrounded by a low, stone wall, there were only a few thatch-roofed houses, so picturesque and charming they might have been made of gingerbread.

From there, the land sprawled out into farms, hedgerows and rolling hills.

It was quiet. They'd been out here ten minutes, parked in the shade of an oak tree at the edge of the green, and not a single car had driven by since they arrived.

In the front seat, Zelazny talked into his mobile phone. The driver sat next to him, eyes on his watch.

They'd planned as much as they could. Now they had to wait.

Raj was at St John's Fields, waiting for Nine to leave. If he'd stuck to the same schedule as yesterday, he'd be here by now. But he hadn't kept to that schedule, and now everyone was trying to decide what to do.

Come on, Nine, Allie thought. *Just show up.*

She bit nervously on the edge of her increasingly ragged thumbnail. If he didn't come tonight, the whole plan was thrown into disarray. They had eight hours left on Nathaniel's clock. *Eight.*

At one in the morning, it would all be over.

Nine had to show.

Two escort vehicles were nearby – one a short distance behind them. Another some way ahead.

They must have gone over the plan a hundred times throughout the day. Up to, and including, role-playing, with Dom playing Owen Moran, sitting at a table telling Allie to go to hell.

Her opening lines, her polished answers to his inevitable questions, were drilled into her memory. They hadn't left the school until Isabelle decided she was ready. The answers they'd worked on rolled off her tongue more easily than her own thoughts.

Now she just needed someone to say them to.

She glanced at her watch – it was twenty minutes to six. Maybe he wasn't going to show at all.

The driver glanced at Zelazny. 'I'm stepping outside to keep watch. Just in case.'

The history teacher gave a sharp nod. 'Understood.'

The driver stepped out, shutting the door behind him gently, as if he didn't want to disturb the stillness. Allie stared through the car window at the picture-perfect village around them. It was so green and tiny. So tranquil. It didn't seem possible such a place could exist.

She could understand why a war veteran might come here every day to sit by himself and observe such peace.

'Are you ready?' Zelazny's voice broke the silence as he turned in his seat to face her.

'I hope so,' she said.

'You are,' he assured her. 'You keep a cool head when things get dangerous – that'll see you through this.'

Allie studied the back of his head curiously. There'd been a time when she loathed Zelazny. For a while, she'd even suspected he was Nathaniel's spy.

But things had changed. He'd fought relentlessly for her and Lucinda. He hated Nathaniel and everything he stood for. And he loved Cimmeria Academy the way some men love their country – with a kind of religious fervour.

She didn't doubt for a minute she could trust him completely. It meant a lot that he had faith in her.

'Thanks,' she said. 'I'll do my best.'

Time ticked by.

It was so quiet that when Zelazny's phone buzzed, they both jumped. Muttering to himself, he pushed the answer button.

'Zelazny,' he barked.

He listened for a minute as the caller spoke. Allie held her breath; her heart thudded so loudly in her ears she was sure he'd hear it in the front seat.

'Copy that.' Shoving the phone back in his pocket, he turned to look at her.

'Get ready. He's on his way.'

Allie's hand shook as she pushed open the heavy wood door of the Chequers. She tried to keep her expression serenely disinterested. As if she came here every day at precisely this time.

But her knees felt unsteady as she stepped inside.

A wave of warmth and scent hit her – frying meat, spices. A rumble of conversation filled the air.

It was just after six o'clock, and the dining room was half full.

Normally she'd have noticed what a lovely old place it was – thick columns and a low, beamed ceiling, a gigantic fireplace on one wall, with iron cooking pots hung around it for decoration.

But she was focused on a man sitting near the window, his light brown hair short and neat, just as it had been the other night.

Nine was here. And he hadn't seen her yet.

A huge man in an apron bustled by carrying two plates.

'Sit anywhere you like, luv,' he said in a thick Hampshire accent. 'I'll be with you in a thrice.'

Allie's lips tried to form the words 'Thank you' but couldn't quite manage it.

Silently ordering her legs to work properly, she made her way across the stone floor towards Nine.

He sat with a cup of tea in one hand, his eyes fixed on some green point outside.

Music played quietly in the kitchen – interchangeable pop songs Allie barely knew after so long without access to a radio.

At one table she recognised two of Raj's guards, disguised, as she was, in jeans and unremarkable pullovers. Neither met her gaze.

Raj himself sat at the back of the room, a pint on the table in front of him, newspaper spread out, apparently absorbed. But she knew he'd be watching everything.

The thought was heartening, and she hurried her pace.

Too soon she stood in front of Moran's table, the words she'd memorised the night before circulating in her head as if on a loop. He hadn't seen her yet – or was hoping she'd go away.

'Mr Moran?' Her voice was low but clear. Steady as a rock.

His head turned slowly until he was looking at her, his hazel eyes tinged with disbelief.

Her heart stuttered.

He recognised her.

When he spoke, though, he gave nothing away. 'Do I know you?'

The low, gravel voice was much more familiar than the face.

'Kind of.' Without waiting for an invitation, she slid into the seat across from him.

Strike fast, Raj had said. *Use honesty as your weapon.*

'My name is Allie Sheridan. Nathaniel would like you to kidnap me. I'm here to tell you why you shouldn't.'

'You must be joking.' Moran's face darkened. 'What the hell are you playing at?'

'I'm not playing,' Allie assured him. 'I'm deadly serious.'

As she talked she watched him closely. He didn't look happy to see her but he wasn't lashing out, either. Mostly he appeared irritated.

'We're in a difficult position, Mr Moran,' she said, words that were not her own rolling out with perfect smoothness. 'You should know that most of the people in this room are here to protect me. I've told them I believe we can trust you. That you're not like Nathaniel and Gabe. They think I'm wrong. They think you'll do something to hurt me. I hope you'll prove them wrong and just hear me out.'

He shook his head, slowly lowering it to his hands. 'Why does this kind of thing always happen to me?'

Allie decided to ignore this.

'I know you can't be seen with me. But I need two minutes,' she said. 'Give me one hundred and twenty seconds to convince you. Then if you want to run to your car and report this to Nathaniel, you can. We'll be gone before he gets here.'

He let out a long sigh. For the first time since she'd sat down across from him, he met her gaze directly.

'Please, kid. Give me some credit. If I wanted you to stay here you'd never leave.'

The thin skin of ice on his voice sent a chill of fear down Allie's spine.

She tried not to show it. 'Does that mean you'll listen?'

'First I want you to answer some questions for me.' Rocking back on his chair, he crossed his arms, studying her with disconcerting intensity. 'How did you find me? No, wait.' He held up one hand before she could reply. '*Why* did you choose me in the first place? There are other guards you could have chosen to approach. I'm not exactly top of the pack.'

'We've been monitoring your communication for some time,' she said.

If this revelation surprised him he didn't let on – his expression was steady as she continued.

'I listened to all of you. I know Gabe Porthus was called Number One. You're Number Nine.' She paused. Raj had given her specific lines to say now, but she decided not to use them. Instead, she said it in her own words. 'You seemed sane to me. The best of them all.'

He barked a humourless laugh. 'If I seemed sane to you,

you've got a problem, sister.'

She didn't smile. 'The other night, you warned me. When Nathaniel was about to grab me.'

His smile faded. 'I'd have done that for anyone.' His tone was brusque.

'It was my choice to come here today. My idea to talk to you. To ask for your help. To offer to help you.' She leaned forward. 'The people from my school don't think we can trust you. But I do.'

For an endless moment he held her gaze.

When he finally spoke he picked up on one part of what she'd said. 'How the hell can you help me?'

His eyes flickered across her face. It was a diminishing look. As loudly as if it he'd shouted it, the look said, '*You are just a kid.*'

'I can help you,' she said evenly, 'by getting you away from Nathaniel. And I have already helped you by getting rid of Gabe.'

'Getting rid of…' He stared. 'What does that mean, exactly?'

Allie brushed back her hair to reveal the bandage on her throat.

'Last night Gabe attacked me,' she said. 'He tried to kill me and another girl. A good friend of mine. I…' *Killed him.* 'He didn't survive.'

Moran had been stretched back in his chair. Now, slowly, he straightened.

'You're trying to tell me *you* killed Gabe Porthus? You?'

'Yes.'

'So that's why the bugger disappeared.' Moran ran his hand across his jaw. His whiskers rasping against his fingers. 'No loss to society, I have to say. But…' He met her gaze again, his eyes narrow. 'Do you really expect me to believe someone your size – some posh kid like you – killed someone like Gabe? I'm not sure I buy it. The guy was a tosser, but he could fight.'

'I can fight, too,' Allie said. It wasn't a boast.

Her two minutes must have been up by now but neither of them cared. The news about Gabe had clearly thrown him.

Whatever he'd expected from her when she walked up, it hadn't been this.

'What'd he do to you?' he gestured at her bandage.

'Stabbed.'

He didn't look surprised.

'There was something wrong with that guy,' he muttered mostly to himself. 'Something fundamentally wrong.'

Allie couldn't argue with that.

'How did you kill him?' His gaze was piercing.

Allie swallowed hard, her throat suddenly dry. She hadn't said it aloud to anyone yet.

'I pushed him off the roof.'

His eyebrows shot up.

But all he said was, 'Creative.'

The big man from the kitchen bustled towards them, a plate in his towel-draped hand.

''Ere you go, mate.' He set the plate piled high with pie and mash in front of Moran and glanced at Allie. 'What can I get you, luv?'

She didn't want to ask for anything, but nerves had dried her throat. 'Could I just get a glass of water for now, please?'

''Course you can, luv.'

They both waited as he walked away. When he was out of earshot, Moran took a bite of his potatoes, watching her speculatively as he chewed.

'So what are you asking for, tough girl? And what do you have to offer?'

'Please call me Allie,' she said. 'I'd like to offer you your freedom.'

He choked. Sputtering, he grabbed his mug and took a swallow of tea.

He wiped his mouth with his napkin, studying her with bemusement.

'My *freedom*? Last time I checked I was already free.'

The big man was coming back with a glass of water in his hand. Allie didn't respond until he'd set it down and gone again. Then she leaned towards Moran.

'I believe Nathaniel has control over you through your finances. I know you had a hard time after you came back from the war. I know you've struggled and got into trouble. I know you want to do what's best for your little girl. And I suspect you think the best thing you could do is take Nathaniel's money and give it to her. I think you think this job is your only option after everything you've been through. That Nathaniel is the only person who will hire you.'

Moran's fork hung suspended in the air, halfway between his plate and his mouth. He'd stopped eating. Stopped everything. She couldn't see him breathe.

She continued with increasing confidence. 'I want you to know that you're wrong. There are other people who would hire you, pay you very well, and do whatever they could to help you. My people would do that. They can and they will. They won't make you compromise on your principles, or give up on mankind, or whatever it is you have to do to get up every single day and go work for Nathaniel St John. Who wants to ruin the world.'

His expression was too complicated to read but she was sure she had him.

She was wrong.

'How the hell do you know so much about me?' His expression was pure, cold resentment.

'Wait… I don't…' Allie stuttered. It was hard to talk when he was looking at her with loathing. 'We're good at what we do,' she said, after a second. 'We did our research.'

'You people. You're as bad as him, you know that?' His voice was low and threatening. 'You've got money so you think you've got the right to do whatever you want. Say whatever you want. You may just be a kid but what the hell are they teaching you at that school? That it's just fine to go through someone's bins? Where do you get off invading my privacy? Where do you get off trying to buy me?'

She kept trying to speak but he slammed his hand on the table.

'I think you need to leave. You're not safe with me right now.'

Twenty Nine

'Wait.' Allie held up her hands, panic rising in her chest. 'We just had to know who you were before we came to you. It wasn't like that. What if you were a murderer or… something?'

'From the sounds of it, *you're* the murderer, kitten,' he growled. 'And if you've looked at my records you know I've killed a fair few people myself.'

Every muscle in his body was tense. She kept looking at his hands, which rested flat on the table. They looked strong – dangerous.

From the corner of her eye, Allie saw Raj had set his newspaper down and was watching them closely. Until that moment she'd almost forgotten he and the others were there.

She let out a breath.

'That was war,' she said quietly. 'Not murder.'

She didn't specify which of them she was talking about.

Nine was unmoved. 'Call it whatever you want, kitten. Killing's killing.'

'Then we're both murderers,' she said.

It felt strangely liberating to say that. How odd that it was so easy to confess her crime to the only person who really understood – somebody else who'd done the same thing.

'Just… please don't think I'm as bad as Nathaniel,' she said. 'I'm not. I want to do good things with my life. I want to help people. I don't want to spend my life making my money. I want to spend my life doing good work. Being useful. Changing things.'

They were completely off-script now. She was winging it. Which was exactly what Raj had warned her not to do. None the less, her instincts told her Moran would see right through their carefully prepared lines. He seemed to have an instinct for honesty.

So honesty was what she'd give him.

'I want you on my side,' she continued. 'But if you don't want to be on my side, if you want to keep working for Nathaniel, that's fine, too. You don't owe me anything. I just don't understand it. Because I know you hate him.'

He studied her for a long minute, as if making up his mind about her.

'How do you know I hate him?'

He picked up his fork again. Allie took a long, relieved breath. And hoped he wouldn't stab her with it.

'Look, don't freak out at me, but I've spent hours listening to you talk about him,' she said. 'I think you hate him as much as I do.'

He chewed his food thoughtfully, swallowing before he answered.

'He's as mad as a box of badgers, that much I'll allow you.'

Allie's lips twitched. 'That's a nice way of putting it.'

Moran turned his attention to his plate – he didn't speak again for a few minutes. Allie suspected this was a tactic to throw her off, but she didn't try to interrupt his meal.

He ate with mechanical thoroughness. Fast. Not messy, just efficient. Like a soldier.

When he'd finished, he pushed his plate away and picked up his mug of tea.

'I didn't know what he was on about that night,' he said. 'Some papers he wanted you to sign. Something crazy like that. I think he might have killed you if he got his hands on you.' He took a sip of tea. 'Just didn't want to have to clean up the mess.'

'He was asking me to sign away my rights to him,' Allie explained. 'My legacy from my family. From my grandmother. She left it to me. He wants it. I don't want it, but I won't give it to him.'

It was a miscalculation.

'Family money.' He spit the words out. 'You rich people, squabbling over who gets how many millions. Living in your mansions. You don't have a clue. You're just a kid and look at you.' He thrust a finger in her direction. 'Already fighting over money. Clawing each other's eyes out. Using working people like we're not humans, too.'

Allie flinched. She was beginning to worry this wouldn't work at all. His rage always seemed to be simmering, just beneath the surface. She had to do something to win his trust.

'It's not the money I want,' she insisted. 'I've never been rich. Don't you see? This isn't about money. It's about power.'

He watched her narrowly. 'Explain.'

'There is a group of people who run things. The government, the courts. Not directly – you couldn't find them if you wanted to. But they're there. My grandmother was one of them until she died. Nathaniel is too, now. He wants the power she had. If he gets it…' She shook her head. 'I don't even know what he could do. You know he's crazy. I know he's crazy. I just…' She exhaled slowly. 'I want to stop him. Then I want to get away from him. I want…' She picked up her water. 'I want to live a little while longer.'

He didn't speak immediately. Seconds ticked by. Everyone in the restaurant seemed to have gone quiet. The big cook had disappeared, presumably into the kitchen. It was as if the whole building held its breath.

A complex array of emotions crossed Moran's face. Resignation. Worry.

At last he sighed. 'What do you want me to do? Tell me that, then I'll tell you my decision.'

It was what she'd been waiting for. Allie leaned forward eagerly.

'Nathaniel's holding a friend of mine. A boy. His name is Carter West. He's locked up somewhere in that farmhouse right now.'

Moran's unsurprised expression told her he knew all about it.

'I need you to unchain him,' she said. 'And get him out of the building. Tonight.'

'Oh,' he said. 'Is that all? I thought it might be hard or something.' His tone was sardonic. 'Jesus Christ, kid. You don't ask much, do you?' He raked his fingers through his hair. 'Even if I wanted to do that, I'm not sure I could. Nathaniel has guards watching that kid. Constantly.'

'One of those guards is you,' Allie said reasonably. 'And you know the others. How many watch him overnight?'

He held up two fingers.

'Can you get a shift tonight so that you're one of them?'

'Maybe,' he said. 'Probably. I don't know.'

He was close. Allie could tell. She nearly had him. He

didn't want to – the job was dangerous. But he would do it. If she didn't blow it.

'You know what Nathaniel's doing is wrong,' she said. 'I can tell you do. And I think you're a good person. You don't want to work for him anymore. I think you're trapped.' She leaned towards him. 'We will help you. Get Carter out of that room tonight at 1 a.m. Take him to the side door – the one leading to the stables. We will have people there waiting for you. They will get you and Carter to safety. For this, my people will pay you one million pounds. Cash.'

His jaw dropped.

'That is the deal we're offering you, Mr Moran,' she said quietly. 'We will change your life.'

If she'd punched him in the stomach he couldn't have looked more stunned. Perspiration broke out on his brow.

It took him a second to reply.

'How do I know I can trust you?'

It was a loaded question. But Allie didn't blink. 'I think you're a pretty good judge of character, Mr Moran. Do *you* think you can trust me?'

For a long moment they stared at each other across the table. Then he pushed back his chair and stood up. She couldn't read his expression.

'One o'clock,' he said. 'I'll get the kid out. I can't promise any more than that.'

It was well after seven o'clock by the time they got back

to the school.

Raj rode back to the school in the car with Allie and Zelazny so they could go over everything Nine had said. By the time they reached the front gates, they'd formulated a plan.

They had no choice but to work fast. They had less than four hours.

When the SUV stopped at the front door, they leaped out, jogging together up the front steps. Isabelle met them in the entrance hall – Raj had filled her in by phone along the way.

They ran upstairs to Dom's office, planning as they went.

Allie could never remember them working like this before – with such urgency. As if all their own lives depended on it. Not just Carter's.

When they arrived, Dom already had the maps up on the wall.

'Update?' Raj snapped as they stormed into the room.

'Nine is back at work,' Dom said. She glanced at Allie. 'He appears completely normal.'

'Any news on Carter?' Allie asked.

The American shook her head. 'Not a word from anyone.'

In a way, it was good news. If Nathaniel was suspicious of what they were planning – if he had any inkling – he'd be moving Carter, or protecting him.

'What's the plan, Raj?' Isabelle asked.

They gathered around a map. The boundaries of Nathaniel's farm had been carefully measured and marked on it.

'We leave here at midnight,' he said. 'Arriving at St John's Fields, we have thirty minutes to set up. My teams will be here, here, here and here.' Raj pointed at four locations widely spaced around the farmhouse.

'Ten vehicles will wait on this road.' He pointed to a slim

white line that ran past the front of the complex.

Allie, who had seen it on the satellite feed many times, could visualise the narrow country road.

'Isabelle and Allie will wait here.' He pointed to a location about a quarter of a mile from the farmhouse. 'They'll coordinate communication and provide backup assistance.'

Allie's heart gave a flutter of excitement. This had been decided in the car on the way over. With her injury, she couldn't run well enough to be out on the ground, but they'd agreed she could be close.

That had to be enough, this time.

'Presuming Moran does as he's said,' Raj continued, 'once Carter is secured, we separate, travelling on foot to the vehicles in multiple teams. Each team acts as a decoy for the others, in case the security system is alerted.' He glanced up. 'We need to keep them divided and confused.'

All the instructors were arriving now as word spread of their return, along with senior Night School students and a few of Raj's guards.

Raj, still dressed in jeans and the casual grey top he'd worn to the Chequers, was in his element. Confident and focused, but relaxed. Next to him, Isabelle was tense, her forehead creased with worry.

'How many guards will you take?'

'Thirty.' Raj's jaw was set. 'If we're going in, we're going in mob-handed.'

'Good.' The headmistress gave a terse nod. 'The rest will remain here, guarding the grounds.'

The plan was solid. Everything had been carefully thought out on their side, at least.

But Allie was increasingly worried about how Nine could

pull this off. He was alone against all of Nathaniel's well-trained guards.

If he failed, Carter was dead.

Raj called for questions.

'This plan relies heavily on the cooperation of one of Nathaniel's guards.' Zelazny's sharp voice cut through the low murmur of conversation in the room. 'What's your plan if this Moran sells you out? What if it's not Carter who comes to the door but thirty of Nathaniel's guards?'

It was a question he'd asked more than once in the car on the way back from the Chequers, and Raj was ready for it.

'Then we fight.' His voice was cool. 'I'm bringing ten guards into the grounds. Twenty will remain hidden just outside the fence line. If I call for backup they are to move at speed to our location.' He glanced at Isabelle. 'I estimate we could have everyone on the grounds in less than twenty seconds. I've been watching the grounds for days. There are never more than fifteen security personnel on site. We will outnumber them two to one.'

Isabelle glanced at the history teacher. 'Does that satisfy your concerns, August?'

'It will have to do,' the history teacher replied, but he didn't sound mollified. Allie knew he was worried, and she couldn't blame him.

Isabelle was already moving the conversation along, though. 'What's happening on the ground now, Raj? Dom?'

'I have ten guards at various locations surrounding the farm – they've been there all day,' Raj said. 'They report normal activity. Nathaniel is not believed to be inside the house. He was seen to leave at 1600 hours. He has not returned. The house is quiet.'

Dom added, 'Comms are normal at this time – no sign

Moran's warned them what we're planning.'

Isabelle glanced at Raj. 'Is there anything you need?'

He shook his head. 'The vehicles are being fuelled and prepped now. We leave at midnight.'

The room had gone still. Everyone knew how important this moment was. Everyone knew what was at stake.

Isabelle turned to face the crowd, which now filled the converted classroom and spilled into the hallway. It seemed every person in the school had come to see what was happening.

'This is a crucial operation.' Her voice was strong but tinged with sombreness. 'Our future depends on what happens tonight. Once we have Carter back, we can begin to plan our next steps as a school. As a *family*. For we are the family of Cimmeria Academy. This is our home.' For a brief second her gaze met Allie's. They both knew how short-lived this home could be. 'I think we all realise it's time to end this battle with Nathaniel once and for all. But we cannot do that until all our people are safe.'

She turned to Raj.

'Bring Carter home. We're counting on you.'

Thirty

The planning continued into the night.

When Allie finally slipped outside for a breath of fresh air just after eleven o'clock, ten black cars were already parked on the long gravel drive. Waiting.

It was a cool, clear night, with a hint of autumn in the air. The moon hung low on the horizon, casting just enough light to see, but not enough to reveal what needed to remain disguised.

A perfect night for hiding, she thought.

It was so strange, what her life had become. She'd been Allie Sheridan, trouble-maker, angry girl. And now she was Allie Sheridan, heiress, fighter, rebel.

She wasn't entirely certain how she'd got from there to here. It happened so fast.

With a sigh, she lowered herself down to the top step and pulled up her knees, wrapping her arms around them. She wondered if Carter could see the moon from his room in that farmhouse. If he knew they were coming.

If he believed in her as much as she believed in him.

She didn't know how long she'd been there, lost in her thoughts, before a familiar French-accented voice broke the silence.

'Are you afraid?'

Sylvain stood in the open doorway. The light framed him from behind, adding hints of gold to his wavy, brown hair.

Allie's heart lurched.

He kept his eyes on the sky.

'A little,' she confessed.

It was a lie. In reality, her stomach was tied in knots. So much hinged on this night. Everything was in the balance. Carter's life, most of all.

'Me too.' A self-conscious smile touched the corners of his lips. 'It's a dangerous plan. Maybe we're foolish to trust this man.' For the first time he met her gaze. 'But every courageous person is also a fool, no? You have to be stupid to jump out of a plane. Or climb a mountain.'

It was oddly nice to talk to him. She'd missed his accent. His oddly formal way of speaking.

I will hate it, she realised, *if we can't figure out how to be friends.*

She stood up, to be on the same level as him. 'What do you really think? Is this going to work?'

His turned his gaze back to the moon.

'I don't know. I hope so. For Carter's sake. But there's no way to know with Nathaniel involved. Everything is a game to him. And he always seems to predict our next move.'

'I just wish I understood how we got here,' she said, frustration in her voice. 'How everything got this bad.'

Sylvain stayed silent for a long moment. 'Things got bad one step at a time. The way they usually do.'

Allie wondered if they were talking about the same thing.

'Sylvain,' she said. 'I am so sorry about everything.'

He closed his eyes, his lashes soft shadows against the

planes of his cheeks.

'Don't, Allie. I don't want to talk about that. It's done.'

'I know,' she said. 'But you and I both know that, whatever happens tonight, we don't have much time left here.' She gestured at the dark grounds around them. 'We could all be split up. You'll go home to your family. I'll go wherever Isabelle goes. Our lives are going to change. Who knows when we'll see each other again?' She took a step towards him. 'I know we broke up but… I don't want to lose you from my life. I will always be your friend. If you let me.'

He let out a long breath and turned his eyes back to the moon.

'Allie, I don't…' His voice trailed off.

She held out her hand to him. He dropped his gaze to it, hesitating for a long time before finally taking her hand in his strong, steady grip.

Allie fought back a sudden urge to cry for both of them. For Cimmeria. For Jo. For everything that had been lost in the last two years.

'I am so, so sorry I hurt you,' she said, her voice low. 'Please be my friend.'

He pulled back. For a second she thought he would say nothing. That he'd just walk away. But then, as so often was the case, he did exactly what she hadn't expected. He leaned close and brushed his lips against her cheek, light as feathers.

'*Toujours*,' he whispered in French.

And then he was gone.

She spun around just in time to see him disappear inside, his back straight, walking fast into the light.

At midnight, Allie followed Isabelle and Raj down the wide hallway to the front door.

Outside, a crowd of black-clad guards waited. Among the faces looking up at them, Allie spotted Zelazny and Eloise, and, in the back, Sylvain, Nicole and Lucas.

Allie was to stay with Isabelle in the control car – thanks to the stitches in her neck, she couldn't go into the grounds with the others. Being nearby would have to be enough. Zoe had been forbidden to accompany them. She was upstairs in Dom's office with Rachel – sulking.

As soon as their boss appeared in the doorway, the group snapped to attention.

Raj paused, surveying his team with cool assessment.

'You're trained. You're ready.' His gaze was predatory as he looked out at them. 'Let's roll.'

The low, ominous roar that came back from the group made the fine hairs on the back of Allie's neck rise. It was a bloodthirsty sound.

With swift efficiency, the group divided into the cars. Seconds later, the rumble of powerful engines filled the air.

Allie and Isabelle climbed into the back of a black SUV. The driver nodded to acknowledge their presence but, after that, kept her gaze straight ahead.

Throughout the thirty-minute journey, Isabelle sat stiffly, arms crossed, eyes straight ahead. Both of them had earpieces, connected to the comms system. Dom fed through constant updates from the team already on the ground at St John's Fields.

'Nathaniel has not yet returned,' Dom said, as they drove

down a dark country road. 'House and grounds are quiet. No activity. All appears normal.'

'Copy that.' Raj's voice responded.

The roads were nearly empty and at half past midnight they turned into a tiny country lane, bookended on both sides by high hedgerows, and slowed to a crawl. After a short distance, they pulled off the road.

The driver cut the engine.

In the sudden quiet, Allie could hear the other two women breathing, and the ticking of the cooling car engine.

'Where's the target from here?' Isabelle's voice broke the silence.

The driver pointed across the dark, adjacent field to a cluster of lights a short distance away.

'Those lights are the farmhouse,' she said.

Allie stared at the light cluster, trying to guess how far away it was. It was hard to tell in the dark, but she figured she could probably get there in ten minutes, running fast.

Isabelle pressed her microphone button. 'Control in position.'

Raj's voice crackled through Allie's headphones. 'Alpha Group in position. Lima Group, state your status.'

Seconds later, an unfamiliar male voice spoke: 'Lima Group in position.'

Raj responded. 'Copy that. Romeo Group, state your status.'

A female voice responded. 'Romeo Group is in position.'

'Copy that,' Raj said. And so on, through all the three groups assigned to enter the property and the three who would remain outside the fenceline.

When all had responded Raj said, 'All groups remain in

position until you receive further orders from me.'

Now, all they could do was wait.

Time seemed to stretch. Allie forced herself to breathe. Next to her, Isabelle was staring into the darkness, unblinking.

Allie kept looking at her watch. It was nearly one o'clock. Nathaniel could come back at any moment.

Come on, Nine, she thought. *Don't let us down.*

But nothing happened. Five minutes ticked by. Then ten.

Suddenly Dom's voice crackled urgently in their earpieces. 'We have action. I'm patching Nathaniel's comms through to you.'

Nine's deep, gravel voice boomed into Allie's earpiece. 'Repeat. Intrusion alarm sounding in Quadrant Nine. All personnel report to Quadrant Nine immediately. Intrusion alarm sounding.'

'Any visual?' A voice Allie thought she recognised as Six asked him.

'Negative.' Nine's reply was curt. 'I'm inside the building. I will stay behind. Everyone else report to Quadrant Nine for possible intrusion.'

Allie turned to Isabelle, eyes wide. 'What's happening? Have they spotted us?'

The headmistress kept her gaze on the lights in the field. 'This could be a decoy to get the other guards out of the way. It's not us. It can't be us. We wouldn't be spotted.'

But her hands knotted into fists in her lap.

'Copy that,' Six said after a moment. 'Heading to Quadrant Nine now. All personnel to follow.'

Raj's voice overrode Nathaniel's guards. 'Teams Romeo, Alpha, Lima, we have a *go*. Move in now. Repeat move in now. Alpha Group moving in. Others, please respond.'

Seconds later a woman's voice. 'Romeo Group, moving in.'

A man's voice followed. 'Lima Group, moving in.'

Allie squeezed her hand hard against the handle of the car door, digging her nails into the smooth plastic.

A minute passed, then: 'Romeo, Lima and Alpha Groups have reached the location.' Raj's voice was a whisper. 'No sign of target.'

Allie closed her eyes. *Please, God, let this work. Please…*

Silence fell. Then, Raj's voice broke over the speakers. 'Alpha Group, on the move.' His voice shook, as if he was running. 'We have the target. Repeat target in custody.'

Allie drew in a sharp breath and covered her face with her hands. Something held tight inside her let go.

They'd done it.

Next to her, Isabelle punched her right fist into her left hand. '*Yes.*'

'Copy that, Raj,' Dom said, and Allie could tell she was smiling. In the room with her, people were cheering.

Allie dropped back against the leather seat of the car. It was over. Carter was coming home.

Suddenly, Raj's voice appeared again. He was shouting, breathless. 'We are under pursuit. Repeat. Alpha Group on the run. All groups take evasive action…' Allie could hear him running, his voice shook with every step. 'Alpha Group…'

There was a sound like a gunshot. Then the radio went silent.

Thirty One

Allie couldn't seem to make herself breathe.

Isabelle covered her lips with her hand but showed no other emotion. She leaned forward.

The radio crackled into life when a woman spoke, breathless and clearly running.

'Romeo Group on the run.' There was a sound of gunshots, and Allie couldn't tell if they came from the radio or from the field outside. The woman was shouting, 'All groups are taking fire. Return to vehicles. Move, move, *move.*'

Panicked, Allie spun to look at Isabelle. 'We have to *do* something.'

But Isabelle was already on it. She leaned forward towards the driver. 'Start the car. Take us to St John's Fields.'

The driver shot her a surprised look. 'But my orders…'

'Your orders are to take us to St John's Fields and help our people,' the headmistress snapped.

The driver started the car.

In Allie's ears Dom's voice was insistent. 'Alpha Group, verify your location. Alpha Group, are you reading me?'

There was no reply.

They shot down the narrow road, tyres spinning. Allie

rolled down the window and stuck her head out, straining to hear anything above the engines. In the distance, she thought she heard shots. She definitely saw lights in the field, swinging wildly.

The narrow road curved and undulated sharply through the darkness; the driver took every bend as fast as the vehicle would allow.

Come on. Come on, Carter. You can do this. Run for your life. Run for me.

They rounded a turn at speed, just as a man, clad all in black, burst out of the darkness into the road.

Allie screamed. The driver slammed the brakes, throwing them forward hard and then back again. The wound on her neck throbbed.

Clearly recognising the driver, the man ran to her window.

When he saw who was in the car, the guard's eyes widened.

'Which way are they headed?' Isabelle barked.

He pointed down the road ahead of them. 'That way. I was trying to pull the guards off Raj's trail, but they ran right by me.' He held Isabelle's gaze. 'I think they know he's got the target.'

They all heard more gunshots in the distance. The guard took a step back. 'I gotta go.'

He took off running, Allie heard his voice in her earpiece. 'Lima Group unable to locate Alpha.'

Allie stared out the open window. At first, all she could see in the darkness was trees and pastures. But then, just ahead, she saw something else. A blur of motion.

'There!' She pointed. 'Someone's running.'

Isabelle looked where she indicated. Her lips tightened. 'Driver, stop the car.'

She spoke into her microphone. 'Dom, this is Control. We

can see Alpha Group from the road. We're going after them.'

Allie reached for the door handle. Isabelle gave her a look. 'Your neck.'

'My neck will survive,' Allie said, unbuckling her seatbelt.

They both leapt from the car at the same moment.

It was dark, but they were used to darkness. Side-by-side, they crashed through a gap in the hedgerow, leaping over a narrow but deep stream bed to get to the field where they'd seen the others.

Allie climbed a fence to get a view of the field. Again, she saw the oddly disconcerting blur of black clad runners moving against the night.

'There!' She pointed to the movement. The runners were heading to the right, running low and fast. It was impossible to see from here who it was. They had to hope it was Raj.

Allie and Isabelle moved quickly to intercept them.

'If we get to those trees,' Isabelle whispered, pointing to a cluster of pines, 'we can catch them. It will be easier to lose the guards with cover.'

Running in the pasture was difficult – it had been used by cows or horses, who'd left deep pits and ruts in the mud. The uneven steps jolted her, putting pressure on her stitches – her neck burned but she ignored the pain. Carter was out there somewhere. In the dark.

She could hear shouts in the distance – there'd been no gunfire for some time now, and she hoped that was a good sign.

The trees were close. She put her head down, and increased her speed.

Just as they reached the edge of the woods, though, someone grabbed her with such force her feet left the ground.

Struggling in the man's grip, she swung around, fists

raised.

It was Nine.

They stared at each other. He spoke first. 'What the hell…?'

'Let her go.' Leaping between them, Isabelle swung a perfectly targeted swing kick towards Moran's face.

'Wait!' Allie called out, as Nine dodged the blow at the last second. 'This is him. This is Owen Moran.'

Isabelle didn't move out of her defensive stance. Her eyes locked on his.

'Which side are you on, Mr Moran? Are you here to free Carter? Or to take him back?'

He held up his hands. 'Lady, I just risked my bleeding neck to get your kid out of the sodding house. Now if you'd let me run the hell away before someone blows my stupid head off, I'd appreciate it.'

'Where are the others?' Allie asked impatiently. 'Where's Carter?'

'I'm not sure – we got separated in the pasture,' he explained. 'The other guards came back sooner than I hoped. They saw us heading for the fence and took off after us.'

'So they're near.' Isabelle frowned, squinting in to the darkness. She seemed to have accepted Moran's honesty, for now, at least.

Allie still wore her earpiece; she'd been tuning out Dom's updates but now she heard her voice grow insistent. 'Control, please respond. Control: your location.'

'Isabelle,' Allie said, 'Dom's trying to reach you.'

Isabelle pressed her microphone. 'This is Control. We're in the pasture 500 metres from St John's Fields.'

'You've got to get out of there,' Dom said. 'Nathaniel's

coming back.'

Allie's heart seemed to stop. She turned to Nine before realising he couldn't hear what she'd just heard.

'Nathaniel's on his way back,' she said. 'We have to get out of here. Isabelle…' She looked at the headmistress, who shook her head.

'I'm not leaving without my people.'

'Well, seems to me, one of your people's standing right here.' Nine pointed at Allie. Seeing the looks on both their faces, he sighed. 'All I can tell you is, if I was in the position your people are in right now, I'd loop around through these woods,' he pointed at the trees behind them, 'lose the guards here and then head straight into that thicket to the main road and double back.'

The thicket he referred to was just a darker shadow against the black night –Allie hadn't even noticed it before now.

Isabelle was also studying the route he'd suggested, worried lines creasing her forehead. 'It makes sense,' she said, mostly to herself.

There was no time for discussion.

'Let's go.' Allie shot off across the small dark wood – Nine and Isabelle flanked her.

Nothing moved in the forest – there was no sign of life. Soon they were shooting across the flat grass, heading straight towards the line of thick growth Nine had indicated. They were nearly to it when Allie saw the shadows running far ahead of them.

Glancing over, she caught Isabelle's eye and pointed. The headmistress nodded.

There was no way to know if that was Raj or Nathaniel's guards, but they were nearing the road now, anyway. Isabelle pressed her microphone button and whispered into it.

'Dom, have our driver turn on the headlights.'

'On it now,' Dom replied.

A few seconds later, lights lit up the roadway in the distance.

Isabelle whispered instructions. Allie was focused on running, but she saw the lights move closer.

Behind them they heard shouts.

'Shit,' Nine muttered. He grabbed Allie's arm, pulling her low but keeping them both moving.

The crack of gunfire split the air. They increased their speed. Allie's lungs burned. She felt a trickle of warmth down her throat that was probably blood leaking from her wound. Still, she ran faster than she'd ever run, crashing through the hedgerow, ignoring the branches that sliced at her arms and legs as she leapt out into the road.

Where she ran straight into Raj.

'Raj!' she gasped the word. 'Where…?'

He pointed to the SUV waiting behind him. 'No time. Get in. We've got to get out of here.'

'Carter…' she said, panic beginning to swirl inside her. They couldn't leave him behind. Not again.

'He's safe.' He held her gaze. 'In the car.'

Allie fought back tears as she ran to the SUV. They'd come *so far*. And now they were going back without even the chance to see him.

Her vision was blurred as she jumped through the vehicle's open door and slid across into the seat by the window, leaving room for Isabelle and Nine on the seats beside her.

As she did, the guard in the front seat turned around to face her.

'Hey,' Carter said, a grin spreading slowly across his face. 'I was wondering when you'd show up.'

Thirty Two

The cars rolled into the school grounds in a triumphant procession. They arrived to find the students and teachers gathered on the front lawn in the dark, cheering.

When Carter stepped out of the SUV with Allie at his side, they roared.

Zoe launched herself at him, as Lucas patted him hard on the back.

Allie stepped back to let the others have a chance to greet him, but she never took her eyes off him. He looked OK – thin but not damaged.

He hadn't talked much on the way back. When Allie asked him how it had been, he'd gone quiet.

'They weren't much for hygiene. I'd kill for a shower,' he joked, dodging the serious undertone of her question.

But he had leaned forward to where Owen Moran had taken his original seat in the front, and held out his hand.

'I want to thank you for saving my life,' he said. 'You're a brave man.'

Moran had taken his hand with reluctance. 'I'm a stupid man,' he said. 'But you're welcome.'

Dom informed them through the comms system that

Nathaniel had reached his house about fifteen minutes after they'd departed.

'He is *not* happy,' she reported.

After the triumphant return to Cimmeria, they all gathered in Dom's office, while Raj and Carter told them everything that had happened at St John's Fields after Moran freed him.

'Everything was clockwork,' Raj said. 'We got into the grounds without a hitch. Everyone was in position. At midnight exactly, Moran opened the door and he and Carter came out.' He glanced at Allie. 'He didn't let us down. None of what happened next was his fault.'

'Tell us what happened next,' Isabelle urged Raj. 'How were you discovered?'

'It was bad luck,' he said. 'The plan called for us to cross over the fence fifty metres south of the farmhouse. The only problem was, on our way to that location, we ran straight into Nathaniel's guards, heading back from the diversion. We were almost to the fence when the firing started.' His face darkened. 'That was when all hell broke loose.'

'You disappeared from comms,' Dom pointed out. 'Scared the hell out of me.'

Raj shot her an apologetic look. 'I lost my microphone in the pasture.'

'How did you get away from them?' Zoe stared at Raj, her hazel eyes like saucers.

Carter glanced at Raj, a wry smile lighting up his face. 'We ran like hell.'

'Having the decoy groups helped,' Raj said. 'It divided and confused Nathaniel's guards. Some followed the decoys, some followed us. But we still couldn't get to the cars, so we headed into the pasture to try to lose them.' He glanced at Isabelle. 'That's where we were when you arrived.' He leaned back in his chair. 'The rest you know.'

'How did Nathaniel treat you, Carter?' Isabelle studied him with concern.

He hesitated for just a second before speaking. 'To be honest, he was nothing like I expected. Those three days when you saw me with the chains?'

She nodded.

'That was the only time it was like that. Nathaniel straight out told me he was hoping to upset you. The other days I was locked in a room. It wasn't fun but at least I wasn't chained up. The guards weren't friendly but – I wasn't beaten.'

Allie didn't know what to think. She'd been so afraid when she saw Carter chained to a wall like an animal. She was sure he'd been suffering the worst kind of torture.

'Nathaniel and his games.' Isabelle gave a tired sigh. 'He never wearies of them.'

'They did question me a lot,' Carter volunteered. 'About you.' He glanced at Allie, who sat next to him. 'And Allie.'

This caught Raj's attention. 'What kind of things did they want to know?' he asked. 'Who interrogated you?'

'Nathaniel,' Carter said. 'I never saw Gabe after the first couple of days. What happened to him? Anyone know?'

Allie flinched, tightening her grip on his hand.

'We can talk about that later,' Raj said smoothly. 'Let's talk about the interrogation first.'

'He wanted to know how often Lucinda came to visit Allie and Isabelle. How close they were. What their plans were.' He looked at the headmistress. 'He seems obsessed with the idea that you have some big plan for the Orion Group. He thinks you're plotting to undermine him. To turn his supporters against him again. He's really insecure about everything, as far as I could tell.'

Raj rubbed a hand across his jaw, his face dark with thought. 'I'd like to go over all of this with you in private.'

'But not tonight.' Isabelle stood up. 'It's nearly three in the morning. Let's get some rest and start again in a few hours. There is much to discuss.

'Let's do it with clear heads.'

Allie and Carter strolled down the wide, formal hallway towards the stairs, talking in low whispers. After they'd left Dom's office they'd let the others go on ahead. It was their first chance to be alone.

The school was so silent. It was as if they had the entire building to themselves – maybe even the whole world.

Carter looked around, taking in the faint shadowed gleam of the oak-panelled walls, the barely visible oil paintings on the walls, the heavy marble-topped tables, huge vases of roses. He sniffed the air, inhaling the faint perfume of wood smoke that always seemed to permeate the building, even in the summer.

'You know, I know this sounds stupid but… sometimes I wondered if I'd ever see this place again.' He smiled, embarrassed by his own sentimentality. 'It seemed so… far away.' He reached out, running his fingers across the walls. 'I had a lot of time to think, you know? And one day I realised this is the only home I've ever known. I was born here. Leaving it would be like… I don't know. Losing a limb.' He tilted his head to see the crystal chandelier floating above the sweeping curve of the staircase. 'It would break my heart.'

Allie's throat tightened.

She would have to tell Carter about their plans to leave. But she wouldn't tell him now. He needed time to be home. To feel safe.

'I love it here, too,' she said, meaning it.

Turning into the grand, curving staircase, they began to climb. Their steps were perfectly in sync. She kept peeking at him out of the corner of her eye. His gaze was straight ahead; he appeared lost in thought.

At the top, they stopped and turned to face each other. This was traditionally where the genders parted. Girls turned left towards the stairs to the girls' dorm. Boys turned right, towards their own quarters.

Carter looked down into her eyes. His lips curved into a wicked smile. The look in his eyes sent butterflies swirling inside her.

'Want to break the Rules?'

His room was just as she remembered it, much like hers, with an arched window above the desk, a narrow bed and desk. It had dark blue bed covers, and a white blanket was folded neatly over the foot of the bed. Someone had turned down the bed and left the bedside lamp on.

His pyjamas had been set out for him as well, along with a dressing gown and a stack of fluffy white towels.

It was just so Cimmeria, Allie thought fondly.

Welcome back from your kidnapping. Here's a soft towel.

'This is going to sound odd,' he said, his tone unexpectedly cautious, 'but would you mind if I took a shower?' He tugged at the plain grey t-shirt. 'I want to wash all the Nathaniel dirt off and just be me again.'

Allie could understand that completely.

'Go,' she said, leaning back against the desk. 'Don't worry about me. I'll just be in here and going through your stuff.'

Laughing, he grabbed a towel and his shower things.

'Happy snooping,' he said, before closing the door behind him.

As soon as he was gone, though, Allie's smile faded. Without him in it, the room felt empty. She didn't know what to do with herself.

For a while she sat in his chair, staring out the window. Because of the darkness outside, she saw mostly her own reflection.

She leaned forward, mildly horrified. Her hair was a *mess*.

She smoothed it with her fingers, getting rid of the wilder tangles.

When she didn't want to look at herself any longer, she climbed up on the empty desktop, unlatched the window and pushed it open, letting in the cool night breeze.

It was very late. But she didn't feel tired anymore. She'd never felt more awake. Her body thrummed with happiness. Carter was *home*.

They were still in trouble. The same problems they had yesterday would be there to greet them tomorrow. But she would get through them. Now that she had him back.

She sat cross-legged on top of his desk, her chin on one hand, looking out over the quiet grounds. In the distance, a night bird sang a mournful song.

Her mind flipped through all that had happened while he'd been gone. Her grandmother's funeral. Her inheritance. Rachel.

Most of all, Gabe.

Her heart twisted at the memory. She'd have to tell Carter what she'd done. What if he didn't understand? What if he looked at her differently?

Behind her, the bedroom door swung open. Allie spun around.

Carter stood in the doorway, a towel over his shoulder, his dark hair damp and curling. He wore navy Cimmeria trousers. He'd left his shirt unbuttoned, and her eyes were drawn to his finely muscled chest, the flat plane of his stomach.

Just looking at him made her pulse race.

He was perfect.

His eyes traced her face, the lines of her body.

He didn't say a word. Dropping the towel to the floor, he crossed the room in four long steps. She slipped from the desk and they met in a kiss.

It was the kiss she'd dreamed about. Longed for.

He must have dreamed of it too, because his lips were demanding. Passionate. He crushed her in his arms, pulling her tightly against him. His body was warm and shower damp.

His lips teased hers until her lips parted. He tasted of peppermint toothpaste. His soft breath filled her lungs and she never wanted to breathe anything again except him.

She pressed her hand against the warm skin of his chest and felt his heart beating beneath her fingertips. Its rhythm was strong and so fast – as fast as her own.

His eyes darkened.

'Allie,' he whispered. 'I've dreamed of this a thousand

times. Tell me I'm not dreaming now.'

The longing in his voice made her stomach muscles tighten. Something deep inside her ached when he looked at her like that.

'This is real,' she said, as much to herself as to him.

Reaching up, she ran her fingers through his damp, tangled hair, and pulled his head down until his mouth met hers again. 'Completely real.'

She couldn't seem to stop touching him. She slid her hands across his warm skin, feeling the hard definition of his muscles. The nubby line of his spine.

Taking this as invitation, he slid his hands underneath her untucked top, stroking the sensitive skin of her lower back until she gasped.

With a ragged breath, he raised his head, gazing down at her, his dark eyes fathomless.

'You are the most amazing person I have ever known,' he whispered. 'I would be held prisoner for a hundred years if I knew I'd see you at the end.'

Allie's eyes blinked back tears.

When she'd first arrived at Cimmeria Academy, she didn't believe there was one true person left in the world. Now, at last, she knew she'd been wrong.

'I love you, Carter.'

It still felt weird to say it; some part of her twisted in agony waiting for him to say it back.

He pressed his forehead against hers, looking deep into her eyes. There was nothing in his face but truth. She'd never seen anything more beautiful.

'Allie,' he whispered. 'I will love you forever.'

Thirty Three

Allie slipped from Carter's room just after dawn, leaving him sound asleep.

She hated to leave his side even for a second, but there was no way Isabelle would look favourably on this sort of extracurricular activity.

Even in days like these.

The night before they'd talked for hours. Kissed for hours. Revelled in the glorious unfamiliarity of being *together*.

He told her more about being held prisoner.

'The worst part was the isolation,' he said, running his fingertips down her shoulder. 'Some days no one talked to me at all. Twenty-four hours of silence. It messes with your head.'

He kept insisting it wasn't as bad as it sounded. But something about the way he avoided her gaze told her he was protecting her from the reality of it.

He wanted all of her news, too. When she told him about Rachel and Nicole, his eyebrows climbed.

'Are you seriously telling me you *didn't know*? Bloody hell, Allie. They were the most obvious couple I've ever seen.'

'Oh God, you knew, too?' She couldn't believe it. 'And you didn't mention it?'

'Tomorrow,' he'd said, 'remind me to point out the blue sky and the green grass and some other really obvious things.'

She'd hit him with a pillow.

Sometime later, she told him about Gabe.

They were lying in his bed, side by side. His skin was warm against hers.

He'd been dozing off as she began, but when she got to the part where Gabe appeared on the roof, his eyes snapped open.

She kept her voice steady, as emotionless as possible; still, he watched her closely as she told him how Gabe had threatened her. The icy terror she'd felt.

'I was so scared,' she whispered. 'He'd have killed Zoe, Carter. I know he would have.'

With a gentle touch, he pushed a strand of hair out of her eyes so he could see her face. 'What happened?'

She swallowed hard. 'I hit him at just the right angle, I guess. He was watching Zoe so he didn't see me coming and he just… fell.'

She didn't describe the look in Gabe's eyes – the way he reached for her as if she could save him. Or perhaps to take her with him.

She'd never tell anyone that.

But Carter seemed to know there was more than she could say. He folded her in his arms and held her tight.

'You did the right thing, Allie.' He whispered the words against her temple. And she hoped it was true.

He'd finally fallen asleep just as the sun rose. But Allie didn't want to rest.

She was in the dining hall early for breakfast, but the others were already there – Lucas and Katie, sitting next to Zoe, Rachel and Nicole sharing a plate of toast.

'There you are,' Katie said. Her green cat's eyes were knowing. 'Busy night?'

Lucas snorted a laugh and Allie flushed.

'Shut up, Katie,' she said mildly.

'No classes today,' Zoe announced, as Allie took a huge bite of eggs.

'Really?' she asked, her mouth full. Although, to be honest, actual education seemed to be the thing Cimmeria Academy was least interested in lately.

Nicole nodded. 'Planning day. So we have the day off. I think we should do something fun.'

'I think we should fight,' Zoe said.

'I think we should sleep.' Lucas winked at Katie.

Planning Day. Allie swallowed hard. She had a bad feeling she knew what Isabelle meant by that.

Carter was back. Isabelle had said they would wait until then, but once he'd returned they'd need to move fast.

She lost her appetite.

As the others talked and laughed and the sunlight filtered through the towering windows, Allie's thoughts swirled. She still hadn't told anyone – not even Carter – that they planned to leave Cimmeria. Now that the moment was here, she didn't want to go.

'What's wrong?' Rachel nudged her. 'You look like someone stepped on your grave.'

'That's a horrible saying,' Nicole chided her.

Everyone was looking at Allie now; she had to say something to explain why she looked like she'd just bitten into her own foot.

'What if…' She hesitated. 'What if we couldn't stay here?'

Zoe frowned. 'That's a stupid question.'

But the others were watching her with increasing wariness.

It was Katie who got it first.

'Here it comes,' she said quietly. Allie saw her take Lucas' hand.

'What do you mean?' Rachel asked. 'Is something happening?'

'Something has to happen,' Katie said, before Allie could speak. 'We can't keep going on like this. I've been saying that for weeks.'

'No.' Lucas shook his head, his jaw suddenly taut. 'Are you saying what I think you're saying?'

'I'm saying…' Allie took a deep breath. 'I'm saying we might not have any legal right to this building.' She tapped her hand against the heavy wood of the table. 'Even if we did, we can't keep putting people's lives in danger for it.'

Rachel was watching her closely. 'What's the plan, Allie?'

'We have options,' Allie said, although her voice sounded hopeless even to her own ears. 'There's a place in Switzerland – Isabelle says it's amazing…'

Her voice trailed off as the others exchanged disbelieving looks.

'*Switzerland...*' Lucas said, as if she'd suggested Mars.

Allie wanted to argue with them, but her heart wasn't in it. She didn't want to go, either.

'I guess it doesn't matter where we go. We just can't stay here anymore. Not like this,' she said.

'It wouldn't be the same,' Nicole said, looking at Rachel.

'Some people couldn't go,' Katie pointed out. 'Their parents won't want them to leave the country.'

'We'd be split up,' Rachel said.

Zoe, who suddenly looked miserable, frowned at her orange juice.

They'd all been so happy just moments before, and now all the joy had left the group. They were huddled together as if the end might happen at any second.

Allie hated this. Why couldn't they have even a day to be normal kids in a normal school, with their A levels the biggest obstacle ahead of them? There had to be another way. A way to keep the school *and* end this fight with Nathaniel at the same time.

She thought of Julian Bell-Howard asking her to join Orion and continue the fight. There'd been something about him – something trustworthy. He wanted the same thing she wanted, to end this. To make Cimmeria what it was again.

In the back of her mind, an inkling of an idea began to take shape. It seemed impossible but then everything seemed impossible when you first thought about it. Imagine being the person who first thought up the television.

She stood so abruptly her chair squawked against the floor. 'I've got to talk to Isabelle.'

Isabelle was in her office, reading glasses delicately perched at the end of her nose, laptop open and a stack of papers at her elbow.

'Oh Allie, good,' she said, glancing up. 'I was going to send for you.'

'I have an idea,' Allie said without preamble. 'Or kind of an idea. The beginning of an idea, anyway. And I need your help.'

Isabelle arched one eyebrow and gestured at the chairs

facing her desk.

Allie sank into the deep leather chair. Isabelle removed her glasses and reached for the cup of tea at her elbow.

Her office was as familiar to Allie as her own bedroom – maybe more so. She loved Isabelle's big, antique desk, the romantic tapestry on the wall, the creamy Persian rug that covered the floor, the way it always smelled faintly of Earl Grey tea and Isabelle's lemony perfume.

In fact, she loved this whole school building. She didn't have a lifelong connection to it, the way Carter did. He'd been born here. But she'd chosen to make it her home. She couldn't imagine not waking up and seeing the arched window, with the light flooding through it. The green grounds stretching out to the forest.

The idiosyncratic teachers. The students in their dark blue uniforms.

She loved Cimmeria Academy.

It wasn't worth dying for. But it was worth saving.

'I don't want to go to Switzerland,' Allie said, choosing her words carefully. 'I thought about it all night, and I don't want to do it. The thing is… I might have another idea.'

The headmistress set down her cup and waited for her to continue.

'The thing we wanted in Switzerland was a fresh start, right?'

Isabelle nodded, but her eyes were cautious.

'That's what made me think of it. Julian, when he was here, he was talking about the same thing – fighting Nathaniel for Orion so we could start over. What if we could have a fresh start…' she tapped the arm of her chair, 'right here.'

Isabelle was watching her narrowly. 'I don't understand

what you're getting at.'

'I think it's been in my head ever since the Orion Group came to meet me, but I couldn't, like… see it,' Allie said, leaning forward eagerly. 'This morning I was talking to the others about leaving and it came to me. You remember the papers Nathaniel asked me to sign? The ones that said I would never fight him for control of Orion?'

Isabelle inclined her head, a hint of impatience in the gesture.

Allie tried to get to the point. 'What if I signed those papers,' she said. 'And all I asked in return is that we keep Cimmeria Academy?'

Instantly the headmistress shook her head. 'There's no way Nathaniel would agree to that. He is obsessed with the school.'

'I think so, too,' Allie said. 'But what if we not only agreed not to fight him for Orion, but we also agreed to leave Orion forever? Not just me, but you. All of Lucinda's supporters. Julian. Everyone who was in that room after her funeral. We would *all* leave. He would have power. He wouldn't have Cimmeria, but this isn't the only Orion school. He could have the others. Give them to him. Give him everything.' She held Isabelle's gaze. 'All we would ask in return is to keep Cimmeria and be left alone.'

Her fingers pressed to her lips, Isabelle sat very still. Allie knew she was thinking it through. Looking for flaws.

'Cimmeria would just be a school, in that case.' Isabelle spoke slowly. 'It would lose all of the organisation that once gave it purpose.'

For the first time in this conversation, Allie let herself smile. 'Not exactly,' she said. 'Because here's the part we wouldn't tell Nathaniel: we'll start a new organisation.'

Isabelle looked over at her sharply. 'What do you mean?'

'I was thinking about it. All this time, we've been fighting Nathaniel for power and control we don't actually want. Look. Between us, we have a ridiculous amount of money. I'm guessing Julian's loaded?'

Isabelle gave a bemused nod.

Allie gestured at the door behind them. 'Out in that school, all those kids have families with money. Sylvain's family are like freaking *kings*. If we pooled our money…' She shrugged. 'We could be the new Orion. Better than the old one. Without Nathaniel.'

This was what seemed to get through to Isabelle.

'I see what you mean. Yes…' she said, excitement dawning in her eyes. 'We could form an alliance with the European Group through Sylvain's family. We'd be backed by Demeter.' She flipped through the papers on her desk. 'There's a new group in India and so far Orion hasn't reached out to them. We could welcome them.'

Grabbing a pen, she began to scribble notes. 'I have contacts in the Far East, there are people who could help us.' She glanced up at Allie, fighting a smile. 'Do you know what? This could really work.'

'I think so, too,' Allie said. 'Although I'm kind of afraid to think it, after everything. I don't want to be wrong again.' She sat up straighter, waiting until Isabelle looked up from her papers again. 'The main thing is, we have to know what we want from it, Isabelle.'

She remembered what Owen Moran had said to her the day before. The look of horror in his eyes when he found out what she knew about him. The control she had because of who she was.

'I don't know about you but there are things about Orion that aren't right. If we do this – if I'm going to be involved – we can't be like that.'

Isabelle stopped writing. 'What do you want from the group, Allie? Do you want what Lucinda wanted? A fairer version of the same thing?'

Allie shook her head. 'It can't be the same. There's no reason for a group of one hundred or two hundred people to run the government and the courts. It doesn't make sense. We can be there, and we can still help and listen, and… I don't know. But we can't try to be Orion. We have to be something else. Something new.'

Isabelle tapped her pen against her desk.

'If you're going to have a secret society, Allie, there needs to be a reason to do so. Orion's reason was to preserve the interests of its members against the vagaries of democratic government. If some tyrant was inclined to be elected prime minister, Orion would put a stop to that.'

'And elect its own tyrant.' Allie held up her hands. 'How is that OK? It's meddling in democracy and it… bothers me.'

'So, tell me what you want, then. You want to be part of a group that advises and listens…?' Isabelle's eyes challenged her.

'I want to be part of a group,' Allie said slowly, 'that advises in areas where it has knowledge, lobbies for what it wants, but doesn't just *take*. I'm not saying we can't run for office, of course we can. Anyone can. But we shouldn't be organised just to get our people elected. We should be set up to try and make the country better. Not just our bank accounts. Improve education, so it's not just rich kids going to schools like this.' She waved an arm at the beautifully appointed room. 'Most people probably have no idea schools like this are even real, you know? And maybe we could work to stop corrupt politicians from getting elected. Make sure people find out when things are being covered up. There's a lot we could do that would help other people, while helping ourselves, too. It's like a balance.'

Isabelle's expression was enigmatic – Allie couldn't tell if she hated everything she was saying or not.

Heat rushed to her face. She didn't think she was presenting this well at all. She felt put on the spot. She hadn't had any time to really think about it before now.

'Anyway,' she said, losing confidence. 'We could start with that.'

For a second, the headmistress didn't speak. Then, a smile lit up her features.

'I've never been more proud of you than I am right now, Allie Sheridan. And I believe Lucinda would have been proud of you, too. She would have disagreed with you about the bank accounts, mind you. But she would have been proud of where your heart is on this. And you're right. It's a bloody good start.'

Allie sagged back in her seat. Maybe she hadn't sounded completely stupid after all.

'If we can get the others on board,' Isabelle said, 'this could work. It might not be everything you're dreaming of, but these are good people, Allie. People I believe in. We could make a difference. I really believe we could.'

Allie wanted to feel hopeful. Wanted to believe it was possible. But there was still a huge obstacle to overcome.

'The thing is, I don't want to end up just fighting Nathaniel again,' she said. 'He's torn this school apart. Torn Orion apart. Torn my life apart, actually. How do we avoid that? Is there something I could do to make him just… stop?'

Isabelle set down her pen with a thump. 'It saddens me to

tell you this, Allie. But whether you became a high court judge, a cocktail waitress, or a street sweeper, Nathaniel will always be obsessed with you. He will always harass you and threaten you. You see, you have what he wanted – Lucinda's love. As I had my father's love. He will never forgive you as he has never forgiven me.'

Leaving her chair, she walked around to Allie's side and leaned back against the desk.

'Here are your options as I see them. You can run from Nathaniel for the rest of your life. He will never tire of chasing you, I can assure you of that. Or you can live your life, with me at your side, as part of one of the world's great new secret societies.' She leaned back in her chair, still holding Allie's gaze. 'Only you can decide what's best for you.'

There was never any question what Allie's answer would be.

She'd tried running away from her troubles many times. But that's the thing about trouble: it's fast. It's relentless. It always finds you.

She was through running.

She raised her chin. 'Let's do it.'

Thirty Four

She and Isabelle talked for nearly an hour, sorting through the details. Getting the plan in place. The headmistress wanted to have it all figured out before she broached it with the others.

'Julian will have many questions,' she said. 'I have to be ready for that.'

The longer they talked, the more feasible it seemed, and the more hopeful they both became.

How could this not work? Everyone got something they wanted.

It was perfect.

There was one wildcard. And Allie brought it up. 'What about Nathaniel? How do we get him to agree to it?'

Isabelle considered this. 'We have to convince him it's something he'll benefit from. The only good Nathaniel sees in the world comes from power and profit. I think… if the others agree to this, we have to invite him here. And talk to him together.'

'*What*?' Allie couldn't believe what she was hearing.

Isabelle was unbending. 'It's not the sort of thing you can discuss on the phone, Allie. If we're going to do this, we have to be brave enough to look him in the eye. We're going to have to sell this to him. It won't be easy. We'll keep it on our home turf, we'll call in others to back us up. We'll do it properly. But there's no getting around it.'

'How do we keep everyone safe, though?' Allie demanded. 'Carter and Zoe – everyone. How do we make sure he doesn't try something?'

'We will take care of that,' Isabelle said. 'You worry about making your case. You're going to have to win Nathaniel over.' She shot Allie a warning look. 'It won't be easy. We need him to *want* to do this. He needs to believe the battle is over.

'And that he's won.'

By the time Allie left Isabelle's office, the sun was bright and high, almost blinding her when she stepped out of the building on to the front lawn. Everyone was taking advantage of the late summer warmth, and the lawn was filled with students. She found the others, standing in a cluster by the wall of the east wing, talking quietly.

At some point, Carter had joined them. Seeing him there – all dark hair and muscles – made her heart leap.

As if he'd felt her gaze, he looked up. Their eyes locked. She felt that look in every part of her body.

The others must have told him what was going on, though, because as she got closer, she could see the worried lines on his forehead.

'You know?' she asked him quietly, and he nodded, squeezing her hand lightly.

'I've got the gist of it.'

'Something's happening,' she told him, raising her voice so the others could hear. 'Isabelle's got a plan and I think it could work.'

'What's going on?' Rachel asked. 'You were in there for ages.'

'We're going to try…' Allie stopped as a skinny, dark-haired boy dashed up to them.

'Come on Zoe,' he said. 'We're going to play football.'

It took Allie a second to recognise Alec, the junior student from Night School. His glasses were crooked and his tie hung loose, and he looked at Zoe with a tenuous mixture of admiration and hope.

She could see the temptation in Zoe's eyes, as she looked from him to Allie then back again. Finally, she sighed.

'Allie has to tell us something boring,' she explained. 'Then I'll come. I don't want to be on your team.'

He looked only slightly crushed. 'OK.'

'Zoe,' Nicole chided her. 'Remember what we said about too much honesty.'

'Yes.' Zoe's brow lowered stubbornly. 'Honesty is good.'

Rachel interceded. 'But you have to balance it with niceness.'

'No I don't,' Zoe said.

'My God, *enough*,' Katie said, raising her voice. 'I don't have time for young love. Allie, just tell us what's going on, for heaven's sake.'

But there were too many people around. They needed somewhere to argue in private.

'Let's go to the summer house,' she decided. 'There won't be anyone there.'

'Oh good,' Katie said, her tone heavy with sarcasm.

'Secrets. We don't have enough of those around here.'

'Cimmeria,' Lucas said, draping an arm across her slim shoulders, 'is Greek for "Place of Secrets".'

'No it isn't,' Nicole murmured to Rachel, who smiled at her.

They struck out across the soft green lawn. Zoe was in the front, as usual. Carter was talking to Lucas and Katie a few steps away. Rachel and Nicole were walking hand in hand.

All around them laughter and excited voices swirled in the summer breeze. From somewhere, Allie could hear the thwack of a racquet against a tennis ball. The cheers of participants in some unseen game.

It felt like the start of summer, not the end.

Suddenly Sylvain appeared at Allie's side. His gaze swept the group. 'Something's happening?'

Guilt coloured Allie's cheeks with red. She hadn't even thought about looking for Sylvain to include him in this meeting.

'Yes. Come with us,' she said, over-compensating with eagerness. 'You should hear this, too.'

'Intriguing,' he said, and strode away to walk with Rachel and Nicole.

Carter cast a curious glance at Allie, but she kept her gaze straight ahead, tightening her grip on his hand as they left the smooth grass to move into the velvet shadows of the trees.

The sun fought its way through the thick branches, shooting shards of light here and there. Thick emerald ferns covered the forest floor, brushing softly against their knees.

The steep, peaked roof of the summer house rose out of the treetops ahead of them like an elves' castle – the pale stone, adorned with elaborate, colourful mosaic tiles gave it a fairytale look, especially from a distance.

Up close, there was nothing to it, really, except the roof, and, up a few steps, a circle of stone benches and ledges, where they gathered.

Rachel sat close to Nicole, Katie, as usual, was almost in Lucas' lap. Zoe sat on the steps, looking out into the trees. Sylvain sat alone in the shadows. Carter sat across from Allie, giving her space.

She took a breath. 'Nathaniel was elected the new leader of the Orion Group yesterday.' A murmur swept the group as she continued. 'That's why he was away when we went to St John's Fields to get Carter. He was being "elected".' She made air quotes around the last word. 'This school is the lead institution of the Orion Group. It is funded by the Orion Group, which is now run by Nathaniel. And they don't want us here.'

She could see the awfulness of this news on their faces.

She had them right where she wanted them.

'We thought we were going to have to leave,' she said. 'But now we have a better idea.'

She told them about the plan, watching as their sadness turned to doubt. Then hope.

Her gaze kept returning to Carter. She needed him to back her on this. This was her school but it was his home.

His face was hard to read. She knew he'd need time to think this all through.

'You're really going to let Nathaniel come *here*?' Zoe was standing next to Carter now, her gaze fixed on Allie.

'We've got to get him to agree to sell the school to us,' Allie said. 'Isabelle says he'll only do that if we meet him in person.'

'Will the others support this?' Sylvain stepped into the light. 'Has anyone spoken to my group?'

'It's all happening now,' Allie said. 'Isabelle's on the phone with Lucinda's supporters within Orion. If they agree, she'll take it out to the other groups, including Demeter… your group.'

Sylvain's father was technically the head of Demeter, the European equivalent of Orion. But he was still in the hospital, recovering from an assassination attempt.

'What do you think?' she asked, searching his face. 'Would your group be willing to support us if we did this?'

He looked into the distance, his brow furrowed. 'I'd need to talk to my father. After what happened to him – what Nathaniel did… I think he'll be looking for any way to undermine him. He would support this, I think.' His gaze flickered off hers. 'I can speak to him. I'll be returning to France in a few days.'

Something about the way he said it made it sound permanent.

'You can't,' Zoe argued. 'Nathaniel's coming.'

He studied her soberly. 'I'll stay for that, Zoe. But then I must go back – my family needs me.'

Katie's judgemental gaze swung from Sylvain to Allie.

Look what you've done, it said.

Allie's emotions were confused. She hated for him to go – hated the idea that, whatever he said, it might really be her fault. And yet…

It made sense that he should go. He was an exchange student of tremendous wealth. If being here made him unhappy he could literally go anywhere.

After all, he had his own jet.

The others, perhaps not attributing the same permanence to Sylvain's announcement, had already gone back to talking about the new group.

'We're actually going to start our own secret society.' Rachel marvelled. 'It seems so strange. New world order.'

'We just need to not make the same mistakes our parents did,' Katie said. 'Otherwise, what's the point?'

'We must make it fairer,' Nicole said. 'I hate how unfair Orion is. It treats ordinary people like cattle.'

The others nodded.

'Can we have more real people at Cimmeria?' Carter looked around the group. 'Does it have to be people from the same background all the time?'

'Everyone's real, Carter,' Katie reminded him tartly. 'I didn't ask to be born into my family, believe me. No one would ask for that. And I want to make things better, too. Just like you.'

He winced. 'Sorry. That came out wrong. But you know what I mean, don't you?'

'Yes,' Rachel agreed, dispelling the tension. 'We want good people. And your bank account is just your bank account. It's not your worth.'

Allie looked around the circle of familiar faces and wanted to hug everyone. For the first time in a very long time, her heart felt light.

'This is what Lucinda always wanted,' she said. 'She thought Orion was messed up because it was so unfair. Obsessed with last names.'

'Can we really do this?' Nicole struck a note of caution. 'We're just kids. Will they listen to us?'

'I can't promise we'll get everything we want,' Allie admitted. 'But we'll be part of something. We have a chance.'

Rachel glanced at Allie. 'If Nathaniel's keeping Orion as a name, I wonder what the new group will be called?'

'We need a cool name,' Zoe said. 'Like the Avengers. Or

the Sisterhood of Pain. We could do it in Latin or something. For the old people.'

Allie opened her mouth to argue but Lucas got there first.

'I like the Avengers,' he said unhelpfully.

Katie shot him a withering look. 'I think it's taken.'

'That doesn't matter,' Zoe argued. 'It's not like there wasn't someone called Orion before.'

'All the other groups are like Greek and Roman gods, aren't they?' Rachel tapped her forefinger against her lip. 'Orion, Prometheus, Demeter…'

'How about Medusa?' Katie's tone was dry. 'I think that one's free.'

Rachel ignored her. 'There must be one. A good one…'

Nicole leaned over and whispered something. Rachel's eyes widened. 'Oh my God, that's *perfect.*'

'Share, please.' Katie crooked her fingers.

'Aurora.' Rachel took Nicole's hand. 'The goddess of the dawn.'

The others fell silent.

'I love it,' Allie said.

Even Katie looked pleased. 'It could be worse.'

Zoe stared at them in disbelief.

'You think *that's* better than the Sisterhood of Pain?'

Thirty Five

By the time they got back to the school building, work was already underway. Isabelle and the teachers met to discuss the plan and decide how to proceed, while, in London, Julian agreed to take the idea to the rest of Lucinda's supporters within Orion.

Everything seemed to be happening very quickly, fuelled by concern about Nathaniel and what he might do now. So far, there'd been no word from him. And his silence was somehow chilling.

No one doubted how furious he must be.

Dom was still making sure his communication system was monitored at all times.

They were, in a way, in a race against his revenge.

Despite all this, Allie found it hard to stay on edge. With Carter back and everyone together again, she wanted to let herself be happy. She wanted to go to class and study. To get back to normal.

She wanted it all to be over. It just wasn't, yet.

That evening, she was walking down the wide main hallway to meet the others in the common room, when she saw Christopher turn into the library.

She followed him in, but kept a distance away, watching

as he sat down at a table covered in books. He didn't notice her standing by the door, as he pulled a book from atop it, and sat down to read it.

After a second, she walked over. 'Hey,' she said. 'Can I join you?'

He looked up and smiled. 'There you are. I was looking for you earlier.' He gestured at the seats across from him.

She slid into one.

Christopher wore a Cimmeria uniform now, a white button-down shirt and navy trousers. Seeing her checking out his clothes, he flushed self-consciously.

'I know, I'm too old to be a student here, but I took what I could find.' He brushed invisible lint off the leg of the trousers. 'It'll do for now, anyway.'

'It looks good,' Allie said, honestly. 'You would have been an awesome Cimmeria student.'

'Maybe.' He changed the subject quickly. 'Hey, I heard everything went well last night, and your friend's back. Well done.'

'That's what I came to talk to you about,' she said. 'I wanted to just… thank you. For helping us with the guards, and telling us all you did.'

He held her gaze. 'I'm glad it helped. And I hope you believe I'm on your side now.'

'I do,' she said. And, to her surprise, she really did. Her doubts about her brother had faded every time his information had proven right. Now she was certain he really was trustworthy.

'What are you going to do now?' Allie gestured at the books on the table. 'This is a lot of reading, by the way.'

He looked down at the books as if he'd just noticed them.

'Well, to be honest, I was thinking of taking my A levels.

After I left home, I kind of missed out a year of lessons. So I've been studying, a bit.' He gave an embarrassed laugh. 'Finding out how thick I am.'

Allie tried not to appear as surprised as she was. She'd never thought about what running away meant to her brother's life. She'd been focused on how it had impacted her and her parents. But, of course, he'd missed his last two years of school, and had never taken his exams.

'That's really great,' she said, meaning it. 'Are you thinking of going to university?'

'Maybe,' he said, a bit shyly. 'I'd like to, if I can get through this stuff. I kind of want the chance to find out what it's like to be you guys.' He gestured at the vast library, where rows of bookcases soared to the ceiling. 'To study some place like this.'

Somehow, this was flattering. Before he'd run away, Allie had always looked up to Christopher. He was everything she'd wanted to be.

Now maybe she could help him.

'If Nathaniel doesn't do something crazy,' she said, 'maybe you could stay and study for a while. Until you take your exams. I could ask Isabelle, if you'd like.'

The hope in his eyes broke her heart.

'I'd really like that,' he said. 'The thing is, I'm not really sure where to go from here.'

She couldn't suppress a grin.

'Don't worry,' she assured him. 'None of us are.'

That night, Nathaniel called.

The students were gathered in the common room, when Isabelle summoned Allie and Carter to her office. When they walked in, Raj, Zelazny and Dom were already there.

'Nathaniel is insisting on coming here, tomorrow night,' Isabelle said. She looked preternaturally calm – as if she'd ordered herself to be unafraid. 'I tried to get him to give us a week so we could get everything in order, but he refused. He threatened to send the bailiffs to evict us if I didn't.' She paused. 'The publicity from such an eviction would be devastating to anything we might want to do with the school in the future. He knows I can't allow that.' She glanced at Raj. 'So he's making his move.'

'Yes, he is.' Raj's expression was dark. 'We're not ready.'

She held up her hands. 'We'll have to get ready.'

'How could he send the bailiffs?' Allie asked, looking around the room.

It was Zelazny who explained. 'Technically, Orion has ownership of the school. Nathaniel now has control of Orion. So we are trespassing.'

Allie glanced over at Carter. He looked as worried as she felt.

Nathaniel must suspect they were planning something.

'Do you think word got back to him somehow?' Allie asked. 'Someone Julian talked with?'

'It's possible,' Isabelle said. 'We need to move quickly now.' She turned to her security chief. 'Raj, I know there's not enough time. But do all you can.'

He nodded. 'I'll bring in some extra guys, secure the grounds. We'll be as ready as possible.'

She turned to Zelazny. 'August, I'll need your help to prepare the staff and students.'

'Whatever you need, Isabelle.' He spoke with uncharacteristic gentleness.

They all knew this was the beginning of the end, one way or another.

Isabelle turned to the students. 'Allie, you will need to prepare with me, as you'll be meeting with Nathaniel directly.'

Allie nodded. Her mouth had gone so dry, she didn't trust herself to speak.

'Carter.' The headmistress gave him a sad smile. 'I want you to stay as far away from Nathaniel as you can. All of this could be a ruse to try and get you back.'

He didn't argue, even though Allie knew he'd hate that. He wouldn't want her to be in danger if he wasn't there, too.

'We have a lot to do and very little time.' Isabelle looked around the room. 'We'd better get started.'

Nobody got much sleep that night.

Word spread quickly among the students about what was happening.

Senior Night School students spent much of the night working with Raj, Eloise and Zelazny, concocting an elaborate security plan.

Allie tumbled into bed with her uniform still on at half three, and was up again just after six to start again. Everyone looked as tired as she felt. But nobody talked about stopping.

There was an overwhelming sense throughout the school that this would be the end – one way or another. When Nathaniel left that night, either he would have Cimmeria, or they would.

It was a fight for everything.

For Allie it was all too soon. They hadn't had time to gather support for their plan – hadn't even begun to iron out its weaknesses or identify its strengths. It was still just a fuzzy idea.

Maybe that's why Nathaniel was doing this, she thought. If he'd heard what they were planning – if word had somehow got back to him – he'd want to stop them early. Cut them off at the knees before they learned how to walk.

The thought made her angry. And anger gave her energy.

Just after noon, Allie and Isabelle were working in her office when her mobile buzzed.

'Isabelle,' she answered shortly, her eyes still on the document in front of her. Then her tone changed. 'Oh,' she said. 'How odd. Yes. Open the gates.'

Allie, who was seated on one of the chairs in front of her desk, looked up in surprise.

'It's Julian.' Isabelle was already heading for the door. 'This can't be good news.'

'What? *Here*?' Allie scrambled after her. 'Why can't it be good news?'

'Why would he just show up without calling first?' Isabelle said as they half-ran down the hallway. 'Good news can be given any way you like. But you deliver bad news in person.'

Allie's stomach flipped. Would Julian Bell-Howard actually drive all the way from London to Cimmeria just to tell them he wouldn't help them?

It seemed cruel. But anything was possible. She didn't understand adults, sometimes.

Julian pulled up a short while later in a glossy silver sports car.

'This is ridiculous,' Isabelle exclaimed as he climbed out, all long legs and elbows in a Savile Row suit. 'You didn't have to come all this way.'

'Don't be absurd.' He kissed both her cheeks smoothly, as if they were about to go to dinner together in Kensington. 'We have important things to discuss. Besides, I'd never let you face Nathaniel alone. Allie, my dear.'

He held out both hands to her. 'I cannot tell you how happy I was to get Isabelle's phone call and hear about your plan.' His mouth was too wide for his face, his dark hair flopped forward into his eyes. There was something wonderfully off-kilter about him. 'I knew the two of you would think of some way to get us out of our Orion predicament. I think the idea is brilliant. Nathaniel will be backed right into a corner.'

'How was the idea of the new group received by the others?' Isabelle asked. 'We need their support or we have nothing to fight for.'

'You've got it.' Julian's reply came without hesitation. 'You have them all.'

Allie wasn't sure she'd understood that. 'Wait. They're *all* going to support us?'

'All of them,' Julian said. He glanced at Isabelle. 'It turns out a lot of people are very eager to leave Orion.'

This was brilliant news, but Isabelle still looked worried.

'But first we have to get Nathaniel to agree.'

'Indeed.' Julian tilted his head at the front door, which stood open behind them. 'Well Izzy? Shall we just stand in the driveway fretting? Or should we go inside and get to work? Do you know, I'm absolutely gasping for a cup of tea.'

'Oh, for heaven's sake.' Isabelle turned on her heel and headed up the steps, her low heels clicking. 'Fine. Come in. You can join in the chaos.'

Seeing them together like this, Allie got the impression they'd once been a couple. They seemed absolutely at home with each other.

And Isabelle was wrong. Julian had *not* come with bad news.

The rest of the day passed in a blur of work and planning. Allie spent most of the day with Julian and Isabelle. Occasionally Raj and Zelazny would join them to go over finer points of security planning.

It was decided that the meeting would take place outside the building. Isabelle insisted Nathaniel would be impossible to control if he was actually inside. But Allie suspected she simply didn't want to see the man who would like to take the school from her within its doors.

They would meet by the front steps. The meeting would be as short as possible.

Raj was placing guards among them, and hidden in the shadows.

Everything had been decided, down to who would do most of the talking.

'Dealing with Nathaniel is always tricky,' Isabelle said at one point. 'I shouldn't speak much – my presence upsets him.'

'Hmm, yes,' Julian agreed. 'I must say, he and I have always been able to speak with some rationality, so I feel comfortable talking with him, if you'd prefer? I'm happy to stand in for our side, as it were.'

'Good. And he seems to like Allie.' Isabelle glanced at her. 'She can handle some negotiations.'

'Of course he likes her,' Julian said cheerfully, 'she's wonderful. But I think it would be wise if she stayed out of his… reach. If you will.'

'Yes,' Isabelle agreed. 'I'll make sure the guards know he's not to touch Allie. She must be kept away from him at all times.'

The implication of this made Allie's blood run cold. Everyone suspected Nathaniel would hurt her, given the chance.

Throughout the day, Dom had sent down periodic updates.

At half past nine, Rachel knocked on Isabelle's office door. She was breathless, clearly having run down from the top floor office.

'Dom says to tell you they're coming.'

When they walked out into the hallway a short time later, they were greeted by a group of fifteen guards, dressed in black. Allie saw Sylvain and Nicole among them.

Carter, still in his school uniform, stood a short distance away, just inside the door of the common room.

Relieved, Allie ran to his side. It was the first chance they'd had to talk all day.

He pulled her into his arms. 'I wish I could go with you. Be careful,' he whispered. 'Promise?'

'I promise,' she said. 'And don't you dare get kidnapped.'

He grinned at her. 'Like *that* would ever happen.'

Further down the hallway, the guards had formed a "v", with Isabelle and Julian in the middle.

'It's time,' Isabelle said, looking at Allie.

'Good luck,' Carter whispered.

Allie ran to join the headmistress.

The guards opened the front door, and they walked out into the night.

Thirty Six

Nathaniel's black BMW rolled up the drive. Two escort cars drove behind it.

'Three cars?' Julian tutted quietly. 'Will he never think of the environment?'

The three of them stood amid a phalanx of Raj's guards. He'd never made the security more obvious.

He was sending a message.

Nathaniel stepped out of the car with athletic lightness, and strolled towards them.

At the sight of him, Allie's stomach twisted.

Behind him, two guards got out of each of the two escort cars. They formed a line behind Nathaniel, as he headed straight towards Julian.

'Julian,' he held out his hand. 'Lovely to see you.'

'Always a pleasure.' Julian smiled.

Allie wondered how Julian managed to appear so relaxed.

She was so nervous she thought she might hurl at any moment.

'Isabelle.' Nathaniel nodded at her.

'Nathaniel.' Her reply was emotionless.

Then he turned towards Allie, and smiled. 'Lady Allie.

How lovely you're looking.'

He said the title with a hint of sarcasm, and held out his hand.

Allie felt the guard next to her stiffen. But she couldn't not shake his hand.

Tentatively, she reached out until their hands met. His grip was firm, his palm dry and smooth. He shook her hand just once, and then let her go.

She yanked her arm back.

His lips curved into a Cheshire Cat grin. She got the distinct impression he knew exactly how terrified she was. And he thought it was funny.

The guard next to her nudged her back, and she took an involuntary step away from Nathaniel.

'Shall we get on with it, Isabelle?' Nathaniel's tone was impatient. 'I'm in no mood to play games. There was a break-in at my house yesterday, you see. Something very… valuable was taken.'

'Really?' Julian looked concerned. 'How ghastly. I trust no one was hurt?'

'Nothing serious,' Nathaniel said. 'One of my men is missing, however. So it's possible it was an inside job.'

'Beastly business.' Julian tutted. 'Look, old man, we are sorry to drag you out, but this did seem to be a conversation we should have in person.'

'What conversation is that?' Nathaniel asked. 'Precisely?'

Julian gestured towards Allie. 'I believe Miss Sheridan has something she wants to say to you.'

Nathaniel turned his cool gaze towards her, and Allie forced herself not to recoil.

'Is this true, Allie?' Nathaniel's voice was silky. 'What

could you have to say that requires the presence of fifteen guards and Julian Bell-Howard?'

Stay calm, she told herself. *Don't show fear.*

'I wanted to apologise,' she said. 'You came here some time ago and asked me to sign the agreement I'd made with you. I refused. And I was rude about it.' She forced herself to hold his gaze. 'I shouldn't have done that.'

'No,' he agreed amiably. 'You really shouldn't have.'

'I'm sorry, and I hope you'll forgive me.' She kept her voice low, humble, as she'd practised all day. 'And I wanted to tell you that, if you're still interested… I'm happy to agree now. I will do what you want. Leave Orion, and never challenge you for control of the group.'

'How very interesting.' Nathaniel studied her as if he'd never seen her species before. 'Might I ask what brought about this change of heart?'

Allie bit her lip.

'Julian and I discussed it, and we both felt I was… hasty. That I'd acted in anger.' She held his gaze. 'The truth is, I never wanted to be in Orion. I don't want any part of it. And I don't want anyone else to get hurt. This has to end. So I think I should just sign your paper. End this fight.'

She reached into her pocket and pulled out the papers he'd brought to the gate that night days ago. The papers had been repaired, and she'd already signed them.

She handed them to Julian, who held them out.

Nathaniel ignored the papers, cocking his head to one side and studying Allie intently. Finally, he plucked the pages from his hand and unfolded them. Then he slipped them into the pocket of the tasteful grey blazer.

'Well this is unexpected,' he said, not hiding his suspicion.

'I'd love to know what made you change your mind.'

When Allie said nothing, he turned his attention back to Julian. 'What do you stand to gain from this, Julian?'

While he was distracted, the guard next to Allie pulled her back again, putting more space between her and Nathaniel. Allie didn't glance up at him; her attention was focused on Nathaniel.

'Nothing in particular,' Julian was saying mildly. 'I'd like to see the end of this unpleasantness as much you.'

At that moment, Nathaniel's phone buzzed. Frowning, he pulled it from his pocket and glanced at the message. His face darkened and he held the phone up – its screen glowed blue in the night.

'What the hell is this, Julian?'

This was the moment they'd been waiting for. The key to Isabelle and Julian's plans.

Allie held her breath.

'That,' Julian said, 'is the other issue we wish to discuss with you.'

'These are resignation notices,' Nathaniel said, as if Julian hadn't spoken. 'From Orion. Including yours.' He scrolled through them faster and faster. 'There are dozens of them.' He glowered at them. 'Explain yourself Julian or I swear to God…'

Julian held up his hands. 'This is why we're here, Nathaniel. As you can see, Miss Sheridan is not the only person leaving Orion. Many of us will be leaving with her. Those who have unfortunately disagreed with you over the direction the organisation should take.'

'This is insane.'

But Allie thought Nathaniel had begun to look pale. He clearly hadn't expected anything like this.

His sudden nervousness emboldened her.

'You should be happy, Nathaniel,' she said. 'We'll be out of your way forever. I will never vote against you in Orion because I won't be in it. You can run the group as you wish, without interference from now on.'

'Think of it, Nathaniel.' Julian's voice was warm, convincing. 'You'll have absolute control. The power will be… immense.'

Nathaniel let that sink in. His eyes glittered.

'What do you want in return?' he asked. 'You won't just give me everything I want and walk away. There's bound to be a price.'

'Oh of course.' Julian's tone was mild. 'It's nothing much.' He held up both his hands, his long fingers stretched out flat. 'You're standing on it.'

'You want the school.' Nathaniel's voice was flat.

Allie hazarded a glance at Isabelle. She was watching him closely, eyes intense.

'That's right,' Julian said. 'It's all we ask. Sell Cimmeria to us for a very fair price, and we will give you everything you ever wanted.'

'And if I don't sell it to you?' Nathaniel's voice was tight.

'Oh, I'm certain it won't come to that,' Julian said. 'But if you refused you should know there would be ramifications. Our combined wealth exceeds yours. We would fight you every step of the way. Devoting ourselves to making the organisation so dysfunctional and unhappy your leadership would become infamous. Leaving you, in the end, with no organisation. No school. Nothing.'

Allie couldn't imagine where the ruthlessness in his tone had come from. It had just appeared, bone-chilling and devastating.

She shivered.

The guard nudged her again. Another step back.

This was getting irritating. Everything was going smoothly but he'd now pushed her back so far it was difficult to see what was happening. She'd ended up behind all the guards. Julian and Nathaniel were both hidden from her view.

Why was he being so protective?

Puzzled, she glanced up at him. He was staring at Nathaniel, utterly alert. His face wasn't at all familiar.

The fine hairs on the back of Allie's neck rose. It was her only warning.

He grabbed her, wrapping a hand tightly across her mouth so she couldn't scream and lifting her off her feet. Spinning her skilfully away when she kicked.

Even as she struggled in his grip, Allie was working through what had happened.The guard behind her must have been one of Nathaniel's men – they dressed largely the same as Raj's. He'd slipped in behind them while everyone was focused on Nathaniel.

In all the excitement, no one had noticed an extra guard.

She struggled in the man's grasp, but he was very strong. Her feet were off the ground. She hated the feel of his fingers against her mouth, she could taste the salt of his skin on her tongue.

She kept thinking someone would notice but he'd carried her behind a line of decorative hedges now, and no one could see them.

His hand over her mouth and nose was making it hard for her to breathe. They were getting closer to Nathaniel's cars.

Allie looked around desperately. Someone had to notice she wasn't there.

But the truth was, as long as Nathaniel didn't talk to her no one would think to look for her.

She tried to cry out but she didn't have enough air.

'Quiet,' a voice said in her ear. And she froze. She knew that slightly high-pitched voice. She'd heard it a hundred times.

It was Six. Nathaniel's guard.

Allie seethed with helpless rage. Her efforts to end this pointless, bloody fight had failed. Nathaniel would never let it end. This was all he lived for. He loved this battle. These little brutalities gave him purpose.

But he couldn't have her.

She raised her right arm and thrust her elbow into the flesh below his ribcage with all the force she could muster.

Six made an odd, strangulated noise. And let go.

Allie landed on her feet in a crouch, hands raised defensively. But she wasn't alone.

Sylvain stood next to her.

He lowered himself to a crouch, his hands curled into fists, his intense blue gaze fixed on Six.

'Back off, kid,' Six snarled.

Sylvain watched him with the curious interest of a cat eyeing a bird that had landed in its path.

'Backing off is not what I have in mind,' he said calmly.

He leapt at Six with such force, the man never had a chance. Allie watched in horror as the two hit the gravel with a thud. Six grappled for Sylvain's throat, but couldn't get a grip. He was so unprepared for the power of Sylvain's assault, he could do little more than ward off the blows that now rained down on him.

Allie had never seen Sylvain so angry. So violent. His fists hit Six's face with an awful crunching sound.

'Someone *help*,' she heard herself say, quietly at first but then louder. 'Raj! Someone!'

Footsteps pounded towards them. In seconds, guards surrounded them. It took two to pull Sylvain off of Six. The others seized the wounded man and took him away.

'I'm fine. Let go.' Sylvain jerked free of the guards' hold. His hands were bleeding but he didn't seem to notice.

His eyes searched the crowd until they found Allie. For a long moment, they stared at each other across the chaos.

Her heart twisted in her chest.

Then he turned and walked away.

She took a hesitant step after him, but Isabelle grabbed her arm, pulling her in the other direction. 'Allie – are you hurt?'

'I'm fine.' Allie insisted. 'It was nothing.' Craning her neck, she tried to see past the headmistress. 'Where's Nathaniel? Is someone watching him?'

'Raj has him,' Isabelle assured her.

Through the crowd, in the hazy light flowing from the open school door, Nathaniel stood with stiff impatience. Muscular guards flanked him, each holding one arm tightly.

Raj was in front of him, hands on his hips.

When things were calm enough, the two guards looked at Raj, waiting for his command. With a sigh, he nodded.

Each dropped Nathaniel's arm and stepped back one step.

Freed, he straightened the cuffs of his crisp white shirt, and smoothed his tie with an irritated brush of his fingers.

Allie and Isabelle returned to stand next to Julian. Isabelle stuck very close to Allie's side.

'As I said, we need your signed agreement.' Julian's voice was unruffled, as if nothing at all untoward had just occurred.

Allie was amazed at his sheer level of cool.

He pulled a folded sheet of paper from his pocket. 'Before

you leave tonight. The school in exchange for Orion. You'll see the money on offer is more than fair. This offer is only on the table now.'

Nathaniel considered him narrowly. 'You know, if I agree to this, I will never forgive you, Julian.' His voice was menacing. 'You will be on my list.'

Julian smiled. 'Your list is filled with so many of my favourite people. I'd be delighted to be among them.'

'You fools.' Nathaniel looked around the group in front of him. 'All of you. You could have had everything.'

His gaze lingered on Allie's face. She thought she saw puzzlement in his eyes, amid the cool calculation.

'Indeed,' Julian agreed, as if Nathaniel had said something reasonable. 'I think the price we're paying to Orion for the school and grounds constitutes highway robbery. But property prices in Britain are out of control.' He straightened his jacket. 'Someone should really address that issue.'

Nathaniel glowered at him. 'I'll ruin you, Julian.'

'Well,' Julian said, 'all you can do is try.'

Nathaniel reached for his breast pocket and the two guards stepped towards him instantly. When he raised his hands, one held a silver pen.

'All right?' he said to Raj.

Eyeing him suspiciously, Raj nodded. The guards stepped back.

Allie couldn't believe it. Was he really going to do this? Had they actually won?

Under cover of darkness, Isabelle took her hand, squeezing it tight.

Nathaniel unfolded the document and read it over. Then he signed it with a flourish. Julian plucked it from his fingers.

'You think you've won.' Nathaniel looked around the circle of faces. 'You think this is over. Well, I have news for you. This will *never* be over.' He pointed at Allie. 'I will dedicate myself to destroying you the way I destroyed Lucinda. Your inheritance will be blood and pain.'

It was too much.

'Stop it,' Allie snapped. 'Will you just *stop*. Stop this stupid vendetta. You have your victory. You won Orion. You have full control. Go and be happy with it. Leave us alone to live our lives. We'll stay out of your way. You stay out of ours. We are no threat to you. '

She thought he would shout back. Instead, Nathaniel studied her face.

'Lucinda always said you were clever,' he said after a long pause. 'She also said you were reckless. She was right on both counts.'

With that, he turned on his heel and walked to his car. He climbed into the drivers' seat. The engine roared to life; the headlights lit up the trees. Tyres spinning, he sped away.

And just like that, it was over.

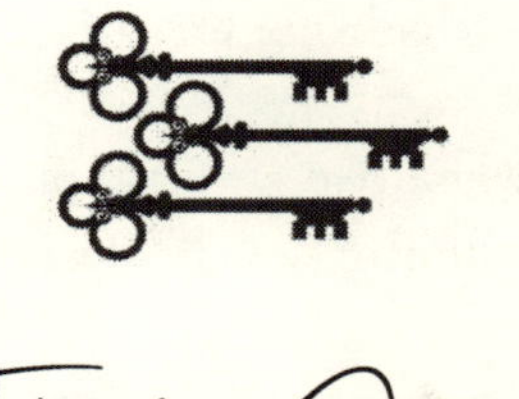

Thirty Seven

'Come on,' Allie said. 'We have to go.'

She tried to rise, but Carter pulled her back down. She landed on his chest. He smiled at her lazily.

'There you are.' His lips teased her mouth, softly nibbling at her bottom lip until she turned her mouth back to his, parting her lips so his tongue could brush lightly against her teeth.

His arms tightened around her. In a single smooth move, he flipped her over until he was above her, and she lay on her back, looking up at the high, ornate ceiling of the great hall.

The vast ballroom was empty – no one ever came in except the staff, who dusted and swept it once a week. Tucked away behind stacks of chairs and tables, they were perfectly hidden.

'Now I have you right where I want you.' He whispered the words against her cheek, his warm breath feather-light against her skin. 'But I'll stop if you want.' His lips traced a line along her jaw.

Each syllable sent heat rushing into her veins.

'All you have to say…' He reached her ear, tugging the soft skin of her lobe between his teeth. His tickling breath was maddening. '… is stop.'

His lips moved to her neck now, and Allie whimpered,

arching her back as he made his way in a line of fire down to her shoulder.

'Do you still want to leave?' He raised his mouth from her skin to look at her enquiringly. The desire in his eyes made her shiver.

She reached for his neck and pulled his mouth roughly back to hers, parting his lips with her tongue as her answer.

He groaned deep in his throat and pressed his body against her. The muscles of his chest were rock solid and she ran her hand across his shirt, threading her fingers between the buttons to feel the warm skin beneath.

'We can be late,' she breathed.

He raised himself on to his hands, lifting his weight off her. One hand rested on the warm skin of her thigh and she was very conscious of that hand. Its every movement made her twitch. Right now his fingers traced slow circles on her skin there, raising a Braille pattern of goosebumps.

Even after two weeks, it was still a wonder to her to have Carter back. To see him at her table at breakfast in the morning. To have him appear at her bedroom window after curfew, standing on the ledge smiling at her with eyes like the night.

She never wanted to be apart from him again.

When they strolled into the library a few minutes later, Rachel shot Allie a knowing look.

'You're late,' she complained.

But her indulgent smile belied her words.

'We lost track of the time.' Carter's arm hung loosely across Allie's shoulders.

'Again,' Allie added apologetically.

Rachel was not alone. Katie and Lucas sat across from her, their faces illuminated by the low glow of the table lamp in front of them. Zoe was at the end of the table ignoring them all as her pencil flew across the page, creating long, complex equations.

Christopher sat in a far corner, engrossed in a book. Allie was getting used to seeing him there. He kept to himself, most of the time. Although occasionally he let himself be included in their conversation.

The one person significant in his absence, in fact, was Sylvain.

As he'd warned them, he went home to France a few days after the meeting with Nathaniel. He'd left without saying goodbye. One morning the students got up, and he was already gone.

It wasn't clear if he was coming back this term at all. His father's recovery was slow, and Isabelle told Allie he was considering trying a Paris school for a while.

Like Orion in Britain, Demeter ran several boarding schools in France and Switzerland. He'd only ever stayed at Cimmeria because he wanted to be there.

After the fight with Six, Sylvain had avoided Allie. When she did manage to catch him alone, he wouldn't let her thank him.

'I would have done it for anyone,' he said, then he'd made his excuses and slipped away. A few days later he left the school.

Although she said nothing to the others, Allie felt responsible for his decision to go. Whatever his public reasoning for the move – and his father's injuries were real – she knew in her heart he'd left at least in part because he didn't want to stay and watch her and Carter together.

When she'd first heard he'd gone, though, she couldn't believe it. She ran up to see for herself, finding his room neat and empty. The bed perfectly made. Still, she told herself, he'd surely come back. But then she spotted the bare space on the wall where once there'd hung an ornate, romantic painting of an angel. As soon as she saw that, she knew. He was gone for good.

That had happened ten days ago. She hadn't yet got used to the idea that she might never see him again.

She kept thinking she saw him in the hallway. Or heard his smooth stride behind her.

But it was never him.

In the time he'd been away, the school had begun returning to a new kind of normal. Classes were small but they were *classes* – run fiercely by demanding teachers, and resulting in mountains of homework.

Night School training still happened, but not for everyone. It was small and select, and only for senior students. They no longer trained with weapons.

Rachel had been allowed to drop out of it. She devoted her time to studying and working with Dom, who was tutoring her in coding. Shak had also left Raj's company and now worked fulltime as Dom's assistant.

The biggest surprise was Nine. He'd joined Raj's company, and was now working as one of his guards. Raj said he had real potential. Allie sometimes saw him on the grounds.

'Hello, Trouble,' he'd always say when they passed.

It was late afternoon and the library was busier than it had been in a long time. A few of the study tables were occupied. Students strolled across the thick, Persian rugs through the forest of tall bookcases and rolling ladders.

'How am I supposed to help Allie become a science genius if she doesn't show up for our tutoring sessions?' Rachel chided them.

'Allie,' Zoe said without looking up, 'will never be a science genius.'

'Pessimist.' Allie pulled a notebook out of her bag and dropped it on the table. 'I could learn.'

The new science teacher was already infamous. His lessons were intense. She was struggling with his homework.

'Sometimes I miss Jerry,' she sighed, leaning on her elbow.

Zoe's pen stopped moving. She shot Allie a furious look.

'I mean *nice* Jerry,' Allie added hastily. 'Not crazy, Nathaniel-spy Jerry. The Jerry we thought he was. Jolly, here-have-a-good-grade Jerry.'

'Pretend Jerry was much better than real Jerry,' Katie agreed, leaning against Lucas' shoulder.

Rachel flipped through the pages of her biology text until they reached a section on cell development and spun the book around so Allie could see.

Looking at the incomprehensible drawings, Allie wrinkled her nose.

'Why do I have to learn science if I hate science?'

'Schools aren't here for learning,' Lucas explained patiently. 'They're here to torture you until you're eighteen and then send you out into the world to suffer in a suit for the rest of your life.'

Allie picked up a pencil. 'When you put it like that it all makes sense.'

Rachel waited until everyone was focused on their own work and then spoke to Allie quietly. 'Still no word from Nathaniel?'

Allie shook her head. 'Nothing. Julian says he's sticking to the deal. I can't wait until the first Aurora meeting next week. You're coming, right?'

Rachel nodded, her cheeks reddening. 'I'm so excited

about it.'

They were still putting together the rules for the new organisation, and creating a framework for it. But one of Julian's first acts was to allow Night School members to attend annual board meetings and be part of the decision-making process.

'Me, too,' Allie admitted.

Across the room, the library door opened and Nicole burst in. She ran towards them, her long hair a dark cloud around her face.

'You guys, you have to see this.'

She was breathless.

Allie's stomach tightened; Zoe started to stand.

A worried frown creased Rachel's brow as she hurried towards her girlfriend. 'What's the matter? Did something happen?'

Realising she'd scared them, Nicole's gave them a reassuring smile. She reached for Rachel's hand.

'It's good news. But you have to see for yourselves.' She beckoned for them to follow. 'Come with me.'

Exchanging puzzled glances, the group rose slowly and followed her out into the corridor in an uneven queue.

'This better be good,' Katie murmured. 'I was very into that article I was reading about couture dresses at the Oscars.'

Just ahead, Nicole reached the end of the wide corridor, outside the entrance hall and stopped. They crowded around her.

The entrance hall was packed. Young people – some in Cimmeria uniforms, some in street clothes – milled with their parents, teachers and guards. Suitcases were piled in chaotic stacks.

Their excited voices echoed off the stone floors and the old walls.

'What the hell?' Lucas said.

'Who are these people?' Zoe muttered, frowning.

The front door stood open and, through it, Allie could see a long line of cars, stretching down the drive.

Isabelle stood near the front door with Zelazny. Sunlight poured through the stained glass window above their heads, flooding the room with swirls of gold and blue. A crowd fluttered excitedly around them, gesticulating and explaining. Isabelle was beaming at them.

When Izabelle noticed Allie and the others standing in the doorway, she ran over to them.

'Can you believe it?' she asked. Her eyes were bright.

'It's wonderful,' Nicole said, her smile widening.

'What's going on?' Rachel asked.

'They're coming back.' Isabelle gestured at the crowded room. 'The students who left when Nathaniel split Orion – they're coming back. And more besides.' She pointed to a group who stood somewhat shyly to one side, beneath a tapestry of knights in armour.

'They're Polish students,' Isabelle explained. 'Their parents called this week to ask if they could attend Cimmeria on exchange. They've heard about Aurora and they want to be a part of it. Apparently a new group is starting up there.' She took a breath. 'And there will be more. I just got off the phone with some American students who want to enrol in the autumn term. I'm getting emails and calls from Canada, Australia, Germany, Belgium…' She gave a giddy laugh. 'We'll have to expand the school if this keeps up.'

Her cheeks were flushed with excitement – Allie couldn't remember ever seeing her look so happy.

It was contagious. For the first time in months, the school

felt alive. The returning students began streaming down the wide hallway with their parents in tow, lugging suitcases and chattering. Ahead, Allie could see staff rushing around – they'd be hurrying to prepare rooms and meals for the unexpected influx.

It was like fresh blood pouring into the school's veins.

With this many students, she could imagine full classrooms again. A packed dining hall – Cimmeria Academy, as it always should be.

Allie thought her heart might explode. She wanted to hug everyone.

As if he knew how she felt, Carter wrapped his arms around her waist, and rested his chin lightly on her shoulder.

'Unbelievable,' he murmured.

When they trooped back to the library a few minutes later, Allie looked up at him and asked the question she'd been afraid to verbalise since this all began.

'Tell me the truth: do you think we're going to do it? Do you think it's really possible to change things? To make things better?'

He didn't hesitate for a second. 'I think we're going to change the world.'

The way he said it, with absolute conviction, made her heart leap. The thrill of it was overwhelming. He had to be right.

They could do this. It wasn't impossible. After all, people had changed the world before.

Why shouldn't we?

Still, the simple truth was, she wouldn't get the chance to change the world without first passing chemistry.

'I've got to get back to science torture,' she said glumly. 'Rachel has a cattle prod waiting for me.'

Carter's lips twitched. 'Good luck,' he said. 'I've got to

talk to Raj about what all this means for Night School. I'll come find you after. I'm guessing you'll be in the library?'

'For the rest of my life,' Allie said.

He brushed his lips against hers, and headed off. 'See you in a while.'

For a moment, Allie just stood where he'd left her at the foot of the curving grand staircase, watching his distinctive, loping stride.

No one else moved like that. Like he was going somewhere important, but he'd get there in his own time. In his own way.

'Stay cool, Carter West,' she called after him softly.

She could hear his smile in the reply that floated back to her down the long, sunlit corridor, past the oak-panelled walls, under the crystal chandelier, for her ears alone.

'Always.'

CIMMERIA ACADEMY

Here's your chance to read the thrilling first chapter of

NUMBER 10

C J DAUGHERTY

BEWARE THE
ENEMY WITHIN

MOONFLOWER

ONE

'Want to do some shots?'

Gray could barely hear Chloe's question above the bass thumping from the speakers.

It was nearly midnight and the Bijou nightclub was in full swing. Lights spun and collided around them – purple, blue, yellow, green – and then whirled away, dizzyingly. The effect was so blinding that she had to squint to see the small, glittering glasses Chloe held.

Taking one, Gray peered at the clear liquid inside.

'What happened to the punch?' she asked, nearly shouting to be heard over the music.

There'd been some fruity punch around earlier – a technicolor concoction of juice so tooth-achingly sweet it was hard to detect the alcohol in it.

'This's all I could get.' Chloe slurred her words slightly as she leaned closer so Gray could hear her.

She didn't have to explain. They were underage, which meant they had to rely on older clubbers to buy their drinks.

Raising the glass, Gray sniffed the contents, wrinkling her nose at the sharp, astringent smell. 'What is it?'

'Dunno. Vodka, maybe?' Chloe's shrug told her how little she cared. 'Everyone else is drinking it so it must be fine.'

'Are you doing shots?' The Bolino twins walked up, with Aidan in tow, grinning at the two girls. 'Down in one!'

They were all here for Aidan's birthday – his dad owned the Bijou, and had arranged for everyone to get in regardless of age, as long as they promised not to drink alcohol. It was one of the trendiest clubs in London right now for the younger set, so this was the party of the year. It seemed like half the school had lied to their parents and come here tonight. From the moment Gray had heard about it, the whole thing had seemed exciting and illicit. She and Chloe had spent a week deciding what to wear, settling on skin-tight minidresses in silver (Chloe) and blue (Gray), paired with terrifyingly high heels. Gray could hardly walk, but she thought she looked at least eighteen, if not older.

There was no way her mother would have given her permission, so she'd used the oldest trick in the book, saying that she was spending the night at Chloe's. Meanwhile, Chloe's mother thought they were at Aidan's.

The lies only made it more exciting. They'd both been on a high from the moment they'd arrived to find their classmates similarly buzzing. Earlier, they'd all sung happy birthday to Aidan and danced around him as he turned the same russet colour as his freckles.

Now, though, it was getting late. Gray was tired. She'd borrowed high heels from Chloe and her feet hurt. She was also starting to feel a bit queasy. Their plan for the night had not included food and right now she was regretting that.

Chloe had no such concerns. Holding up her shot glass, she shook it until the liquid sloshed. 'Come on, Gray,' she cajoled. 'We're here to have fun.'

'Yeah,' Tom Bolino said, nudging her. 'Don't be a buzz kill.'

'I *am* having fun,' Gray insisted. 'I just don't want to drink mystery booze and wake up to everyone saying, "Why on earth did she drink that? She didn't even know what it was. Now, she's in a coma. What an idiot."'

'This is the *Bijou*.' Chloe said it as if this fact were emphatic evidence of safety. 'It's something like vodka. It's not *toxic*.' She swung an arm to take in the room, crowded with sweating dancers, gyrating under the strobing lights. 'Everyone here isn't going to wake up in a coma.'

'My dad's club is safe,' Aidan agreed, taking unexpected offence.

Gray bit back an argument about how people get their drinks tampered with in nice places all the time. There was a lot she could have said but the music was too loud and nobody was in the mood to listen. So all she said was, 'I just don't think so.'

Chloe shrugged. 'Well, I'm not wasting this.' She raised her glass, smiling. 'To better grades. And wilder parties.'

The boys cheered as she downed the shot. She winced at the taste but as soon as she finished, she laughed, slamming the little glass down on the sticky table next to them.

'That was *awesome*.'

Closing her eyes, she began weaving to the music, which was so loud Gray could feel the beat of it in her chest. Chloe's glossy dark curls shimmered in the magenta lights, and her body moved sinuously.

Across the room, Gray saw a group of men nudge each other and point at her, hunger in their grins.

Standing abruptly, she angled herself until she blocked her friend from their view. Misunderstanding this move, Chloe beamed at her and gestured at the glass Gray had almost forgotten she was holding.

'Come on,' Chloe said, slurring her words slightly. 'I haven't died yet so it must be safe.'

The boys laughed.

'Yeah, come on Langtry. We're all still alive,' Tyler Bolino goaded. 'Don't be so boring.'

That stung. Gray never wanted to be boring. Her mother was boring. Her stepdad was boring. She was nothing like them.

"Fine," she said.

Just as she raised the glass though, Jake McIntyre walked out of the fog of fake smoke billowing across the dance floor. Gray froze, the glass hovering in front of her lips.

In jeans and a dark shirt, he looked as cool and bored as ever, surveying the room with an air of disapproval. He was too thin. Too arrogant. And so stuck on himself.

When his eyes found her, she saw his gaze flick to her shot glass. His left eyebrow lifted.

Heat rose Gray's face. Without thinking, she hastily lowered her drink. Instantly, she regretted it.

He was always doing this. Giving her superior looks. He was always looking for ways to make her feel like an idiot. He wasn't going to decide what she did tonight.

Defiantly, she turned to Chloe.

'To wild parties,' she said, and threw her head back to down the drink. The others cheered as she slammed the glass down on the table next to Chloe's.

It wasn't vodka. It had a strong liquorice flavour that made her stomach burn.

She coughed, her eyes streaming. Her throat felt like it was on fire. Before she could recover, the music changed. Chloe gave an excited scream. 'I love this song!'

Grabbing Gray's arm, she dragged her to the dance floor,

where a hundred other bodies were already bouncing to the beat. Surrounded by laughing, gyrating young people, with the beat all around, Gray suddenly did want to dance, and she held Chloe's hand, laughing as they moved to the music. Tyler and Tom had followed them to the floor, and they all danced in a circle.

Out of the corner of her eye, Gray noticed Jake walk over and stand next to Aidan, who offered him one of the shot glasses. Jake shook his head. Shrugging, Aidan downed the shot and then ran out to dance. Jake stayed where he was, watching them with a frown.

Conscious of his gaze, Gray threw herself into dancing. The powdery fog rose around her. Her body felt light and lithe. She was part of the music. She whirled easily, soon oblivious to whether anyone was watching.

Chloe's face was damp with perspiration as she gyrated, singing the words of the song aloud. Closing her eyes, Gray raised her arms above her head, letting the music take her. Letting herself be free.

Ten minutes later, though, the music abandoned her. Her lips were dry, and her head was woozy. Her stomach didn't feel right.

'What's wrong?' Chloe shouted over the noise. 'You look weird.'

'Feel a bit sick,' Gray said and immediately wished she hadn't. Talking about it made it worse.

'Let's get some air.' Chloe grabbed her hand and led her across the bar.

Strands of hair clung unpleasantly to Gray's face as they made their way through the crowds, towards the exit. Her stomach lurched with every step.

Maddeningly, Chloe didn't seem queasy at all. She just

looked worried.

It was quieter as they neared the door, and noticeably cooler. Wiping the sweat from her face, Gray took deep breaths, trying to steady her stomach. Her mouth felt Sahara dry.

'Need somethin' to drink,' she muttered.

She barely noticed when Chloe disappeared for a minute, returning with a bottle of beer that she shoved into Gray's hand. 'Drink this. You'll feel better.'

It didn't seem like great advice.

'I need water,' Gray insisted.

'The bartender wouldn't give me any. He said he only sold it in bottles and I couldn't buy anything because I'm underage. Tyler gave me this. He thought it would help.'

Gray wasn't going to drink any more alcohol. The cold bottle felt good against her overheated skin, though, and she held it up to her face, pressing the glass against her cheek.

'Gray.' Jake's northern accented voice was unmistakable.

She spun around to see him a few feet away, his expression dripping disapproval.

'What do you want?' she asked.

His brows furrowing, he glanced from the bottle in her hand back to her face. 'Maybe you should go easy on that. You don't look so great.'

This was insulting on multiple levels. But before Gray could think of a devastating reply, Chloe stepped between them, bristling.

'Why don't you mind your own business, Jake?' she asked. 'You're always messing with Gray. Giving her looks. It's so obvious you're jealous of her. It's ridiculous.'

Even in heels she was so tiny she had to stand on her toes to bring her face to the same level as his. She looked like a really angry butterfly. He gazed at her with cool, infuriating detachment.

'I'm just trying to help.'

Chloe, fuelled by alcohol and a determination to protect Gray, wasn't backing down.

'She doesn't need your help. You're always picking on her. Why don't you get over it?'

Jake's lips tightened, and he turned to Gray. 'Look,' he said steadily, 'I'm not trying to insult you or anything. But you don't want to get drunk here. There are too many people watching. Too many eyes.'

Maybe on a different night she would have taken this advice differently. Right now, it made her furious. He was so patronising.

Ignoring the churning in her stomach, she threw him an imperious look.

'Thanks for your concern. But I'm perfectly able to decide how much I want to drink.'

For a second, he held her gaze, and she thought he'd argue. But then, shaking his head, he walked away. As Gray watched, one hand on her unruly stomach, he paused at the coat check to retrieve his jacket, and then, without looking back, disappeared out of the wide glass door.

A cool autumnal breeze flowed in as he departed. It felt good against Gray's hot skin. When the door closed, the damp heat returned.

Gray's stomach flipped. She covered her mouth with her fingers.

'He's so arrogant.' Chloe was still fuming, but as soon as she saw Gray's face, her anger faded. 'Is it worse?'

Mutely, Gray nodded. 'Have to go home,' she said, thickly. 'Gonna be sick.'

She didn't trust herself to say more, and Chloe must have seen the seriousness of the situation in her face, because her only reply was, 'I'll get our coats.'

Gray leaned against the wall as Chloe ran to the cloakroom and handed over the small white ticket. A minute later she came rushing back, clutching their jackets, which they'd checked together at the beginning of the night, when everything was so exciting.

But Gray couldn't wait for her coat. She needed air. Now.

The bouncer stepped aside with a wary look as she bolted, her borrowed high heels skidding on the cement. Under the black and white awning with the illuminated word 'BIJOU' in magenta neon, she paused for a split second.

Then she took two steps to the right and vomited into the base of a giant potted palm tree.

'Gray!' Chloe ran to her.

'She can't be sick there,' the bouncer objected.

Pulling Gray's hair back, Chloe fired a glare at him over her shoulder. 'Leave her alone.'

The two of them argued across Gray's back as the sickness slowly subsided and Gray began to straighten, wiping her mouth with the back of her hand.

What happened next happened fast.

'Bloody hell, is that Gray Langtry?' A male voice came from a few feet away.

'That's her!' Another man responded.

A blinding series of flashes lit up the night. The *rat-a-tat-tat* of camera clicks came from everywhere, like weapons being fired at them.

Chloe gasped and stumbled back as voices barraged them.

'How are you feeling, Gray?' An adult male voice with an

Essex accent taunted her. 'Bit tired and emotional?'

'Who's your friend? What's your name, sweet 'eart?'

'Had a bit too much to drink, love?'

Flash. Flash. Flash.

Blinded by the camera flashbulbs, Gray couldn't see the men, but she knew instantly who they were. *What* they were.

Her heart sank.

'Does your mother know you're drinking?' the first man asked. The others laughed.

'You're underage, young lady,' one of them said. 'I should take you over my knee.'

Through it all, the flashes lit up the night.

'Gray.' Chloe's voice sounded strange – high and nervous; her hand gripped Gray's fingers hard. 'What do we do?'

Desperate, Gray looked for escape. Behind them, the black-clad bouncer stood blocking the doorway, his arms crossed impassively. They couldn't go back in to their friends.

Behind the paparazzi, London's Park Lane was busy with late evening traffic.

Gray looked at Chloe.

'Run,' she said.

Acknowledgements

This new edition of Night School was an absolute joy to work on. Huge thanks to the small but mighty team at my new publishing imprint, Moonflower Publishing, especially to the multi-talented Jasmine Aurora, who was responsible for the fabulous cover and the interior design. I cannot imagine what we would do without her.

Thanks always to my amazing agent, Madeleine Milburn, who was the first person to love Night School who wasn't actually married to me. Without her, there would be no Cimmeria Academy. She is a hero in stilettos.

As always thanks to Jack Jewers. He is the first reader of every single book I write, and the first person I want to talk to when everything is great, and the first one to fix things when everything is terrible.

Most of my thanks, though, go to the readers who have supported the series from the beginning, and stayed with me on Instagram and Facebook for years. You are the Night School family, and I love you.

About the Author

A former crime reporter and accidental civil servant, C.J. Daugherty began writing the Night School series while working as a communications consultant for the British government. The series was published by Little Brown in the UK, and went on to sell over a million and a half copies worldwide. A web series inspired by the books clocked up well over a million views. In 2020, the books were optioned for television. She later wrote The Echo Killing series, published by St Martin's Press, and co-wrote the fantasy series, The Secret Fire, with French author Carina Rosenfeld. Her books have been translated into 25 languages and been bestsellers in multiple countries. She lives with her husband, the BAFTA nominated filmmaker, Jack Jewers.

Links

Follow C. J. DAUGHERTY on…

INSTAGRAM @cj_daugherty
YOUTUBE /nightschoolbook
TWITTER @cj_daugherty
FACEBOOK /CJauthor

Join her book club at…

www.christidaugherty.com

Christi CJ Daugherty

Manufactured by Amazon.ca
Bolton, ON